City of Jade

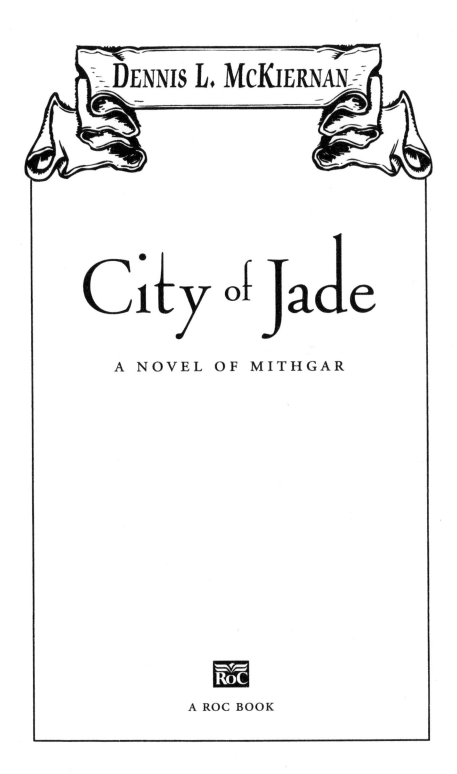

DENNIS L. MCKIERNAN

City of Jade

A NOVEL OF MITHGAR

RoC

A ROC BOOK

ROC
Published by New American Library, a division of
Penguin Group (USA) Inc., 375 Hudson Street,
New York, New York 10014, USA
Penguin Group (Canada), 90 Eglinton Avenue East, Suite 700, Toronto,
Ontario M4P 2Y3, Canada (a division of Pearson Penguin Canada Inc.)
Penguin Books Ltd., 80 Strand, London WC2R 0RL, England
Penguin Ireland, 25 St. Stephen's Green, Dublin 2,
Ireland (a division of Penguin Books Ltd.)
Penguin Group (Australia), 250 Camberwell Road, Camberwell, Victoria 3124,
Australia (a division of Pearson Australia Group Pty. Ltd.)
Penguin Books India Pvt. Ltd., 11 Community Centre, Panchsheel Park,
New Delhi - 110 017, India
Penguin Group (NZ), 67 Apollo Drive, Rosedale, North Shore 0632,
New Zealand (a division of Pearson New Zealand Ltd.)
Penguin Books (South Africa) (Pty.) Ltd., 24 Sturdee Avenue,
Rosebank, Johannesburg 2196, South Africa

Penguin Books Ltd., Registered Offices: 80 Strand, London WC2R 0RL, England

First published by Roc, an imprint of New American Library, a division of Penguin Group (USA) Inc.

First Printing, October 2008
10 9 8 7 6 5 4 3 2 1

ROC REGISTERED TRADEMARK—MARCA REGISTRADA

LIBRARY OF CONGRESS CATALOGING-IN-PUBLICATION DATA:
McKiernan, Dennis L., 1932–
    City of jade : a novel of Mithgar / Dennis L. McKiernan.
        p. cm.
    ISBN: 978-0-451-46231-2
    1. Mithgar (Imaginary place)—Fiction. I. Title.
    PS3563.C376C58 2008
    813'.54—dc22   2008012568

Set in Adobe Garamond
Designed by Ginger Legato

Printed in the United States of America

To Martha Lee McKiernan
The heart of my world

Acknowledgments

To Martha Lee McKiernan for her enduring support, careful reading, patience, and love. Additionally, much appreciation and gratitude goes to the Tanque Wordies—John, Frances, and Diane—for their encouragement throughout the writing of *City of Jade*. Lastly, I would say of all the languages used herein—some of my own devising, others of known nationalities—any errors in their usage are entirely mine.

Contents

Foreword

B ack when I began the Mithgar series, I didn't know about Aravan and his Elvenship, the *Eroean*. I wrote *The Silver Call* and *The Iron Tower* completely ignorant of that magnificent ship. Then I wrote *Dragondoom*, followed by *Tales of Mithgar*, and it was in *Tales*, in the very last story—"When Iron Bells Ring"—that the name Aravan first appeared, though we only saw the name and little else of that Elf.

But then I wrote *The Eye of the Hunter* and there he was—Aravan, a crucial member in the search for Baron Stoke. It was here we first learned of the *Eroean* and of some unknown tragedy that lay in Aravan's past, and of the disappearance of that splendid ship. What had happened, none knew . . . but Aravan held subdued grief in his eyes, and his ship was among the missing.

It was when I went back in the history of Mithgar and wrote *The Voyage of the Fox Rider* that we first got to sail on that Elvenship—with its crew of forty men and forty Dwarves, and a Pysk and two Mages—and sail we did, over much of the world. It was also there that we discovered why grief dwelt deep in Aravan's gaze, and where the *Eroean* had gone when it vanished from the world.

Once I discovered where the *Eroean* was, I realized then that Aravan had indeed sailed on the *Eroean* during the Winter War, a war at the center of the story told in *The Iron Tower*. And so when the book was revised, I added a single paragraph telling of Aravan's mission during that conflict.

However, after *Voyage of the Fox Rider*, we didn't get to sail on the Elvenship again through three more Mithgarian novels—*The Dragonstone* and the two books of the Hèl's Crucible duology—but finally we reboarded that craft in *Silver Wolf, Black Falcon*, and then once again in *Red Slippers: More Tales of Mithgar*.

And so, of the many books about Mithgar, in only two (or perhaps three) have we really spent time with the crew on the decks of the *Eroean*.

This story—*City of Jade*—is about to rectify that dearth, for an untold adventure in that mislaid city was first mentioned in the opening chapter of *Red Slippers*, and many of you have pestered me to recount that tale, for once again you would voyage across the seas of Mithgar on the fastest ship in the world, with her Elven captain and Mage mistress and crew of forty men and forty Dwarves, and her scouts—a fox-riding Pysk and a Warrow or two. So unfurl all sails and heel to the wind and we'll get under way.

—Oh, and yes, bon voyage, my friends. Bon voyage to all.

—Dennis L. McKiernan
Tucson, 2008

Background

Events in the Last Years of the Fifth Era

In the year 5E1009, in the Boskydells, three Warrows dreamt the very same dream—or was it a ghostly visitation? Regardless, they beheld the specter of Aurion Redeye, who told them that he was redeeming a pledge made long past. Redeye called for the Warrow Company of the King to be reassembled, formed as it was in the Winter War, for a great storm was coming from the east, and the Gjeenian penny would soon be seen on the borders of that small land, summoning the company to the side of the High King.

And so, the word went out, and Warrows flocked to the cause. Among those who volunteered were two buccen—Binkton Windrow and Pipper Willowbank, who slipped away from their uncle Arley, and went to the village of Rood to see the local Thornwalker captain to join the ranks. The captain turned them down and sent them packing, for Pipper Willowbank was but thirteen summers old and Binkton Windrow just three moons older. Fuming in disappointment, they went back into the care of their uncle, who was training them in their professions yet to come.

And as to this uncle Arley, his own past was shrouded in mystery; it was something he spoke little of, though the skills he taught to his nephews would be most useful in many ways.

Regardless, Pipper Willowbank and Binkton Windrow resolved to run away and join the Company of the King, once it was on the march.

In that same year of 5E1009, as foretold by Redeye's apparition, a dreadful threat to the High King's realm came from the east: it was Kutsen Yong, the Dragonking, and he would destroy all, he and his Golden Horde. He would be joined in this endeavor by the ancient enemies of the High King—the Lakh of Hyree, the Chabbains, the Rovers of Kistan, and the Fists of Rakka—Southerlings all. But the most terrible foes the High King's Host would face were not the Southerlings nor the Golden Horde, but the Dragons under the sway of the Dragonking, for nought could withstand the might of Drakes . . . none but the gods, that is, for other forces were at work, other powers in motion.

The Gjeenian penny arrived at the Thornwall, and the Warrow Company of the King set out to join the Host on the banks of the Argon. Binkton and Pipper then made preparations to follow after. Yet they were thwarted by a great blizzard that enveloped the Boskydells, and by the time the thaw came in the spring of 5E1010, the Dragonstone War was over.

Even so, the end of the war was not the end of things to be done, for an Impossible Child—Bair by name—was yet to challenge those very same gods to stop their meddling in the fates of Man and Elf and Dwarf and Mage and all other beings as well.

Caught up in this aftermath precipitated by Bair were Aravan and Aylis and others, later to include Binkton Windrow and Pipper Willowbank.

This is their story.

"Nervous, me? Pah. I mean, after all, what can possibly go wrong?"

BINKTON WINDROW
EARLY AUTUMN, 6E6

1

Cold Anger

Dark Designs
Late Autumn, 5E1010
[The Final Year of the Fifth Era]

In a tall tower hidden deep in the Grimwalls, that long and ill-omened mountain chain slashing across much of Mithgar, a being of dark Magekind sat in his dire sanctum and brooded about retribution. In the time since the end of the Dragonstone War, the Ban had been rescinded and the ways between the Planes had been restored, though most of those crossings were now warded by Elves and Humans and even Magekind to prevent the passage of Foul Folk from Neddra into the High and Middle Worlds. But none of these things were what occupied the seething thoughts of Nunde. Instead, his rage was directed at the vile Dolh—vile Elf—who had slain the Black Mage's god, to the ruin of all Nunde's plans.

Well he remembered that day, when Gyphon's silent scream of the dying had sounded across the Planes; it had driven Nunde and all of Black Magekind to their knees in agony, the unbearable pain affecting all Drik and Ghok and Oghi and Vulpen, along with other fell beings, all the creations of the Dark God.

How to take vengeance, how to gain redress, occupied all of Nunde's thoughts. *Aravan must die, that is certain, but the method of it is the question; for he is surrounded by staunch and powerful allies, and slaying him will be no easy task. Oh, there are ways the Dolh can be killed outright, but that isn't the point at issue; instead agony and grief and unbearable despair must overwhelm Aravan before he suffers a dreadful death. Hence, stripping him of all he values comes first, and doing so in a fitting—some would say unspeakable—manner must precede the Dolh's own demise.*

How to do it, how to accomplish what most certainly had to be done, *that* was the question, *that* was the issue, and that was what the Necromancer pondered throughout the long tides of night.

Indeed, I could bring an army from Neddra to Mithgar, but where would be the pleasure in that? No subtlety, no iron taste of cold revenge? Pah! With the ways between the Planes now open, it isn't like that time I slew ten thousand on Neddra to gain enough <fire> to bring a rout of Chûn and others through the temple in Drearwood despite the Sundering. Ah, what surprise upon the faces of those who sought to purge the 'Wood of Gyphon's minions. They did not know that a small measure of Mithgarian blood flows in my veins along with the blood of Neddra, as well as that of Vadaria. Nor did any know that I could capture the rout in my <fire>, my aura greatly expanded by those I had slain. And we fell upon those Humans and Elves in a great killing; had it not been for Aravan's crystal-bladed spear and Riatha's cursed Darksilver sword, we would have slaughtered all ere Silverleaf and the others arrived, and we would have butchered them as well. But with the Gûk and their steeds and the Vulpen all brought down by Aravan and Riatha, the remainder of my Chûn were no match for them, and I had to flee. Even so, Riatha's blade nearly was my undoing. Nunde's fist smashed down upon the arm of his dark chair. *This is another reason to render vengeance upon Aravan and all of those he cherishes.*

As dawn broke in the eastern sky, Nunde rose from his seat at the slit of a window, preparing to descend to his quarters. It was not as if he had to flee from the light of day, for, thanks to that fool of a boy Bair, the cursed Rider of the Planes, not only were the in-between ways now open, but Adon's Ban had been lifted as well, and no longer did the Black Mage and his ilk suffer the withering death.

No, instead Nunde, by force of ingrained habit—a habit many millennia long—was a creature of darkness, as were his minions, all beings of Neddra.

Down the stone steps of the shadowy stairwell Nunde descended to his torchlit quarters below, and there he fell into a restless sleep, his mind still churning with thoughts of revenge, as it had done for weeks on end, ever since word had come that it was Aravan, wielding a Silver Sword, who had put Gyphon to death.

But as the sun came up on this day, Nunde would set aside his scheming and rest, for in the dusktime morrow night he would begin the long journey to the crossing to Neddra to meet with a small conclave of Black Magekind, where, if his immediate ruse came to fruition, the conclave would be under his heel. After all, he had plans to wrench their power from them.

Aravan could wait.

2

Training

It was a blustery day in the Boskydells, with the wind swaying the lofty pines to and fro and the tall grass in the adjoining field rolling in undulant golden waves. An eld buccan stood back from the edge of the woods, his cloak whipping in the air. Behind him sat a stripling in chains, his wrists shackled, his legs in irons. But the elder paid no heed to the youngster on the ground; nor did the chain-wrapped stripling seem concerned over his own fate. Instead both Warrows looked up high at a rope spanning the gap between two of the swinging pines, the line alternately looping slack and then snapping taut.

Between clenched teeth, the black-haired youngster gritted, "Come on, Pip, come on. You can do it." Yet the worried look on his face said otherwise.

The eld buccan stood stock-still and muttered under his breath, "Wait for it, bucco. Wait for it."

And the trees swayed upright, the rope drawing tight, and in that moment, from the pine on the right, a fair-haired stripling ran out on the line. Across the space he dashed, but just ere reaching the far end, a misplaced foot gave him pause, and he teetered precariously, and in that same moment a gust caught the Warrow and the trees. Even as the buccan fell, the rope drooped and swung away. Wildly he grabbed for the line, but missed. And he plummeted down and down, to land in the net far below.

"Rats!" spat the chain-wrapped Warrow. He sighed and, with a lock pick, began probing the innards of his left-foot shackle.

The oldster trudged across the space and to the net, to find the fair-haired buccan lying on his back and looking at the swaying rope above.

"Well, lad?"

"I would have made it, Uncle Arley, but for a stupid wrong step."

"You would have, at that."

The youngster turned over and made his way to the brink of the net, where he grabbed the edge and somersaulted over to land on his feet on the ground.

"It's no easy task, Pipper," said the eld buccan. "But it's one to be mastered, for there might come a day when you'll have no net whatsoever."

Pipper nodded and sighed and said, "I'll give it another go."

Uncle Arley grunted his assent.

"How's Bink doing?" asked Pipper.

"I dunno," said Arley, looking back toward the chain-wrapped stripling. "He hadn't even started until after you fell. —Binkton worries about you, you know."

"I know. But it's Bink I worry about. I mean, that thing with the chains and the knives and the breaking links . . . well, it just gives me the blue willies."

Arley smiled, and then turned and started toward Binkton, as Pipper trotted to the right-hand pine and began climbing.

With the smile yet on his face, Uncle Arley slowly walked toward where Binkton sat. Though they had much left to learn, the lads—Pipper, now at fourteen summers, and Binkton, three moons older—were making good strides toward the professions Arley would have them master. Not that he hoped they would follow in his own footsteps; oh, no, that would be too perilous. Yet they were deft, and skill would come, for both had quick hands, especially Binkton, and they were very agile, especially Pipper. And they were exceptionally good with sling and bow and arrow. Why, just last year they had tried to join the Company of the King, and perhaps would have run away to do so, but for the blizzard.

As Arley came upon Binkton, that stripling had managed to get his feet freed, and now he was working on the shackle at his left wrist.

Perhaps within a year or two, Binkton would be quit of all locks and chains in but a heartbeat or three; even so, and at this time, he was quite skilled for one of his young years.

Arley nodded at the dark-haired buccan, then turned and looked toward the tall swaying pines again, with the rope strung between.

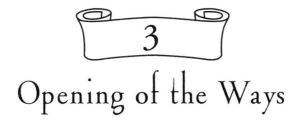

3

Opening of the Ways

Three months after the end of the Dragonstone War, and four days after returning to the Elvenholt of Arden Vale, a young giant of a man—a tall, gangly youth, some six-feet-ten in height—took it upon himself to confront yet another god. The young man's name was Bair, son of an Elf and a Baeran—Riatha and Urus their names. Bair was no ordinary being, for he was the Impossible Child, the Dawn Rider, the Rider of the Planes. And just like his father, Bair was a shapeshifter, but into a Draega—a Silver Wolf—rather than into a Bear.

Though he was yet a youth, the lad had a storied past, for he and the Elf named Aravan had recovered the long-missing, legendary Silver Sword from the bowels of the Black Fortress at the Nexus on Neddra. Together they had used the weapon to save not only Mithgar, but all of creation as well; to do so they had slain the god Gyphon with that very same sword.

Bair arose from bed in the middle of the night and made ready to go on the mission he had set for himself, and as he stepped from his chamber the aroma of freshly brewed tea was on the air, and from the shadows Riatha said, "Wouldst thou have a cup with me?" She brushed her golden hair from eyes such a pale grey they seemed almost silver, and looked up at her son. At a slender five-feet-six she was tiny by comparison.

Bair nodded and sat, and she poured. As the lad took up the earthenware mug, Riatha said, "Thou art dressed as if to hie on a journey, and I deem I have seen in thine eyes a lingering from the war."

Bair nodded. "Ythir, the mission I took up with Aravan is not yet fulfilled. There is still that which must be done, perhaps as important—or even more so—than that which we have done so far."

Riatha raised an eyebrow, and Bair plunged on. "I need to speak with Adon Himself."

Now Riatha's silver eyes flew wide. "Speak with—"

"Adon, Ythir. Adon."

Riatha took a deep breath and then slowly exhaled, and she calmly asked, "About . . . ?"

"About Durlok's staff and Krystallopŷr and the Dragonstone. About prophecies and auguries and redes. About a stone ring and an amulet of warding and a falcon crystal. About tokens of power fashioned long past with destinies set to come to fruition in these days. About a debate long ago concerning free choice versus control. And about what Redclaw said to Dalavar concerning Adon, the Drake naming Him Adon Plane-Sunderer, Adon Meddler, Adon Falsetongue. For all those things I have named and more do I need to speak to Him."

Riatha turned up both hands. "But why?"

"To take Him to task."

Riatha leapt to her feet. "What?"

"To take Him to task," repeated Bair. "Oh, don't you see, Ythir? Redclaw was right, but only partly so." Bair threw out a hand to forestall Riatha's objections. "Hear me out, Ythir: no matter Adon's intentions, the full of the tale is, we have all—all Elves, Hidden Ones, Warrows, Baeron, Dwarves, Humans, Dragons, Mages, Utruni, and even the Foul Folk—we have all been used as mere pieces in a vast tokko game played by those we name gods. And it's time it stopped."

"But, Bair, surely thou canst not believe—"

"But I do, Ythir. I do. Look, if Adon and Gyphon had settled this between themselves long past—by combat to the death, if necessary—then we wouldn't have been mere pawns in that long-played game."

Now Riatha did frown and sit again, her look thoughtful. She sipped her tea and then said, "What thou dost say is in part true, but let me ask thee this: if it had come to combat to the death, and if Adon had lost, then what would the world be like under the heel of Gyphon?"

Bair's eyes widened, for clearly he hadn't thought of such. And from a doorway to the side, Urus said, "Mayhap, lad, mayhap all the things you name, the things which you and Aravan and we and many others did, in this time and in the past, mayhap that *was* Adon's and Gyphon's combat to the death, and only by Adon using us could Gyphon be defeated."

Bair turned to his sire. Like all Baeron, Urus was a large man, some six-feet-eight and well muscled and weighing in at twenty-two stone, and much like the creature he at times became he had brown hair, grizzled at the tips, and amber eyes.

As Riatha poured a third cup of tea and set it before Urus, Bair fell into deep thought. But at last he said, "Nevertheless, Da, I need to speak to Adon still, for I am the only one who can do so and return."

"But what is it that you would say to Him?" asked Urus.

"Just this: things have been done which now need undoing, the Sundering of the Planes for one."

Riatha gasped, and then said, "Oh, Bair, if the ways between the Planes were opened, then we could . . . we could all once again . . ." Her eyes filled with tears.

Urus reached out and took her hand and stroked it, and then said to Bair, "I deem she would have you do so."

Bair nodded and then said, "I will ask Aravan to go with me, for as I say, this is but a continuation of the same mission we took on times past, he much longer than I."

Bair and Aravan were gone from Mithgar for nearly three months, elar and kelan travelling to the Ring of Oaks in the Weiunwood to cross the in-between, Aravan in the shape of a black falcon and borne across by Bair. And when they returned, a host of Elves came, too—Daor and Reín among them, Riatha's dam and sire—for the ways between the Planes had been made whole again. . . .

"What?" Riatha looked at Bair in puzzlement.

"I said, Ythir, that the ways to and from Neddra have been made whole as well, and the Ban has been rescinded."

"But why?"

"Oh, don't you see, Ythir? Any interference subverts free choice, free will, not only for us but for all."

Bair looked toward the black-haired Elf who lounged against the wall. Like all Lian, he was slender, but at six feet he was a bit taller than most of his kind. "Help me out, kelan," said Bair.

"His argument was quite eloquent," said Aravan, fixing Riatha with his sapphire-blue gaze, "and in the end he not only persuaded Adon, he persuaded all who attended: Lian, Dylvana, and the gods."

Riatha turned to Urus. "But to free the Foul Folk to work their will . . . ?"

"Mayhap without Gyphon and His agents driving them," said Urus, "they will be less inclined to do their ill."

"For that, Bair has a plan," said Aravan, grinning. "One with which I am in hearty accord."

"What?" asked Faeril—the damman Warrow—who had served as a loving aunt to Bair from the very day he had been born. "What is it?"

Bair ran his fingers through his long, silvery hair. "Just this, Amicula Faeril . . ."

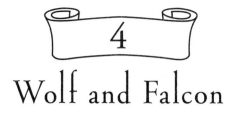

Wolf and Falcon

NEXUS

LATE AUTUMN TO EARLY WINTER, 5E1010
[THE FINAL YEAR OF THE FIFTH ERA]

Through fall-yellow grass and past brown-leaved thickets and over the rolling hills of Adonar sped the Draega, the Silver Wolf as large as a pony. High above and sailing across the azure sky a dark falcon flew. Around the ruff of the running 'Wolf dangled a stone ring on a chain, an ebon inset gleaming. Something as well glistened about the neck of the falcon above, the bird itself black as night, the glisten as from silver and glass, though it was a crystal instead. A small blue stone on a leather thong rested beside the glisten. And wherever the Draega ran, the falcon above followed, for they were travelling together, or so it seemed.

Through patches of forests the Silver Wolf wove, and it dodged around hoary old moss-laden trees and splashed across swift-running rills, while the falcon above rode the chill breeze blowing o'er the land. Not once did they slow their pace, league after league after league, until evening drew nigh, that is, and then the falcon above gave a *skree*, and veered leftward, the Draega below pausing to watch the dark bird above.

Along the edge of a woodland the falcon soared, and then winged over in a tight turn, and sailed down to land high up in an oak, its brown leaves rustling in the wind forerunning the oncoming winter. The Silver Wolf loped toward the broad-limbed tree where the dark bird had settled, and the moment the Draega arrived, the falcon once again took to the air.

After lapping up water from a nearby small burbling stream, the 'Wolf, yet panting, its ears pricked alertly, lay under the oak and watched as the bird shuttled back and forth above the tall grass in the field. And in but moments the falcon stooped, its wings nigh folded, the tips alone guiding its plummeting dive, and but a bare distance above the ground it flared its pinions and extended its talons and disappeared into the grass.

Up the Draega sprang, and loped to where the bird covered the fat coney it had downed. The 'Wolf whuffed, and the falcon, its wild eyes glaring, for a moment did not move, but at the second whuff, the bird released its prey and leapt into the air again.

The Draega snatched up the rabbit and loped back to the streamside oak, arriving just as the falcon came to ground. The 'Wolf dropped the coney, and from a flash of platinum light and a blooming of darkness, Aravan and Bair emerged: Aravan from the light; Bair from the dark.

It was but a year or so agone that Aravan, working with shape-shifting Bair and a winged Phael—a Hidden One named Ala—and a powerful being whom all of the Phael called the Guardian, learned to evoke the inherent power of a crystal, one with a falcon incised within, a crystal that now depended from the chain Aravan wore about his neck.

It was a crystal given some twenty-four years past to Faeril by Riatha, who told the damman of the scrying powers of such. At the time Faeril received it, no falcon was incised within. Faeril tried her hand at <seeing>, using that selfsame crystal, and once she succeeded, almost to her doom. Much later and within a ring of Kandrawood she met the oracle Dodona, and he took her spirit within the pellucid stone itself. Dodona showed her many things, and told her that all shapes were possible within the crystal. That was when Faeril had said she had always wanted to fly like a falcon, and of a sudden she shifted to the form of that bird, again nearly to her doom. But Dodona rescued her from permanently becoming a thing wild. And when Faeril finally returned to herself, the incised form of a falcon lay inside the crystal clear.

Upon her return to Arden Vale, Faeril mounted the crystal on a platinum chain and gave it to Bair as a birth gift.

On his quest with Aravan to find the yellow-eyed murderer Ydral, Bair had worn the crystal into the Jangdi Mountains, where the Guardian and the Phael and Bair, working in concert with Aravan, had taught the Elf to master this token of power, which allowed him to assume the form of a black falcon.

As a black falcon and a Draega, they had managed to run down Ydral, where he had holed up in a Foul-Folk-infested black fortress on Neddra, a bastion that lay at a nexus of four in-between crossings. Respectively, three of the in-betweens connected Neddra to Mithgar, to Adonar, and to Vadaria; the fourth one they knew not where it led—perhaps to the Hidden Ones' world of Feyer or to the Dragon world of Kelgor, or somewhere else entirely—for at that time only the bloodways were open, and Bair, in spite of his stone ring, could not make that crossing: he had not the blood in his veins that would allow him to do so.

Regardless as to where that fourth crossing led, it was the black fortress that concerned Bair and Aravan's current mission, for it controlled vital in-between ways that would allow Foul Folk access to Free Folk lands.

Bair and Aravan had returned to Adonar to make certain all was ready and to set in motion the final stage of Bair's plan. They had found the Elven host assembled and eager, and so the order was given to march to the in-between. And now the two fared ahead of the army to ensure that their even more powerful allies had assembled as well.

In moments Aravan had dressed out the rabbit and had set it to roast above a small fire.

"Kelan," asked Bair, "how far to the in-between, do you reck?"

"Thirty leagues, I deem," answered Aravan.

"Then nigh the mark of noon on the morrow, neh?"

"Aye, elar. Wouldst thou could run as fast as I can fly; then 'twould be midmorn."

"Ah, you're just anxious to get to Aylis, I ween," said Bair, grinning.

Aravan laughed. "There is that."

They sat without speaking for long moments, watching the coney sizzle above the flames. Bair's mind recalled the last time he had seen Aylis, and the stratagem she proposed. Alamar had quickly accepted it, but he wanted another Seer to accomplish the deed. Yet Aylis would have none of that, saying it was her plan and she would be the one to carry it out. Finally, Bair said, "I am both sad and glad that she has decided to join in the battle."

"As am I," replied Aravan. Then he sighed and added, "Not that either of us could have prevented it; she's quite reckless at times, you know. 'Tis one of the things I love about her, and one of the things I most dread."

As fat sizzled and dripped, Bair slowly turned the spit. He glanced across at Aravan and said, "She surprised me with her plan."

"Aye," said Aravan. "Still, it will let us know what we are up against and perhaps tell us the best time to attack."

Bair nodded and turned the spit. "Before Aylis made her proposal, I had thought a Seer would give the best aid by peering into the past and noting when guards change and when the sentries are most likely to be lax, or by looking into the future and telling us the moment to launch."

Aravan nodded and said, "I am told looking ahead is quite difficult, with many forks to winnow among."

"Forks?"

"Points of decision," said Aravan. "Where deciding one way causes *this*, and deciding a different way causes *that*. And with each person involved, the possibilities grow. In the venture before us, with hundreds upon hundreds involved, the possibilities are beyond reckoning, or so I would think."

"Ah, I see," said Bair.

It was just after the mark of noon and snowing in Adonar when Bair crossed the in-between, with Valké on his shoulder, Aravan's falcon shape. Bair bore the Elf in this form to ease his way to Neddra, for the best time to cross *into* that world was at the mark of midnight, just as the best time to leave that Plane was in the strokes of noon. And so, for Aravan to make that crossing at a different time would have been difficult for him; but the stone ring on a chain about Bair's neck seemed somehow to ease the lad's way through, no matter the mark of day or night. And so, Aravan had shifted to falcon shape, sealing most of his own <fire> in the crystal he wore; and captured in Bair's own aura, the lad had borne the falcon and the token of power across with ease, from the High Plane to the Low.

With Neddra's bloodred sun shedding precious little light down through an umber overcast, snow fell in this world as well, the white flakes bearing a faint yellow-brown hue as they drifted from the dismal, sulfur-tinged sky.

Bair cast Valké into the acrid air and shifted in darkness to Hunter, his Silver Wolf form. Then Draega and falcon raced in a wide arc to the north and east, heading for the crossing to the Mage world of Vadaria.

Out of view of the black fortress they sped, that bastion a league and a mile up the vale from the western crossing. And flying high above the running 'Wolf, Valké remained silent, for no pursuing Spawn did he spy—no Vulgs, no Ghûls on Hèlsteeds, no Rûcks, Hlôks, or Trolls giving chase—hence no warning did he cry.

As to the fortress itself, it sat atop a high-rising hill in a long vale, a basin surrounded by crags. Roughly square it was, the bastion, an outer wall running 'round, some twenty feet high and three hundred feet to a side and fifteen feet thick at the top, wider at the base, with bartizan after bartizan along its length full about, some fifty feet in between any given pair. To the south a barbican sat atop a gate midmost along that outer wall, a smaller barbican at the north, with a road running up in a series of switchbacks to the main gate of the central stronghold, and a like road ran down from the postern gate opposite. Between the bulwark ringing 'round and the inner fortress itself, there lay an open space, a killing ground for any who had won their way up the hill and had breached the outer wall.

Centered within, the black bastion stood: some sixty feet high it was and also built in a square, two hundred feet to a side with a great court-yard in the middle, towers and turrets and a massive wall hemming the quadrangle in.

Within the courtyard was a broad stable, wherein scaled Hèlsteeds shifted about, indicating the presence of Ghûlka in the mainstay below.

Two outer and two inner towers sat in a small, close-set square and warded the passageway into the dark fortress, with great outer and inner gates and portcullises barring the way. At the northern wall of the bastion, likewise another tight cluster of four turrets warded the rear entry as well.

With a tower at each corner of the main fortress and towers midmost along each of its walls, defenders could bring great power to bear against any and all assailants who sought to claim the stronghold as their own.

And the walls warding the central fortress were well patrolled—Hlôks and Rûcks at each corner with a small rout slowly walking the rounds.

All this did Valké see as he soared above Hunter loping below.

Four leagues and a mile did the Draega run, circling wide of the dark stronghold and into the steeps in the north. Up he ran and up, the falcon sailing above. And then the 'Wolf came to a sharp rise, and up this he sped, and he topped the slant to trot onto a circular flat, and ahead and curving three-quarters 'round to the sides towered the hard face of a sheer stone bluff, trapping the small plateau in its looming embrace. To the midpoint fared Hunter, Valké spiraling down from above. And darkness enveloped the Draega, from which Bair emerged.

The lad stretched out his arm, and Valké landed on the padded leather sleeve.

Bair glanced to the south, where a league and a mile away stood the black fortress, central to the four in-between crossings—central to the nexus—for equidistant to north and west and south and east respectively lay the way to Vadaria, to Adonar, to Mithgar, and to a land unknown.

Bair shifted Valké to the pad on his shoulder. Then, gripping the ring in his left hand, Bair began chanting, canting, pacing, turning, pausing, singing, gliding, while Valké on his shoulder glared down at the distant dark bastion, rage in the black raptor's eye. . . .

. . . And then they were gone from Neddra, their disappearance witnessed only by the yellow-brown snow drifting down from the umber-clad sky.

5

Vadaria

Yet stepping and chanting the rite of the crossing, Bair and Valké emerged onto a nearly identical stone plateau to the one they had left on Neddra; but, unlike the brown-tinged air of that world, here the chill atmosphere was pellucid and bore the faint aroma of the clean-smelling pine forest drifting up from the vale below. Snow lay upon the crests all 'round and along the slants 'neath, the white winging scintillant glitter to the eye in the light of the bright sun above.

Valké sprang up toward the cerulean sky, while darkness enveloped Bair, from which Hunter sprang forth to run. Down the slope and across the vale he sped and toward a distant knoll, snow cascading in his wake, Valké above following, watching, warding. They were heading for a mountain cabin in which a Seer dwelled—Aravan's beloved, Aylis.

And in and about that cottage an assembly had gathered, Magekind all, and they waited for a falcon and a Draega to appear. Some rested before their tents, while others ranged the slopes, and a foursome sat at an oak-wood table out beside the steep-roofed cottage. But all watched the skies for the appearance of a black raptor.

And as they did so, bearing a tray of steaming mugs, Aylis stepped out from the cabin. Reed slender she was, and dressed in brown leathers. Her light brown hair was cropped at the shoulders and seemed shot through with auburn glints in the bright sunlight warming the day. Her complexion was fair and clear, but for a meager sprinkle of freckles high on her cheeks, and her eyes were green and flecked with gold. She was tall for one of Magekind, the top of her head but a hand or so less than six feet. She bore the tray to the table.

Sitting at the board were Alamar and Dalor and Branwen, all of whom had been at the in-between crossing when Bair and Aravan had first come on Winterday a full year past, with Valké terribly wounded nigh unto death. Dalor the Healer had managed to keep the bird from dying, and Branwen the Animist had discovered how to change the unconscious falcon back into an Elf, after which Dalor had saved Aravan.

As Aylis began handing out the steaming mugs, "A Silver Wolf, a Draega, you say?" asked the fourth one sitting at the table—a somber-faced Mage. "The boy a shapeshifter?"

"Aravan, too, Sorcerer Cadir," said Aylis, "though he does not come by it naturally, as does Bair."

"<Wild-magic> for one and a token of power for the other," said Dalor, the short and portly Mage accepting a cup from Aylis.

"I don't know why we have to wait for them," said dark-haired Alamar, an irritated glint in his green eyes. "I mean, we are assembled and ready to strike, and so should just get on with it ourselves."

"Father," said Aylis, "Bair's plan is well thought out."

"She's right," said Branwen, stirring a dab of honey into the tea.

"Pah!" snapped Alamar. "Why, I alone can destroy that fort." He gestured toward the Mages downslope. "Any one of a dozen of us could."

"Ah, but what if it is teeming with Black Mages?" asked Dalor. "Then who would take on the Foul Folk while we do battle with our kind?"

"Black Mages are *not* our kind," growled Alamar. "Besides, if it came to it, as I said before, we could simply destroy the fort."

Aylis sighed and said, "Father, the mission is not to destroy the fort but to capture it intact."

"I know that, daughter," snapped Alamar. "I am merely saying we *could*. Nay, but even so, I think we need no Elven aid to capture that stronghold undamaged." Then he grinned. "After all, I am to be commander when it's in our hands."

"Co-commander," said Cadir, "or am I wrong about this captain of the Elves? Um . . . what is his name again?"

"Captain Arandor, I believe," said Branwen.

"Yes," said Aylis. "Arandor has agreed to be co-commander of the Black Fortress."

"Captain of the guard, you mean," said Alamar.

"And co-commander, Father," replied Aylis.

"Yes, yes, but you see—"

"Falcon!" came a cry, and both Dalor and Branwyn turned to see. High above and spiraling down the dark bird glided.

Although Aylis knew Valké's sight was keen beyond reckoning and he could find her in any crowd, still she would separate herself from the others to make it a bit easier for him to espy her. And so, she rose up from the table and coolly walked to the doorstone of her cottage and stood upon it waiting, her heart leaping with joy.

"Draega!" called another voice, and bursting forth from the pine trees came a great Silver Wolf running, clots of snow flying in its wake.

But the bird reached the cottage first, and even as it landed a silvery light bloomed, out of which stepped Aravan, and he took Aylis in his arms and kissed her long and deep.

Some of the gathered Mages laughed, while others applauded, and Alamar snorted and said, "Canoodling."

The Draega came loping to the doorstone, and from a blooming of darkness Bair emerged. And he stood waiting until at last Aravan and Aylis released each other. Then Bair hugged the Seer and kissed her on the cheek.

As Bair did so, Aravan's deep blue gaze swept over the assembly, lighting at last on Alamar, who sat and sipped tea at the outdoor table, along with Dalor and Branwen and a Mage Aravan did not know. Nodding their way, the Elf turned to Bair and said, "Alamar sits yon."

Smiling, Bair handed Aylis over to Aravan, and set off to speak with the Mage, the Elf and the Seer following after. When they reached the board, Bair paused a moment and surveyed the gathering along the slopes, then turned to Alamar and said, "It appears Magekind is ready."

Alamar looked up at the sixteen-year-old whose plan they followed. "Of course it is, you young whippersnapper. After all, I am in charge."

"Still crotchety, I see," said Bair.

Dalor and Branwen whooped in joy, and Aylis giggled and Aravan grinned, though Cadir gasped in astonishment.

Alamar leapt to his feet. "Now look here, boy, just because you faced down a god—"

"Two gods, old man," interjected Bair.

Alamar could keep up the pretense no longer, and he joined the others in laughter even as he embraced the lad.

Branwen, too, got up to hug Aravan and then Bair, while Dalor raised a hand of greeting. Alamar then introduced Cadir the Sorcerer, saying, "Should we need a conjoinment, Cadir will be our focus."

Again Bair surveyed the assembly. "It looks to me as if there are but fifty or so of Magekind. Is this enough?"

"There are seven nines gathered here, my boy," said Alamar, "and most assuredly that is enough."

"And the kinds . . . ?" asked Bair.

Alamar gestured toward the gathering. "Each of the nines will have three of us to throw fire or blasts of light or to control the wind and other such; one Sorcerer to destroy various things; one Seer to look where none else can and to intercept the commands of the enemy; one who can bend light and sound to disguise or to frighten the foe out of its wits, assuming that Foul Folk have wits; two who can control any beasts they send against us—Hèlsteeds and the like, and perhaps even Trolls—they are mindless enough to be animal-like; a Healer for the obvious reasons; and one of the nines will include an Alchemist instead of an Animist."

"Alchemist?" asked Bair.

"Well, lad, you never know what you might find in a black fortress, especially on Neddra," replied Alamar.

"Well, then, let me meet with each of these nines, for I would express my gratitude that they have taken up the cause."

"Lad," said Alamar, "it is cause enough that you have found a way for us to travel the Planes." The Mage gestured back toward the way Valké and Hunter had come. "And since passing through Neddra is the only way we can do so, 'tis meet that we control the nexus."

"With our allies, the Elves, and whoever else might come," said Aylis, hugging Aravan's arm.

"Yes, yes, daughter," snapped Alamar. "With our allies."

"Speaking of the Elves," said Cadir, "are they now on the march?"

Bair nodded. "Captain Arandor leads them. And in that company are

Vanidar Silverleaf, Loric, Phais, Tillaron Ironstalker, Ancinda Soletree, Ellisan, Inarion, Gildor Goldbranch, his sire, Talarin . . ."

Bair was yet naming Elf after Elf as he and Alamar and Cadir went down the slope to introduce the lad to the individual members of the seven nines.

Aravan turned to Aylis. "Would that I had thought to bring Drimma to the cause, for they are fighters nigh beyond compare, as thou hast seen on the *Eroean*."

Aylis beamed up at Aravan and said, "Oh, Aravan, sailing with you on that ship, those were days of splendor."

"Aye, they were, though they ended in tragedy, and I thought you gone forever."

Aylis took his face in her hands and said, "Oh, my love, I am so sorry. Still, you cannot get rid of me that easily."

"Get rid—? Never." And now he kissed her long and tenderly, caring not who might be watching.

When they finally broke for air, Aylis said, "Even so, voyaging with you o'er the vast seas, I would do so again."

"Fear not, love, for the vessel is in good hands and awaits us at Arbalin Isle."

"Is it yet Long Tom who cares for her? You spoke of him when last spring you were here."

"The very same, Chier, and thou wilt meet him anon, for I would have thee in my cabin again and sailing the oceans of all Mithgar after this business is done."

Dalor cleared his throat. "Speaking of business, Aravan, is the plan yet the same?"

"Aye, Healer," replied the Elf. "Mages and Elves cross over at the mark of midnight on Winterday two days hence."

"And the number of Elves in the assault?"

"At least fifty tens, all told, just as intended, though since others have discovered our aim, I believe that number might grow. From the High Plane they come, for, because of the Sundering, it has been long since any on Adonar took part in a battle against the *Spaunen*, and they would do more than their share. Yet Elves who have dwelt on Mithgar would not be denied, and they have crossed from the Mid to the High World to join the ranks as well."

"Good," said Dalor.

Branwen then looked at Aravan and said, "So you would have Dwarves in this fight?"

Aravan nodded. "Aye, the Drimma are mighty warriors."

"But how would they cross the in-between? I mean, they know not the ritual."

"Branwen, thou dost forget, the Drimma cannot lose their feet. And once they tread a path, it is with them forever. Hence, once through the steps of the crossing rite, they would repeat it without error."

"Oh, I see," said Branwen. "Then you are correct: we should have asked the Dwarves."

"And you say you have them on your ship?" asked Dalor.

"None at the moment," said Aravan, "but soon, I hope. A warband of forty will sail with us."

"Oh, my, the *Eroean*," said Aylis, her eyes lost in softness. "I remember it well."

They sat in silence for long moments, but at last Aylis said, "Come, Aravan, there is something in my cote I would have you see."

Together they strolled to the small mountain cabin, and when Dalor heard the lock click shut behind them, he turned to Branwen and said, "As Alamar would say, canoodling."

Together they broke into laughter.

In the black marks of the darktide, Elves on Adonar and Mages on Vadaria canted the chant and stepped the steps and crossed into the Untargarda, into the world of Neddra. The moment he reached the plateau, Aravan knelt and, shielded by Bair's cloak to conceal the flash of light, transformed into a black falcon and took to wing. Up he soared and up, and then sailed o'er the crags, his flight curving on a long arc to another cardinal point of the nexus, a league and a mile due west the Black Fortress. There he settled down in an open area deliberately cleared in the midst of the Elven host where the captains waited for him. One of these captains, Silverleaf, whipped off his cloak and coaxed the near-wild bird to huddle beneath, the falcon *keck*ing in irritation at having to do so. Finally, though, shielded by the garment, Valké transformed back into Aravan, the argent flare flickering under the edges. When the light died,

Aravan stood and looked about to see not only Lian Guardians but Dylvana as well, the Elven race of the woodlands, come to join in the fight.

Aravan turned to Arandor and said, "The Mages are across. Cloaked by illusion they are on their way here."

Arandor nodded and said, "How many, all told?"

"Seven nines."

"Then I will divide my force into sevenths," replied the captain, "a century and a half for each nine."

"Thou hast over one thousand?" asked Aravan. "I thought fifty tens was the count, though I suspected there would be more."

"Aye, our ranks have swelled," replied the captain, grinning. "Wouldst thou care to command one of the companies?"

Aravan shook his head. "Nay, for Valké is best as a scout."

Arandor spread his hands wide. "Aravan, 'tis a marvel that thou canst do such a thing."

"The crystal makes it so, Arandor." Aravan paused a moment and then said, "When Valké is no longer needed, then will I join one of the companies, the one wherein Aylis marches."

Arandor shook his head. "Nay, Aravan. Thou art too valuable a warrior to spend thy time ever fretting at her side."

Among those gathered immediately about, two stepped forward—both Dylvana. "Vail and I will take Aylis under wing," said Arin Flameseer, her bow in hand, as was Vail's.

"As will we," said Ruar, touching his own chest and then canting his head toward Rissa and Eloran.

Disappointed, yet understanding why Arandor would rather he be at the forefront instead of withdrawn and protecting Aylis, Aravan smiled and said, "Dylvana all, I see, and I could not ask for better."

Arandor nodded his agreement, and then said, "Dawn on this miserable world comes but six candlemarks hence. Let us form up our seven companies to be ready when Magekind arrives."

As Arandor went about the task of assigning one hundred and five tens among seven companies, one for each of the seven nines, Aravan paced and paused and paced again as he waited for his beloved to appear.

And dimly silhouetted against the stars, the sinister black moon of Neddra stole across the dark skies above.

6

Reconnaissance

They came as a whisper through the night, a soft murmuring not unlike that of the wind. And of a sudden and before the Elven army, a Silver Wolf and seven nines of Magekind appeared: first they were not, and then they were, the illusion of vacant land falling away.

Even as a pall of darkness gathered 'round the Draega from which Bair appeared, Alamar, at hand, sought out Arandor and, espying the leader, strode away.

Aylis, with eight others trailing, passed among the Mages and stepped to Aravan's side and welcomed his embrace. "How long, Chier, till dawn?"

"Four candlemarks."

"Good, then we are right on schedule and I've plenty of time to explore the interior."

Aravan sighed, and though they had had this discussion many times, still he asked once again, "Canst thou not let another do it?"

Aylis shook her head. "Nay, love, for I have trained. Fear not; your Elves and my nine will protect me. Now, get me close."

Aravan turned and signaled his squad even as Aylis gestured toward the eight Mages who had come with her. Quickly they assembled, for all knew the plan, and once again Bair became Hunter. At Aravan's whispered command, they set out westerly, twenty Elves and nine Mages, an illusionist in their midst casting cover, and a Silver Wolf in the lead.

Fretting, Alamar watched them go. "Fool of a daughter," he muttered.

"Thou art anxious?" asked Arandor. "Should we have sent someone else?"

Alamar shook his head. "Nay. She is the best at this."

"Then why dost thou call her a fool?"

"Because I love her," snapped the Mage.

Though the Elven captain said nought in reply, he nodded in understanding.

Within a candlemark, Aylis and her escort reached the near side of the knoll from which she would do her exploration. It stood no more than five hundred paces from the outer wall beringing the bastion.

As two Dylvana made their way to the crest, once again the Draega vanished and where he had been Bair now stood.

"Hunter scented only distant Spaunen," said the lad.

Aravan's hand strayed to the blue stone on the leather thong about his neck. "My amulet runs chill, yet I deem it does so because of so many *Rûpt* within the Black Fortress."

"Might I see this stone?" asked Delynn, the Sorcerer of the nine.

Aravan pulled the thong up over his head and handed it to her. A small blue pebble depended thereon, the thong running through a hole piercing the center. "It grows cold when peril is nigh," said Aravan.

Delynn peered at it a long moment and then said, "<Wild-magic>," and she handed it back to Aravan.

"'Twas given to me by a Fox Rider named Tarquin, when I rescued him and his mate from a fire."

"That explains it then," said Delynn.

"Explains what?" asked Bair.

"Why it is <wild-magic>," said the Sorceress. "It comes from the Hidden Ones, and that is the <magic> they have, a form we do not understand."

"Oh," said Bair, sounding somewhat disappointed, for he had known this all along, but, it seemed, he had been expecting a deeper insight from the Mage.

One of the Dylvana, bearing a spear, came back down from the crown of the knoll. "'Tis all quiet in yon fortress, Aravan, but for the wall patrols. Vail remains on watch above."

"Well and good, Melor," said Aravan, and he turned to Aylis. "Chier."

Aylis gave him a quick kiss; then she sat on the chill barren ground, and the remainder of the nine took places, sitting in a shallow arc about her, Delynn midmost along the curve.

Aylis looked at Delynn and nodded and then closed her eyes, and the Sorceress in turn looked about the arc and one by one called out the names of the others, and Mage after Mage in sequence murmured a word—"*Coniunge*"—and then remained silent thereafter.

"What are they doing?" asked Melor.

Aravan looked at Bair, the only one among those watching who could <see> the effect. Bair said, "<Fire> flows to the Sorceress from each on the arc, and she in turn channels it to Aylis at the focus, each in the curve giving up a bit of life essence to power the <seeing> spell."

Melor nodded, for he knew that castings required the use of <fire>, a form of life force, the loss of which caused the caster to age, unless the <fire> of others was employed. Most Mages spent their own life force, except when several agreed to combine, each to deliver some of his own <fire> to power a particular spell; in which event a Sorcerer was needed to handle the conjoinment. On the other hand, some Mages, without any prior agreement, wrenched away life force from their victims to drive their own spells; those who practiced such evil were named "Black" Mages.

"And what is it she does?" asked Melor.

"She is sending her essential self—her spirit, her soul, the very core of her being—into the Black Fortress to assess the number and kind of foe," replied Bair.

"I would think that quite dangerous," said Melor.

Bair nodded, but did not otherwise reply.

Finally Melor said, "I will go back up and keep watch with Vail."

As the Dylvana turned and quietly made his way up the slope, Bair stood at Aravan's side and stared at the arc of Mages, Aylis cupped within. And as a nimbus of jade-hued <fire> flowed to the Sorcerer and from her to the Seer, he wondered at what Aylis saw.

Disembodied, Aylis flew up and over the knoll and across the space toward the Black Fortress. Above the outer wall she soared, Spawn below standing at stations, a small rout marching widdershins along the banquette, the Rûcks in the band jostling one another and cursing. Over the killing field she swept and to the main wall of the bastion. There more Spawn stood ward, and another small jostling rout marched along the battlements. Aylis espied a closed door at one of the turrets, but this would be no bar to her spirit, and she swooped through it and into the chamber beyond.

There, she slid *behind* a shadow—not in the wall aft of the darkness, nor in the shadow pressing against the stone, but *between* the darkness itself and the wall—for there <sight> could not penetrate. If any of Magekind was in the fortress, then none could see her. Yet Aylis herself could not see ought beyond the black unless she pressed her face forward to peek out from the umbra.

Down she spiralled, now and then pausing to peer from in back of the shadow to see and count the numbers and kinds of foe. Floor after floor she descended, passing by arrow slits and by Rûcks casting bones, some shouting in glee while others cursed at the outcome of the throw.

Within the corridors and aft of the darkness lying against the walls, Aylis sped a complete circuit of the fortress at each level, checking, counting, safe for the most part from any who could <see>. Down through the strata she went—five, six, seven levels, and more—surely by then she was underground. Corridors branched off, and along these she flew, keeping behind the clinging dark, but momentarily stopping at intervals to peer out. At these pauses she noted barracks with sleeping Spawn, a mess hall with Hlôks and Rûcks gorging down gobbets of a dark and stringy meat swimming in an ocherous liquid of some sort; and in another place—a huge chamber—six monstrous male Trolls seemed to be wrestling, though when Aylis looked closer, it wasn't wrestling they did at all. Disgusted, she flew farther within, and popped up and out into the central courtyard, and making a circuit she found a stable of Hèlsteeds; and in quarters above the mews she discovered an unmoving band of Ghûls, each one sitting with its back to a wall and staring straight ahead with unblinking dead eyes, a cruel barbed spear at hand. Like the corpse-folk they were called, each one seemed to be utterly without life, but Aylis knew it was not so. With but barely a glimpse, quickly she fled the place of the Ghûls, for if they were indeed undead, whether or no she hid aft of shadows, they would catch sight of her, for unlike the living, the dead could not only see through darkness but behind it as well.

As Aylis passed back into the open courtyard, a dreadful howling sounded, and she followed it to its source to find a kennel of Vulgs worrying at the corpse of a large animal so mangled Aylis could not identify what it might have been, though it somewhat resembled a Troll.

Back across the quadrangle she sped, and as she flew in the darkness over the cobblestones, she sensed an arcane power below. *At last! 'Tis a sign of Magekind! Those who I came to find and count.* Into the ground she slipped, and she eased down into a chamber, an arena, and recalling the tales that both Bair and Aravan had told, she recognized it as the mating field of Spawn. But it was totally empty at this time, no wild, unfettered coupling taking place; perhaps the females were not in heat. Yet the dark force she felt did not emanate from this hall, and down she went into the structure below.

She descended into a chamber filled with mutilated corpses: some rotting, some fresh, some flayed, some missing limbs or heads, while others were gutted or had further atrocities performed upon them, as if some dreadful experiments were taking place. At one end of the room a curtained archway stood, and from the chamber beyond, a dreadful chanting sounded.

Aylis approached the opening, and she peered within a candlelit room to see <dark fire> flowing. She slid behind a shadow and into the vile sanctum. And she peeked out from in back of the blackness to see what might be taking place.

It was a ceremony, a rite, a ritual, for there assembled in a circle was a group of eleven, no, twelve Mages, one of whom—a Magus with long black hair down to his hips—called out arcane words. The other twelve were arrayed about a large geometric figure scribed on the floor—somewhat like a spiked wheel—and six of the Mages stood at each tine, and six more stood in the gaps between. At the hub of the wheel lay the corpse of a Hlôk, and <dark fire> flowed down and into the dead body, <fire> wrested from a score of screaming Rûcks shackled to the walls.

And the corpse twitched and shuddered and then sat up; its jaw dangled agape, and its head tilted on its neck at a broken angle, and it opened its eyes all milky and dull. With the crackling of bone it wrenched its skull upright to look about at the Mages, and then swiveled its face toward Aylis as she jerked back behind the shadow; and she heard what seemed to be a thousand voices all crying out together, as if a myriad of dead souls were crowding forward to scream through the single mouth of the corpse and cry out a warning.

Even as the shrieks wrenched out from that throat, Aylis bolted up and away, and as she passed from behind the shadow and into the ceiling above, she saw the corpse pointing at her as she fled, while Magekind turned or lifted their gazes as if to see what the dead Hlôk saw; and she sped up through stone and chambers and halls and soil and cobbles to emerge in the center of the courtyard.

Back to the knoll she raced, to flee into her own body, and as she regained possession of herself she managed to cry out, "Discovered!" before she slumped forward into a faint.

And from somewhere within the Black Fortress, a huge gong began tolling out an alarm.

7

Black Fortress

"Aylis!" cried Aravan, starting forward, even as she slowly toppled sideways to lie as one asleep. But Bair grabbed onto Aravan's arm and held him back, saying, "Nay, kelan, the <fire> yet flows. I think it would not do to break the stream."

Though agitated, nevertheless, Aravan waited, shifting from foot to foot, straining to hold back, while a league and a mile away, the alarm gong in the Black Fortress continued to sound out a deep tolling.

Moments passed, and moments more, but at last Bair said, "Now."

Quickly, Aravan stepped through the arc of Magekind and unto Aylis's side, where he knelt and cradled her in his arms. "Chier. Chier," he whispered.

Mages of the arc got to their feet, all but Delynn, who remained seated. "Fear not, Aravan," said the Sorceress. "It taxes a Seer to do what Aylis did, and I am surprised that she managed to speak ere she swooned. But she will waken soon, for her spirit is now fully within her form."

Several more moments passed, and at last Aylis opened her gold-flecked green eyes to stare into Aravan's sapphire blue gaze.

"Love?" she asked, frowning.

"Just counting the freckles 'pon your cheeks, Chier," said Aravan, smiling. Then he kissed her lightly.

Even as he aided her to her feet, Aylis's eyes widened in alarm. "Oh, my, I was discovered. We must get to my father, for there are more than we guessed might be."

"Twelve, daughter, twelve?"

"Yes, Father," replied Aylis, now fully recovered from the strain of her casting. "Twelve Black Mages. Yet whether there are additional dark Wizards, I cannot say." She stood among a small gathering of Elves and Wizards, Aravan at her side, Bair across from her, the allied forces nearby.

Still, the alarm gong in the Black Fortress rang.

Cadir sighed. "We planned for one or two, but twelve?"

Dalor shook his head. "As jealous as they are of one another, for that many Black Mages to be together is a rarity. I wonder why they might have gathered?"

Fedor, a tall, skinny Mage standing next to Alamar, glanced at Bair and then at Aravan and said, "Mayhap it has to do with the death of Gyphon. Perhaps they yet have ambitions."

"Of course they have ambitions," snapped Alamar, "but without a god at their beck, we are more than a match for Black Magekind."

"All of us on Vadaria can defeat them," said Dalor, "but here with the numbers we have versus theirs?"

Fedor glumly nodded. "Twelve Black Mages in the bastion is certainly more than we bargained for, and if there are others, well . . ."

"Why would this be a problem?" asked Ruar. "I mean, there are seven nines of you Mages among us. Is that not enough to counter twelve?"

Aylis shook her head. "It isn't the number of Mages we have, but rather the amount of <fire> at our beck." She sighed and gestured at the fortress. "Those vile Mages will wrest what life force they need from the Foul Folk within, whereas we will use only our own."

Dalor nodded in agreement, then said, "And since more <fire> can be wrenched from those in agony, from those who suffer, and because there will be plenty of pain, anguish, and distress in the battle to come, then even more fuel will be at the beck of Black Magekind."

"So twelve can overpower sixty-three?" asked Ancinda Soletree.

Fedor glumly sighed and said, "Mayhap."

"If they prevail, then likely they will defeat our army as well," said Arandor.

"And they were raising a corpse?" asked Cadir.

Aylis sighed. "They were. A Hlôk."

Cadir turned to Alamar. "Then they will know all about us: that an army of Elves and Mages is on Neddra, as well as our numbers and kinds."

"They will?" asked Ruar.

"Nothing can be hidden from the dead," said Cadir.

"True," said Branwen. "But only if they can single out that particular slain Hlôk's voice from among the myriad other dead all vying to speak."

"What we need is a plan," said Bair.

"And before dawn, I think," said Arandor.

Aylis frowned in thought and then said, "What if we hold off our assault on the fortress until after the Mages are slain?"

Aravan turned up a hand and looked at her. "Chier?"

"That way they won't have the agony of the dying to draw <fire> from," said Aylis.

"They'll pull it out of the living, regardless," said Dalor.

"Aye, but Aylis is right: less life force will be at their disposal," said Cadir.

"Look," snapped Alamar, "I say our plan changes little: we seven nines, especially those of us who can wield the elements—fire, water, earth, air, and aethyr—specifically take on the Mages, and let Elvenkind deal with all else."

Branwen took in a deep breath and slowly let it out. "We thought there might be Black Mages in the fortress. Still, I think it is as Alamar says: the plan changes little, no matter that there are twelve. Yet I and my kind are better suited to dealing with the Hèlsteeds and Vulgs, rather than trying to bring down the Mages. Likewise, Dalor and those of his training are suited to healing rather than battling dark power. And the ones of us who can cast illusions are more adept at taking on the Foul Folk, for Black Magekind can winnow through such visions and sounds, whereas the Spawn cannot."

Alamar nodded in agreement. "I and my like will meet them head-on, while all else support us."

Cadir said, "Forget not that my school can do great damage as well, and we will join you in the direct battle."

Aylis said, "We Seers will locate them for you."

Arandor glanced at Bair and said, "I deem there should be a change in my plan."

Bair frowned. "How so?"

"My forces are divided in seven companies, one for each of the nines. Instead of an immediate assault against the fort, we will stand back and defend Magekind from the Foul Folk until the nines are victorious, after which we will take the battle to the Rûpt."

"Yet what if the Spaunen bring the battle to us?" asked Tillaron.

"Then in spite of loosing fire for the Dark Mages to use," said Arandor, "we must fight."

Bair slowly nodded, and turned to the other captains and the leaders of each nine and asked, "Are we in agreement then?"

Silverleaf said, "Would that we could get right at the Spaunen, but that must wait until the greater threat is put down, unless, of course, the Rûpt come to us."

Other Elven captains murmured their accord with Silverleaf's words, and they nodded their concurrence to the plan of attack.

None of Magekind voiced any opposition, and so Bair said, "That, then, as far as the Black Mages are concerned, is our strategy. Yet heed: I was once told by another, a plan is good only until the first arrow is loosed, after which we can only act and react to the needs at the time. In this case, I suspect the plan will be good only until the first spell is cast." Then he turned to Aylis and said, "Now as the follow-on to dealing with the Mages, tell us of the kind and count of Foul Folk you did see."

In the last marks before the Neddran dawn, the combined force of Elves and Mages had taken their positions on the shallow slope leading down toward the main gate of the outer wall.

And as the ruddy light of the oncoming dull red sun began to broach the dismal overcast, the seven companies drew closer downslope.

Seers went into trances, and after but moments reported that all twelve Black Mages were upon the walls and none were elsewhere within. Yet ere the Seers reported such, Bair as well as the Mages could see the glut of <fire> on the parapets.

"Adon," asked Bair, "have we enough Mages to combat that much life force?"

"It will take everything we have," replied Cadir.

"Lit up like the targets they are," muttered Alamar, and he looked at the umber-clad sky and said a single word—*"Adfligere"*—and a huge bolt of lightning flashed down to blast among those on the battlements and to strike the midmost Mage among them. Body parts and fragments of stone flew outward, and a wild flare of released <fire> shuddered across the sky, and a great clap of thunder hammered throughout the vale to echo over and again among the peaks to the north and the crags to the south.

"Heh!" Alamar snorted. "That's one; eleven to go."

But then lightning jagged out from the dull brown above and toward the assembled army; yet even as death flashed down, a tendril of aethyr twisted up from the killing ground between the outer wall and the fortress to intercept the bolt and lead it to crash into the barren soil, where sallow snow and dirt geysered up in a great spew, most to fall back, some to drift away on the sulphurous air.

"Next time, Fedor, deflect it to the ramparts," shouted Alamar to the nearby Mage. "Kill them by their own castings."

"I barely had time to think," shouted Fedor in return.

Great gouts of flame flew out from the crenels to blast among the assembled army, and Elves and Mages died. As more fire blasted outward, it was met by walls of water conjured up from the snow.

"Adon, but they have such great power at their beck," shouted Cadir, even as he pointed his staff, and where he aimed one of the merlons directly before the Mages exploded, the blast hurling sharp fragments among screaming Foul Folk, but none of the dark Wizards was touched.

Lightning flew at both sides to be deflected by aethyric tendrils; the ground heaved below the army; stone exploded along the battlements; floods roared down from the steeps behind, to be deflected by earthen walls ripped up from the terrain; and rocks detonated within the arrayed ranks of the allies.

"Spread out!" commanded Arandor, and the army and Mages spread widely to reduce the concentration of Free Folk at any one place.

But even as they dispersed, as if the foe had been waiting for such movement, a great drum pounded out a heavy beat and the fortress gates swung wide. Ghûls on Hèlsteeds rode from the bastion and led ranks of Rûpt out—Rûcks and Hlôks all armed and armored for battle. Massive Trolls, ten and twelve feet tall, trod 'mid the oncoming foray, and a pack of black Vulgs ranged to the fore. Yet when the Spawn reached the gates along the outer wall, they could not open them, for Sorcerers among the allies held the portals shut.

But then the Ogrus strode forward and smashed the gates wide, and, howling Slûkish battle cries, Foul Folk poured through, Hèlsteeds and Vulgs leading the charge.

A darkness bloomed where Bair stood, from which Hunter emerged, and with a howl the Silver Wolf rushed down to meet the age-old dark enemy.

Elven archers flew sleets of arrows into the oncoming Spaunen ranks. Rûcks and Hlôks died screaming; some bolted back toward the safety of the fortress, yet most, yowling wordless cries, charged onward up the slope toward the Elven army while the great drum pounded out a frenzied beat.

Arrows pincushioned the Ghûls, but most were ineffective, for only a few wooden shafts lodged directly in the hearts of given corpse-foes, those Ghûls to fall dead.

"Silver points!" cried Aravan, and the special arrows then flew at the nearly unkillable Ghûlka, and where these struck, corpse-folk shrieked in pain and black ichor flowed. Even so, still they hurtled onward, cruel barbed spears couched and aimed.

Of a sudden the Hèlsteeds began squealing and bucking, and throwing their Ghûl riders, as the force of the Animists' spells struck these snake-tailed, hairless, scaled, cloven-hoofed mounts, panic filling their bestial minds, and they fled away, some yet with clinging corpse-foe upon their backs.

And, in spite of the fact that agony and death released life essence for the Black Mages to use, still arrows flew, and Spaunen fell slain as up the slope they charged.

The silver form of Hunter slashed among the Vulgs, and the entire pack of the virulent black beasts veered toward the Draega and leapt upon him in a slashing, howling swarm. Elven archers flew arrows at the

pony-sized dark creatures, killing some. Yet others were too close to
Hunter to risk loosing a shaft at them. But then the spells of the Animists
filled the Vulgs with dread, just as the Hèlsteeds had been, and they, too,
fled away, even as Hunter, his jaws locked upon the nape of another of the
beasts, broke the spine of the creature. And the Silver Wolf stood snarling
amid slain Vulgs, their throats torn out and necks broken. But then the
Draega sped back to the Elven ranks, where once again Bair emerged
from a darkness and took his flanged mace in hand.

Leading the onrushing Rûpt army, ponderous Trolls, swinging their
massive warbars, with arrows simply shattering against their skin, thudded toward the now-closing ranks of the Free Folk.

Gildor stepped to the fore and drew his sword, Bale, and the weapon's
blade-jewel blazed with scarlet werelight as if to ignite the length of steel,
for Foul Folk were nigh. Preternaturally sharp-edged, the sword had been
forged long past in the House of Aurinor in the Duellin for use in the
Great War. Yet Gildor's wielding of Bale at the Iron Tower proved to be
even more critical in the Winter War than in the War of the Ban, for the
weapon was deadly to Trollkind in spite of their stonelike hides.

Others took up their weapons as well—swords, maces, spears, flails.
And as the yowling Spaunen hurtled up the slope toward the army, Aravan took up his spear and glanced at it and said, "Elven-forged thou art
and worthy, yet would that thee were Krystallopŷr, but it is gone into the
Abyss, taking its <fire> with it, and so thou and I must do." And he lowered the point of the weapon to meet the oncoming foe.

The howling wave of Rûcks and Hlôks and Ogrus smashed into the
Elven files, and, roaring, the Trolls swung their great bars to left and
right. Elves met the Spawn head-on, swords riving, spears stabbing,
shields bashing. And they danced back or ducked under cumbersome but
lethal swings of the Troll weaponry, yet not all, for the dreadful warbars
struck among them, felling many. And even as Rûcks and Hlôks rushed
by him, Gildor waited until the huge iron rod of the Troll before him
swept past, and then he stepped forward and, with a two-handed swing,
drove Bale through and across the Ogru's gut and out the other side, and
with his steaming entrails spilling forth and to the ground, the Troll
gazed down in disbelief, and then fell forward dead. But with Rûcks and
Hlôks following in their wake, other of these monstrous foes waded in

among the allies, flailing, slaughtering, crushing; they alone could devastate the Elven army. Grimly, Aravan stabbed and slashed with his spear, hacking his way through Spawn and toward one of the Trolls, yet even as Aravan neared, the behemoth espied him and, snarling, turned his way and raised his massive warbar to smash down upon this puny being, the Troll's gaze wide in triumph. But in that moment, an arrow sprang forth from the eye of the monster, and as the Ogru crashed down, its brain pierced by the shaft, Aravan glanced aside to see Silverleaf fitting an arrow to his silver-handled white-bone bow while turning to seek yet another one of these dreadful creatures, rampaging among the allies. And as a shrieking Hlôk charged at a group of Magekind, only to be skewered by Vail and fall dead at Alamar's feet, the Mage looked away from the parapets above and down at the slain Hlôk. Then his gaze swept across the roiling battlefield to see the Ogrus laying waste to the Elven host. *"Dicere!"* evoked Alamar, casting a spell, then shouted "Fedor! Bremar! Cadir!" and called other names as well. And in spite of the uproar of battle—the screams and bellows and cries—those he named heard his spell-cast voice. "Trolls! Trolls! We must deal with the Trolls!" And the Ogrus were met by flame, as Mages took precious moments from their own bitter struggle to hurl bolts of fire at the behemoths, their greasy hide garments to burst ablaze. Shrieking in fear, the monsters fled, flinging away their weapons and ripping and rending their burning clothing from themselves, for fire they feared, and away they ran, now pursued by spectral flames cast by Illusionists; they did not flee back toward the fortress, but bolted toward the distant crags instead.

Even so, with Magekind distracted by having to deal with the Trolls, lethal blasts and bolts of the dark Wizards fell among the allies and took a grim toll. Swiftly, Alamar and his Elementalists and Sorcerers again took the fight to the battlements above, hurling lightning and fire or exploding the stone of the shielding crenels.

As the Trolls fled from the ranks of Elves and Mages and ran among the Spawn and away, and as Ghûls afoot fell down, killed by silver-headed arrows, the nerve of the Rûcks and Hlôks broke, and they bolted away screaming, most back through the broken gate in the outer wall and across the killing grounds and around the far side of the bastion, though some scrambled into the fortress itself.

Even as the Spawn fled back through the allied ranks, Elven swords rived and spears stabbed and Bair's mace crushed many who sought escape.

As the last of the foe fled down the slope, arrows felling many as they ran, Gildor wiped Bale's length clean of Rûpt ichor and sheathed the blade again, and the Elves stood ready, though the foe was now gone. But still the Mage-versus–Black-Mage fight went on, as water battled flame, and dark, whirling winds came roaring out of the mountains to be met by howling air twisting counter; hailstones and sleet hammered down from the skies amid lightning and thunder and upheavals of land and exploding stone. Mages were slain, and Elvenkind fell, and Black Mages died in spite of their glut of <fire>, for there simply were too many casters opposing them, Mages of greater skills.

And as the arcane battle raged, Healers moved among the wounded, and they snatched many back from the brink of death, but others they could not save.

Yet finally all of the occult resistance from the battlements ceased, as the last of the dark Wizards fell.

Now the Elven army charged the fortress, the gates yawning open before them.

But the Foul Folk were fled out the rear postern and away, and the Elves came into an abandoned stronghold, but for a few quailing Rûpt, and these were quickly dispatched.

When a count of the dead was taken, nearly a thousand Spawn had been slain, fully half by arrows on the battleground, most of the rest by allied steel.

Yet four hundred ninety-eight of Elvenkind had fallen, some to the Trolls, some to Rûcks and Hlôks, but most to the dark Wizards' castings. And on Adonar and Mithgar and even among those on Neddra, Elves grieved, for they had received the death redes of those whose lives had been quenched . . . death redes, a unique Elven gift, both a curse and a blessing of Elvenkind, a final good-bye from a slain Elf that somehow winged to a loved one. Though the ways between the Planes were now restored, not even when they were sundered had they prevented such messages from reaching the intended. And for an Elf to die was particularly grievous, for no matter the count of a given Elf's years, it was but a single step along an endless life.

Thirty-two of Magekind were also slain: no school had been spared. But Aylis and Alamar yet lived, much to Aravan's relief.

Though they had been but twelve Black Mages, they had been devastating, given their glut of <fire>. Had there been more of them, the fight could well have gone the other way. Yet in the final tally only eleven slain dark Wizards were accounted for. The Necromancer with the black hair down to his hips was not among the bodies found.

8

Flight

DARK DESIGNS
WINTERDAY, 5E1010
[THE FINAL YEAR OF THE FIFTH ERA]

Through a long and low and narrow tunnel a Black Mage fled, dreadfully shaken by the unexpected attack upon the fortress. Until the moment the aethyric intruder—the disembodied spy—had been discovered, not one of the dark Wizards had known that an appalling force of Elves and Mages was on Neddra to assail the bastion; yet the dead Hlôk the Necromancer had raised had told all. And although the Wizard could have used his occult arts to send slain Drik and Ghok and Oghi back into the fray, when the battle had begun and the Necromancer had seen the skills and force of the opposing Magekind and the prowess of the Elven army, the dark Wizard had known it would be hopeless. His fears had been borne out by the onslaught, and he quickly saw that nought could be done to keep the fortress from falling into the hands of the foe, and so he had fled in the confusion of battle. Yet just before the fight had begun, he had glimpsed the one who had slain his god, had seen the murderer in the fore of the Dolhs: Aravan, killer of Gyphon.

Aravan and his ilk had upset all of the Necromancer's plans, not only by killing his god, thus ruining the Black Mage's certainty of dominion over a significant part of Mithgar, but also on this very night had interrupted the conclave of Black Mages, where the Necromancer had fully expected to be elected the very first leader of the first *Siniihi apo Thætheha*—Covenant of Twelve—of dark Wizardkind.

Someday, someday, that Dolh would suffer vengeance; someday Aravan would meet his doom, or so again swore Nunde the Necromancer, even as he fled down the long escape tunnel, running for his very life.

Trickery

BOSKYDELLS

WINTERDAY, 5E1010

[THE FINAL YEAR OF THE FIFTH ERA]

As the snow blew and a chill wind rattled the sides of the barn, with cold air drifting in through the cracks, Pipper ran up the long slant of the rope tied between the first stall and the hayloft above the far end. Binkton, not needing to look at the five balls he kept in the air, their graceful arcs crisscrossing and not colliding, watched as his cousin made the ascent.

"Well and good, Binkton," said Uncle Arley. "Give them over and we'll revisit your sleight-of-hand skills."

Binkton waited until Pipper reached the top and alighted on the loft and turned and bowed to an imaginary audience below. Then, one after another, Binkton let fly the balls to Arley, the eld buccan gracefully catching each of the colored spheres and dropping them into the box at hand.

Pipper then slid down the length of the line and backflipped to the floor planks just ere reaching the end.

As Pipper stepped over to watch, Arley said, "'Tis claimed the hand is quicker than the eye, yet I say, not so. Instead, the art of successful legerdemain is twofold: distraction and a stealthy touch, like so. —Oops!" Arley dropped a fetter that fell with a clang, and both Binkton and his uncle bent down to pick it up. As the stripling rose with the irons in hand, Arley said, "Thank you, bucco," and he took the shackles while at the same time giving over to Binkton the lad's own belt.

Pipper laughed and clapped and said, "Nicely done, Uncle."

Somewhat embarrassed, Binkton scowled as he rethreaded the belt through the loops on his breeks.

"Now, since there are two of you," said the eld buccan, "the filcher can slip the taken object to the other, and, when accosted, the filcher can show he hasn't got it."

Arley then demonstrated how this was done, this time using Pipper as the dupe.

For the next candlemark or so, uncle and nephews practiced this form of trickery, until Arley seemed satisfied that they had got it right; then they moved on to other sleights of hand.

Time after time, Arley put the striplings through their paces, as he had been doing ever since they had come to him, or so it seemed. With both sets of parents lost in the raid upon Stonehill some four years back, he had inherited these two rascals, being their only remaining kin, and a granduncle at that. It was when he had shown them a few of his skills that they had insisted on learning all he knew, after which, they maintained, they would see the world.

Oh, well, perhaps someday they would, yet Arley hoped it would be in different and less perilous circumstances from those in which he had done.

And so, he set out to teach them all he knew of the picking of locks and pockets, of misdirection and stealth and guile, of walking upon ropes and swinging through the air and other feats of aerial skill, of trickery and sleights of hand, and of making something seem other than it was.

"All right, buccoes," he finally said, "that's enough for the day. Now, let us go have some warm soup."

With that, they made their way through wind and snow to the stone cottage at hand, a cottage a league or two north of the small town of Rood in Centerdell, the Bosky.

10

Securing the Watch

On Year's Long Night the brigade of Elves at the Black Fortress held no ceremony to celebrate the passing of the seasons. Instead, throughout the day they had gathered the dead and laid three great pyres outside the killing grounds: one for the fallen Elvenkind; a second for the slain Mages; and a third one for Black Magekind as well as the corpses of the Foul Folk, including those mutilated cadavers found in the vile sanctum below. Too, Healers tended the wounded, bearing some back across the in-betweens for further treatment in a less noxious place than Neddra.

That night under the black moon, Elves sang their slain into the sky; Mages mourned their fallen by conjuring brief images of each within the flames to rise in the smoke and vanish; none shed any grief whatsoever for Black Magekind or Foul Folk.

The following day, messengers were sent beyond the in-betweens, and Mages came to replace those who had been slain and those who had expended much of their <fire>, the latter to return to Vadaria to <rest> and regain their life essence. Aylis was not among those who had spent a deal of her <fire>, for the conjoinment of her nine for her aethyrial spy mission had spared her greatly. So she stayed at the fort with Aravan to help with whatever she could. Elves also came to replace those of their Kind who had been slain. Supplies as well flowed to the fortress, for much would be needed to maintain the outpost.

Bair had crossed into Adonar, where swift Hunter loped toward another in-between, a difficult crossing that connected the circle of stone to its counterpart on Mithgar. Yet Bair planned for Hunter to pause at any Elvenholts along the way to the stone circle; at these the Silver Wolf would briefly become Bair to spread the word of the victory. But at the stone circle in Adonar, Bair would step in-between unto the land of Lianion, now called Rell. From there Hunter would head north, intent upon reaching Arden Vale, where he would tell of the fall of the fort and name the casualties taken. It was in Ardenholt where Riatha and Urus waited, for they had taken on the task of governing the vale while Inarion and others joined the assault on the Black Fortress.

Even as the word went forth across Adonar and Mithgar and Vadaria, the allies on Neddra spent twelve full days—all the days of Yule—making the Black Fortress habitable: Animists sent the ubiquitous vermin to flight, rats and mice scrabbling away, while insects and serpents and worms and spiders went flying and scuttling and wriggling after, a veritable horde of fleas and lice coming last. Elves carted various items out into the lands beyond and set them ablaze, although they retained serviceable furniture. After chambers were temporarily emptied, Alamar and his kind then scoured them with vortexes of boiling water. And as the fort was cleansed, Alchemists and Seers examined the abandoned tomes and scrolls and other writings, as well as the devices found in laboratories and various chambers, keeping some, destroying others, setting others aside for further study. Seers also used their powers of <sight> to sweep the corridors and rooms for hidden doors and panels and such, and in this manner they discovered the escape passage most recently used by a long-haired Black Mage. Where he had gone, none knew, though they managed to <see> his flight out and away and south to the in-between to Mithgar. After that he had used his own power to completely obscure his trail.

When the fortress was clean enough to be lived within, Elves moved furniture back into chambers, and all settled into their assigned duties.

The battle had begun and ended on First Yule, the day of Year's Long Night, and now it was Last Yule—Year's Start Day—the first day of the first year of the Sixth Era. And after dinner on this new beginning, Arandor and Alamar sat down to review what was yet to be done, Aravan and Aylis joining in.

Alamar poured each of them a glass of dark Vanchan wine from a bottle he had been saving for the occasion.

"To victory," declared Alamar, lifting his goblet.

"Aye, to victory," replied Arandor, raising his own, but Aravan looked into his glass and added, "And to absent friends."

Arandor took a sip and then said, "We'll not hold this fortress unless we remain vigilant and well supplied."

Alamar nodded but said nought.

"Logistics," said Arandor. "Food and drink are now coming in from Adonar along with a supply of arrows and other such armament. Vadaria, too, is sending goods. Yet, Alamar, art thou certain that Magekind can do nought to bring wagons across the in-betweens? Carrying items by backpack and horseback is a tedious chore, and should we be able to use wains, well, then . . ."

Alamar shook his head. "Captain, I know of no spell that will increase the reach of the essence of one who is crossing, and as you know—"

Aylis said, "But for tokens of power, if a thing cannot be captured in one's aura, it cannot cross an in-between."

"Ah, well," said Arandor, "too bad the gods made no wagons of power." Then he and the others broke into laughter, and Alamar hoisted his glass to the captain.

Aylis then asked, "Speaking of crossing the in-betweens, have the next steps begun?"

Alamar nodded. "Even now Magekind is preparing to travel to the High Plane and the Middle. There Seers will seek out crossing points into Neddra, and Illusionists will block them with dreadful spells and phantasms triggered by Foul Folk. Some crossings we will destroy by razing the likenesses between."

"Just as we shattered the temple in Dhruousdarda during the Purging of that foul place," said Aravan.

"Indeed," said Alamar.

"What of those in-betweens we leave open?" asked Aylis.

Arandor said, "We will set ward upon them, particularly here at the nexus. But the opposite sides need warding as well." The captain gestured out toward the valley and said, "Even now on Adonar an Elven stronghold is being fashioned in the matching point to the west cardinal here at the nexus; 'tis a vale in the reach of the Durynian Range nigh Lyslyn Mere, and so that side will be guarded. Also, I have dispatched an emissary across to Mithgar to ask High King Ryon to build a garrison on the Middle Plane side of the nexus. Too, I would have him send a proper share of supplies across as well—an annual levy—food and drink and such."

"Just make certain that it includes Vanchan wine," said Alamar, grinning as he refreshed all goblets.

"That goes without question," replied Arandor, his smile matching Alamar's.

"We're also doing our part," said Alamar, turning the bottle up to get out the last drop of the dark liquid. "A Mageholt is under way on Vadaria just north of the crossing. We'll staff it with some of our finest casters."

Even as Alamar set the empty bottle down, "Drimma!" exclaimed Aravan.

Arandor cocked an eyebrow. "Drimma? What would the Drimma do?"

"They cannot lose their feet. Once through the crossing rite and it will be with them forever."

"Has this been done ere now?" asked the captain.

Aravan nodded. "Aye, Bekki did learn from Phais and Loric the rite during the Great War."

The captain held up a hand. "Yet crossing the Planes requires more than just knowing the steps. One must also be at an in-between at the right time, as well as become lost in the rite."

Aravan frowned and then said, "As for reaching the proper state of mind, I am certain the Drimma might do so whenever they celebrate Elwydd at the changing of the seasons. If so, 'tis a small matter to have them repeat that rite to go in-between."

"I agree with my chier," said Aylis. "The paean to Elwydd will put the Dwarves in the proper state to make the crossing."

Alamar nodded. "My daughter is right, I think. And besides, Dwarves are the proper ones to teach."

"I concur," said Aravan.

"Thy meaning?" asked Arandor.

"Just this, Captain," said Aravan. "I think we do not want Human-kind learning the way to pass from Plane to Plane. As I once told Lady Faeril, look at how Humans despoil the land. Although Humankind can do little more to ruin Neddra than the Rûcks and such haven't already done, to let them loose in the High Plane, well . . ."

"I understand," said Arandor, nodding.

"This, then, I propose," said Aravan. "If the Drimma do agree, we teach them the necessary steps, and can they get into the needed frame of mind to make the crossing, they will be the ones to ferry supplies from Mithgar to here. Besides, if this works, some might even agree to help staff the fortress, and as I have oft said and seen as well, they are mighty warriors."

Arandor nodded. "Ah, then, Humans staff the garrison on the Mithgarian side, there in the vale north of Inge, but Drimma bear supplies across."

"Just so," said Aravan.

Arandor thought a moment and then said, "Kachar is the deeve of the Drimma nearest to that crossing; who is DelfLord there?"

"Borak," said Aravan.

"Good, then," said the captain. "I will send an emissary to DelfLord Borak."

Aravan turned to Alamar. "Wouldst thou ask one of the Seers to go with the envoy? Together they should be able to convince Borak to agree. I mean, after all, it is a great boon we offer."

Arandor frowned. "Great boon?"

"Why, the manner of the crossing of the Planes," said Alamar.

"Ah, yes," replied Arandor.

Alamar glanced at Aylis. "Now, as to a Seer to send on that mission—"

"I will go, Father," said Aylis.

"No, daughter. I can see that you and that young sprout of a ship's captain are eager to rejoin the *Eroean* and set off to who knows where. Instead, I will ask Delen to go. He's eager to visit Mithgar."

"As you wish, Father," said Aylis, her gaze downcast, though she squeezed Aravan's hand in delight.

Arandor said, "Then we are in accord: if High King Ryon and Delf-Lord Borak also agree, it seems we have a framework for the upkeep of the black fortress, as well as the plans to assure the ways into Mithgar and Adonar and Vadaria are warded against Spawn escaping from Neddra."

Alamar looked at the empty bottle before him and said, "We'd drink a toast to that had we a bottle of good brandy." Then he laughed and added, "Or even a bottle of swill."

11

Warding

A sevenday later, as the dull red sun stood at the zenith—neither morning nor afternoon, but the in-between time necessary for beings to cross out from Neddra and unto Vadaria—Aravan and Aylis began the chant that would take them over to the Mageworld. They were going to collect some of Aylis's belongings—auguring cards, a viewing bowl and dark dye, a finding needle, a small crystal globe, and other such Seer's gear—for she and Aravan were on the first leg of their journey to Mithgar, to Merchants Crossing in Jugo, where the Elvenship *Eroean* was moored and her crew patiently waited for their captain to return.

As the pair emerged on the plateau in Vadaria, the clanking sounds of a hammer against a chisel against stone split the air, along with some venting of oaths. Aravan frowned and looked up and about, and on the heights cupping the flat he saw several Mages standing ward. Aylis waved up at them, and one sketched a salute while the others nodded or raised hands in greeting. Then she and Aravan moved onward. As they rounded the shoulder of the bluff hemming in the table, they saw the reason for the cursing: by pulley and rope, Mages were hoisting a large block of stone up to a scaffold above. Down below, others worked with hammers and chisels, dressing the next block. Still others led horses drawing wains up the slopes below, and bringing more stone to the site. Magekind was at work building a tower, a bastion to ward the in-between.

Aravan glanced up at the barely begun fortification and laughed. "I thought I would see stones floating free through the air to be precisely maneuvered into place. But instead I see high-rising platforms and ropes and pulleys and mortar-filled hods and trowels and hammers and chisels and sweating and straining people."

Aylis grinned and said, "It would take much <fire> to erect it by castings. The loss would not justify the gain."

Aravan frowned and said, "Methinks ye Mages should have asked the Drimma to build the tower."

Aylis turned up a hand, a rueful grin on her face. "You are right, Chier. I ween none thought of it."

"'Tis all the more reason for Durek's line to learn to go in-between."

Aylis looked at Aravan and said, "I suppose across the nexus from Neddra to Adonar whatever fortification is being raised there also is not being built by Dwarves."

Aravan chuckled and shook his head. "I suspect that none thought of asking the Drimma to erect that bastion, either."

Aylis then said, "Let us suggest to whoever is in charge here that he ask the Dwarves to come."

As they started across the slope, Aravan smiled and said, "Knowing the Drimma, they will tear down whatever they find as being shoddy and start from the bedrock below and make the structure Drim-solid to the very top."

Aylis and Aravan spent the next two fortnights in her cottage, talking, making love, laughing, making love, cooking, making love, sleeping, making love, making plans, and making love. It was as if they were, in part, trying to make up for the many millennia they were separated—from the destruction of Rwn to the time when Aravan and Bair crossed into Vadaria right after recovering the Silver Sword, a total of seventy-two hundred and twenty-nine years.

On the day before departing Vadaria, Aravan and Aylis sat at the table out in the open air. Aravan gazed at the scintillant glitter of the stream tumbling past and said, "'Tis an altogether impossible task."

Aylis looked at her black-haired lover and asked, "Impossible task?"

"Trying to catch up to what we missed."

Aylis smiled. "As the old adage goes: you can never catch up and get even, and certainly not ever get ahead. Still, I enjoy every moment we strive to do so." Even as she said it, Aylis blushed furiously.

Aravan laughed and looked at her, a gleam in his eye, and then he stood and offered her his hand and asked, "Shall we, my demure maiden, put that eld saying to another test?"

At the end of those two fortnights, Aylis took up her small bundle and Aravan took up his spear, and as the bright moon of Vadaria stood at the zenith—an in-between time, neither yesterday nor tomorrow, yet the easiest time to make the crossing—the pair canted the chant and paced the steps, and within moments they stood beneath the black moon of Neddra, sailing above through the dark broken clouds.

And the air rang with distant cries and blasts; for a league and a mile to the south, fire bloomed and lightning flashed from dark fortress walls, while a stark illumination lit up the killing ground and the land beyond, revealing a vast Rûptish army surrounding the bastion.

A nighttime battle was under way.

Arrows flew from the walls, to be met by arrows flown in return. Hundreds of Spawn lay dead on the killing grounds, and more shrieked and died in the volleys, while on the darkened walls above, archers loosed shafts and Mages threw bolts, and Healers rushed hither and yon and treated wounded allies.

Spawn raised long scaling ladders against the walls and began clambering up, but Elves above waited until the Rûpt were nearly to the top ere using long forked poles to push the ladders out and away, Rûcks and Hlôks to tumble down screaming.

From within the shelter of a roofed-over battering ram, Trolls hammered at the fortress gates. But fire rained down upon them, and they flinched and cowered, yet the wetted, hide-covered roof protected them, and they and their garb had been thoroughly soaked and did not burn, and so they rose up and hammered on. Flaming oil flowed out from under the gate, but grounded iron plates formed a wedge and fended the fire away.

In the dimly lit courtyard beyond the gate, an Elven army stood assembled, ready to do battle were the entry to be breached.

"My kindred," said Aravan, shifting from foot to foot, his knuckles white against the haft of his spear. "I need do something. I cannot just stand here. Valké must fly to the western crossing and bring reinforcements from Adonar. We can attack the foe from the rear. Yet I cannot leave thee unprotected."

But Aylis shook her head. "I will be well enough, Chier. Yet 'tis not the in-between time for crossing into Adonar from Neddra."

"Rach!" cursed Aravan, frustrated in even this.

And still the battle raged.

But then out from the ragged clouds above, four bellowing Dragons came sweeping, their battle cries drowning out all others. Across the skies they hurtled and swooped down toward howling ranks of the Rûptish army encircling the black fortress

Aravan gasped, "How did Drakes come into this—?"

Aylis spoke an arcane word—"*Evulgare!*"—and peered at the Dragons, and then said, " 'Tis illusion, Chier. —The Dragons, I mean. The conjured fire and lightning are real, but the Drakes are not. 'Tis a deception Magekind brings to bear."

As the Dragons plummeted toward the Spawn, claws extended, fire licking out from the corners of their mouths, Aravan slammed the butt of his spear against the stone and said, "Aylis, I have to do *something*. I cannot leave thee, yet I also cannot just stand here and—"

"Nay, love, look," she replied. "Even now the foe is routed."

In the face of the Drakes, the ranks of Rûcks and Hlôks and Trolls and Ghûls broke, and Spawn fled, the Dragons roaring in pursuit, spewing illusory fire, augmented by real Firemage castings. Rûpt burned and died screaming, yet some aflame ran on. Then the Drakes veered away from the chase and returned to settle atop the four towers at the corners of the fortress, where they bellowed challenges into the air, their thunderous echoes to slap among the crags and peaks.

"It takes much life essence to conjure a Dragon," said Aylis, "one with movement and dimension and fire and sound. Those Illusionists who have done so will need to be replaced by other Mages, and soon." Even as she spoke, the Drakes took to wing and flew up above the clouds to vanish.

Aylis smiled. "Good. The Dragons went as true Drakes would, and didn't simply fade away. That will give the enemy pause ere they try to assail the fortress again."

She turned to Aravan. Clearly he was agitated that he had had no part in this battle. Aylis took him by the hand and said, "Come, love, let us to the fortress, where we will celebrate with the others."

Aravan inhaled deeply and slowly let his breath out. Then he shook his head. "The Rûpt scattered in all directions. We need wait till the coming of the dismal day on this ill-begotten world ere we start for the bastion. I would not have us encounter remnants of that army."

In less than a candlemark, Aravan and Aylis heard heavy treadfall thudding across the slopes below.

"Trolls," murmured Aravan.

Moments later, many feet pattered by down in the narrow vale running past.

"Rûcks?" whispered Aylis.

"Rucha or Loka or both," breathed Aravan.

Though Aylis and Aravan stayed alert the rest of the night, no other Spawn passed in the darkness.

At last drear dawn seeped into the sky, and Valké took to wing. Up and across the brown-tinged air he soared, and after but moments he spiraled down and landed at the rear of the plateau, where a flash of silvery light brought Aravan in Valké's stead.

" 'Tis clear. Let us hie to the fortress."

And together Aravan and Aylis hastened down the slope and toward the dark stronghold below, where new fires burned outside the walls, pyres for hundreds upon hundreds of slain Spawn.

"How many battles have ye fought while we were away?" asked Aravan.

"This was the first," said Alamar, "though I doubt it'll be the last."

"It took them some while to assemble again and to collect even more Spaunen to come and assault the bastion," said Arandor.

" 'Twas nigh a full Horde," said Aravan.

"Next time it might well be that," said the captain.

Aravan sipped from his wine and looked at Alamar and then Arandor. "The crossing points here on Neddra need be warded as well as the fortress, else the Foul Folk could set ambuscades for those entering or leaving. Yet to have guards at the crossings has two drawbacks: they advertise to the Rûpt exactly where the in-betweens are, and it puts the warders at risk. And so, I suggest that at the critical times of crossing—mid of night when arriving on Neddra, and mid of day when leaving—that patrols 'just happen' to be in the vicinities of the nexus points."

Alamar shook his head. "Not necessary, my boy."

Aravan frowned. "Not necessary?"

"That's what I said," snapped the Mage.

"Father," cautioned Aylis, glaring at her sire, then adding, "You'd better explain."

Alamar gritted his teeth, then took a deep breath and let it out. "A Seer looking one day ahead or even a half is altogether enough."

Aylis frowned, then nodded in agreement. "If all that is being examined are the times of the crossings and whether or no the enemy is nigh, it should be simple enough."

"I told you it wasn't necessary," said Alamar, somehow preening while seated, a self-satisfied cast to his face. "We have things well in hand."

Aylis looked at her sire and shook her head and sighed. "Well in hand or not, Father, I think a good leader would lay his cards on the table ere jumping down someone's throat."

Alamar rolled his eyes as if asking, *Where's the fun in that?*

Arandor laughed and said, "Lady Aylis, it was through a Seer that we knew the assault was coming. And so, we had the plan in place. My battalion stood assembled, and archers and repellers were on the walls as well as Magekind."

"The Dragons were my idea," said Alamar, again preening though he sat in a chair. "Scared the spit out of them, too."

"But we didn't foresee the fact that the Trolls would be protected such that fire did them no harm," said Arandor.

Alamar made a negating gesture. "Pah! Next time we'll ask the Sorcerers to simply destroy their shelter, and then use lightning."

They sat for moments, none speaking, but then Aravan asked, "Thinkest thou they will attack again?"

Alamar shrugged. "As I said, I doubt if this will be their last assault, yet if this didn't scare them off forever, then when they come again we'll do even more."

"We can stay on, Father," said Aylis, glancing at Aravan, who nodded his agreement and added, "I am a fair hand with bow and spear."

Alamar snorted. "What? You think we can't do it without you two? I told you we have it well in hand." Then his gaze softened and he looked at Aylis. "You two go on. The *Eroean* is waiting, and I would not have this fortress come between you and that."

"Art thou certain?" asked Aravan, swinging his gaze to Arandor.

"Aye, Aravan," said the captain. "Thou hast done more than thy share in defending the Planes. 'Tis time thou and thy lady were off to sail the Mithgarian seas."

Aylis and Aravan spent the next two days at the fortress, but the mark of noon on the third day found them at the western crossing, and as dim light shone down through a yellow-brown overcast, they were gone in-between.

12

Vows

Aravan and Aylis emerged upon Adonar in a copse in a small hollow of a matching vale in the Durynian Range. Unlike the valley on Neddra, here the air was crystal clear and the soil fertile, with winter-dormant grass underfoot and slender, new-budded saplings on the slopes rather than the dead brown weeds in the meager thicket of barren trees of that devastated underworld.

With their bows drawn, Elven warders stood among trees, guarding the in-between. Aravan raised a hand and, above the distant sound of hammers and saws and other echoes of construction, called out a greeting to the Lian: "*Hál, valagalana! Vio Aravan! Vi estare Dara Aylis, vo chier.*" The warriors shifted the aim of their bows to point their arrows down and away as each relaxed his draw, then smiled and sketched salutes to the pair.

"Your love, eh?" asked Aylis, a smile crinkling the light sprinkle of freckles across her cheeks.

Aravan grinned and reached out and took her hand and drew her up the slant of the hollow. "I would have it no other way."

Aylis laughed and shook her head. "You called me 'Dara,' though I am not of Elvenkind."

"Thou art and ever will be my Dara, Aylis."

"As will you be my Alor, Aravan."

Hand in hand, up the slope and out from the copse they went, to emerge upon the floor of a greening vale trapped between forested mountains to the right and moss-laden crags to the left. In the distance before them, they could see Elves at work constructing a large, palisaded fortress, heavy timbers making up the pales of the long, surrounding barrier. Towers stood at the midpoints of the walls as well as at each corner, with arrow slits positioned to cover the grounds without as well as those within. Contained by the palisades they could see a building rising, where Elven woodwrights turned augers to bore holes through the cladding and into the crossbeams beneath, while others hammered tight-fitting wooden pegs into the just-made holes. A heavily built main gate stood open along the wall facing Aravan and Aylis, revealing low barracks and other buildings across a quadrangle.

And just as was the tower on Vadaria, the fortress sat well away from the in-between to not interfere with the match of the crossing point.

As Aravan and Aylis passed through the gate and onto the fortress grounds, a slender, golden-haired Dara stepped out from one of the buildings and came toward them across the quadrangle.

"Faeon!" called Aravan.

At the sound of her name, a brilliant smile filled the Dara's features, and she called back, "Aravan!" and hurried her gait.

As Faeon neared, Aylis could see by her very movement she seemed to radiate grace.

Aravan warmly embraced Faeon, and she kissed him on the cheek. "'Tis good to see thee," said Aravan, now holding her at arm's length.

Faeon smiled up at Aravan, and then turned her clear blue-eyed gaze toward Aylis. "And thou must be the one who holds Aravan's heart."

"Um," replied Aylis. *Adon, I said "um"?* Even though she knew it was not so, still she felt ungainly and cloddish next to this elegant creature. Amending her "um," Aylis smiled and added, "So he tells me."

Aravan released Faeon, and she stepped to Aylis and embraced her, whispering, "I am so glad he found thee again."

"As am I," murmured Aylis in return, and at that moment the awkwardness fell away from her.

Aravan said, "Dara Faeon, I present Dara Aylis. Aylis, Faeon is Gildor's *jaian*—his sister."

"He is your *jarin*?" asked Aylis. "A splendid brother to have."

Faeon smiled. "Though I agree, Aylis, say it not overmuch in Gildor's presence, for I would not have him take on an unseemly strut."

All three laughed, and then Faeon said, "When we saw you coming through the gate, Inarion asked me to fetch you."

Aylis frowned. "Inarion?"

"My trothmate," said Faeon. "He is overseeing the construction of the fort."

"Ah," said Aravan, "just the one I would speak to."

Faeon led them back to the building from which she had first come, and inside at a table, mulling over scattered drawings, stood a black-haired Elf. He looked up at the sound of the door closing, his piercing grey eyes lighting with warmth at the sight of Aravan, though Aylis sensed that behind that affection a deep sadness lay. Aylis then looked at Faeon, and saw the same hint of grief behind her eyes as well.

"Aravan," the Alor said, stepping 'round the table to greet them.

"Coron Eiron," said Aravan, giving a slight bow.

"Ah, my friend, Coron no more. My days in Darda Galion are long past." He embraced Aravan, and they were of like height. Releasing Aravan, he turned toward Aylis. "And this is . . . ?"

Aravan introduced the two, adding, "She is my chier and trothmate to be." Aylis's gaze flew wide, and a blush suffused her cheeks. *Trothmate to be?*

Aylis, her heart pounding, gave a deep curtsey, but Eiron stepped to her and took her hands and raised her up. "No more, my dear. I left all that behind when I returned to Adonar after the Winter War."

"As you wish, my lord," said Aylis, finding her voice at last.

Eiron smiled and asked, "Did I hear correctly; thou art Aravan's trothmate to be?"

"I had not known it until just now," Aylis replied.

Faeon looked at Aravan and shook her head and then broke into laughter, managing to say amid her giggles, "And here I thought Aravan the most sensitive of souls, yet I find he is just like all males."

A puzzled look fell upon Aravan's face. He turned up his hands and asked, "What?"

"Didst thou ask her?"

"Well, no, but—"

"Then how dost thou know whether she will say yea or nay?"

"Well, I always—"

"Yes, Aravan, I will marry you," interjected Aylis. Then she turned to Faeon and added, "There was never any question that I would."

"Ah, I was but twigging him, Aylis, and ne'er before have I seen Aravan nonplused. He stood gaping as would a fish out of water." Faeon's silver laughter filled the air, and Eiron joined her as Aylis suppressed a grin. Aravan sighed and managed a discomfited smile.

Finally, Eiron said, "Faeon, my love, wouldst thou see these two to suitable quarters?" He gestured toward the scattered drawings. "I must get back to these plans."

Aravan asked, "Wouldst thou rather this fortress be built of stone? In fact Drimmen-built?"

"Indeed," replied Eiron. "None are better at stonework than the Drimma. I would welcome such."

"Then heed, for Alamar, Arandor, Aylis, and I have a plan. . . ."

That eve, as Aylis lay in Aravan's embrace, she said, "I sensed a deep sadness within Eiron, a reflection of sorrow echoed by Faeon as well."

"They yet mourn their *arran*," said Aravan.

"Their son?"

"Aye. 'Twas Galarun," said Aravan. "He was like a *jarin* unto me, the brother I ne'er had. E'en so, my grief is but a shadow next to theirs, for Eiron is Galarun's athir, as is Faeon Galarun's ythir."

"Galarun? The one Ydral killed to take the Silver Sword?"

Aravan sighed. "'Twas in the days of the Great War of the Ban."

They lay without speaking for long moments, but at last Aylis asked, "If it does not yet pain you, can you tell me how it happened?"

"It will always pain me, Chier, but I will tell thee regardless.

"We were on our way back from Black Mountain in faraway Xian, where the Mages had given Galarun the Silver Sword to bear back to Darda Galion. Our small band had come a long way, and finally reached the Dalgor March, there on the wold east of the Grimwall and west of the Argon some sixty leagues north of the Larkenwald. There we were joined by a company of Lian patrolling that part of Riamon, Riatha and her *jarin* Talar among them. As we made our way across the fen where the outflow of the Dalgor River widens into a wetland of many streams to spill into the Great Argon, a strange fog enveloped us—spell-cast, I ween. It was then that . . ."

In the silver light of dawn, into the delta marshlands they rode, horses plashing through reeds and water, mire sucking at hooves, the way slow and shallow, arduous but fordable, unlike the raging upstream waters of the Dalgor, hurtling down from the high Grimwalls to the west. Deep into the watery lowland they fared, at times dismounting and wading, giving the horses respite.

It was near the noontide, that late fall day, when the blue stone on the thong about Aravan's neck grew chill. He alerted Galarun that danger was nigh, and the warning went out to all. On they rode and a pale sun shone overhead, and one of the outriders called unto the main body. At a nod from Galarun, Aravan rode forth among the tall reeds to see what was amiss. He came unto the rider, Eryndar, and the Elf pointed eastward. From the direction of the Argon, rolling through the fen like a grey wall rushing came fog, flowing over them in a thick wave, obscuring all in its wake, for Aravan and Eryndar could but barely see each other less than an arm's span away. And from behind there sounded the clash and clangor and shout of combat.

"To me! To me!" came Galarun's call, muffled and distant in the mist there in the Dalgor Fen, confusing to mind and ear.

Though he could not see, Aravan spurred his horse to come to his comrades' aid, riding to the sounds of steel on steel, though they too were muted and remote and seemed to echo where no echoes should have been. He charged into a deep slough, the horse foundering, Aravan nearly losing his seat. And up from out of the water rose an enormous dark shape, and a webbed hand struck at him, claws sweeping past Aravan's face as the horse screamed and reared, the Elf ducking aside from the blow. *"Krystallopŷr,"* whispered Aravan, Truenaming the spear. He thrust the weapon into the half-seen *thing* looming above him, and a hideous yowl split the air as the blade burned and sizzled in cold flesh. With a huge splash, the creature was gone, back into the mire.

Still, somewhere in the murk a battle raged—clang and clatter and outcries. Again Aravan rode toward the sound, trusting the horse in treacherous footing. Shapes rose up from the reeds and attacked—they were Rucha and Loka alike—but the crystal spear pierced them and burned them, and they fled screaming, or fell dead.

Of a sudden the battle ended, the foe fading back into the cloaking fog, vanishing in the grey murk. And it seemed as if the strange echoing disappeared as well, the muffling gone. And the blue stone at Aravan's neck grew warm.

"Galarun!" called Aravan. "Galarun! . . ." Other voices, too, took up the cry.

Slowly they came together, did the scattered survivors, riding to one another's calls, and Galarun was not among them.

The wan sun gradually burned away the fog, and the company searched for their captain. They found him at last, pierced by crossbow quarrel and cruel barbed spear, lying in the water among the reeds, he and his horse slain . . . the Silver Sword gone.

Three days they searched for that token of power, there in the Dalgor Fen, as well as for sign of the ones who did this dreadful deed. Yet in the end they found nought but an abandoned Ruchen campsite, a campsite used less than a full day, and no trail leading outward. "Perhaps there is an in-between somewhere nigh, and they went back to Neddra," suggested Eryndar.

At last, hearts filled with rage and grief, they took up slain Galarun and the five others who had fallen and rode for Darda Galion across the wide wold. Two days passed and part of another ere they forded the River Rothro on the edge of the Eldwood forest. Travelling among the massive boles of the great trees, they forded the Quadrill the following day and later the River Cellener to come at last unto the Coron-hall in Wood's-heart, the Elvenholt central to the great forest of Darda Galion.

Aravan bore Galarun's blanket-wrapped body into the hall, where were gathered Lian waiting, mourning. Through a corridor of Elvenkind strode Aravan, toward the High Coron, and nought but silence greeted him. Eiron stepped down from the throne at this homecoming of his son, moving forward and holding out his arms to receive the body. Desolation stood in Aravan's eyes as he gave over the lifeless Elf. Eiron tenderly cradled Galarun unto himself and turned and slowly walked the last few steps unto the dais, where he laid his slain child down.

Aravan's voice was choked with emotion. "I failed him, my Coron, for

I was not at Galarun's side when he most needed me. I have failed thee and Adon as well, for thy son is dead and the Silver Sword is lost."

Bleakly, Coron Eiron looked up from the shrouded corpse, his own eyes brimming, his voice whispering. "Take no blame unto thyself, Aravan, for the death of Galarun was foretold—"

"Foretold!" exclaimed Aravan.

"—by the Mages of Black Mountain."

"If thou didst know this, then why didst thou send thy son?"

"I did not know."

"Then how—"

"Galarun's death rede," explained Eiron. "The Mages told him that he who first bore the weapon would die within the year."

Aravan remembered the grim look on Galarun's face when he had emerged from the Wizardholt of Black Mountain.

Kneeling, slowly the Coron undid the bindings on the blankets, folding back the edges, revealing Galarun's visage, the features pale and bloodless. From behind, Aravan's voice came softly. "He let none else touch the sword, and now I know why."

Coron Eiron stood, motioning to attendants, and they came and took up Galarun's body, bearing it out from the Coron-hall.

When they had gone, Aravan turned once again unto Eiron. "His death rede: was there . . . more?"

The Coron sat on the edge of the dais. "Aye: a vision of the one responsible. It was a pale white fiend who slew my Galarun; like Man he looked, but no mortal was he. Mayhap a Mage instead. Mayhap a Demon. More, I cannot say. Pallid he was, and tall, with black hair and hands lengthy and slender and wild, yellow eyes. His face was long and narrow, his nose straight and thin, his white cheeks unbearded."

"And the sword. Did Galarun—"

Aravan's words were cut off by a negative shake of Eiron's head. "The blade was yet with my son when he died."

Frustration and anger colored Aravan's voice. "But now it is missing. Long we searched, finding nought."

After a moment Eiron spoke: "If not lost in the fen, then it is stolen. And if any has the Dawn Sword, it is he: the pallid one with yellow eyes. Find him and thou mayest find the blade."

Aravan stepped back and unslung his spear from its shoulder harness; he planted the butt of the weapon to the wooden floor and knelt on one knee. "My Coron, I will search for the killer and for the sword. If he or it is to be found—"

Aravan's words were cut short, for the Coron wept. And so the Elf put aside the crystal blade and sat next to his liege lord, and with tears in his own eyes, spoke to him of the last days of his valiant son.

Aravan took a deep, shuddering breath. "That was some five millennia agone . . . and it was but a year past that Bair and I together finally fulfilled that pledge."

Aylis nodded. "You recovered the Silver Sword and slew Galarun's killer, to say nought of slaying Gyphon."

"Strictly speaking," said Aravan, "'twas Bair who slew Galarun's killer, Ydral."

Aylis gave Aravan a quick peck on the cheek and said, "Methinks you were busy at the time dealing with Gyphon."

At Aylis's words, Aravan's embrace tightened about her. "Oh, Chier, we nearly lost it all: not only the pledge and our lives, but the whole of creation."

"But you did not." Aylis gave him another quick kiss. "Now let's talk about something more cheerful . . . our trothing perhaps?"

Surrounded by winter-dressed aspens and silver birch, the crystalline waters of Lyslyn Mere lay mirror-smooth in the high, still air of the mountains. On the far side of the mere a cupping massif of alabaster stone rose sheer unto the sky, and mist twined among the trees along the shore. Snow lay upon the ground, but the broad, limpid pool held no ice; instead the waters embraced a clear reflection of stone and woodland and sky.

On a smooth outjut of pale grey granite lying along the brim, an assembly of Elvenkind stood, a female of Magekind among them, and the horses they had ridden to reach this place were tethered among the birch, their breath blowing white in the chill air. To the right of Aravan stood Inarion, for he had vouched for the Alor, and to the left of Aylis stood Faeon, who had done the same for the Dara.

Facing the four as well as the assembly stood Valar—second in command of the fort—for that Lian Guardian had been chosen to conduct the ceremony. And he had spoken the venerable words of plighting, conceived long past and pledged by trothmates ever since. He now came to the last of his guiding words and their replies and affirmations: ". . . Hence, to keep thy bond strong ye must share equally in the cultivation of the common ground and in the nurturing of the promises between; and ye must sort among all duties and participate willingly and fully in all which can be shared."

Valar then took Aylis's right hand and Aravan's left and asked, his voice soft, "Do ye comprehend all that ye have declared?"

Both Aravan and Aylis looked into one another's eyes. *We do,* they said in unison.

"Then speak true: Do ye vow to each other to tend the common ground and to cherish the pledges given and received?"

I do vow, they said in unison.

"Then speak true: Will ye plight thy troth to one another, forsaking all who would come between?"

I do vow.

Valar then placed Aylis's hand in Aravan's and clasped their joined hands in his. "Then, Dara Aylis, then, Alor Aravan, each having spoken true, go forth from here together and share thy joys and thy burdens in equal measure until thine individual destinies determine otherwise."

Valar embraced each of them, first Aylis, then Aravan, and then called out to all: "*Alori e Darai, va da, Dara Aylis e Alor Aravan, avan taeya e evon a plith.*"

And even as Aravan and Aylis kissed, a great shout went up from all and echoed among the mountains of the Durynian Range.

They rode back to the fort, Elves singing the leagues away, and as they entered through the main gate, they were greeted by cheers from those who had remained on ward. Into the partially completed assembly hall they escorted the new-pledged pair, where they found a feast waiting. The celebration lasted long, Elven bards taking turns, while lyre and lute and drum and flute filled the air with music. Poems were spoken and songs were sung and dances sedate were stepped and dances wild were flung.

Each in turn, all the Alori danced with Aylis and all the Darai with Aravan. And there was much laughter and cheer. But at last even Elvenkind had to call it a night, though they led Aravan and Aylis to their quarters, and sang them a pleasant eve.

Two days after, amid farewells and trailing packhorses, Aravan and Aylis rode out from the fort, heading for the Eldwood forest of Darda Falain, lying some three hundred leagues away. There they would cross over to the Eldwood forest of Darda Galion on Mithgar on their way to their beloved Elvenship *Eroean*.

Standing on the banquette along the palisades, Eiron and Faeon watched them ride away. And when the last of the trailing horses vanished among the distant trees, Eiron took Faeon by the hand, and they turned and went down the ramp and back to the business essential.

13

Darda Galion

In a tiny glade by a crystalline mere in the dawntime upon Mithgar, canting and chanting, their horses dancing an arcane sidle step, Aylis and Aravan came riding out from the in-between and into the Eldtree forest of Darda Galion. In the air above and winging across on their own came silverlarks singing, their carols heralding the onset of a new day, for a new day indeed had come. And in spite of a gentle rain, a warm spring breeze purled among the soaring giants, the trees shedding twilight down upon the woodland below, for within the Larkenwald Elvenkind dwelled, which the Eld Trees somehow sensed and responded to.

Aylis and Aravan were some three hundred leagues from Merchants Crossing in the south, there where the *Eroean* lay. Yet that Elven ship was not their immediate goal, but the Dwarvenholt of Drimmen-deeve instead, for Aravan would collect a Dwarven warband for his ship, and Drimmen-deeve held another treasure he needed as well as the warriors he would have.

Aravan glanced at Aylis and smiled and said, "This way, Chier." And he heeled his horse and set off easterly, leaving the mere behind. Through long twilit galleries they rode, and the limbs and foliage far above formed a canopy o'erhead, sheltering them somewhat from the light rain carried on the air, more of a mist than a shower. Now and again, however, where great clusters of leaves on high overlapped to form a broad cover, the water collected and runneled together across the dusky green layer to come tumbling down through the dawn light in a long, streaming cascade.

And as they rode, Aylis marveled at the size of the soaring behemoths, some rising nigh nine hundred feet into the air, the girths of their boles many paces around, their broad limbs widely reaching. She knew, too, that the wood of the Eld Tree was precious—prized above all others—and she wondered how it was harvested. As if reading her thoughts, Aravan said, "None of these have ever been felled by any of the Free Folk, though long past, in the First Era, some were hacked down in malice by *Rûpt*. 'Twas the Felling of the Nine; but Elven vengeance was swift and without mercy. Examples were made of the ax wielders, and their remains were displayed to *Spaunen* in their mountain haunts throughout Mithgar; and never again has an Eld Tree been hewn in Darda Galion."

"But I have seen dear things made of this wood," said Aylis. "If not hewn, then how—?"

Aravan gestured at the surround. "At times a gathering is made in the forest, for occasionally lightning or a great wind from the south sweeping o'er the wide plains of Valon will cause branches to fall; and these are collected by the Lian storm-gleaners, and treasures dear are fashioned of this precious timber."

"What of storm-felled trees?" asked Aylis. "Or those that simply topple of old age? Surely now and again a tree falls in the forest."

Aravan nodded. "Thou art right, my love: Eld Trees sometimes die. And for each that does so, we mourn, for the trees somehow know when Elvenkind dwell nigh and shed their twilight down. And there are among Elvenkind those who in turn are attuned to the trees and feel the passing of each."

"Some of you can sense the loss of one of these giants?"

"Aye. Arin Flameseer of the Dylvana was one. In fact, she felt the deaths of the Nine, or rather I should say their murder."

They rode in silence for a moment, and then Aravan said, "When an Eld Tree falls, the master carvers long study each branch and twig, each root and nub, and every inch of the full of the bole, sensing the grain, sensing the shapes trapped within, ere setting ought to ought."

"Do these grow elsewhere on Mithgar?"

"But for the Lone Eld Tree in Arden Vale, they do not." Then Aravan added, "This entire forest was transplanted here from Adonar. 'Twas the work of Silverleaf."

"Oh, my," said Aylis. "It must have taken forever."

Aravan laughed. "Not quite, Chier. Not quite." Then he sobered and added, "There are, however, some events that last forever, and the Felling of the Nine was one of these."

"Signal events," said Aylis. "Though some do not last, as you say, 'forever,' still in every life they occur. At times they change the destinies of those involved."

Aravan nodded his agreement and said, "Some events sweep up many in their wake—wars and such—while others affect only one."

Aylis looked at him and asked, "What were some of yours? —Signal events, I mean."

"The first time I laid eyes on the sea is one," said Aravan.

"On Adonar?"

"Nay, on Mithgar. 'Twas dawn when I first rode out of Adonar and into Mithgar in the early days of the First Era, coming to the youth and wildness of this new world, leaving behind the stately grace and beauty of ancient Adonar. As I knew I would, when I emerged I found myself in a misty swale, with grassy crowns of mounded hills all about, for, as all such in-between crossings must be, the cast of the terrain was fair matched to that I had left on Adonar. But what I did not expect was the distant sound that to my ears came: *shssh*ing booms. Intrigued, I turned my horse toward the rolling roar, riding southerly among the diminishing downs. Upward my path took me, up a long and shallow slope, the sounds increasing, the wind in my face, a salt tang on the air. And I found myself on a high chalk cliff, the white bluff falling sheer. Out before me as far as the eye could see stretched deep blue waters to the horizon and beyond. It was the ocean, the Avagon Sea, its azure waves booming below, high-tossed spray glittering like diamonds cast upward in the morning sun. My heart sang at such a sight and my eyes brimmed with tears, and in that moment something slipped comfortably into my soul, for it seemed I was home at last."

"Oh, Aravan, how beautiful."

Aravan grinned and said, "Not as beautiful as when thou didst come climbing o'er the rail of the *Eroean*. 'Twas the most signal event in my life."

As she had done on that day, Aylis blushed, remembering the time. For she had seen Aravan ere then . . . or his image, rather. As a neophyte in her first year at the College of Mages in Kairn, the City of Bells on Rwn, like many young maidens with Seer Talent she had cast a spell upon a small silver mirror, asking to see her truelove; in her case, Aravan's visage had come into view. And so, years later when she had intercepted the *Eroean* and had clambered over the rail and set eyes upon him, her heart hammered and her face flushed, and Aravan had reached out to steady her, and a spark leapt between the two, startling both. And so, that first meeting had been a signal event for her as well.

Even as Aylis relived the experience, Aravan's smile vanished and a bleakness stared out from his eyes. "But the second-most-important event of my life was when I thought thou wert gone forever into the deeps with Rwn. The loss of Galarun was hard, but the loss of thee was worse. It was then I gave up the sea, right after thy 'death' was avenged."

"Oh, Aravan, I would not have had you forsake the ocean and certainly not the *Eroean*."

"But for the time of the Winter War, the *Eroean* sat idle in the Hidden Grotto in Thell Cove."

"You sailed her in the Winter War?"

"Aye. A crew and I took on the Rovers of Kistan during those terrible days. But afterward, we put her back in the grotto, and there she sat until the Wolfmage drew her forth and sailed her unto Port Arbalin for Bair and me to use in the time of the Trine."

"No more, Aravan, no more," said Aylis. "You must promise me that should ought happen, you will—"

"Chier, my heart went out of me when I thought thee gone forever. I had no love for ought, not e'en the sea or my ship."

They rode in silence for long moments, and surreptitiously Aylis turned her face away from Aravan to wipe away her tears.

Noting her attempt to hide her shared desolation for Aravan's long years of despair, Aravan said, "But then, mayhap e'en more signal than when first we met came but two winters past, for that was when I discovered that thou wert yet alive and not gone down with Rwn, and my heart and my love were restored unto me."

Aylis smiled, her eyes again brimming, but this time at remembered joy. "It was so for me as well, yet I thought you might die, wounded as you were."

Aravan reached out and briefly touched her hand, and they rode side by side in quietness, and only a soft sound of a nearby cascade showering down from the canopy above broke the peace of their shared solitude.

But at last Aylis asked, "Speaking of the time of the Trine, what about the death of Gyphon? Was that not a signal event in your life?"

A rueful smile twitched Aravan's mouth, and he said, "It was, Chier. But even more signal was what Raudhrskal did right after; that will be with me forever."

"Raudhrskal the Dragon?"

"Aye. He not only saved Bair and me, but the whole of Mithgar as well."

"Tell me, love."

Aravan took a deep breath and then let it out and said, "Gyphon was slain, and Ydral dead, and the Crystal Cavern began to collapse. Bair and I fled, but the Great Abyss was yet agape, with the entire world being sucked down and in. . . ."

A furlong or two from the in-between, just as Aravan came to the last of his story, they passed by Lian sentries to come into Wood's-heart, the Elvenholt at the core of Darda Galion, where thatch-roofed white cottages nestled among the trees of the soaring Larkenwald.

Even as they dismounted before the central hall, they were met by the newly crowned Coron of all Elves on Mithgar: flaxen-haired Tuon of the ice-blue eyes. And from the dais in the great hall, Aravan spoke to a gathered assembly of the winning of the Black Fortress on Neddra by a battalion of Elves and seven nines of Magekind. He spoke of the occupation of the stronghold and the plans to guard and control the nexus to keep it out of Rûptish hands, for one of its in-betweens was now the only known crossing to the Mage world of Vadaria, and to lose that would be to lose much.

Aylis then told of the subsequent massive attempt to regain the fortress by nigh a full Horde of Spaunen two fortnights and a sevenday later, and the victory achieved by allies, by might and main and Magery, and by the use of illusory Dragons, their intangible flames augmented by the castings of Firemages. She added, however, that it was almost a certainty that the Spawn would have been repelled even without the phantasmal Drakes: not only did Arandor's company of Lian and Dylvana hold the fortress upon the high ground, but the reserve <fire> of defending Magekind was and is considerable; along with this she mentioned that using the illusions of Dragons simply meant less overall expenditure of <life essence> by the defending Wizards.

"What of Trolls among the Foul Folk?" asked slender, black-haired Dara Irilyn. "Could they not shatter the gates, given a ram like the one known as Whelm?"

Aylis smiled. "Aye, they could, yet my father says if Trolls ever again come to knock at the door, they will be greeted by searing lightning that will stroke their hides and send any survivors screaming into the hills."

After the laughter died down, another Dara rose to her feet and asked, "Were there Draedani among the foe?"

Aylis shook her head. "Nay, yet there are Mages among those at the fortress who might be powerful enough—though that is not at all a certainty—to banish a Gargon back to the Demon world. If that proves not to be feasible, the Healers among the allies can cast calmness upon our forces, enough so that the Elves at the ballistas could launch spears at the Fearcaster, just like the ballista-flung lance slew the Gargon at Dendor during the War of the Ban."

"Even so," said the Dara, "with many Draedani among the foe would they not pose a dreadful risk?"

"They would," replied Aylis. "Yet my father says that it would require a very powerful Black Mage to summon each one from Grygar, and for a number of Dread Ones to be called, it would take many powerful dark Wizards. Modru, Durlok, mayhap Ordrune: they were powerful enough to do so. But they were in a class of their own; yet all three are now dead. Mayhap there is not a living Black Mage powerful enough to draw forth a Gargon from the Demon Plane, much less enough to summon several."

A look of relief swept over the faces of many in the assembly, for they well knew the terror such monsters could bring.

A ginger-haired Alor asked, "Aravan, what are the plans for rotation of

Lian and Dylvana in and out of the Black Fortress company? It cannot be pleasant living upon Neddra."

"For the nonce, Theril, by choice that duty falls to our kindred on the High World; they cite the fact that it has been long since they were in battle against the Rûpt, whereas the Dylvana and Lian on Mithgar have since engaged in two great wars—the Winter War against Modru, and the War of the Dragonstone against the Fists of Rakka and the Golden Horde of the so-called Dragonking—while they sat idle on Adonar . . . through no fault of their own, I add, for in those times the Planes were yet sundered one from the other."

At Aravan's side, Tuon said, "Would that we of the Darda Galion ward had been in those battles, those of us who were here at the time. Yet we could not leave the Larkenwald undefended." Tuon smiled and shook his head and added, "Though with the small company I had after Inarion and the others went unto the High Plane, we would have been hard-pressed to defend this realm against a force of any size."

"Thou wert here in the Eldwood when Bair and I crossed to the Larkenwald from Adonar?" asked Aravan.

Tuon nodded. "Aye, though on patrol when the Dawn Rider and thee and the silverlarks came, though afterward Silverleaf told us of the event that he and the Dylvana had seen here in Wood's-heart."

When the questions had run their course, with Aravan and Aylis responding, Tuon called for a halt, for the mark of noon had come. Then Aylis and Aravan joined Tuon for a midday meal. As they retired to a bench under the spread of one of the giants, "Your weapon, Tuon," said Aylis, gesturing at the dark spear Tuon set aside, "its aura bears strange <fire>."

"'Tis named Black Galgor," Tuon replied. "Some say it has a destiny to fulfill, though none knows what it might be."

"What of the Well of Uâjii?" asked Aravan.

Tuon shrugged. "Mayhap that was Black Galgor's destiny, though Silverleaf claims it was his arrows brought down the wyrm, while Halíd claims it was his great shamsheer did the creature in."

"You must tell me this tale," said Aylis, curiosity filling her gaze.

"Aye, that I will," said Tuon. But then he shook his head, saying,

"'Twill pale by comparison to the story of the Dawn Sword. Hai, would that I had seen that blade." He glanced at Black Galgor and then at Aylis. "I ween its aura was filled to bursting with what you name <fire>."

"Nay, not that sword," said Aylis. "Though it was a token of power, it had no <fire> whatsoever."

"But it slew Gyphon," protested Tuon.

"Aye, it did," agreed Aravan. "But Bair, too, saw no aura on it."

"Nor did my father, Alamar," said Aylis. "Nor did Dalor and Branwen, who were there as well. Father thinks mayhap *that* was its power, for all other things I have ever seen have had at least a flicker of aethyr, yet the sword had none. And mayhap by having no aura whatsoever, that's why it could not be diverted by Gyphon, and why it could penetrate his <shield> and rip his <fire> from him."

"Where now is that fabled blade?" asked Tuon.

Aravan shrugged. "'Tis gone forever, down into the Abyss along with Gyphon and Ydral and the Crystal Cavern and most of the Great Swirl and a monstrous gulp of the Sindhu Sea."

Two days after, Aylis and Aravan rode out from Wood's-heart and headed northward. They were bound for Drimmen-deeve, or as the Drimma called it, Kraggen-cor. They crossed the Cellener and late that eve came to the Quadrill, where they turned their mounts to follow along that watercourse. Two more days passed ere they emerged from the forest and came into sight of the Grimwall Mountains lying some four leagues to the west, the dark peaks heretofore shielded from view by the massive boles of the trees. The range ran beyond seeing to north and south; grim in its fastness it was, and said to be filled with the dens of Foul Folk. Yet those fetid holes lay not nigh the Eldwood, nor in the sweep of Drimmen-deeve, for neither Elves nor Dwarves abided Spawn to live in their immediate grasp. Southward the mountains ran toward the Great Escarpment, forking in twain: the main spine to turn westerly and head for far-off Gothon and Tugal and Basq to finally end in Vancha, the other to dwindle into the Gûnarring, to arc about the land of Gûnar and eventually rise once more to rejoin the main run of the range. Northward the peaks ran toward Gron and Jord, to turn easterly and flow all the way to Jinga and nearly reach the Shining Sea. But in the distance, mayhap three or so

days away at the pace they were riding, they could see four peaks towering above the rest—'twas the Quadran, consisting of Greytower, Grimspire, Loftcrag, and Stormhelm, this last towering above all.

Below these four mighty mountains lay their goal—the Dwarvenholt
of Drimmen-deeve—and Aravan and Aylis heeled their horses and rode
onward, leaving Darda Galion behind.

14

Kraggen-cor

JOURNEY TO THE *EROEAN*
LATE SPRING 6E1

"I can see why Greytower is so called," said Aylis, pointing at the ashen rock of that peak, "and the blackness of Grimspire would seem to give that mountain its name. But given the tint of the stone, I would think Loftcrag would be called Bluecrag or Skycrag, while ruddy Stormhelm ought to be called Bloodhelm or some such."

"'Twas Humankind that gave them those names, hence I cannot say why they are called as they are. Elves, on the other hand, name them respectively, Garlon, Aevor, Chagor, and Coron."

"Coron, as in the High King of Elves?"

"Aye, for it is the mightiest mountain in the Grimwall."

Aylis laughed. "You think much of Elvenkind to name it so."

"Ah, Chier, I did not say it was the mightiest mountain in all of Mithgar, for I have seen giants of mountains in the Jangdi Range."

Again Aylis laughed and added, "I take it that Elvenkind is not the mightiest in all of Mithgar, then."

"Oh, my love, surely I would not say that," replied Aravan, and his laugh joined hers.

Again Aylis looked at the four peaks. "What do the Dwarves call them?"

"Uchan, Aggarath, Ghatan, and Ravenor."

"And Drimmen-deeve lies under those four?"

"Aye," replied Aravan. "And it is a mountainfast no foe could penetrate until the Gargon was set free from the Lost Prison. Then it lay open to enemies, though only the Rûpt took advantage, for they were sent to occupy the Deeves by Modru. 'Twas he who summoned the Draedan to deal with the Drimma."

"Ah, again Gargons," said Aylis.

"Shall I tell thee the tale? How the Drimma, when mining starsilver, weakened the wall of the Gargon's Lair? I know but part of it, not all."

"Nay, love, let me <see> for myself; then I will tell the whole of it to you."

"Ah, for the nonce I had forgotten thy calling," said Aravan with a smile.

Aylis's gaze swept over the four peaks of the Quadran. "A formidable fastness, you say?"

Aravan nodded. "Nigh impenetrable."

"Well, then, I do hope they let us in."

"Fear not, Chier," said Aravan, "for I am Châk-Sol—Dwarf-Friend—so named long past by Tolak. After several perilous encounters during the many journeys to obtain that which was needed for the construction of the *Eroean*, it was by his decree that I became Châk-Sol. He also vouched for me when I went to the third Khana Durek in Drimmen-deeve for a pound of starsilver needed to paint the hull of the *Eroean* to keep barnacles and other such away from her bottom. And I intend to ask DelfLord Balor for another pound when we reach Drimmen-deeve."

" 'Twas a priceless gift they gave you," said Aylis.

Aravan shrugged and said, "Paid back more than tenfold by the experience and knowledge the Drimma gathered in return, to say nought of a share of the goods received at the end of each voyage. Well-earned, I add, by each and every Drimmen warband that has served on my ship."

"And now we go to recruit a new one, eh?"

"We do," replied Aravan . . .

. . . and on they rode.

Three days passed and a part of another ere the golden sun in a high blue sky found Aravan and Aylis riding up the Pitch, a long slope of land rising into the embrace of the Quadran—four mountains lying more or less in a square: To the left flank stood ashen Greytower, and just to the west loomed ebon Grimspire; to the right soared azure-hued Loftcrag, while straight ahead towered ruddy Stormhelm. It was toward this latter they were headed, for there stood the Dawn Gate, the eastern entry into Kraggen-cor.

They had followed a pave past a rune-carved realmstone, announcing that from this point forward they trod upon a Dwarven domain.

They passed by another realmstone, this one broken, the top half of the column missing. It stood on a stone ledge jutting out from the shore of a small lakelet fed by the flow of the Quadrill down from the steeps lying between Stormhelm and Loftcrag. "Here at the Quadmere it was that First Durek declared this realm to belong to the Drimma of his line," said Aravan, looking toward the shorn pillar.

Aylis frowned and turned her head to the right. "What is that distant roar?"

" 'Tis the Vorvor, Durek's Wheel, a whirlpool in a fold of stone along the flank of Loftcrag. There a furious river bursts forth from the mountain and spins 'round a stone basin to disappear down through a central cavity, like unto a drain in a vat. Whence from there, none knows. 'Tis said First Durek was cast by Rûpt into that wrath and drawn far below the earth. 'Twas then that the Drimmen war with the Spaunen began, and has raged so ever since."

"Not a pleasant way to leave this life," said Aylis.

"Oh, he survived," said Aravan, "yet whether he died or merely came to Death's door is in some dispute among the Drimma. Some contend he passed into that realm, but fought his way back out. Knowing the stubbornness of the Drimma, I would not dispute that claim."

Aylis laughed and on they rode, and within a mile they crossed a stone courtyard to come before the eastern gate into Drimmen-deeve, its massive iron leaves standing open and warded by four armed and armored Dwarves.

Escorted by the captain of the gate ward, a dark-haired, dark-eyed Dwarf named Brekk, past the great iron doors of the portal known as the Dawn Gate and into an entry hall they went, the hooves of their horses clattering upon rock. Delved out of the red granite of Stormhelm, and with the smell of stone in the air, the chamber before them was huge: perhaps two hundred yards in length and nearly as wide. The ceiling above stood some thirty feet high and was covered with machicolations, murder holes from which would rain death—burning oil and melted lead and crossbow bolts and darts and other such—in the unlikely event an invader breached the formidable outer gates. All along the walls were slots in the stone, arrow slits, through which more bolts would fly; they were steel-shuttered from behind and closed at this time.

Past these formidable defenses Aravan and Aylis followed Brekk toward an exit at the far end, an outlet which led into a broad corridor and down, gently sloping into the interior of Drimmen-deeve. And with the shod hooves of the trailing horses echoing from the nearby stone walls, they passed into this roadway. As if she were using her <sight>, Aylis looked overhead, where stood a wide slot above, in which she could see the bottom edge of a thick, black-iron slab, and deep grooves ran down the walls to mate with another slot across the floor.

Aylis whispered, "A gate, a great iron plate, set to drop down the grooves and into the channel below and seal the way?"

Aravan nodded.

Aylis murmured, "How do they lock it down, and afterward pull it back up?"

"I ween they have latch bolts in a corridor above and a geared winch to haul it back up," said Aravan.

Along the wide corridor they went, the hallway lit blue-green by phosphorescent Châkka lanterns, casting a ghastly aspect over all. Down through this spectral glow they trod, along the gentle descent, more murder holes overhead, with the faint hint of an odor of oil drifting down. A furlong or so they went this way, when the corridor came to an end at last, with another floor channel and more wall grooves, while ensconced in an overhead slot a thick iron slab awaited. They issued out onto a broad landing at the top of a short flight of wide stairs leading down to a broad shelf of stone, which in turn came to an abrupt end at a wide rift cleft in the rock. Black and yawning, the deep abyss barred the way: the ebon gape split out of a vast crack in the high rock wall on one side to jag across the expansive stone floor and disappear into another great crack on the opposite wall. It was a mighty barrier, some fifty feet across at the narrowest point, a hundred or more at the widest. Over the immense chasm spanned a broad wooden drawbridge, and a shielded winch on the far side stood ready to hale the counterweighted bascule up and away and lock it in place at need. Dwarven warriors warded the hoist and the bridge.

Beyond the mighty fissure the wide stone floor continued, and by the light of Dwarven lanterns affixed in wall sconces Aylis could see the whole of a vast chamber: its extent was a mile or more, its width may-hap half that, its high-vaulted ceiling some hundred feet up, the roof of the chamber supported by four rows of giant pillars marching away to the end.

"Yon is the War Hall," said Aravan, "a mustering chamber should en-emies march up Falanith to threaten this holt."

"Falanith is the Pitch?"

"Aye," replied Aravan.

Brekk nodded his agreement and said, "We have mustered here many a time when the Grg tried to conquer this place. Some have managed to breach the old outer gates, but none has ever won across the Great Deôp against the assembled Châkka."

Aylis said, "I was told an army of Spawn once occupied Drimmen-deeve."

"Aye, it is true." Brekk glanced at Châk-Sol Aravan, and then at Aylis. As if making up his mind, he took a deep breath and slowly let it out and then said, "It was after the Ghath—the Gargon—was set free and we were driven from this place. During the Winter War, Modru sent a Horde of Squam to Kraggen-cor, making ready to conquer this part of Mithgar. But his Ghath was slain by the Deevewalkers, and afterward Modru was defeated. There passed two hundred years and some, but at last Seventh Durek brought an army to reclaim our holt, and the Squam were con-quered in the War of Kraggen-cor."

Aylis turned to Aravan. "Deevewalkers?"

"I could tell you that tale, Chier, but in the library of the *Eroean* is a copy of *The Ravenbook*, wherein the entire story is recorded. It is a grip-ping saga, and one that you will find to your liking."

"Then I will wait," said Aylis. "But the story of the Gargon in this stronghold is one I will winnow out for myself."

A dark look crossed Brekk's features, as if speaking of those long-past days filled him with shame, for, just as in the story of Blackstone, wherein the Châkka had fled their holt, stolen by the Dragon Sleeth, here the Dwarves had abandoned their homeland, too, had fled from an enemy they could not defeat.

"Come," he said. "Mayhap DelfLord Balor will be free. If not, I will show you to quarters while you await an audience."

Rather than risk the horses to the steps, Brekk turned leftward. Down a ramp all went, at the bottom of which they swung to the right and thence to the drawbridge. As they passed over, Aylis looked down. The walls of the abyss were smooth and sheer and dropped straight for as far as the eye could see and vanished into dark depths below. "How deep is this?"

"I know not," said Aravan, while just ahead of them Brekk turned up a hand as if saying, *Who knows?*

As they reached the floor of the War Hall, Brekk called a Dwarf to him, and bade him to lead the horses to the stables, as well to deliver the possessions of the visitors unto the guest quarters. Then rightward he turned to escort the travellers across the hall, toward one of the many exits leading off into passages carved through the stone. On the way to the opening they passed two of the many giant red-granite columns supporting the roof of the chamber. On each pillar the figure of a Dragon was carved twining up and around the great fluted shaft.

Into the passageway they stepped, and up a flight of stairs and then another and another, the group turning left and right and left and . . . At the top of yet another flight of stairs, they came into a long, narrow chamber, where a rune-covered archway athwart the midpoint spanned the full of the width. Aylis looked about, a slight frown of concentration on her face. "The aethyr of this stone is different from that which we have passed through ere now."

"Bair said something of the like when last I was here," said Aravan.

"This is the Hall of the Gravenarch," said Brekk. "Here it was that Braggi and his warband made their last stand, but the Ghath came and slew him and his valiant raiders. Some years later, during the Winter War, to hinder the Ghath, the Deevewalkers broke the arch and the ceiling collapsed. Some two hundred and thirty-one years after that war, we retook Kraggen-cor from the Grg. A decade or so later, we restored the chamber."

"I assume this tale is in *The Ravenbook*," said Aylis.

"Not Braggi's tale, but that of the Deevewalkers is," replied Aravan. "Also in the book is appended the story of the War of Kraggen-cor. Last summer, Faeril gave me a copy of the combine. I sent it by messenger to Long Tom to place it in the *Eroean*'s library. Thou canst read it there."

Out from the Hall of the Gravenarch they passed, turning leftward along a corridor. "Here we are on the Sixth Rise," said Brekk. "The Great Hall lies just ahead."

Now they came into a huge, dimly lighted chamber, fully a half mile from end to end and a quarter mile across. And in the center and surrounded by glowing, phosphorescent lanterns sitting on pedestals of stone, mid a seated gathering of Dwarves armed and armored for battle, stood DelfLord Balor, explaining a particular tactic of war.

"We train here," explained Brekk.

Balor, his dark hair shot through with silver, and dressed in black-iron chain, warmly greeted Aravan and was introduced to Aylis. Leaving Brekk to continue the lesson, the DelfLord led the visitors to a side hall, wherein they were served tea and scones to assuage their appetites until the evening meal. When the Dwarven page left them to themselves, Balor asked, "What brings you to my holt?"

"With your permission, DelfLord, I've come to recruit a warband to serve on the *Eroean*," said Aravan.

Balor smiled. "So you are returning to the sea." Then a look of puzzlement filled his grey eyes. "But why Kraggen-cor? Is it not true that your warbands of the past came from the Red Hills?"

"Two reasons, my lord: first, many of the Red Hills Drimma came here after you retook this holt from the Rûpt. And as is my wont, I like to have the descendants of those who served with me in the past be the ones to serve in the present, for the strength of proven blood ofttimes runs true."

Balor nodded. "Indeed. And you may gather your forty from among my warriors. The experience will benefit them, I would think."

"Thank you, my lord," said Aravan.

Balor frowned, as if trying to capture an elusive memory; then he brightened. "Captain Brekk can assist you, Aravan, for I believe that one of his ancestors sailed on the *Eroean* long past."

"Oh," said Aravan. "Dost thou recall his name?"

"Bokar, it was, I think."

"Ah, yes. Armsmaster Bokar. I remember him well," said Aravan.

"As do I," said Aylis, for he had been the Dwarven warband leader in those days millennia agone when she had sailed upon the *Eroean* ere the destruction of Rwn.

Aravan's gaze lost its focus as he remembered times past. Then he said, "A mighty warrior was Bokar, and if Brekk is anything like his ancestor . . ."

"He is one of my finest captains," said Balor.

"Then done and done," said Aravan. "Brekk will be my new armsmaster."

Balor then cocked an eyebrow and asked, "And the second reason you are here . . . ?"

"I need a pound of starsilver," said Aravan, grinning.

Balor broke into laughter and said, "As you did Khana Durek, so you do me. But must it be a whole pound?"

"Aye, for 'tis time the keel and underside coat of the *Eroean* needs replenishing."

Balor shook his head and sighed. "Starsilver used as an ingredient in paint for a ship's hull. It seems a waste."

"Not a waste, my lord," said Aravan, "for barnacles cannot cling to starsilver and it rejects growth, hence my ship will run all the faster with her argent bottom. And as you know, you will profit well beyond the measure of the silveron's worth."

Balor smiled and said, "We are currently working the lode nigh the Lair of the Ghath. I will send a message for a pound to be newly delved and refined for your use."

Just after breaking fast the next day, as Aravan, with Brekk's aid, began recruiting a warband, Aylis sought out Balor.

"Starsilver mining and refining: Might I go and see how this is done?" asked Aylis. "Besides, Aravan said that the Gargon broke free of its lair, and I would see that place, if I might."

Balor swept a hand toward the far reaches of Kraggen-cor and said, "It would be my pleasure to guide you myself."

Balor and Aylis saddled two ponies and, following a trade road that had one terminus at the Dawn Gate and the other at the Dusk Door, they set out along the road, with its twisting but gently sloped up and down stone passages that would take them nigh the silveron vein lying some thirty-six miles away. As they journeyed, Aylis spoke of the taking of the black fortress, and the need for the Châkka to learn the rite for the crossing of the Planes. The morning waxed as they rode, though, underground as they were, Aylis could but guess as to the mark of the day; nevertheless, she took Balor at his word when he said that the noontide had come. They stopped by an undermountain stream for a meal and to feed and water the ponies, but took up the ride shortly after. "Even though we are pressing the pace," said Balor, "it will be two candlemarks after sunset when we arrive. My lady, I would not have you overtired, and so we will stay the morrow and return the day after." Onward they rode, and Aylis spoke of the days she and Aravan had had on the *Eroean*.

At last they came to a small underground community, where the starsilver miners were quartered. As they arrived at the stable, two young Dwarves—no more than teens, for their beards were not yet in evidence—took the animals back into the stalls to care for them. Balor then guided Aylis to a mess hall, where they took a meal along with Dwarven miners, after which to the gathering therein, Aylis told of the taking of the Black Fortress, this time speaking fluent Châkur.

The next morning Balor guided her along a pathway and over a bridge under which water flowed, and thence they went along a shelf toward where starsilver lay. Just ahead was a breach in the stone, and beyond that stood a chamber, one whose floor and walls and ceiling were crisscrossed with jagged silveron veins. As Aylis entered she noted a faint foul odor on the air, which seemed to emanate from a huge stone slab centered in the room. Rectangular it was and with a flat top, rather like a dais, and it held carvings along the sides. And along the sides as well were runes smeared in dark ichor. Aylis frowned and then said a word, then translated aloud, "Tuuth Uthor."

"That was the name of the Ghath," said Balor.

"This then is the Gargon's Lair?"

"Aye."

"And you did not remove his name?"

"It reminds us of our shame," said Balor. "We fled."

"It is no shame to flee a Gargon," said Aylis. "They are Fearcasters."

"Nevertheless," said Balor.

At the far end along one side a wide stone doorway gaped, and from beyond came the sounds of hammers striking chisels and the chanking and clanging of a working mine.

Balor led Aylis through the opening, and there she saw Dwarves cutting silveron-laden rock from the walls.

"Here lies that which is more precious than diamond," said Balor, gesturing widely.

"And you are giving a pound to Aravan," said Aylis.

Balor merely nodded.

After a moment, Aylis looked back toward the Gargon's Lair. "Yet you do not mine the starsilver in that place?"

Balor shook his head. "As I said, it serves to remind us of our shame. Mayhap if such a thing happens again, we will not flee."

And perhaps you will die needlessly, thought Aylis; she did not say it aloud.

At a gesture from Balor, one of the miners brought a small sample of the stone to the DelfLord, who handed it to Aylis. She looked at the rock with its scintillant glitter, then handed it back.

Balor said, "We find it five ways: veins, sheets, flakes, nuggets, and as an ore. The veins, flakes, sheets, and nuggets take little or no refinement, but this"—he held up the stone—"is the hardest to separate from the rock. We crush it to a fine dust and wash it down a very long sluiceway, and the heavier starsilver sinks to the bottom and is trapped by retaining bars, while the lighter stone powder is carried away."

"I see," said Aylis, and again she looked back at the Lair.

"Would you like to examine the Lost Prison?" asked Balor.

"Indeed. In fact, if you don't mind, I would use my powers to <see>."

Balor turned up a hand and inclined his head in assent.

As Aylis stepped back into the Lair, Balor followed and stood silently by.

Aylis laid a hand on the upraised block, and then muttered an arcane word and after a moment said, "Four. There are four events of significance here."

She fell silent and closed her eyes. Heartbeats passed, and then she smiled and said, "Ah, that's how it was made."

More moments passed, and she gasped. "It comes, the Gargon." Her heart raced, for once before she had faced such a Demon, in a dreamwalk with the Pysk Jinnarin. "It is but a vision of things long past," Aylis murmured a time or two, the mantra settling her fast-beating pulse. Then she smiled and said, "The trap is sprung."

After still another moment she gasped and with unseeing eyes looked toward the gaping hole and cried, "Oh, Adon, it's loose! It's loose! No-no-no-no, the slaughter, the terrible slaughter." Aylis, weeping, broke free of the vision and turned to Balor and, sobbing, leaned into him.

At a loss, Balor stood rigid for a heartbeat or two, but then embraced the Seeress and silently held her till the weeping subsided.

Finally, Aylis took a deep breath and Balor released her. She stepped away and said, "Forgive me, DelfLord, but it was a terrible thing I <saw>."

"The Châkka, they could do nought?" he asked.

"Nothing," replied Aylis. "The Fearcaster's gaze froze them."

"As we thought," said Balor.

Long moments passed in silence, but at last Aylis said, "There is one more event I would <see>, the fourth and most recent one of those I detected."

But Balor held up a hand of caution. "My lady, are you certain you would see this thing? I would not have you suffer again."

Aylis's heart went out to the stalwart Dwarf who sought to protect her from perhaps a vision of sorrow. "Lord Balor, I thank you, yet whether it is a revelation of distress or joy, it is one which I must <see>."

Balor sighed and inclined his head in acquiescence.

Aylis braced herself and laid a hand on the slab and whispered an arcane word. Once more she wept, this time softly, at the <sight> of seven allies who were trapped herein, only to escape Foul Folk and fire, though not all made it out alive.

The following day, Aylis and Balor returned to the eastern end of the Dwarvenholt. But Aylis was not finished with her <seeing>. She paid a visit to the Hall of the Gravenarch, where she witnessed two more events, the first one again leaving her in tears, for she <saw> Braggi and his raiders go down to defeat. The second event concerned the Deevewalkers and the destruction of the hall, this latter leading to her third place of <seeing>: the bridge over the Great Deep. And there she <witnessed> the demise of the Gargon, though it was a close thing, and it took all four Deevewalkers to do the Demon in, more by accident than design.

In all, Aravan and Brekk needed three days to choose the thirty-nine other Dwarven members of the warband, and they had just begun making preparations for the journey south to the *Eroean*.

That night Aravan said, "Thou didst vanish, Chier. I slept alone yesternight and the night before."

"I was learning about starsilver, love, and winnowing out signal events. Perhaps one day I will tell you what I gathered. Besides, you were busy, and what better way for me to while away the time? And as for sleeping alone, well, so did I."

"Thou art not yet ready to tell me what thou didst glean from thy study?"

Aylis smiled and said, "Not yet," but Aravan noted her eyes were glistening, as of tears unshed. He said nought, but simply took her in his arms and held her close.

That night they made tender love, and the next morning Aravan left the holt and took to wing as a falcon and flew toward Darda Erynian, the Great Greenhall, that forest lying eastward nigh fifty leagues and across the River Argon. It was therein where Aravan hoped to recruit a special scout.

The next morning as well Aylis closeted herself with DelfLord Balor and the holt's Loremasters and she related to them what she had learned concerning the Gargon's Lair and the relevant events thereafter. Even then her eyes filled with tears, as did those of the Châkka listening, and they cast their hoods over their heads at the telling of when the Gargon broke free and slew the miners who had inadvertently set it loose. They wept as well when she spoke of how Braggi and his raiders were slaughtered by that dreadful monster. Yet they cast back their hoods and shouted,

"Châkka shok! Châkka cor!" and "Brega, Bekki's Son!" and "Hál, Deeve-walkers!" when she told how that Fearcaster had met its doom.

That evening, as Aylis returned to her quarters, lost in contemplation, she took a wrong turn and wandered into corridors heretofore untrodden by her. And as she started down another of these, at the far end she noted several veiled and graceful beings shepherding a number of chattering Châkka offspring at the distant end of a long corridor. Without thought, Aylis spoke an arcane word invoking her <sight>.

Oh, my, they are all male children, and those with them—females they are, and long past their childhood—yet their <fire> is completely different from that of Châkka males. Are these Châkia? The hue of their <fire> would make them be of the Kind I learned about when I studied in the City of Bells. If so, what are they doing here?

Of a sudden, Aylis realized that these were indeed the Châkia, and exactly who and what these graceful creatures were. *Oh, my, could this be a punishment set by Elwydd in atonement for a long-past dark deed?* In that moment she realized why they were in the Dwarvenholt, and she wondered if the male Dwarves knew these things or if it was instead a long-held secret.

All this Aylis grasped with but a single glance, and she quickly turned away and said another arcane word to lessen the level of her <sight>, for she would not further pry into the privacy of those she had seen.

As she retraced her steps to reach her own quarters, Aylis knew that it would be unlikely she would ever tell anyone ought of what she had inadvertently learned.

The next morning, Aylis and forty-two armed and armored Châkka assembled in the East Hall at the Dawn Gate, along with Aylis's horse and all the ponies and supplies they needed for the full of the trek. Forty of the Dwarves formed the warband that would serve on the *Eroean*; the remaining two would bring the animals back to the Dwarvenholt once the far goal had been reached. Easterly they would ride in cavalcade, aiming for the ferry at Olorin Isle and Darda Erynian beyond, where, at the ruins of Caer Lindor, they would meet with the scout Aravan had recruited, were he successful in doing so. From there they would turn south and journey to the hidden grotto in Thell Cove, where they would meet the *Eroean*.

In saying farewell, Aylis embraced Balor and whispered, "Thank you, DelfLord, for letting me see the Gargon's Lair, and for being there when I needed a friend."

Balor awkwardly returned her embrace and harrumphed a gruff growl and said, "It is I who owe thanks, Seer, for your visions have told us much of what we did not know of the Lost Prison as well as the deaths of Braggi and his raiders, and the final slaying of the Ghath."

Then the DelfLord moved back and nodded to Brekk, and at a command the Dwarves mounted up, Aylis stepping to her horse and mounting as well.

Balor then strode forward and said, "Forget not this," and he handed up to Aylis a well-tied leather pouch filled with a pound of starsilver ground to a fine argent powder. "Open it not in the wind," he added, "else that black-haired Elf of yours will come and ask me for more."

Aylis laughed and momentarily considered putting the pouch into her saddlebags, but knowing that what it held was more precious than diamonds, she knotted the pouch to her belt.

And they rode out from mighty Kraggen-cor and down the Pitch, called Baralan by the Dwarves, and out through the foothills and onto the wide wold they fared, heading for the mighty Argon River and the Great Greenhall beyond.

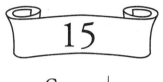

15

Scout

On the evening of the seventh day and some fifty leagues after leaving Kraggen-cor, Aylis and the Dwarven warband reached the banks of the Argon River upstream from Olorin Isle. To the south some five leagues away lay the vast forest of Darda Galion. Yet that twilit woodland was not their goal, but Darda Erynian instead, the Great Greenhall lying just across the wide flow. They made camp at the embarkation point of the ferry, for they would cross in the light of the morrow rather than in this day's darkening eve and its ensuing depths of night.

As they had each sunset along the journey, within a perimeter of Dwarven guards they set up camp and took a late meal of jerky and crue. And by one of the small fires, Brekk turned to Aylis and asked, "My lady, who is this scout we will meet in the ruins of Caer Lindor?"

Her mouth full of the waybread, Aylis shook her head and continued chewing. After a moment she took a gulp of tea and then said, "I know not, for Aravan said nought to me, other than I might find it a pleasant surprise."

"But, my lady, you are a Seeress. Can you not know?"

"Ah, Brekk, I like to be nicely surprised. Besides, looking into the future is somewhat difficult and shows many paths. To winnow out the true one is not simple."

Brekk grunted, but otherwise did not reply.

Aylis looked across the water at the island lying a mile short of two leagues downstream. From the northern tip of the isle, smoke rose into the air, for there lay a small cluster of dwellings. "Who plies the ferry?"

"The Baeron, this year," said Dokan, Brekk's lieutenant, sitting across the fire from her. "Next year it will be ours to do. —We Châkka, that is."

"Baeron and Dwarves alternate?"

Dokan nodded. "Aye. Long past, it was the foul Rivermen who worked the ferry, but they were thieves and robbers and worshipers of Gyphon. Rivermen would waylay boats upstream, cast the cargo overboard, and let it float to the isle, where their kith would snag it and take it as their own. They tried to blame all on the Race, a furious set of rapids and rocks where the river pinches down in a narrow canyon twenty-five leagues to the north. But they were revealed for the vile folk they were"—Dokan clenched a fist—"and the Châkka and the Baeron dealt with them.

"Even so, there were among them some who declared innocence, and those were spared, and they then plied the ferry. But during the Great War of the Ban, Rivermen came to Caer Lindor, claiming that Foul Folk had floated downstream and onto their isle and had raided and slain, and they asked for sanctuary in the fortress; it was these very same Rivermen who aided the Foul Folk to overthrow the bastion, long a thorn in Modru's side." Dokan paused and ground his teeth in rage over vile deeds done during his distant ancestors' time. Finally he took a deep breath and said, "After that war came to an end, we Châkka and the Baeron trade off operating this crossing."

Aylis nodded and then asked, "Is it necessary at all to even have a ferry here?"

Brekk vaguely gestured upriver and down-. "Except for boats, it is the only crossing between here and Argon Ford far to the north, and the Argon Ferry far to the south. We need it for trade, as do the Lian in the Larkenwald and the Dylvana of the Greenhall yon."

"Just the Dwarves and the Baeron ply the ferry, and not the Elves?"

Dokan barked a laugh, then said, "Skinny Elves? Pah! Might as well send women. Nay, only the Châkka and the Baeron have the strength to manage the ferry."

Aylis looked at Dokan, with his broad shoulders half again the width of those of a Man, and, even relaxed as he was, still his muscles were like unto iron knots. "But surely the Rivermen were no stronger than Elves."

Dokan frowned, as if this were a completely new concept. Finally he shrugged and conceded, "Perhaps the Rivermen had among them a few Humans of strength."

Aylis laughed. But even as she fell silent, from the tip of Olorin Isle, across the waters there came the faint sound of singing, yet she could not quite make out the words. She stepped away from the campsite the better to hear, and long she stood at the water's edge, listening. Song after song came floating o'er the slow-running river as baritone male and soprano female voices sang sagas of valorous deeds done.

Aylis was yet enraptured by last eve's singing when the first of the ferry barges floated onto the far downstream landing in the early morning light. Huge Baeron men off-laded mules, and they drew the barge nearly two full leagues up the tow path until they reached the ferry boarding point. As the Baeron secured the ferry to the dock and set a gangway in place, Aylis marveled at the size of these men, all of them towering nearly seven feet into the air, each one as tall as Bair. At a gesture and a soft word from one of the Baeron, Aylis and her horse, along with ten Dwarves and fifteen ponies, embarked, and the gangway was drawn in and the barge then cast off. Baeron rowers plied oars to bear the ferry to a landing on Olorin. They began some five miles upstream from the holm, but the current bore them southward as the men rowed east, the Baeron now and then pausing to gauge their progress, so as to come to ground at the proper place. They eased into a landing on the northwestern brim of the island, and Aylis and the Dwarves then disembarked and rode for the opposite side of Olorin. As they passed through the Baeron village at the northern tip of the isle, lanky children, chattering, tagged after and plied them with questions, and tall Baeron women and huge Baeron men paused in whatever they were doing, as if watching a passing parade. When Aylis and the Dwarves reached the eastern landing they boarded another oared barge waiting there.

As the ferry pushed away, Aylis turned to Brekk and asked, "What happens if by chance we don't reach the shore? What if we lost our oars?"

"It would be a bad thing," said Brekk. "Ctor—what you might know as Bellon Falls—lies downstream, my lady. A thousand-foot sheer drop over the Great Escarpment, the entire river pours over. We would be nought but flinders were that to happen."

"How far downstream?" asked Aylis.

"My lady?"

"How far downstream lies this monstrous fall?"

"Thirty-three leagues."

"Ah, then, we would have time to swim ashore were the ferry to sink."

Brekk laughed. "Aye, we would at that."

Once again Baeron men plied oars, until they reached the eastern bank, some distance downstream from the isle. Aylis led her horse and the Dwarves their ponies across the gangplank to the shore, followed by two Baeron men leading a pair of mules. The drovers hitched the mules to the ferry to begin hauling the barge upriver to the embarkation point well north of Olorin, where it would again be cast adrift into the flow and rowed back to the island for a change of crew and to await the next group of Dwarves.

In all, it took most of the day to ferry the full of the warband across, for the river was wide and much time was spent in towing the barge between the downstream disembarkation point and upstream embarkation one. Aylis and the warband and animals spent the dregs of the day and the full of the night encamped on the eastern shore.

With Dwarven scouts riding ahead, the main body of the band followed and fared easterly through the long, shadowed galleries of the Great Greenhall. Birds sang and flitted thither and yon; insects hummed as they went about their daily business; and now and again an animal bounded across their path or fled crashing away—deer, foxes, rabbits, and such—while limb runners chattered and scolded and scampered above. At last they came to the waters of the River Rissanin. They followed along the banks of this flow, heading northeasterly upstream. As they went, Dokan, riding beside Aylis, said, "Something is passing among the trees to the left and keeps pace with us."

Aylis turned and looked long, and then said a word . . . and gasped.

At her sudden intake of air, Dokan's hand flew to his crossbow, but he relaxed slightly when she murmured, "Oh, how marvelous."

"What is it?" growled the Dwarf, his hand still on the weapon.

"'Tis a Hidden One, a guardian of the forest, a Woodwer, this one a female, a Woodwife, what the Dylvana call a Vred Tre."

"I have heard of those you name Vred Tres, but I see nought but a tangle of leaves and twigs and vines," murmured Dokan, now releasing his grip on the bow.

"That tangle is her," said Aylis. "She's making certain that you evil axe-bearers haven't come to slaughter her wards."

"E-evil axe—?" sputtered Dokan, followed by a more subdued "Oh, I see."

The Woodwer tracked them most of the day, yet as eve drew nigh, there seemed to be no sign of her. Nevertheless, at Aylis's insistence, Captain Brekk commanded the Dwarves to collect only deadwood for the campfires, and to take no axes in among the trees, and to hew nothing whatsoever.

In late afternoon of the second day of travel alongside the deep-running flow, Aylis and the warband came within sight of the ruins of Caer Lindor. On an isle mid the Rissanin flow sat the remains of the fortress, nought but a shambles of tumbled-down granite blocks overgrown with ivy.

Brekk threw up a hand to halt the cavalcade. But in that moment one of the Dwarven fore riders stepped out from among the jumble and into the open, where he gave a piercing whistle.

"Huah," grunted Brekk. "All is clear." And he heeled his pony and gestured for the others to follow.

Across a pontoon bridge they rode, to enter the remains, where the hooves of all animals rang upon the stone flag.

Now riding alongside Aylis, Dokan said, "A full Horde of Foul Folk came sneaking down the Rissanin, along the border between the Greatwood south and the Greenhall north, and Caer Lindor was betrayed, her sentries slain by traitors within, by foul Rivermen. They flung wide the gates to the massed Horde hidden among the bordering trees. Into the bailey they rushed and swarmed up to the battlements, seizing nearly all before the defenders mustered. Valiantly the Free Folk fought, yet they were overwhelmed, and but a few escaped. The Horde did not pursue, but instead stood on the walls and jeered, and then Trolls plied great hammers and mauls and rams to destroy the battlements from within. And before a day passed Caer Lindor lay in ruins."

"What happened after?" asked Aylis, dismounting.

Dismounting as well, Dokan smiled and said, "The Horde had taken a chew too large to swallow, and they choked upon it, for, alerted by the Groaning Stones, the Hidden Ones rallied, my lady. They were enraged that the Foul Folk had encroached upon the Greatwood and stood on the borders of the Great Greenhall. They mustered, I am told: Fox Riders, Living Mounds, Shamblers, Vred Tres, Sprygt, Tomté, Ände—Fey and Peri of all kind. It is said that very few of the Foul Folk managed to escape alive, and most of those who fled the forests ran out screaming in the madness of unbearable fear."

As Aylis unsaddled her horse, Brekk strode to her side. "My lady, where might this scout be? I see nought but overgrown ruins and find no evidence of a campsite where he might have stayed."

Aylis took a deep breath and looked about. She then spoke an arcane word and used her <sight>. Finally she spoke another word and then said, "I don't know, Captain. Aravan said the scout would meet us here, but I see no sign whatsoever of any person. I suppose we'll simply have to wait."

Brekk grunted and turned on his heel and began assigning sentries and setting about making camp.

In the depths of the nighttide, a whisper awakened Aylis. By the light of the dying embers of a nearby campfire, she saw three small shadows standing at her side. And she used her <sight> to see—"Jinnarin! Farrix!"—and one other. Dressed in mottled grey leathers, they were three Pysks, three Fox Riders, three tiny people, two females, one male, each standing no more than twelve inches tall, two of whom she knew.

Nearby, one of the Dwarves, disturbed by Aylis's exclamation, propped up on one elbow and looked about. But seeing nought of suspicion and hearing nothing of alarm, he dropped back down and once again fell into slumber.

"Aylis," murmured Jinnarin, tears gleaming in her eyes. "It has been long since last I saw you, my sister."

Nigh the end of the First Era, some seven millennia agone, on her one and only but very long voyage upon the *Eroean*, Aylis had sailed with Jinnarin some two years in all in a desperate search for Farrix, Jinnarin's lost mate. It was during that voyage that Jinnarin and Aylis, in spite of their differences in physical size, had become pledged sisters to one another. As to their mission, along with Aravan and his crew and Aylis's father, Alamar, they had succeeded in finding Farrix at last, but at great peril, and it seemed only by the grace of Adon had they prevailed. But then the Island of Rwn was sunk beneath the waters of the Weston Ocean, and along with it Aylis and her father vanished from Mithgar, after which Aravan and Jinnarin and Farrix and the crew of the *Eroean* took their revenge upon the one responsible: Durlok the Black Mage.

"Oh, Jinnarin, Farrix," said Aylis, keeping her own voice low, "I would hug you both, but I'm afraid I would—"

Farrix, the male Pysk, laughed quietly and said, "Crush us? You probably would at that."

Jinnarin grinned and said, "Aylis, I would have you meet our daughter, Aylissa, named after you, of course, though mostly we call her Lissa. Lissa, this is your aunt Aylis, or rather your adopted aunt."

"I know the tale well," whispered Aylissa. Just under twelve inches tall and with mouse-brown hair, she looked much like her mother, for Jinnarin's hair, too, was mouse brown, though Farrix's was coal black. A tiny glitter of some kind of stone on a silver chain hung about her neck and carried a trace of odd <fire>. Yet whether it was a token of power or simply something imbued with an unknown essence, Aylis could not say.

"I am so glad to see you," said Aylis, "but how did you come to know we were here? Was it the Woodwer who told you?"

Farrix again muffled a laugh and shook his head. "Nay, Aylis, 'twas instead a dark bird—"

"Aravan?"

"None other. We thought it was out to snag one of us, a black falcon there in the woods. We readied our bows in case it flew nigh, but it lit on a sturdy limb well up in the trees. Imagine our surprise when in a flash of light it transformed into Aravan. Like to have shocked me silly."

"Perhaps thinking we might take him for a shape-shifting Black Mage, he remained up in the tree out of range of our arrows until he had explained all and why he had come," said Jinnarin, taking up the tale.

"A good thing that," said Aylis, for she knew how deadly were the tiny shafts with their tips of nearly instant lethality.

"Indeed," said Jinnarin.

"I am so glad he sent you for a visit," said Aylis, "though I'm afraid the warband and I cannot stay overlong."

"Not just a visit, my dear," said Farrix.

"No?"

"Nay." Farrix then gestured to Aylissa and said, "I would have you meet the *Eroean*'s new scout."

Tiny, brown-haired Aylissa then bobbed a curtsey and smiled.

16

Greatwood

JOURNEY TO THE *EROEAN*
MID SUMMER, 6E1

"How very splendid," said Aylis. "You are Aravan's new scout."

"With Vex, that is," said Lissa, "else not much of a scout would I be."

"Vex?"

"My fox," she replied.

"Ah, yes, you do need your mount," said Aylis, smiling, imagining tiny Lissa trying to scout afoot, battling her way through weeds and such, rather like someone of Human size trying to pass through an entangled jungle. No, a Fox Rider without a fox would be at the mercy of many things, the least of which were plants. "Speaking of foxes," said Aylis, looking about, "where are they?"

Lissa gestured westerly toward the darkness cloaking Darda Erynian. "Rux and Rhu and Vex are just at the edge of the forest. We didn't want some silly Dwarf spitting any of them with a crossbow bolt, thinking they were vermin."

Aylis spluttered and slapped a hand over her mouth to keep from laughing aloud. Finally she mastered herself and said, "Silly Dwarf? I think I've never seen one ever do even the slightest harebrained thing."

"True," said Jinnarin, "though when deep in their cups they can be quite rowdy."

Aylis smiled and nodded, but Farrix asked, "When did you see Dwarves deep in their cups?"

Jinnarin said, "It was wintertime in the port of Arbor in Gelen. It was twelfth day of Yule—the first day of a new year, as the High King measures time—and that evening a gentle snow began falling. The hole in the hull of the *Eroean* had finally been repaired, and two days after, when all had recovered from the labor, a grand celebration was held in the common room of the Blue Mermaid Inn. All of the Elvenship crew were there—sailors and warband alike—as well as Aylis and her father, Alamar. —Oh, and me and Rux. I was lurking in my darkness at the top of the stairs. There was singing and dancing, and Lobbie played his squeeze box and Rolly his pipe and Burden banged away on his drum. All the sailors and warriors stomped in time and clapped their hands, while Aylis and Aravan danced a wild, wild fling, stepping and prancing and whirling about and laughing into each other's eyes. Châkka chanted marching songs, the words in a brusque language strong. Mage Alamar made the air sparkle with untouchable glitter in a rainbow of dazzling colors, and he caused a strange musical piping amid the sounds of ringing wind chimes. And then Aravan played a harp and voiced stirring sagas, odes to make your heart pound and your blood run hot. And Aylis sang in a high, sweet voice, and not an eye was dry when she finished. And while Dwarves or Men stood guard at the bottom of the steps, allowing no townsman to go up to where I was, many a member of the crew came and sat by me in the darkness, and they laughed and joked and shared their sweets with me. And the Dwarves began arm wrestling with any and all, and bets were laid and war cries shouted and they did become quite rowdy.

"And when the celebration came to an end, it was in the wee hours of the morning. All had by this time fallen silent but for the snores, with sailors and warband sleeping in chairs and on benches and on the tops of tables and under them, too, as well as atop and behind the bar. Outside the gentle snow had become a storm. It was the second of January, and the twelve days of Yule were ended."

As Jinnarin spoke, Aylis's eyes filled with remembrance, and a tear trickled down one cheek.

"Are you all right?" asked Jinnarin.

"It was a splendid time," said Aylis.

"Would that I had been there," said Farrix, "instead of trapped in my dreams in a crystal cave."

"Me, too, my love," said Jinnarin, pulling Farrix close and pecking a kiss on his cheek.

Lissa sighed and looked at Aylis and said, "Perhaps something just as wonderful will happen on our voyage."

"One can only hope," replied Aylis.

"Speaking of the voyage," said Jinnarin, "have the members of the warband been pledged?"

Aylissa looked at her mother. "Pledged?"

Jinnarin nodded. "They must take a pledge to keep secret your existence, or, for that matter, any Fox Rider's existence from those not of the crew."

"What?" Lissa looked to her father for confirmation.

"We don't want anyone to know we are real," said Farrix, smiling.

"But everyone knows that Pysks are real," protested Lissa.

"Only in legend, daughter," said Farrix.

"If they knew we were truly real," said Jinnarin, "especially if Humans knew, they might try to trap us. You see, they think we can do magic, and they would like to have us grant them three wishes."

Now Aylissa looked at Aylis, who nodded in agreement and said, "Sometimes Humans can be truly foolish." Then Aylis turned to Jinnarin and said, "If the Dwarves have not already been pledged by Aravan, I will have them do so ere we reveal our scout to them."

"Good," said Jinnarin.

The Pysks and Aylis spoke for long moments more, but Farrix finally said, "We must let our sister and our daughter get some sleep, for the journey ahead is a long one. Besides, we can ride with them through the whole of the Greatwood in the coming days, and surely we will have enough time to catch up with all that has gone since last we saw one another."

And so, cloaked in their <wild-magic> shadows, the three Pysks slipped undetected back past the Dwarven sentries and to their foxes in Darda Erynian to await the coming of dawn.

At the request of Aylis, Brekk assembled the full warband, and they stood in ranks behind him, all but the two sentries perched upon the remains of walls. And to her question, "Aye," replied the stalwart Dwarf. "Pledged us he did in Kraggen-cor, including the two who are to take the animals back. And as to the *Eroean*, we are to keep the secrets of her making as well as her pace locked away in our memories forever. To that Captain Aravan added that no matter what we might see or do or hear while serving aboard the *Eroean*, we will tell no one of whatever befalls without the leave of the captain. Our pledge includes a vow to keep secret the presence of any strange beings or creatures who might sail with us as members of the crew. We are so sworn, and neither torture, drink, death, fever, nor ought else will pry words from our lips and cause us to break our vow. And we took that oath on Châkka honor, as well as swore by Elwydd above."

Aylis smiled and said, "Captain Brekk, I would say that was quite sufficient."

Brekk frowned and asked, "Then, my lady, can you tell us what this is about?"

"Indeed," said Aylis, and she extended her hand in a welcoming gesture toward one of the massive tumbled-down stones. "I give you our scout, the Lady Aylissa."

Of a sudden, one of the shadows at the base of the block vanished, and in the morning light stood a fox, red with black legs. And upon the fox's back rode a tiny maiden dressed in mottled grey leathers, a bow across her shoulders, arrows in a quiver fastened to her hip. And at no urging, it seemed, the fox stepped forward across the pave stones of the ruins of Caer Lindor. Blue-eyed and pale she was, her brown hair bound away from her face by a rune-marked strip of leather 'round her brow, her mane falling to her shoulders. And only the murmur of the faint breeze and the rustle of the leaves of the overgrowth of ivy sounded in that moment, for it was not certain that anyone even breathed. And when she reached the stone before Captain Brekk, the fox came to a stop and Aylissa looked up at the Dwarf.

"Lady Aylissa," said Aylis, "I present Captain Brekk; Captain Brekk, I would have you meet Lady Aylissa and her fox, Vex."

Brekk found his voice at last and knelt on one knee and said to the Pysk, "Lady Aylissa, now I see why Captain Aravan made us swear the oath that we did. This I would say as well: we could ask for no better scout. Welcome to the warband."

Brekk raised a hand, and the assembled warriors with one thunderous voice called out, *Châkka shok! Châkka cor!*

At this roar, even as Vex flinched down, in reflex Lissa's <wild-magic> cloak of darkness sprang up 'round both fox and rider, leaving them hidden in shadow.

Just as Brekk opened his mouth to apologize for startling the tiny Pysk, "I told you they were rowdy," came a call—Lady Jinnarin's—and two more shadows vanished from the base of a tumbled-down block, revealing two more Fox Riders.

Down through the Greatwood they fared, angling a point east of due south, and as they rode, now and then they glimpsed among the trees and tracking alongside them a Bear or a Wolf or at times a hawk or falcon. Aylis could see by their <fire> that these were no ordinary animals, but were instead shapeshifters. When she spoke of them to the Pysks, "They are Baeron," said Jinnarin. "A few of those Folk have the power to become the animals you see."

"Some never become men again," said Farrix.

"And some never shift into the creatures that they can become," said Aylissa.

Aylis smiled and said, "I learned about them at the College of Mages on Rwn, but until I met Bair, I had never seen one—never seen a shapeshifter, that is."

In midafternoon on the fifth day of travel, a distant and continuous roar came into hearing, and the farther they rode the louder it grew.

Riding alongside Brekk, Aylis asked, "What would that be?"

Brekk smiled. "Wait and you will see."

On they fared and still the sound grew louder. At last they emerged from among the trees to find themselves along the lip of the Great Escarpment, a sheer drop falling away for a thousand feet or so to fetch up against the banks of the Great Argon River. As Aylis looked about, her gaze followed the run of the escarpment, and some thirty miles to the west she saw a huge cataract plunging over the brim of the sheer drop and down. —Nay, not one cataract but two. And even this far from the cascades, still the roar was considerable.

"The great one is Ctor—Shouter—also known as Bellon Falls," said Brekk. "There the Mighty Argon plunges over. The smaller fall farther west is Silver Falls, or as the Elves name it, Vanil."

"Now I see why, if the Olorin Ferry got this far and went over," said Aylis, "none would survive the plunge."

They camped that night along the strip of land between the trees of the Greatwood and the verge of the escarpment, and the distant roar of two waterfalls lulled them to sleep.

Over the next several days, league upon league they fared along a gentle downslant of land between the forest and the edge of the escarpment, the great, sheer bluff to decline and decline to finally come to an end. And still they rode southerly between the marge of the Greatwood to the east and the Argon River to the west.

Some three weeks after leaving the ruins of Caer Lindor they came to the Glave Hills, and there did the trees of the Greatwood come to an end.

The next dawn, Aylis and Lissa and the warband said their good-byes to Jinnarin and Farrix, Aylis and Jinnarin and Lissa teary-eyed, Farrix snuffling, his voice quavering, as he embraced his daughter and whispered words of advice as well as words of farewell.

Then the warband turned southwesterly and fared into the grassy plains of Pellar: a Mage and a Pysk and forty-two Dwarves, seventy-six ponies, one horse, and a fox.

Jinnarin and Farrix rode to the top of one of the hills and watched them go. And as the warband dwindled in the distance, after a long while Farrix said, "Well, my love?"

Jinnarin turned to Farrix and smiled through her lingering tears. "Yes, my love."

And they turned Rux and Rhu down the back slope of the hill and rode into the forest beyond.

17

Grotto

Down across the plains of Pellar rode the warband, Aylis and Aylissa in their midst, and whenever they could they stopped at crofters' and replenished their supplies; they especially sought grain for the animals, though Vex provided for her own fare—finding voles and field mice and quail eggs and other such when Aylissa gave the vixen permission to hunt. They stayed on the outskirts of several small towns, taking every opportunity to relax in hot baths and to eat warm meals and to drink a mug or two of ale, good or bad. Yet every dawn found the travellers up and about and making ready to resume their journey.

Some eighteen days after saying good-bye to Lissa's parents, they crossed Pendwyr Road nigh the Fian Dunes and continued on southwesterly.

And fifteen days after that, they came into sight of the broad waters of Thell Cove. Aylis looked leftward, and just as Aravan had said, in the near distance a long stone bluff covered with vines rose up and graced the shore. She led the warband to the place where the sheer cliff began to rise, and there they hobbled the animals, all but Vex. They waited until low tide, and Aylis then took the lead, and, following Aravan's instructions, she guided them wading afoot along the high and solid rock bluff, with its long creepers dangling down. Following immediately after Aylis came Brekk, and riding on his shoulder was wee Aylissa, and he bore Vex in his arms. The fox had suffered herself to be carried only after Aylissa had had a long chat with her. The Dwarves had watched this conversation in amazement, for Lissa had postured and barked, whined and turned and twisted, Vex replying in kind. Aylis smiled, for millennia past in the First Era she had seen Jinnarin do the same. Finally, Lissa looked up at Brekk and said, "She's ready. But if I were you I'd watch my fingers. Vex is likely to nip."

But Brekk reached down and chucked Vex under her chin, and then grasped the top of her muzzle and gave a very slight squeeze. Vex took no action whatsoever when Brekk lifted her up.

And then following Aylis, the warband sloshed along a lengthy but shallow underwater ledge to come to a strange fold in the vine-laden stone, where the bluff curled out into the water and back, to form a wide and deep channel leading toward a thick dangle of the long, trailing plants.

Aylis paused and gestured to the fold and said, "Aravan tells me that this turn in the stone is all but undetectable from the outlying waters of the cove. It makes the entry to the grotto nigh invisible."

Onward they surged, to finally reach the wall of creepers, where Aylis pushed through and into the huge lantern-lit grotto, echoing with voices and the sounds of men working and the splash of water falling in cascade. But just above in a Dwarven-crafted stone-walled niche stood crossbow-armed sentries—Humans, part of the *Eroean*'s crew. As Aylis and the others entered, one of the sentries lifted a horn to his lips and sounded a call.

Voices stilled, and the sounds of mallets and other such fell silent, though the tumble of water persisted.

One of the sentries called down: "Lady Aylis?"

"Who the *kruk* else would it be?" growled Brekk in response.

The sentry laughed and turned to his comrades and said, "The warband is here."

At the far end of the grotto Aylis could see the gleaming face of a narrow dam embedded in what appeared to be a broad ledge receding toward the far back of the grotto. Upon the dam itself, men manned wheel pumps—like those used to suck out a ship's bilge—and water poured over the barrier from the pump outlets in two separate streams. Beyond the dam and jutting above, Aylis saw a part of the stern of the *Eroean*, the ship captured in a long slip of some sort, its masts rising up into the shadows above.

The Dwarves and Aylis continued wading, as the shelf they followed carried on about the wall of the grotto. Slowly the way rose up until it was above the water of low tide. When they reached dry stone they followed the path to come to the wide expanse of the stone ledge, and carved deep into the rock was the long slip—a Dwarf-cut channel—where they found the *Eroean* sitting in dry dock above a bottom of sloping sand. The dock itself was sealed away from the brine of the cove by the doors of the gleaming dam, for the barrier was crafted of brass and was Dwarven-made as well. Aylis and the others then saw that the waters were also kept at bay by periodic pumping to rid the dry dock of slow seepage. Aylis also saw that the *Eroean*—awaiting the renewal of her silver bottom—lay cradled from stem to stern in huge brass trestles mounted on stone pillars—twenty-two in all, or so Aylis later learned. As they crossed the gangway and reached the deck of the ship, Aravan greeted Aylis with a smile and kiss. Brekk set Vex to her feet, and Lissa hopped down and comforted the fox, the vixen somewhat disgruntled at having to have been carried so very far.

At Aravan's side stood an enormous man—he was tall and sandy haired and as broad as a great slab of beef—and Aravan introduced him as Long Tom, the first officer of the *Eroean*, who shuffled his feet and crushed his hat in hand and said in a Gelender accent, "Oi'm moity pleased t'meet you, Miss Aylis. Me 'n' th' crew welcome you 'n' t'others t'this here foine ship."

"Why, thank you," said Aylis, even as she thought that with his massive hands the huge man would twist his well-crushed hat to nought but raggedy threads.

One by one, Aylis and Aylissa and Brekk and Dokan were introduced to various members of the crew: Second Officer Nikolai, Helmsmen Fat Jim and Wooly, and the cook and carpenters and riggers and so on, down to the cabin boy Noddy. And all were agoggle to see a real Pysk actually standing in their midst, tiny little thing that she was. But Long Tom assured Lissa that they would take every precaution "t'keep from steppin' on y'r wee little self, though, if'n Oi were you, Oi moight taike't upon m'self t'be extra alert t'th' clumsy oafs we be."

Using the formula given to him long past by Dwynfor, the legendary Elven weapons master who at the time had been living on Atala, Aravan set aside a quarter of the silveron for future use should the need arise, and he blended the remainder into the ingredients needed to make the starsilver paint. Then Aravan and several sailors began coating the *Eroean's* hull from the waterline on down. The crew marveled over the fact that the bottom was completely clear of barnacles and growth, and that the previous silveron overlay did not at all seem to need renewing. Yet the captain insisted, and so they plied on the paint. As they came to where the ship rested against each trestle, brass lifting levers were sledgehammered off-angle to lower the given cradle into a slot in the stone pillar, the cradle moving down and away from the hull just enough so that the bottom could be painted there. And when the coat at that place had dried, they hammered the levers back on-angle to lift the cradle on the lever cams to share in the support of the hull once more, and they moved on to the next trestle and repeated the process.

In all it took four days to finish coating the hull. During those same four days, the warband completely refitted the ballistas at the bow and amidships and aft, and they made certain that the missiles laid by and those in storage were sound, especially the fireballs. In addition, they re-furbished each of the weapons in the *Eroean's* armory—polishing, oiling, honing, truing, and replacing whatever parts were worn.

A sevenday after Aylis and Lissa and the warband had arrived, the *Eroean* was ready to sail. Men moved the wheel pumps from atop the dam, and then cranked two brass slideways up to let water pour into the dry dock.

Slowly the slipway filled, and by midmorn the *Eroean* floated free from the cradles below. Then the great doors of the dam were unlatched and winched open, and men backed the ship out by haling on lines as well as drawing her out into the grotto by rope-towing dinghies aft.

The few men still ashore then made their way to the vine-covered entrance, and, using fixed hawsers, drew the curtain aside.

Yet towing, sailors in dinghies maneuvered the ship out from the grotto and down the channel well into the open waters, where Aravan had the crew drop anchor.

The rowers then cast loose the towing ropes, to be drawn in by those aboard, and then plied their dinghies to fetch the handful of sailors who had been left ashore. As they rowed back to the *Eroean*, the men in the boats looked on the Elvenship with something akin to awe. Three-masted she was, was the *Eroean*, and swift as a gale in the wind. Her bow was narrow and as sharp as a knife to cut through the waters, the shape smoothly flaring back to a wall-sided hull running for most of her length to finally taper up to a rounded aft. Two hundred and twelve feet she measured from stem to stern, her masts raked back at an angle. No stern castle did she bear, nor fo'c's'le on her bow. Instead her shape was low and slender, for her beam measured but thirty-six feet at the widest, and she drew but thirty feet of water fully laded. Her mainmast rose one hundred forty-six feet above her deck, and her main yard was seventy-eight feet from tip to tip. As to the mizzen and fore masts, they were but slightly shorter and their yards a bit less wide. And dark sea-blue was her hull above the waterline, and silver below, but her masts and silken sails were azure to blend in with the sky. Tinted as she was, nigh invisible she seemed until she was running up another ship's stern or bearing down on her bow or hoving nigh alongside. And no ship asea was swifter, not e'en the Dragonboats o' the Fjordlanders. Aye, this was the Elvenship o' Captain Aravan, and to serve on her was a rare privilege. It brought tears of pride to those who had done so, and tears of envy to those who had not.

When all were aboard and the dinghies lifted on the davits from the water, Aravan glanced back at Aylis, leaning aft against the taffrail. Lissa stood at hand, curiosity in her gaze, for she had never been aboard a ship of any kind. Vex was nowhere to be seen, for the vixen was below and hunting rats. Aravan smiled and winked at Aylis and mouthed the word, *Ready?* Aylis grinned and mouthed back, *Oh, yes.* Aravan then turned to his first and second officers, as well as the helmsman and the bosun standing by. "Tom, set the spanker to help her to come about, and pipe the sails for a larboard run, then up anchor." Against the blue sky above, Aravan eyed the wind pennant streaming in the braw breeze. "We'll take her close-hauled into the wind and make a run for the outlet of Thell Cove and the Avagon Sea beyond."

"Aye, Cap'n," replied Long Tom. He turned to the bosun and said,

"You heard th' cap'n, James; pipe 'em f'r close haul larboard. Nikolai, step to th' fore winch 'n' ready t' up anchor. Fat Jim, spin th' wheel t'steer her f'r th' Avagon. That'd be nigh due sou', I ween."

As James piped the orders and men clambered up the ratlines to bend on all silk but the studding sails, Nikolai leaped down the ladder and ran forward to the men at the winch. Slowly the spanker brought the ship about, and with a rattle and a clatter of chain up came the anchor. Fat Jim spun the wheel, and slowly, majestically the ship got under way, gathering speed as she went, her silken cloud of azure sails harvesting every last breath of air, and soon her hull cut a trough in the water, white wake spinning behind.

Aylis took a moment to peer aft, looking for the entrance to the hidden grotto. But it was as Aravan had said: the vine-laden bluff looked all of a piece, and no entry or channel could she see. She frowned and invoked her <sight>, and then and only then could she see where it lay; otherwise it appeared impossible to find. How Aravan had ever come to know where it was, she would have to ask him one day.

Then Aylis turned once more and faced forward. She looked down at Lissa and said, "Come, Liss, let us go to the bow; there might be dolphins racing, or even Children of the Sea."

And together they made their way forward, dodging this way and that to avoid interfering with members of the crew as they hauled on halyards at the behest of the bosun to trim up the sails to catch the full of the quartering headwind.

And still the *Eroean* gained speed as faster and farther she went. . . .

. . . While far behind and standing ashore, two fairly young Dwarves watched as the craft drew away, each wishing that he could have been one of the warriors chosen for Brekk's warband. And the Elvenship diminished as onward she ran, her hull seeming to sink into the sea with distance, and finally the hull could no longer be seen, though the masts and sails—azure all—yet jutted above the horizon, blending into the sky and just visible . . . if one knew where to look. One of the young Dwarves turned to the other and said in Châkur, ["Ready?"] The other sighed and nodded but said nought in return. And they mounted up and wheeled about and slowly rode toward the remaining seventy-four ponies and the lone horse to begin the long trek back to Kraggen-cor.

18

Plot

DARK DESIGNS
MID AUTUMN, 6E1

Ragged in flight, Nunde had struggled across some six hundred leagues—eighteen hundred miles—to reach his dark tower clutched among the crags of the Grimwall, just east of Jallor Pass, there where the western reaches of Aven cross over to the long steppes of Jord. From the nexus, southerly down into Khal he had fled, emerging from the mountains to come perilously close to the dreaded Skög and the Wolfwood, there where vile Dalavar—the Wolfmage—dwelled. West and away from that dire danger Nunde had veered, to cross Khal and Garia and Aven, to come at last into his domain. And in rage he had slaughtered nearly one hundred Chûn, and had nearly slain his apprentice, Malik. For his plans had been shattered, and all because of Aravan and his ilk. Yet even this bloodletting had not assuaged in the slightest Nunde's terrible rage.

Including the long time of his flight to safety, Nunde had spent nigh nine months in all, seeking a plan to destroy the bane of his existence. He had no doubt at all that the schemes of that vile Elf had led to the downfall of the Black Fortress and the ruin of Nunde's dark designs, a disaster from which the Necromancer had barely escaped with his life.

And at the coming of this day's dawn, down the stone steps of the shadowy stairwell Nunde descended to his torchlit quarters below, and there he fell into a restless sleep, his mind still churning with thoughts of revenge, as it now had done for months on end.

It was as the sun rode across the zenith—though no glimmer of its light reached his chamber—that Nunde bolted upright.

"Radok, to me!" he shouted without thinking, but then he remembered Radok was dead, slain on a raid into Arden Vale a number of years ago.

But from an adjoining chamber, "Yes, Master Nunde," called Malik and, bearing a lit candle casting wavering shadows, he hurried to the Necromancer's side. A not-well-hidden look of anxiety played across the pale white face of the corpulent apprentice—for he never knew where the master's wrath would be directed.

"I have it," declared Nunde, his dark eyes gloating as he ran his long, bony fingers through his waist-length hair, tossing it back and over a shoulder to hang nearly to his hips.

"Have what, Master?"

"The plan, you fool," hissed Nunde, irritation flashing across his narrow face with its hooklike aquiline nose, "the plan for that Dohl Aravan. The way to reave from him all he holds dear. And when I am done with his immediate companions, then will I do him in. After which I will recover his corpse and raise him"—the Necromancer clenched a black-nailed fist—"and ever will he regret that which he did. For then I'll send his rotting remains forth to extract even more of my revenge by having him slay others of those he loves, and he will be able to do nought to gainsay me, even though he will be horrified by that which I will have him do."

With his apprentice bustling at his side, Nunde strode out from the chamber and down a torchlit dark-granite hallway to a corpse-littered laboratory, the flayed bodies on the many tables in various stages of decomposition and dismemberment. But Nunde did not pause to admire his handiwork; instead he stepped to and 'round a large desk made of an esoteric gray wood and sat. Hovering nearby, Malik wondered at what his master intended, but as Nunde pulled a sheet of parchment out from a drawer and began to write—the razor-sharp quill scratching across the vellum, leaving a trail of bloodred liquid behind—the apprentice frowned in puzzlement. The Necromancer brewed no potion, compounded no powder, cast no spell, raised no corpse, and this did not seem to be any arcane scroll the apprentice recognized, so how this could possibly gain Nunde his revenge, Malik did not know.

But at last Nunde passed the parchment across to Malik and hissed, "Bring me these ingredients."

Malik looked at the list, recognition dawning in his eyes, for these things the apprentice did know. Yet how this might further his master's scheme, Malik had not the slightest answer.

The next night, locked and barred in his quarters, Nunde drank the fresh-brewed concoction, and after long moments he slipped into unconsciousness, and sent his aethyrial self winging far eastward.

19

Plans

"Well, buccoes, you've trained extra hard this past year, and, Pip, you're fifteen summers old—"

"I'm three moons older," said Binkton, even as Pipper said, "Bink's three moons older."

Arley laughed. "I was just about to say that, my lads."

"Oh," said Binkton, as Pipper joined his uncle in mirth.

But then Pipper's face took on a puzzled look. "So, I'm fifteen?"

"Of course you're fifteen, Pipper," snapped Binkton. "Have you gone 'round the bend?"

"No, Bink, what I mean is: so I'm fifteen and Bink's three moons older; what has that to do with ought?"

Arley smiled, for ever did Pipper pop up with statements that seemed to drive Binkton to distraction. Pipper never seemed to say or ask what he meant to say or ask, and Binkton always took umbrage when he couldn't follow Pipper's mental leap—one a dreamer, the other more material.

"Oh," said Binkton, and he turned to Uncle Arley. "So, what have our ages to do with anything?"

"Just this, buccoes: next spring, as you approach sixteen summers, I think it's time you put this show on the road and earned a bit of copper for yourselves."

"Yes!" shouted Pipper.

"*Hmph!*" grunted Binkton. "I think we were ready last spring."

"Oh, no," said Arley, "there's much more I have to teach you, and this winter is the time to do it. Besides, I can still see places where you need more skill: you, Binkton, in opening locks with nought but a wire as a pick as well as working while hanging upside down; and you, Pipper, need more practice in sleight of hand, and your juggling could use some sharpening, as well. And both of you need to be able to perform all things in all sorts of weather, when you are dripping with sweat in the heat and your hands are watery slick, or when your fingers and toes and every muscle in your bodies are numb with chill. You never know when sudden winds will blow or the rains pour down or swirling dust and grit will blind you, and you've got to be safe up on the rope or to get out from the trap you find yourselves in."

"Hoy," exclaimed Binkton, "you make this sound like a dangerous business."

Lost in thought, the eld buccan nodded. "Aye, for many a time, I—" Of a sudden, Arley came to himself. "Harrumph. Well, you just never know."

"Oh, I'll work extra hard, Uncle Arley," said Pipper. "I mean, I'll try to get better at walking a coin across my knuckles—though I'll never be as good as Bink, of course—and my filching skills need improvement, and I could get better at—"

"Yes, yes, Pip," said Uncle Arley, interrupting Pipper's stream of words. "I'll help you with all of those, and then next spring and through the summer, but especially the winter after—when the harvests are in and the common rooms are brimming with folks—it's off to the taverns and inns in the Boskydells, where the pickings ought to be good."

That night, Pipper said, "Oh, won't this be the very best?"

Exasperated, Binkton asked, "And what thought flitted through your mind just now?"

"That we'll have our own coppers and silvers and perhaps even a gold or two, Bink," said Pipper, his eyes reflecting his boundless enthusiasm.

"About time, too," grumped Binkton. "I mean, we've taken enough of Uncle Arley's money. We need to be on our own."

"Uncle Arley's money," breathed Pipper, looking about as if to see where the eld buccan might be.

"Oh, come on, Pip, you're not going to bring that up again."

"Wull, it's always been a myst'ry, Bink, and—"

"And you just can't leave it alone," snapped Binkton. The buccan plumped his pillow and jerked his covers up around his neck. "It's Uncle Arley's, and I don't care where it comes from. Now go to sleep."

Pipper lay quietly a moment, but then said, "But Finley Tutwillow, down in Rood, says that once every year a mysterious rider, an Outsider, a Human, no less, comes every Midsummer Day and puts a sack of coins in the Bank of Boskydells. And always about that same time, Uncle Arley says his pension's come. What do you think that's all about, Bink? I mean, why would some Human—?"

Binkton's soft snoring was all the answer that Pipper got, as was usual when he and Binkton speculated in the dark about Uncle Arley's even darker past.

20

At Sail

ELVENSHIP

MID AUTUMN, 6E1

In the Captain's Lounge, Long Tom stood beside Aravan at the map table with Aylis at his other side. Nikolai and Brekk and Dokan stood across the board. Tiny Lissa sat atop the table and sipped tea from a thimble-sized mug, as Noddy poured a cup for Aylis.

"Where we be bound, Cap'n?" asked Long Tom.

Aravan stabbed a finger down to the chart. "Here."

As Lissa got to her feet and strolled across the tabletop to see, all looked, Noddy included, at where the captain's finger touched the map.

A great strew of specks and dots and irregular loops were scattered across where Aravan pointed, his finger resting upon one of the larger shapes.

"Oi see," said Long Tom. "One o' th' Ten Thousand Isles o' Mordain, eh?"

"What be we after, Kapitan?" asked Nikolai.

"White tea," replied Aravan.

Lissa frowned. "White tea?"

Aylis smiled. "Very young tea leaves plucked from the tips of the plant. 'Tis a delicate flavor, much savored in the halls of Caer Pendwyr, or so it was long past."

"It still is, my love," said Aravan. "'Twill bring a fine price for the crew." He glanced at Long Tom and Nikolai and added, "More than enough for all the warband and crew, e'en those who sat idle for many long moons."

An offended look crossed Long Tom's face and he spluttered, "Sittin' oidle, Cap'n? Sittin' oidle? Oi'll have you know we was trianin' 'n' piantin' 'n'—"

Aravan burst out laughing, as did Nikolai, and Long Tom frowned from one to the other, and then a look of enlightenment crossed his face. "Ah. Oi see. You was havin' me on, naow, roight? Wull, y'got me good 'n' well, y'did. Y'got me good 'n' well."

There came a soft knock on the door, and Tarley stepped into the lounge. "Captain, we're entering the Avagon, sir, and leaving the cove behind."

They turned on a westerly run and aimed for the distant outlet into the Weston Ocean, those waters lying some twenty-nine hundred nautical miles away as a gull would fly, but farther than that on the course the ship would run, all depending upon the wind, which blew toward the northwest at the moment, and so close-hauled the *Eroean* would fare.

Still the Elvenship was at long last at sea, and throughout the day and until well after sunset much of the crew remained adeck. And as night grew deeper, the crew not on watch was reluctant to bed down, for they were at sea again and reveling in the fact.

And the Avagon herself put on a show for them, for streaming shoals of phosphorescent fish painted the water with light to glimmer within the reflections of the myriad stars above.

That night, for the first time in more than seven thousand years, Aravan and Aylis slept in the captain's quarters aboard the *Eroean* at sea. And they made gentle love and whispered dear words to one another, for they were home at last.

In her own quarters, Lissa and Vex slept well, the Pysk taking up residence in the tiny cabin made long past for her mother, Jinnarin, by four of the *Eroean*'s crew: Finch and Carly and Arlo and Rolly—carpenter, sailmaker, cooper, and tinsmith. Several times throughout the millennia, Jinnarin had told Lissa of the kindness of these men. . . .

Belowdecks in an aft cabin given over to Jinnarin and Mage Alamar, Finch crawled back from his handiwork, ship's carpenter that he was.

"There you be, Miss Jinnarin, all done up safe and sound, and a pretty job of it, too, even if I do say so myself." Although the man spoke to Jinnarin, his shy eyes looked everywhere but directly at her.

"That little bulkhead panel under Alamar's bunk, it swings both ways, letting you and your fox in and out of the passageway beyond whenever you want. These little dogs . . . well twist them this-away to latch the hatch shut should the sea want to enter, and I've seen it try, rushing down the corridor outside.

"And once I fasten this wood in place . . ." Finch mounted three wide tongue-and-groove boards across the openings left behind when the right-side pair of underbunk drawers had been removed, and he tapped in slender brass nails to hold them in place. "Right. Now you've got your own little closed-off lady's chamber there under the bunk for the privacy you might want, with its own door opening in and out of the passageway, and another door into this here cabin. And, cor, who could use it but you?"

Finch got to his feet. "But as to light, well, I should think a wax taper'll have to do, and I've made these dogged ports out here and in there for ventilation, wot?

"Arlo the sailmaker is making you a bed . . . out of soft blankets. One for your fox, too.

"And as to your very own personal needs"—Finch blushed furiously—"to wash yourself and to relieve yourself, Carly the cooper and Rolly the tinsmith be working on that very thing right even as we speak, though I be going now to help them."

Jinnarin smiled up at the large, humble man. "Oh, thank you, Mister Finch. Rux and I will cherish what you have done for us. And"—the Pysk swiftly stepped into the tiny chamber under the bunk and then back out again—"and my private room is simply perfect for any and all my needs."

Finch shuffled his feet and touched his cap, then turned and rushed from the cabin.

Before the day was done, the carpenter, sailmaker, cooper, and tinsmith delivered to Jinnarin the things needed to furnish her wee "cabin," all new-made to her stature: bedding for her and Rux; a tiny brass candlestick holder, with a striker and straight shavings tipped in pitch and several spare tapers; a small washstand and diminutive tin basin, with a petite tin pitcher for water; a miniature sea chest for her clothing; and a tiny commode chair with a tin privy pot and lid.

As all four men stood about, holding their hats and grinning, Jinnarin *ooh*ed and *ahh*ed, saying, "Why, this is better than I have at home."

Finch removed one of the boards of her chamber wall. "Now you arrange it like as you want it, Miss Jinnarin, and I'll fix it so as it won't slide about in a big blow, wot?"

And over the next few nights, Men and Dwarves alike came to look down the passageway, hoping to see the glow of candlelight shining out through the wee window of the Lady Jinnarin's cabin. This was especially true of Finch and Carly and Arlo and Rolly, even though they knew that she had Fairy sight and probably didn't need the candles; still, she might burn them just to please the crew. And burn them she did, the soft yellow taperlight glimmering, and the four men would look at one another and grin and nod; at other times the tiny portal would be dark, and they would sigh. But always they would go away marveling over *their* Pysk.

Rux quickly adapted to *his* new door, ingress and egress to *his* den, where his mistress also happened to live. Even so, still he spent much time belowdecks hunting, though his take for the day was one or two at most, for the fox found the ratting and mousing on the *Eroean* to be slim pickings when compared to that other ship he had been on. Throughout the full of the *Eroean* roamed Rux, becoming a familiar sight to the crew. From keelson to hold to crew's quarters, from lower deck to locker, from the tiller wheel on the stern to its mate in the sheltered wheelhouse forward of the aft quarters, from bow to bilge ranged the fox. The fact that his hunting ground pitched and rolled and yawed, and canted starboard or larboard depending on the wind, seemed of no consequence to Rux. The only things that mattered at this juncture were rats and mice and exploring.

And now Jinnarin's daughter, Aylissa, occupied these same quarters—she and Vex, that is—under what was now Nikolai's bunk. And like as not over the days and months ahead the crew would come on any excuse to the corridor outside to see if candlelight glowed out from the tiny dogged port to see if their very own Pysk was at home.

Nine days later, they stood in the bow at the base of the stem, Aravan and Aylis and Brekk. To the south and just barely seen, like a long, dark smudge on the horizon, rose the hills of the Isle of Kistan. To the north and unseen just beyond the curve of the world lay a broad river delta marking the marge where the lands of Tugal and Vancha met. And as the hull of the *Eroean* sliced into the perilous waters trapped between isle to the larboard and mainland to starboard, Aravan turned to Brekk and said, "Though we enter the northern strait, until the lookouts call a sighting, the warband can be at ease."

Even as Brekk's gaze swept across the horizon ahead, he grunted and nodded but otherwise said nought, for he knew that Rovers roamed the seas along the path they would take.

Kistan, though an island, was roughly circular and vast, nearly a thousand miles long and eight hundred wide, and it sat in the Avagon Sea like a barely pulled cork east of the narrows where the indigo waters of the Avagon met the dark blue deeps of the Weston Ocean. And both to the north and south of this "stopper" lay straits where the Rovers plied their dhows and flew their maroon or crimson sails, those bloody colors deliberately chosen to strike terror into the hearts of the men of merchant ships.

Throughout history, Kistan had been a thorn in the High King's side, for the pirates had plagued the shipping lanes, interrupting trade and travel. Oft had forays been sallied against these looters, the High King's fleet bearing legions to destroy the brigands. Yet to escape the blades of the kingsmen, the Rovers merely faded back into the rugged hills and dense jungles of their enormous island refuge.

The strait to the north, down which the *Eroean* now sailed, formed a long throat leading in and out of the Avagon Sea, a seven-hundred-nautical-mile-long choke point, varying in width from seventy to just over eighty-five nautical miles.

On the far side of the isle the southern strait lay between Kistan and the treacherous realm of Hyree. There the channel, though just as long, was nearly twice as wide for nigh the full of its length, yet ships from the realm of Hyree plied these waters in league with the Rovers, and together they harassed that route.

West of the isle the two straits merged to form a three-hundred-fifty-nautical-mile run to the Weston Ocean, again choking down to a width of eighty-five nautical miles, and there did many of the Kistanian and Hyrinians lurk, for no matter whether ships came from north or south or went in the opposite direction, through those narrows between sea and ocean they all had to pass.

And so the *Eroean* did enter that perilous stretch, with some one thousand nautical miles of Rover-laden lane lying before the ship. Yet the westerly breeze was off the fore, and tacking would add nigh half again to the full of the length.

"How long will we be in these waters?" asked Brekk, never taking his gaze from the horizon.

Aravan peered down at the furl of bow-split water, then up at the foremast wind pennant above. "When last we measured we were running at some eleven knots. And so, if the wind remains braw and steady from the west, six days at most."

Brekk barked a laugh. "Hai! Now I see why we should remain at ease, for to stand at full ready through the length of these straits would wear quite thin." Brekk then glanced 'round at the Châkka warriors adeck in clusters nigh each of the ballistas, including the ones at hand. He sighed and said, "Time to have all stand down."

For four days they tacked along the northern channel, and not a crimson sail did they see. Aravan leaned against the taffrail and watched Aylis at the wheel, Fat Jim pointing at the mizzen wind pennant and coaching her in helmsmanship. Aravan frowned, puzzled. "Ne'er have I gone this long without seeing any Rovers whatsoever. Where might they be?"

At his side, Long Tom shrugged, but then his features lit up. "The Dragons!" he blurted, by way of explanation.

"Dragons?" asked Lissa, the Pysk sitting atop the compass and drinking tea from a thimble.

Aravan glanced at Long Tom and nodded. "Ah, yes. Now I recall. It was old news in Arbalin, when thou and Bair and I and the crew didst return from the Great Swirl, or what was left of it, that is."

"What was old news?" asked Lissa.

"A spring past and one, on the equinox in the High King's year 5E1010," said Aravan, "at the end of the Dragonstone War, the Drakes not only slew the Golden Horde and the Lakh of Hyree and the Fists of Rakka, but they burned every ship in the Argon—Kistanian, Hyrinian, even the High King's ships . . . they did not discriminate."

"The Rovers were in the Argon?"

"Aye. 'Twas said the full of the fleet of the Rovers brought the southern invaders to face the High King's host along the banks of the Argon, and they were yet in the river when the Dragons slew all the foe, though that slaughter took place where the Red Hills meet the plains of Valon. After that great killing, the Drakes then flew east and turned their fire against the fleets."

Then Aravan looked at Long Tom and said, "I deem thou hast hit upon it, Tom: that's why we've espied no Rovers."

Long Tom grinned and said, "Wull, then, Cap'n, it just moight be that we get clean through th' striats wi'out seein' none."

As the sun sank toward the horizon in late afternoon of the following day, "Sail ho!" came the cry from the lookout above.

"Where away and what color?" shouted Long Tom.

"Sir, a point starboard the bow. She's lateen and scarlet."

Long Tom turned to Noddy. " 'Tis a Rover, lad; sound the alert."

"Aye-aye, sir." Noddy began ringing the bell in the tattoo of warning. And in but moments the full of the crew spilled onto the decks, Châkka warriors to the ballistas, sailors to the sheets and halyards.

" 'Nother sail ho, Tom," cried the lookout. "This one scarlet, too."

Aravan, along with Nikolai, came from the cabins and to the aft deck. Fat Jim puffed up after, though Wooly was manning the helm. Aylis and Aylissa, their tokko game interrupted, stood out of the way on the deck below, Vex sitting calmly at Lissa's side in spite of the bustle all 'round. Yet Aylis held a bow in her hands, a quiver of arrows at her hip. Lissa, too, was armed, her tiny bow and arrows quite lethal, should any foe come within its limited range.

"Three, no, four crimson sails," cried the lookout, "two-masted dhows all. And a white-sailed ship running ahead, three masts—a barque, I think. They're after her, Tom."

"Wi' y'r permission, Cap'n," said Long Tom, "Oi'll arm th' crew. Them fools o' Rovers moight tiak it in't' their heads t' try t' board th' *Eroean*."

Aravan smiled and nodded his approval but said, "More likely we'll be boarding them, Tom, yet we'll need falchions, no matter which."

"I be the one to see it done, Kapitan," said Nikolai, and down the ladder he bounded.

Nikolai rounded up a handful of sailors to disappear below and emerge moments later with their arms full of falchions, the heavy and relatively short-bladed swords ideal for close-quarter, hand-to-hand fighting.

And as Nikolai and the sailors passed among the seamen and handed out cold steel, Dwarves, already armed, stood ready at the ballistas—two of the arbalests in the bow, two in the stern, and three down each side—yet they did not cock the weapons nor load any missiles.

And on hove the *Eroean* . . .

. . . and the sun sank toward the sea.

Like the silent long shadows streaming from the masts and sails and cast far to the aft of the Elvenship by the lowering sun in the west, quietly the *Eroean* drew nearer and nearer to the Rovers, and still the ready Dwarves waited.

And all aboard the *Eroean* seemed to stand stock-still with bated breath, and the only sounds aboard the ship came from the prow cutting through the indigo sea and the *shssh* of the wake astern as well as the creak of Elven ropes straining against pins and yards and blocks.

And as azure sails drew on toward those of crimson, Aravan softly said to the bosun, "James, very soon, when I give the command, pipe the sails for a larboard beam reach against the two aft raiders. We'll cross their sterns and rake the decks."

Intent on their prey ahead, the Rovers had no idea that the hunters were hunted themselves.

Word as to Aravan's plan went whispering the length of the ship. And the Dwarves to the starboard growled in their beards at being left out of the fight, while those to the larboard at last cocked their weapons and laded on fireballs.

And the *Eroean* slipped unnoticed up behind the foe.

"Now!" hissed Aravan, and James piped the command.

Even as sailors hauled the yards about and slipped the sheets of the stays, of a sudden the crews aboard the two Rover ships glanced 'round and began gesticulating and scurrying, their shouts loud over the water, as the Kistanian crews, their faces stark with fear, had finally realized the peril they were in.

Hard over the Rovers hauled the long lateen spars, yet it was entirely too late, and fire sailed o'er the span between the Elvenship and the deck of the first raider, flaming balls to explode across the decks and splash upon rigging and masts and sails and set all ablaze. Swiftly, the larboard ballistas were again cocked and, as the Elvenship crossed the heel of the second raider, five more fireballs were flung. And then the *Eroean* was past this pair and Aravan ordered the sails piped about to run down the other two dhows.

And as the bow veered close to the wind, a single fireball from one of the Rovers flew across the distance to fall short and sink with nought but a splash and the sputter of a fuse extinguished.

And leaving the two Rovers battling against blaze—their masts, sails, and decks afire—the *Eroean* now sped toward the remaining Rovers, whose prey fled just beyond.

And the sun lipped the horizon and began sinking into the sea.

On sped the Elvenship, closing the distance between. Yet, given the hullabaloo aft, the Rover captains had spotted the *Eroean*. And they shouted orders, and Rover crews haled on the lines of the lateen-rigged ships, and they heeled over to flee away southward toward the haven of Kistan, for few captains of the island nation dared take on Aravan's ship.

"Shall I pipe the sails, Captain?" asked James.

"Nay, bosun," said Aravan. "We'll let these two take flight with their rudders tucked under their keels."

Long Tom sighed, but said nought, while Nikolai snorted and headed to the decks to gather a crew to take up the no-longer-needed falchions. He passed Brekk as the Dwarf came storming up to the afterdeck. "Captain, you are my commander, but are we just going to let them run? If so, I mislike it a deal."

Aravan looked at his Dwarven warband leader. "Armsmaster, wouldst thou hie after a snake were it fleeing into the dark?"

Brekk shook his head. "Nay, I would not. Yet if it were an Ükh, I would run it to earth and slay it."

"This is no Rûpt, Brekk."

"Nay, it is not, Captain, but the difference is mere, like one chip of bad stone to another."

"Yet thou dost know, Brekk, stones come in many kinds and forms—whereas some can be shaped, others crumble at a touch."

"You, an Elf, try to teach a Châk about stone?"

"Nay, Brekk, for I know thy kind are masters of such."

"Then what is your point, Captain?"

"Just this, Armsmaster: whereas Rûtcha were made in the spirit of Gyphon, hence are incapable of change, Humans are malleable and can alter their behavior—for good or ill, I admit. Yet, heed: mayhap yon Rovers, though now like unto fleeing snakes, perhaps are frightened enough to give up their vile ways, for unlike vipers and Spaunen, Humans can indeed change. Yet, Brekk, I promise thee this: I have marked them well, and should either of those same ships be plying these lanes when we return, then will we hunt them down, day or night, and slay them to the last man."

The armsmaster growled and glared at the crimson sails of the fleeing pair of ships. "Mayhap *were* it a lethal viper, I would slay it on the spot to prevent it from even the possibility of striking an innocent victim. I think these poisonous Rovers deserve the same fate, for unlike the snakes of which you speak, the brigands seek out the blameless to do them harm."

Aravan nodded. "There is much to what thou dost say, Brekk. Mayhap I have made a mistake after all. Yet there is a ship to the fore that needs our help to gain the ocean beyond."

Brekk grunted and gave a single sharp nod, for at last did he see Aravan's true aim, and on plied the *Eroean* westerly as crimson-sailed Rovers fled southward.

Swiftly, the Elvenship overtook the three-masted barque as twilight overtook the world. As the *Eroean* eased up sails and hove alongside that ship, Aravan called out to the captain opposite, "We'll run ahead and clear the channel."

"Captain Aravan, is it, of the *Eroean*?" called the merchant commander in reply.

Noddy snorted and muttered, "J'st who bloody else moight we be?"

"Aye, I be Aravan."

"Well I thank ye, Captain Aravan. I be Captain Allson of the *Gray Petrel* out of Gelen. Though an escort we would take gratefully, we were headed east for Arbalin when we spotted the brigands."

"Then come about, Captain Allson. The northern channel was clear when we sailed through. And I suspect you won't be bothered by those particular Rovers again. As for us, we're sailing west, and won't be back for many a day."

"Very well, Captain Aravan," called Allson. "The channel west was also clear when we came through. And, Captain, if you are ever in Lindor, I'll stand you and all of your crew to a fine meal and a drink."

"We'll take you up on that, Captain," replied Aravan; then he signaled James, and the bosun piped the orders to tighten up sails again, and the *Eroean* drew away from the *Petrel*, as that ship came about to head east once more.

And, as the nighttide drew down over the world and stars began to appear one by one in the darkening skies above, west sailed the Elvenship, while aft sailed the barque toward the glimmering light of two burning ships that would never ply the seas again.

21

Voyages

ELVENSHIP
LATE AUTUMN, 6E1,
THROUGH MID SPRING, 6E7

No foe did they see as they sailed the remainder of the way through the Kistanian Straits and into the Weston Ocean. And even as they emerged, Aravan, standing at the starboard rail with Aylis, said, "Here is where I first saw thee, Chieran, as thou didst clamber over the rail, and I fell in love in that instant."

Aylis smiled, again recalling that fateful day in her first year at the College of Mages in Kairn, the City of Bells, that she had cast a spell upon a silver mirror, and that was when she had first seen who her true-love would be. Yet those days were long past, and the City of Kairn no more, for it had gone into the sea when the Island of Rwn vanished below the waves.

She looked into Aravan's sapphire blue gaze and said, "And I loved you long before we ever met."

"Cap'n." Long Tom's voice broke into their reminiscences.

"Aye?"

"What be our course?"

"West-southwest, Tom. We'll ride the trades and the coastal current as far as we can, and hope they carry us across the doldrums of the midline."

"Aye, Cap'n, west-sou'west she be."

As Long Tom turned away, Aylis asked, "Are we taking the same route that we took once before, back when we headed for the Crystal Cavern?"

"Nearly the same," said Aravan. "After we cross the doldrums, we'll run a long tack southwest to the line of the goat, where, Rualla willing, we'll not find irons there. Then swing southeast and run for the Cape of Storms, down through the roaring forties and the polar westerlies. Once past the cape, we'll head northeasterly on nigh a straight run for the Ten Thousand Isles of Mordain."

"Rualla willing, of course," said Aylis.

Aravan laughed. "Indeed, for the Mistress of the Winds, fickle though she is, has command o'er the *Eroean*, e'en above me."

When they came upon the waters of the midline, the winds were light and shifty, and the crew was hard-pressed to make the best of the erratic air.

"Did I not say Rualla was fickle?" asked Aravan.

"Capricious, I would say," answered Aylis. "Playful."

"Y'r laidy, Cap'n, she's roight t'call 'er that," said Long Tom, looking about as if expecting that at any moment Rualla would manifest Herself upon the decks of the Elvenship. "Oi mean, laidies don' loik t'be called 'fickle,' naow, do they? Oi mean, capricious is more loike a nicer word, it is, a more nicer word at that. Oi think Rualla would loike that word ever so much better, Oi do, Oi think, Oi do."

Aravan laughed and nodded. "Indeed, Long Tom. Capricious and playful it is."

And on they sailed in the whimsical wind, erratic and difficult to sail as it was.

But then once past the Midline Doldrums, they ran swift and true to the Calms of the Goat, and there the ship found itself in irons. They broke out the gigs, and for three full days both Dwarves and men rowed southerly, and the hot sun beat down upon them, sweat runnelling from brow and pits and crotch. But on early morn of the fourth day, a slight puff of air bellied the sails and, ere the noontide, again the *Eroean* ran full in a brisk wind.

Steadily the winds increased the farther south she fared, and though it was verging upon the warm season south, the shortening nights grew cold and colder, and chill grew the lengthening days as well. The speed of the ship increased, and she ran sixteen and seventeen knots at times, logging more than three hundred fifty miles a day on two days running. And the weather became foul, rain and sleet off and on lashing against the ship, while large breaking waves raced o'er the southern lats of the Weston Ocean, the *Eroean* cleaving through the waters, her decks awash in the cold brine.

In the swaying light of the salon's lanterns, Aravan looked across the table at Long Tom and at Nikolai, third in command. Spread out before them were Aravan's precious charts, marking winds and currents throughout the oceans of the world. Back in the shadows stood Noddy. A knock sounded on the aft quarters door, and Noddy sprang down the short passageway to open it, and in through wind and spray came Fat Jim and Brekk, followed closely by James, bosun of the *Eroean*, all three wearing their weather gear, boots and slickers and cowls.

Noddy took the dripping slickers and hung them on wall pegs in a corner. And everyone, including the cabin boy, gathered 'round the chart table.

Aravan's finger stabbed down onto the map. "In a day or three we will reach the waters of the cape, and I would have ye all remind the crew what it is we face."

"Storms," breathed Noddy. "Storms fierce and wild and cruel."

Aravan smiled at the lad. "Aye, Noddy, storms indeed. Autumn storms at that, though not as cruel as those in the cold season south."

Brekk growled. "Stupid southern seasons. Just backwards! Here, winter in the north is the warm season south, and summer north is opposite as well."

Long Tom laughed. "Hoy, Brekk, back'ard or no, th' polar realm be always frigid, though th' sun may roide the sky throughout a day as nice and peaceful as y' please."

Nikolai nodded, adding, "A bad place, this cape, by damn. Hard on crew no matter season. Snow, ice, freeze rain fall, weigh down both sail and rope. In autumn, there be snow or sleet or freeze rain or anyt'ing, and same be true of spring. Even in heart of warm part of year it be not very different; ha! much time sleet hammer on ship. But in autumn season, like now, storm always seem bear freeze rain and ice, and wave run tall—greybeard all—*Diabolos!* hundred feet from crest to trough."

"E'en so, Nikolai," said Fat Jim, "it ain't like the winter season, when things be double-worse."

Aylis, standing off to one side, nodded, for she had sailed these waters millennia agone when seeking Jinnarin's mate, Farrix.

Aravan gazed down at the chart. "It is ever so in these polar realms that raging Father Winter seldom looses his grasp, no matter the southern season."

Noddy, too, stared at the map. "And the winds, Cap'n, wot about the winds? Will they be the same as wot we came through afore, back when you 'n' Bair 'n' the rest o' us went to the Grait Swirl?"

"Aye, 'tis the very same air—westerlies, and constantly running at gale force, or nearly so. Seldom do those winds rest, and the *Eroean* will be faring with the blow." Aravan looked up at the faces about him. "And I would have ye all remind the crew just what it is that we likely face: thundering wind, ice, freezing rain, long days and short nights fighting our way through. Each of us will have to take utmost care to not be washed over the rails, for like as not, should anyone go into the water he will be lost. Remind them again that tether ropes are to be hooked at all times aloft . . . and, Tom, Nikolai, rig the extra deck lifelines, for surely they will be needed. As for Lissa and Vex, they'll have to remain belowdecks, else she and the fox will be blown into the sea."

"I'll warn her," said Aylis, "and make it my job to see she remains down here with me."

As Aravan nodded, "The sails, Captain," said James, his dark eyes glittering in the lantern light, "is there something special you would have me render?"

"The studs are already down," replied Aravan. "Likely we will furl the starscrapers and moonrakers as soon as we round the shoulder of the cape . . . the gallants and royals as well. I deem that we'll make our run on stays, jibs, tops, and mains, though likely we'll reef them down somewhat. Long ago I ran with all sails full up—not here but in the Silver Straits—and I lost two of the masts in one fell swoop. I'll not risk that again."

"What about the spanker, Cap'n?" asked Noddy.

Aravan smiled at the cabin boy, who even now was showing promise of becoming a bosun. "Aye, Noddy," answered the Elf, reaching out and tousling the lad's unruly hair, "we'll reef the spanker, too."

"Kapitan," said Nikolai, "I t'ink you might talk to crew again about running cape. They no doubt like word straight from you."

A murmur of agreement rumbled 'round the table.

"Aye, Nikolai, I had intended to. Assemble the men, and thou, Brekk, gather the Drimma as well. Shall we say at the change of the noon watch on the morrow?"

Sleet pelted down upon the ship, while in the forward quarters below, Aravan stood on a sea chest and spoke to the *Eroean*'s crew, the weather too harsh to hold an assembly above. And as the hull clove through the rolling waves and brine billowed over the decks, all the Men and Dwarves gathered 'round their Elven captain, all but three remaining in the sheltered wheelhouse—Fat Jim and Wooly, along with Tarley.

Aravan spoke of the cape and reminded them all of the weather at this time of year, for although each had been through this passage before, it was a year and a half past and in a different season. This time, as then, they would make transit from west to east, running with the wind, running with the gale. Aravan spoke of the ice that would form on the ropes, and of the driven snow that would blind them and weigh down the sails, if it should come. "Yet," he said near the last, "we have made this run ere now. The *Eroean* is a sturdy ship, and ye are a fine crew. I fear not that we will see the Sindhu Sea in but a week or so. Still, I would caution ye to take care, for if any be lost to the waters, we will not be able to wear around the wind in time to save ye in those chill waves, and to do so would put the entire ship at hazard. So, buckle up tightly when up top, for I would see ye all when we've passed beyond the cape.

"Be there any questions?"

"What about the Grey Lady ghost ship?" asked Billy, the cook's helper. "I mean, Captain, I hear she runs in weather like this."

An uneasy stir rippled through the crew, for well they knew the legend of the tatter-sail ship, ever cursed to ply these waters, ever searching for the owner's lost son who had washed overboard in a wild storm in these waters.

Aravan sought out Billy's gaze and said, "I think the legend be false. Yet if true, and if the Grey Lady appears, then look the other way."

Now it was a stir of agreement that rippled through the crew, for everyone knew that if you didn't look long at the ship, she would not claim your soul. On the other hand, if one got washed overboard and lost in these waters, the Grey Lady would stop and take the unfortunate one aboard to sail forever this frigid sea, especially in furious blows.

"Be there any more questions?" asked Aravan.

None had any, for they had made this crossing before, and so Captain Aravan called for a round of rum, his words met by a cheer.

They finally entered the South Polar Sea, and around the cape they fared, and the freezing rain and sleet beat upon the masts and sails and rigging, and made the decks treacherous. Men spent as little time as possible above, and Fat Jim and Wooly and Tarley helmed the *Eroean* from the small, sheltered wheelhouse, rather than the aft deck.

And the westerlies hurled the ship onward, her sails reefed half or goosewinged, and those nought but the stays, jibs, tops, and mains, the rest furled and stowed or reefed full.

And the waves she rode across—or those that rode across her—were sixty, seventy, eighty feet high from trough to crest, or conversely eighty feet deep from crest to trough, depending on where the *Eroean* rode, as southeast and then east she ran.

But at last the cape was rounded, and Aravan turned the Elvenship to east-northeast. Even so, sleet and freezing rain yet hammered upon the ship, but the farther north they fared the less ill the weather became.

From the polar westerlies and into the roaring forties the *Eroean* sailed, and there came a day when she broke out into sunlight, and all the crew celebrated and stood adeck admiring the warm light and clear blue sky.

Another two weeks found them wending among mountainous green islands, for they had come into the tea-growing slopes of the Ten Thousand Isles of Mordain.

They spent nearly a month altogether obtaining what they had come for, and the crew reveled in shore leave, yet toiled when the precious and well-sealed cargo was laded.

And then they made the long journey home, this time rounding the cape in the teeth of the wind.

They brought back a ship laden with white tea from the slopes of a dormant fire-mountain on one of the Isles of Mordain, and no Rovers did they see when once again they fared through the Northern Strait of Kistan.

Their next voyage took them to Ryodo, where they delivered fine Valonian horses to the royal court of the Emperor of that insular land.

Throughout the following five years, they sailed west through the perilous waters of the Silver Straits in the South Polar Ocean to reach the Great Island in the Shining Sea. There they took on a single chest as cargo, a small cask filled with fire opals, a fortune in and of itself.

They sailed north through the Shining Sea to the small island where Lady Katlaw lived in her tower, and they exchanged one of the opals for a deck of special cards for Aylis to use in her <seeing>.

In Bharaq, they traded charts to Dharwah, a map merchant in the port of Adras, where they took on a cargo of teakwood, to fare to the carvers and furniture makers in Lindor. While in Lindor they sought Captain Allson to redeem his promise of a meal and a drink, yet the *Gray Petrel* had been lost at sea and none knew the fate of the men.

They made several forays inland at various isolated shores, where rumor said something lost or precious lay within. Here Lissa and Vex scouted as Brekk and the warband and Aravan and Aylis followed. Yet all they found were ancient ruins, usually nought but tumbled-down stones with nothing dear for their effort. Yet these expeditions along remote coasts were the principal reasons why the *Eroean* sailed the seas.

As Aravan said to Aylis and Lissa one night in the salon, "It matters not whether the legends are true, for the seeking is the sum of the game. Had we wanted nothing but wealth, then merchants of the seas we would ever be, for with but a few trips of the *Eroean* we can each make a fortune many times over.

"Nay, comfort and riches suit none aboard, not I, not ye, not this well-chosen crew. For we sail only to fund our quests, setting a little aside for the times after, when many of the crew will leave the sea and settle down to a more staid existence. But that is for later and not for now, and not for the times immediately ahead, for legend and fable yet call to this crew, sweet voices singing in our hearts, in our spirits, and drawing us on.

And so we hie across the sea, the holds laden to the hatches, until we can go somewhere we are called, and mayhap we will find whatever it is that drew us there. If not, so be it, for other ventures lie beyond the horizon, their siren songs luring us on."

Lissa looked up from her jot of brandy and raised the tiny cup into the air. "I'll drink to that, Captain. Lead on. Lead on." She stood and then abruptly fell on her rump. She looked into her cup and muttered, "Perhaps I've had enough."

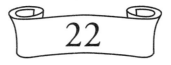

22

Onset

Dark Designs
Mid Spring, 6E7

Nunde again locked himself in his quarters and once more quaffed the bitter brew. And after but moments he fell back as if dead. Yet his aethyrial self flew free, and for the fifth time in as many years, he arrowed east. He soared over land, and to his astral sight all shades and colors were reversed: dark was light; light, dark; crimson shone viridian; sapphire shone ocherous; amethyst, amber; ebon, alabaster; and the reverse. The night skies were bright and speckled with dark stars; the moon, black, reminiscent of Neddra. Faster than any eagle he soared, swifter than even a shooting star. And when he reached his destination, dawn at that place broached the horizon, the skies darkening, the leading arm of the black sun even then beginning to lip the rim of the world. Quickly, he flew to where a man slept, and there upon a workbench, Nunde's aethyrial self saw that the labor had at last been completed.

He swiftly flew out from there and to an adjoining chamber, where another man slept with a woman lying at his side. She gave a small start as Nunde entered, and he was careful not to let his spectral essence touch her. In but a moment, she settled back into sleep. Cautiously, Nunde merged with the man, but in a heartbeat or two he flew free again.

Nunde then darted westward, for he could feel his aethyrial strength ebbing. Out from this land and over Xian and Aralan and down through Alban he soared, arrowing for Caer Pendwyr. At last he arrived, where he momentarily merged with yet another man, one well away from the palace, for he knew that place was warded against creatures such as he. Nunde then flew up and out and fled back to his vile sanctum ere his aethyrial strength gave out.

He rested a full day and all the next, and then went to his laboratory, where he slew several Drik and took their essence into himself.

Then he unrolled a map and called Malik unto him, and when the apprentice arrived, Nunde said, "My vengeance will soon fall due."

"Indeed, master," said Malik, dreading what would come next.

"It is time. Take the Drik and Chûn and Ghok and others that I have assigned to you and march east to here"—Nunde's finger stabbed down to the map—"where you or my chosen one will slay Aravan and all those with him. I care not if he is mutilated, just as long as you bring his corpse to me."

And then Nunde laughed, Malik laughing with him, even as the apprentice's gut churned with dread at what lay waiting at the place he was ordered to go.

23

Risky Business

BURGLARS
MID SPRING, 6E9

*D*ogs. *Rûck-loving, rat-eating dogs.* Binkton slipped back down from the spike-fanged top of the moonlit wall to the shadow-clutched alley below. He came to rest beside his cousin. "You didn't tell me they had dogs," he whispered.

"Huh?" Pipper looked up from the carefully coiled rope as he finished attaching a small grappling hook to one end, a hook with its tines padded.

"Keep your voice low, Pip," whispered Binkton, "else they'll hear us."

"Who'll hear us?" whispered Pipper back.

"The dogs. You didn't tell me they had dogs."

"Dogs?" breathed Pipper.

Binkton growled low in exasperation. "Are you listening, Pip? There are dogs patrolling the yard—a couple of huge brutes with jaws that crush and teeth that bite. We fall afoul of those two, they'll snap us up like we were no more than bits of bacon."

Pipper frowned and shook his head. "Dogs?"

Through clenched teeth, Binkton hissed, "Yes, Pip, dogs; dogs you didn't mention when we planned this."

Dropping the hook, Pipper began free-climbing the ten-foot-high wall by jamming his fingers and toes into the mortar cracks. "Are you certain? I mean, there were no dogs when I—"

"Argh!" Binkton plopped down with his back to the wall.

Moments later, Pipper dropped down beside Binkton and murmured, "Well, Bink, you're right. There are definitely two big dogs patrolling the yard. And a new kennel off to one side."

Binkton sissed air out between clenched teeth, but otherwise made no comment.

"They weren't here when I scouted out the place," breathed Pipper. "No dog poop. No kennel. Nothing. It's not like I'd miss something like dogs."

"Oh, yeah? But miss them you did, even though you watched the house for five days."

"I did watch it for five days, Bink, but I swear there were no dogs. Me, I think they are new."

Binkton unclenched his jaw and drew in a deep breath and slowly let it out. Finally, he said, "Oh, Pip, I believe you. Maybe they *are* new, but it's just that I'm frustrated. Rackburn is off to the Rivers End Theater, and we've not got a lot of time. And with dogs patrolling the yard, even if we escape their slavering jaws, they'll alert Rackburn's household, no doubt a bunch of Rûck-loving, rat-eating ruffians. That'd just put us in another pickle, and we'd not get Lady Jane's money back to her."

Pipper made a gesture of negation. "We can't let that happen, Bink. Let's take another look at the situation."

Pipper started to climb, but Binkton sat still for a moment, brooding. Finally, with a sigh, he got up and followed Pipper, who at that moment gripped two spikes along the top and raised his head just above the wall to peer over. He quickly ducked back down and whispered, "Oh, lor."

"What? What is it?" asked Binkton, his voice a low mutter.

"Another one," murmured Pipper.

"Another dog?"

"Yes."

Grasping two spikes, Binkton lifted himself up to where he could see.

Three huge mastiffs lounged near the rear entrance to the manse.

Binkton flinched down.

Once more Pipper raised up to study the scene. After a moment he murmured, "I think we've enough rope to reach the balcony."

"And . . . ?"

"And I can cast the grappling hook over and snag the rail; then we'll tie it off at this end on one of the spikes and walk across."

"Are you insane, Pip? You're the acrobat, not me."

"Oh, Bink, walking a rope is as easy as falling off a log."

"Good example, Pip, 'cause I'd fall off at the first step. Besides, your rope and hook were to be used to get us up to the balcony only *after* we crossed the yard."

"But, Bink, that was just so we wouldn't have to sneak through the house to get to the room with the strongbox."

"That *was* the plan," said Binkton, "over the wall, across the yard, up to the balcony, through the window to the left, and to the coffer. Well, the dogs have put an end to that scheme, and put an end to your new one, too. I mean, even if I could walk the rope, they'd bark the moment you threw the hook, and that would bring out the ruffians to catch two ninnies: one walking a rope above, the other screaming and falling down into the jaws of the beasts. But even if I didn't fall, don't you see, Pip, no matter what we try, the dogs, they'll raise a hue and cry."

Pipper frowned and then brightened. "You are right, Bink. But remember what Uncle Arley said about turning disadvantages into advantages, like turning hecklers into part of the act."

"So . . . ?"

Pipper began easing back down the wall.

Binkton followed, and when he reached the ground beside Pipper, again he asked, "So . . . ?"

"So, bucco, we'll turn those hecklers into part of the act."

"What in blue blazes are you talking about?"

"Well, Bink," said Pipper, grinning, "I know where we can get a couple of chickens." And he started along the alley.

Binkton momentarily stood still, but then as enlightenment dawned, he murmured, "Oh, I see. For a bit there I thought this might be another one of Pip's harebrained schemes, but I think it might actually work." Binkton hurried after his cousin. As he caught up, they looked at one another in the moonlight and smiled, on the verge of laughter. They'd get Lady Jane's money back if it took all night.

And as they strode on down the twisting way, Pipper fell into reflection. It was but some two and a half years ago—in early autumn, 6E6, to be exact—that they were on their way to make their fortune, and he wondered just how two buccen Warrows had ever managed to get from that beginning to this end, to this unseemly business of burglary. . . .

24

Away

BOSKYDELLS
EARLY AUTUMN, 6E6

As the Red Coach rumbled along the Crossland Road and into the outskirts of Rood, "Here she comes," said Granduncle Arley, the eld buccan sitting on the bench of the pony cart beside his once-removed nephews.

With anxiety lurking in the back of his sapphire blue eyes, Pipper looked at Binkton, as if asking, *I know it was my idea, but do we really want to do this?*

Binkton threw an arm around Pipper's shoulders and said, "It's just to Junction, Pip. I mean, if we find it not to our liking, and even if we don't have the fare for the Red Coach back, at worst we can always hike home."

"But I've never been outside the Bosky before."

"Wull, neither have I, bucco. But, hey, wasn't it you who said, 'Let's take this show on the road'?"

"Yes, but I'm beginning to have second thoughts."

"Well, put them out of your mind, Pip," said Binkton, a glint of fire in his viridian gaze. "After all, we have the blood of heroes running through our veins. Remember, Beau Darby is one of our ancestors."

"Be that as it may, Bink, I'm thinking that after five thousand years, Darby blood is beginning to run mighty thin."

Uncle Arley laughed but said nought.

"Oh, Pip," said Binkton, "it'll be fun."

Pipper looked over at the eld buccan who had accompanied them into the Centerdell village. "Will it be fun, Uncle?"

"It was for me, back in the day," said Arley.

The Red Coach pulled up in front of the way station, and Humans got out to stretch their legs and to relieve themselves and to have a drink and a bite to eat. As Warrows led fresh horses out from the stables to replace the team, the driver and one of his three footmen made ready for the exchange.

As to the passengers and coachmen, these were not the first Humans that Pipper and Binkton had seen, for the Red Coach regularly came through the Bosky, and Rood was a transfer point. Out from the town and to the northeast the Two Fords Road led toward Challerain Keep, and to the southeast the Tineway ran toward Caer Pendwyr, while due east the Crossland Road continued on to Stonehill and past. Back to the west lay the lands of Wellen and the realms beyond.

Even so, the sight of Humans was somewhat intimidating, being as they were nearly twice the height of the average Warrow. And Binkton and Pipper would be travelling with these tall beings, for at the request of Graden Finster, owner of the Black Dog Inn, these two buccen were heading southeasterly and beyond the Thornwall to the small town of Junction, there where the Tineway met the Post Road.

Noting the hesitance of Pipper, Uncle Arley said, "Pip, I've taught you and Bink all I know, and you'll be a welcome sight to the onlookers, whether it be on the streets of a city or in an inn or on the stage of a theater. Seldom do Warrows show up in the cities, and so, if for no other reason, you two will be a novelty, just as I was. Why, I've performed in Hovenkeep and Rivers End and even Caer Pendwyr, as well as little hamlets and villages throughout much of the High King's realms. Yet should your and Bink's acts fail, Bink is a fine locksmith and you a tinker rare. If nothing else, you two can travel through the countryside, mending pots, sharpening scissors and knives, fixing lockboxes, and whatever else needs doing, and you have my old kit for such. Pip, you and Bink will be fine, and there's a world out there awaiting. And the Black Dog will give you a small taste of what you'll discover beyond the limits of the Barrier."

Pipper sighed and said, "Well, I suppose you are right. I mean, folks in the Bosky seemed to like us, and perhaps those Outside will too."

"That's the spirit," said Binkton, looking 'round at the two duffle bags and large case on the bed of the pony cart, the case iron gray with painted red and yellow and orange flames here and there licking up along its sides. "Now let's get our things onto the coach."

With a cluck of his tongue, Arley drove the two-wheeled carriage to the side of the Red Coach, and there one of the footmen tossed the young buccen's duffles up to the man atop. But when the footman lifted the chest, he grunted in surprise and in a strained voice as he hoisted it up he called to the man atop, "Take care, Willam. I think this is filled to the brim with sheet iron."

Pipper laughed and said, "Not iron, but chains and locks, ropes and pulleys and other such tackle, along with mending gear." The footman looked at the Warrows and frowned in puzzlement, as if wondering what such equipment was for.

The coach remained awhile to allow the continuing passengers to take care of their needs, and the new passengers to lade their luggage atop, but finally the driver called for all to get aboard. With final hugs from Uncle Arley, both Warrows passed in among the Humans, who simply towered over the wee buccen—dark-haired Binkton standing three-feet-six, fair-haired Pipper three-feet-four—and they climbed into the coach and took seat.

"H'yup, h'yup," cried the coachman, "hup, my boys," and with the eight horses pulling, slowly the great stage got under way. It rumbled southeasterly out of Rood along the road to Tine Ford.

The Red Coach itself was huge, and divided by a partition into two sections, with seating for eighteen passengers. And Pipper and Binkton found themselves in the aft half and sitting in between two large men, with two more men and a matronly woman across from them. The woman, her dress seemingly mostly ruffles and bows, leaned forward and said, "Why, aren't you two just the cutest of things?"

Binkton sighed, but Pipper said, "Why, yes, madam, yes, we are."

Batting her eyes, the matron asked, "And just what would you two children be doing travelling all alone in the great wide world?"

"Ch-children?" sputtered Binkton. "Children? Madam, I'll have you know my cousin here is a young buccan, just turned twenty summers of age, while I am his senior by three moons or so."

"Twenty?" she exclaimed, taken aback. "Twenty, you say?"

"These are Warrows," said the man to the buccen's left. "Heroes of the War of the Ban, the Winter War, and the Battle of Kraggen-cor, and they served with distinction in the Dragonstone War."

The lady's eyes widened in surprise. "Oh, my, you did all that?"

"Well, not us personally," said Pipper. "But our cousin Trissa Buckthorn served under two High Kings—Garon and then his son Ryon—during the War of the Dragonstone, to say nothing of our ancestor Beau Darby, who fought beside High King Blaine in the Great War of the Ban."

"Goodness, I did not know that," said the woman. "Nor did I know of . . . what do you call yourselves? Warrows? Yes, Warrows. I don't believe we have any Warrows in the city of Lindor on the Isles of Gelen."

"Not many of us travel beyond the bounds of the Boskydells," said Pipper.

"Nor beyond the fringes of the Weiunwood," added Binkton.

The matron frowned. "The Weiunwood?"

"Over by Stonehill," said Binkton, gesturing to the east. "A shaggy old forest caught between the realm of Rian to the north and the land of Harth to the south."

"I say," said the man who had come to their defense, "I'm Raileigh Bains, a historian, and I'm travelling to the libraries in Caer Pendwyr to write a definitive account of the Dragonstone War. If you don't mind, perhaps you could supply me with some details about the Warrows who served under the High King during that terrible time."

"Wull, we all serve under the High King," said Binkton, "but I suppose you mean the Company of the King."

"Cousin Trissa was the captain of that company," said Pipper. "Forty-three Warrows, archers all, who rode to the High King when summoned. What would you like to know?"

The man pulled a case out from under the seat and opened it. It contained a great number of blank sheets of parchment, and to one side a stoppered inkwell sat snugly in a small partition affixed to a corner, and along the other side in their own partition rested a number of sharpened quills. Raileigh took up parchments and flipped down a writing board and unstoppered the ink and dipped a quill and said, "I'm ready when you are."

Pipper turned to Binkton. "Where should we begin? The Gjeenian penny?"

Binkton shook his head. "No, that starts back in the Great War of the Ban, when Tipperton Thistledown helped the dying prince."

"Then how about when Tuck and Danner and Patrel first got the armor?"

"Oh, I know," said Binkton, "we'll start when the specter of Aurion Redeye appeared to Trissa and Kipley and Danby."

"That's Trissa Buckthorn and Kipley Larkspur and Danby Candlewood," said Pipper to Raileigh.

"Who's telling this tale," flared Binkton, "you or me?"

"Why, you are, Bink. I'm just trying to help."

Before Binkton could reply, with her eyes wide in trepidation the matron leaned forward and asked, "Did you say the specter of Aurion Redeye, the High King of ancient days? His ghost appeared? His true ghost?"

"Indeed," said Binkton, glaring at Pipper, who himself had begun to answer.

As Pipper fell silent the woman gasped, "Oh, my," and, seemingly to stave off a swoon, she fell back in her seat and fanned herself with her fingers.

Binkton turned to the historian and said, "You'll recall that Aurion Redeye was the High King at the start of the Winter War, a thousand years ago. And some seven years back his ghost appeared to Trissa and Kipley and Danby, for he was redeeming a pledge made long past. . . ."

Raileigh Bains' pen scratched across the parchment, while Binkton and Pipper took turns telling the tale of the Warrow Company of the King: how it was first formed, how Tuck and Danner and Patrel came to be wearing, respectively, the silver, black, and gold armor, and the terms of the loan of that armor Aurion Redeye made. Then the buccen told of Redeye's shade's visitation a thousand years later to redeem that loan, and how, to retrieve the black armor, Trissa and Kipley and Danby travelled to the distant tombs out before the dreaded Iron Tower in the fearful land of Gron. Following that, they told of the trio returning to the Bosky to take command of the Company of the King, and then on to the Argon Ferry, where they and the High King's Host were defeated in the battle at that place.

The passengers were held spellbound, for both Binkton and Pipper knew the story well, and as they told of the retreat and the coming of the Dragons, the Red Coach continued to rumble on toward the distant ford across the River Spindle.

Some ten leagues south of Rood the coach made a stop at a way station to change teams, and then some ten leagues after that and late in the evening they stopped at the Wayside Inn for an overnight stay, the inn located at the junction where the spur road to Thimble meets the Tineway. The Warrow-run establishment on the Red Coach line had rooms suitable for travellers of all sizes, and was as well the place where the coach would again change teams.

When Denby Willowdell saw Binkton and Pipper enter his establishment, he welcomed them warmly, for oft had these two performed at the Wayside Inn, and he asked if they'd come for a stint.

"Ar," said Binkton in response, "we'd like to stay and put on a show, but you see we're expected at the Black Dog down at Junction Town two days hence."

"Beyond the Thornwall?"

"Aye," said Pipper. "Uncle Arley arranged it with Mr. Graden Finster."

"You'll like Graden," said Denby. "He's a good sort and honest as the day is long."

Pipper grinned. "What about at night?"

Denby laughed and said, "Oh, he's fair the night long, too."

"Well, then," said Pipper, "there's also dawn and twilight to consider, for they are neither day nor night."

All three Warrows broke into laughter, and Denby threw an arm about each and said, "Ah, me, but I've missed you two buccoes, and I'm sorry you'll not be staying a day or so. But be that as it may, come on, let me buy you a drink."

Two evenings later found Pipper and Binkton thirty-three leagues farther along their route. They were ensconced at the Tineway Inn in the village of Stickle, there near the Thornwall.

Looking about, Raileigh asked, "And this is where the Company of the King assembled and waited for the Gjeenian penny?"

Pipper nodded. "Yup. And it came on First Yule."

"What's all this business about a Gjeenian penny?" asked the matron, Mrs. Harper. "I thought Gjeenian money was nearly worthless, and a Gjeenian penny the most worthless coin of all."

"Well, you see, back in the Great War of the Ban," said Binkton, "Tipperton Thistledown took on a mission from a wounded prince to deliver a Gjeenian penny to Agron. He didn't know who or what Agron was, and his only instruction was to go east. But the prince died before he could tell Tipperton more."

"It turned out," said Pipper, "the Gjeenian penny represented a pledge made from one king to another that each would come to the aid of the other with an army and whatever else it would take, and all it would cost was—"

"A Gjeenian penny!" burst out Mrs. Harper. "Oh, how utterly droll."

"Wull, I wouldn't exactly call it 'droll,' ma'am," said Binkton. "I mean, the sight of that penny meant that many good people would die, most likely at the hands of the Foul Folk."

Mrs. Harper's face fell into dismay. "Oh, I see," she said, her manner now subdued at the thought of the consequences attached to the coin.

"Anyway," said Pipper, "at the end of the War of the Ban, the Warrows and the High King made that same pledge to one another, and should we ever be in dire straits, all we need do is send a Gjeenian penny to the King, and all he needs do is the same."

"How many showed up again?" asked Raileigh, scribbling.

Binkton said, "We didn't see one for some four thousand years after the Great War of the Ban, but then a penny came in the Winter War. And we didn't see another one until a thousand years after that, when the Kutsun Yong's Golden Horde threatened Mithgar."

"That was the Dragonstone War, some six or seven years past," said Pipper.

Binkton nodded. "As foretold by the ghost of Redeye when he came to recall the armor into service."

Pipper laughed. "I'll never forget the day we heard of the recall of the

Company of the King. Bink and I went to see the Thornwalker captain in Rood to join up. 'Sorry, buccoes, but you're just striplings,' he said. 'What are you, about ten summers old?' As I gaped, dumbfounded, Bink sputtered and yelled, "What? What? Ten summers? I'll have you know Pip here is thirteen summers, and I am a full three moons older.' And the captain said, 'Well, then, you've got seven summers to wait, 'cause to be a Thornwalker you've got to be a young buccan.' And Binkton shouted, 'What Rûck-loving, rat-eating idiot made that rule?' Well, for some reason the captain got all huffy, and threw us out."

As the passengers broke into laughter, Raileigh scribbling while doing so, Binkton growled and said, 'Well, it *is* a Rûck-loving, rat-eating rule." Then he looked at Mrs. Harper and said, "Excuse my language, ma'am."

Finally getting control of her giggles, she looked at Bink as if to say, *My, but aren't you the cutest little thing.*

Bink squirmed in irritation, but Pipper said, "So, anyway, the Bosky got snowed in, and we decided that come the thaw we would run away and join Cousin Trissa and her company. The melt came the following spring, but by that time, the war was over."

Raileigh looked up from his parchment. "So that's the story of the penny?"

Binkton nodded. "And why the Company of the King was here in the Tineway Inn waiting for the sight of it. And of course, when it came—on First Yule, as foretold—the Company then travelled to the Argon Ferry, where thousands upon thousands of Free Folk died in battle, a number of Warrows among them."

"Oh, my," said Mrs. Harper, "I'll never look at a penny the same way again."

"Well," said Raileigh, talking while scribbling, "let us hope that with the death of Gyphon, a Gjeenian penny will never again need be sent anywhere to summon aid."

"I'll drink to that," said Binkton, and he and Pipper hoisted their mugs in salute.

The next morning, the Red Coach trundled away from Stickle, and within a mile they came to the mighty Thornwall.

Dense it was; even birds found it difficult to live deep within its embrace. Befanged it was, atangle with great spiked thorns, long and sharp and iron hard, living stilettoes. High it was, rearing up thirty, forty, and in some places fifty feet above the river valleys from which it sprang. Wide it was, reaching across broad river vales, no less than a mile anywhere, and in places greater than ten. And long it was, nearly a thousand miles in all, for it stretched completely around the Boskydells, from the Northwood down the Spindle, and from the Updunes down the Wenden, until the two rivers joined one another; but after their merging, no farther south did the 'Thorn grow. It was said that only the soil of the Bosky in these two river valleys would nourish the Barrier. Yet the Warrows had managed to cultivate a long stretch of it, reaching from the Northwood to the Updunes, completing and closing the 'Ring. And so, why it did not grow across the rest of the land and push all else aside remained a mystery; though the grandams said, *It's Adon's will,* while the granthers said, *It's the soil,* and neither knew the which of it for certain.

Toward this mighty rampart, the Red Coach trundled along the Tineway, and all the passengers peered out the windows to see the great, looming, dark mass reaching up toward the sky and standing across the way, extending far beyond seeing to the north and south. Through this mighty barricade the road went, through one of the Warrow-made tunnels, a shadowy vault of thorns leading down into the river valley from which sprang the fanged barrier.

Into the dim passage rolled the Red Coach, and the light fell blear along the path. And long did the coach roll in befanged gloom.

At last, ahead the wayfarers could see an arch of light, and once more into the day they came as the route passed through Tine Ford across the Spindle River. Beyond the water on the far bank again the Barrier grew, and once more a dark tunnel bored through it. Nearly two miles the travellers had come within the spike-laden way to reach the ford, and nearly three more miles beyond would they go before escaping the Thornwall.

Into the water they rolled, and the wheels rumbled as the Red Coach splashed across the stony bottom. And all the occupants stared in amazement at the massive dike with its cruel barbs rearing upward and clawing at the slash of blue sky jagging overhead. Soon they had crossed the shallows and again entered the gloom.

In all, it took nearly two hours for the coach to pass completely through the Spindlethorn Barrier, but at last it emerged into the sunlight at the far side. Passengers leaned out the windows to look, glad to be free of the taloned mass. The countryside they could see before them was one of rolling farmland, and the road they followed ran on to the east, cresting a rise to disappear, only to be seen again topping the crest beyond.

"Well, we've gone and done it," said Binkton, the look on his face stark.

Pipper nodded but said nought, his own face filled with unease.

"Gone and done what?" asked Mrs. Harper.

"Left the Bosky," Pipper whispered.

The Black Dog

FIRE AND IRON
EARLY AUTUMN, 6E6

Just after the sun crossed the zenith, the Red Coach rolled into Junction Town, where it stopped at the depot to change teams, and to allow the passengers to debark and stretch their legs and have a meal and take care of other needs.

As the dust of their arrival settled or drifted away on a gentle breeze, the footmen laded the Warrows' luggage onto a pushcart. Pipper and Binkton said good-bye to Mrs. Harper and Raileigh Bains, and Raileigh thanked them for the tales surrounding the Company of the King in the Dragonstone War, while Mrs. Harper nearly smothered both buccen with an all-encompassing, drawn-out hug against her ample and beribboned bosom.

Released at last, the two Warrows began trundling the cart toward the Black Dog Inn. They trudged by stores with wares sitting out front on display—barrels, pots, dry goods, and the like. They passed a barbershop and bathhouse, a leather-goods store alongside a boot-and-shoe repair shop, and other such establishments. A clanging sounded on the air, and the Warrows fared by a large stable with a smithy to one side, where a man pounded a glowing iron rod into a curved shape. Along the way and on either side of the street there sat a few houses, but mostly business establishments lined the Post Road, a main route between Challerain Keep at its terminus far to the north, and Caer Pendwyr even farther away at the other terminus southeastward. And although Junction Town couldn't by any means be called a full-fledged city, still it was considerably larger than the Warrow village of Rood—not only in the size of the buildings, for all were constructed for Humans, but also in the sheer number of them; for many dwellings and other buildings stood along the streets that crossed or paralleled the main road. The broad scope of the town was due not only to it being along a major trade route and sitting at a junction, but also due to the garrison on the outskirts, where a company of King's men were stationed. These soldiers were assigned to patrol the roads, for although the ways to Neddra were in the main blocked, still there were occasional Foul Folk sighted, as well as brigands and other unsavory kinds roaming the land.

Down the wide way passed the Warrows, their eyes agoggle at the splendor of it all, with people rushing hither and yon, now that a Red Coach had come.

"Lor, Bink," said Pipper, "have you ever seen so many Big Folk?"

"Now how would I have done that?" snapped Binkton. "I mean, just like you, this is the first time I've—"

"Oh, Bink, what I mean is that this is really quite a place."

Binkton took a deep breath and then let it out, calming his irritation. Then he said, "You're right at that, bucco."

"I think our fortune is soon to be made," said Pipper, grinning.

"Wull, I wouldn't exactly say that, Pip . . . fortune or fate, perhaps, but— Oh, look. Up ahead." Binkton pointed with one hand, the cart wobbling in response. He quickly grabbed hold again, and said, "I think it's where we are bound."

The buccen could see in the near distance and standing out before a large red barnlike establishment a painted signboard hanging by hook and eye from a post arm and swinging slightly in the breeze. The words thereon proclaimed the place to be the Black Dog Inn, Graden Finster, Prop. Above the placard a dog stood darkly on the post arm, its ears pricked, and, as if sighting a friend or its master, its tail was awag.

"Good grief. How do they get a dog to do that?" asked Pipper.

"Oh, Pip, don't be silly. It—it can't be alive," said Binkton, hesitantly, uncertainty filling his face.

As they neared they saw it was a carved wooden dog, its tail on a swivel and swinging back and forth in the stirring air.

"See, I told you," said Binkton, his voice taking on a tone of superiority.

"Wull, you had your doubts, too," declared Pipper.

"Did not."

"Did too."

They were still quibbling when they arrived at the inn. And as they pushed the cart to the edge of a roofed-over porch with tables and diners thereon, a dark-haired lad jumped up and asked, "Are you them?"

"What?" asked Binkton.

"Are you them?" repeated the boy. "You surely must be, 'cause you're Warrows."

He turned and bolted through the swinging doors, shouting, "Da! Da! They're here."

As the boy ran into the inn, customers glanced up from their meals. And one burly man looked at his tablemate, a small, skinny man, and declared, "Well, strike me dead, Queeker, but it looks like two pip-squeaks got lost and strayed outside the Boskydells."

The tablemate laughed and in a high-pitched voice said, "Yar, Tark, I do believe you're right. Got all turned about and accidentally wandered out into the world."

Binkton bristled and said, "I'll have you know most of us are not like some of those mossbacks back home."

"Bink's right," said Pipper, and he made a sweeping, theatrical gesture that took in all the others dining on the porch. "We are daring adventurers, and we have the blood of heroes in our veins."

"Heroes? Ha!" sneered the Tark. "Weakling runts like you, heroes?"

The skinny one, Queeker, hooted, as if somehow a victory had been won.

Binkton muttered, "Rûck-loving, rat-eating idiots," and he reached for a rock, but even as he bent down, Pipper grabbed his cousin's arm and hissed, "Remember what Uncle Arley said: Turn hecklers into part of the act." Then Pipper pulled himself up to his full three-foot-four height. "We are descended from the great hero and healer Beau Darby, and Captain Trissa Buckthorn of the Company of the King is our cousin."

At these words, two men, each wearing a scarlet tabard emblazoned with a rampant golden griffin, looked up from their own meals.

"So?" sneered the skinny man.

"So," answered Pipper, "adventurers we are, and quite bold, with the blood of warriors in our veins, as you'll see tonight if you come to the Black Dog and watch."

"Ar," scoffed the skinny one, "as Tark says, y'r nothing but pip-squeaks. Pah! As if you could fight anyone."

Even as this exchange went on, one of the tabarded King's men stood and strolled to the table where Queeker and Tark sat. With a flinty gaze he looked down at them. "I fought beside Captain Buckthorn and her company in the Dragonstone War, and finer or better warriors I ne'er saw. So, if I were you, I'd keep my gob shut."

As Queeker flinched down, Tark looked up, his eyes filled with suppressed rage. Then he glanced at the other King's man, who had also risen to his feet, but who merely stood waiting.

In that moment the lad burst back through the doors, a sheaf of paper in his hands. And on the boy's heels bustled a small, rotund, bald-headed man who burbled, "Binkton Windrow and Pipper Willowbank, I presume? Welcome to my establishment. Graden Finster at your service. Which of you is which, might I ask?"

"Um, I'm Pipper, and this is Binkton," said Pipper.

"Well met. Well met," said Graden, nodding enthusiastically. "Have you brought your gear? Oh, I see you have. Yes, yes. Yes, yes, yes. Indeed, I see you have. If you're anything like your Uncle Arley, well . . ." He turned to all the diners at hand, and even though there were no women present he announced, "Ladies and gentlemen, I invite you, each and every one, to come tonight to see these two perform. All the way from the mysterious and exotic hidden land of the Boskydells they came to delight all. Tonight, sometime after"—he looked at the buccen—"sundown?" Pipper nodded. "Tonight after sundown they'll be here exclusively in the Black Dog. You don't want to miss them." Finster then said to the lad, "Pud, start passing out those handbills. Make certain that everyone in town gets one. And post several down at the Red Coach station"—he glanced at the King's men—"and make sure the garrison gets some as well."

As the boy darted off, Graden turned to the Warrows again and said, "Now let's get your gear inside."

"Um, Mr. Finster," said Pipper, "we'll need some help with the chest. It's quite heavy."

"Right-o," Finster started to answer, but the King's man looked at the buccen and smiled and then turned to Tark and Queeker and said, "These two here will be more than happy to carry your trunk inside, right?"

Queeker leapt to his feet, but Tark said, "Hey! We've got a Red Coach to catch."

"Don't worry," said the guardsman, placing a hand on the hilt of his sword. "You've time."

Tark snarled, and his own hand twitched toward the dagger at his belt, but the burly man did not complete the move and, growling, got to his feet. He and Queeker stepped to the handcart, and, grabbing the leather handles at each end, they hefted up the iron-gray case with its painted-on flames, Queeker grunting under the unexpected load. Following Finster, they toiled up the steps and into the inn, the King's man coming after, Binkton and Pipper, their duffle bags over their shoulders, trailing the parade.

The Black Dog's interior was huge. "Used to be a hay barn, back before Junction Town became a way station," explained Finster. He took a deep breath and said, "Still smells like clover at times. —Anyway, they were going to tear it down, and that was when my great-granddad said to himself that it'd make a fine inn. So he bought it and changed it over, and it's been in the family ever since."

As they wended among the tables, Pipper looked up at the rafters and beams high overhead. "Perfect," he murmured to Binkton.

"Just like Uncle Arley said," replied Binkton, gesturing at a stage sitting well below what must have been a small loft of sorts.

To one side sat a bar, and swinging doors led somewhere—to a kitchen, the buccen guessed.

They crossed the large common room and passed through a door to one side of the stage, where they entered a hallway. Graden led Tark and Queeker along the corridor to a modest room.

As Queeker and Tark set the trunk down, Finster said, "I turned a storage room into this dressing room a while ago when I realized we'd have bards and dancers and such passing through. It's had lots of use, and for the next sevenday it's all yours."

Binkton looked about. "I don't see any cots. Where do we sleep?"

Finster laughed. "The main inn is out back in another building. One of the guest rooms is waiting for you. Come, I'll take you to it."

Pipper said, "First we need to push the cart back to the Red Coach station."

"Oh," said the King's man, "I'm sure Mr. Queeker and his sidekick, Tark, will be glad to do that for you. After all, they have a Red Coach to catch."

"Yessir," said Queeker, heading out, even as Tark, relegated to the status of sidekick to his own hanger-on, glared and followed. As he passed the Warrows, he muttered, "Someday, pip-squeaks. Someday."

"Oh, yeah?" spat Binkton, as the man went onward.

"The blood of heroes beats in our hearts," Pipper called down the hallway after Tark.

The guardsman laughed and looked at bristling Binkton and said, "I believe it does at that."

That evening, the large common room of the Black Dog was full to the walls with King's men and townsfolk, along with most of the passengers on layovers while waiting for Red Coaches to roll through heading toward their various destinations: some would fare north through the land of Harth and toward Rian and the Jillian Tors, as well as the Dalara Plains; other passengers waited for a southbound coach en route to Gûnar, Valon, Jugo, and Pellar; a few travellers would bear west through the Boskydells, aiming for places in Wellen, or Thol, or Jute, or Gothon, or perhaps across the waters to Gelen. But on this eve, the townsfolk and soldiers and wayfarers were not thinking of these things. Instead they were in the Black Dog to see a show. Quite often bards and minstrels came through, and occasionally dancers, and many onlookers came to hear them sing or see them perform, especially if they were Elves. But this show would be different, for these were not singers, not musicians, not dancers, but entertainment of a different sort. Not only that, but this diversion boasted legendary Warrows, a folk seldom seen outside the Boskydells, except in times of strife.

And so the room was crowded, and Graden and his staff bustled hither and thither, bearing platters of food and trays of foaming mugs of ale from the Holt of Vorn and goblets of dark wine from Vancha.

Some in the audience were impatient, and many asked when the performance would get under way.

"In a candlemark or so," someone said.

"Ar, is that one of the 'old' candlemarks, or one of High King Ryon's 'new'?"

That simple question started an argument among those gathered concerning the merits of the old versus the new, an argument hearkening back some seven years past to the time King Ryon had made it so:

It was after the end of the Dragonstone War that the boy King declared that beginning on Year's Start Day, with the onset of the Sixth Era, there would be a new candlemark instituted, where four of the "old" candlemarks equaled just one of the new. He said that with this change, instead of there being ninety-six candlemarks in a full day, there would be only twenty-four. No one knew for certain why ninety-six marks from noon to noon had been chosen as the old candle measure in the first place, and there were several explanations—none of them satisfactory. Regardless, King Ryon set about to partition the day into more readily remembered divisions, and he decided on a four-to-one standard, for that would make it straightforward to institute, since the chandlers could simply alter their existing wares with a red mark every fourth one of the old. Slowly the new standard—twenty-four candlemarks in all—was accepted, but for the most hidebound. In reality, given the quality of the wax and wick, most candles burned at something between twenty-one and twenty-seven new marks in a full day.

But in the Black Dog, even as arguments over candlemarks continued, Graden Finster stepped upon the empty stage and called for quiet. When—but for some murmurs—relative silence fell, Finster announced: "My lords and ladies, sirs and madams, and soldiers and maidens alike, I present to you, all the way from the secret land of the Boskydells, the Incredible Pip and Marvelous Bink, and their travelling show: Fire and Iron!" Graden then made a wide-sweeping one-handed gesture to point up to the rafters, where lines had been strung, along with stationary bars crossing from beam to beam as well as trapezes lightly held up and back by fragile string tethers. And upon a joist high above in the shadows stood Pipper. And even as the crowd turned about and looked toward him, Pipper leapt out into the light and into empty space. Women screamed and men shouted, as the buccan hurtled through the air like a red flame, with yellow and orange streaming after, and it seemed the wee one would plummet to his death. But in the last instant he caught hold of a tethered bar and swung down and through a deep arc, then up to the rafters again, where he released the one only to catch another lightly tethered bar to swing down and just over the heads of the gasping onlookers. Up he sailed once more, to release and somersault through the air, and grab onto one of the fixed bars to whirl 'round and 'round. Then he dropped straight down and onto a tightrope and he ran across to leap to another. And all the while he looked to be a Warrow trailing fire, dressed in scarlet as he was, with a multitude of bright orange and yellow ribands streaming from the backs of his arms and legs, and his fair hair flying out behind. And he spun and whirled and leapt and swung, all scarlet and gold and saffron.

The crowd *ooh*ed and *ahh*ed and called out in fear for the wee one's very life. And women fanned themselves and gasped, while men leapt to their feet and shouted.

But then Pipper swung on a line down and through and up, and he released to land on a rope tied from a high rafter on one end to slant down to the stage on the other. And he glided down to the platform, where he sprang outward in a high-flying leap and flipped through the air like a swirling blaze to land upon a large iron-colored chest painted with flames, a chest that had not been there when Graden made his announcement.

He came to rest and bowed to the crowd, to wild cheers and applause. And he bowed again and then once more, the cheers only growing as he did so. But then, of a sudden, there came a flash and a bang and a great puff of smoke. Some in the crowd shrieked in fear, while others reached toward their waists for a weapon. And when the smoke cleared, Pipper was gone, but high above and dangling upside down from the ceiling and wrapped in dark chains secured with locks slowly spun a Warrow dressed in iron gray. Two men rushed out from the wings, and they took up the chest and rushed off, while two more men, one of them Graden, at the end of a rope dragged a bed of long, gleaming spikes to place them directly below the trussed Warrow.

And even as the men exited, there came a *Ping!* and a large silvery link flew to clatter upon the stage, and the Warrow dropped toward the spikes, only to be jerked up short, having fallen some third of the way.

And as the Warrow slowly twisted like a fly strung up by a spider, "Look!" cried someone—Graden, it seemed. "Look at the silver rings above!" High over the Warrow, the dark suspension chain dangled in two remaining big loops, held together by two more large and glittery silver links among the dark rings of the chain, and one of the silver links was slowly giving way.

Ping!

The link parted and clanged down, and amid a rattle and clatter the Warrow dropped another third of the way toward the gleaming spikes below.

And up above, the gap in the last silver ring began to spread.

"Oh, please, please, get him out of there!" shouted someone, female it seemed.

Men stood, and some started for the stage.

But in that very moment, the Warrow began shedding locks and chains.

But the silver link gave even more, as chains cascaded from the Warrow to rattle down among the spikes.

"Hurry! Oh, hurry!" cried the voice.

The silver link yawned, and by only a slim finger held on.

But the Warrow was now free, and with white and black ribands swirling about him, the dark-haired, gray-garbed buccan began climbing the chain, even as the link finally failed, and the last loop fell.

The Warrow plunged toward the spikes.

Women screamed and looked away.

Men shouted in despair.

Chang!

The chain came to an end, and the Warrow swung safely just above the sharp points of the long and gleaming tines.

The hall exploded in relief, and Binkton swung out from over the spikes and dropped to the stage, and bowed to cheers and applause, and to the relieved tears of many.

After several more bows by Binkton, Pipper came out from the wings, and, as helpers dragged the spikes and chains away, Graden jumped up on the stage and called out, "There they are, folks, Fire and Iron."

As Pipper and Binkton took more bows, Pipper said out of the side of his mouth, "You cut that one mighty close."

"Pah, I would have landed in the safe spot, had anything gone wrong," replied Binkton.

Before Pipper could reply, Binkton held up his hands for quiet, and when it fell, he called out, "Blindfold, please."

Pud, in his moment of glory, rushed from the wings bearing a black cloth. And Fire and Iron began the second part of the act, with Pipper roaming through the crowd and holding up various objects donated by individual spectators and calling out for blindfolded Binkton to identify what it was. Binkton, of course, slowly hemmed and hawed and circled 'round the identity of the object—brooches, daggers, cloak pins, coins, swords, and other such—making it look as if he were struggling to simply discover with his mental abilities what the object was that he could not see, while all the time knowing by Pip's coded responses exactly what it was.

Most of the folks in the Black Dog had never seen such an act before, though one or two soldiers in the audience had come across such in the past. Even so, they were amused by the patter of the Warrows, such as the time Pipper held up a bookkeeper's quill for the audience to see, and Binkton declared that he thought it might be something smaller than a horse. The audience roared.

The next night, Pipper again performed daring acrobatic feats, leaping and turning and tumbling across the stage and through flaming hoops, and he juggled blazing firebrands that it seemed would burn him to a crisp.

And this time at the end of his act, when he did a series of backflips and landed on the trunk, after his bows, he reached down and pulled up a large piece of cloth all 'round, to immediately drop it, but it was Binkton who stood there instead.

As men started to carry the chest offstage, a man leapt to his feet and called out, "Ar, I'll wager t'other Warrow is in the trunk."

Binkton called for the chest bearers to stop and open it up and tilt it forward so that the patrons could see inside, and when they did, Binkton waved his hand through the space within and called out, "Are you in here, Pip?" When he received no answer he turned and said, "As you can see, my skeptical friend, it's completely empty." The challenger grunted in puzzlement and sat back down.

As the men closed the chest and took it into the wings, Binkton invited a couple of soldiers to come to the stage and shackle him. As they were doing so, and much to their surprise and confusion, he handed the first one of them the second soldier's sword that had somehow come free, and he gave the second soldier's suddenly loose purse to the first, saying that he had thought he had heard the one sell his sword to the other for a fee. He apologized and returned the rightful goods to each as the crowd whooped in glee. And then, even as one snapped shut a shackle cuff on Binkton, the soldier discovered he had locked his own wrist. And there were inadvertent losses of the soldiers' belts and pants falling down and other such. It was an "Oops, pardon me," and an "Oh, I am so sorry," and a "Well, how did that happen?" sort of act, the audience laughing themselves to tears.

Finally they managed to get Binkton's wrists into manacles, and as they knelt to fetter his ankles, the Warrow leaned down to help them, handing one of the soldiers the wrist shackles to hold while Binkton helped.

When the soldiers were finally sent back to their seats, the captain of the garrison called out to Binkton and said, "I do believe, my dear Wee One, you do use trick fetters."

"Ah, well, then," replied Binkton, "would you happen to have some of your own about you?"

"No, but if you'll come to the garrison tomorrow, I'll have some waiting. Slap you in one of my cells, too, and I'll bet you one of the Black Dog's finest meals and drinks that you'll never get out of that."

Binkton hesitated a moment, and the captain called out, "Do I see fear on your face?"

Binkton flared. "Fear? Pah! No gaol can hold me, much less a military stockade. I do accept your challenge, Captain. Shall we say at the mark of noon?"

"I will bear witness," called out someone, and when he stood all could see he was the town's Adonite priest, a man the townsfolk knew to be totally trustworthy.

The acts went on, and as they took their bows, Pipper said from the corner of his mouth, "Are you insane, Bink? You've never broken out of a prison before."

"Do not worry, cousin. I mean, how hard can it be?"

"Those are the words of doom, I fear," said Pipper in return.

"Not really, bucco," said Binkton, "for you see, I have a plan."

The sun stood on high, and nearly all of the citizenry of Junction Town, along with a few layover passengers, as well as the soldiers of the garrison, were at hand. Businesses were closed, and a Red Coach driver and his footmen and the passengers who happened to be heading north were in attendance as well.

The captain and the priest greeted Binkton on the steps at the front of the stockade, a humble but sturdy stone building. The King's man held in his hands a pair of small-sized irons. Binkton said, "Might I have a walk about your gaol first?"

The captain led the Warrow and the entire crowd around the modest guardhouse, noting that both iron-barred doors, front and back, were well locked, and all windows—front, side, and back—were iron-barred as well.

When they returned to the door at the front, the officer led Binkton up the steps, where he fitted the irons to the buccan's wrists, while Pipper stood to one side and fretted, clearly nervous for all to see. Then the captain announced, "No one has ever escaped from the cell that I will now lock him in."

"Pah!" snapped Binkton. "I'll be out in a trice."

"We'll see," said the captain, and he took a ring of keys and opened the barred front door, and, with the Adonite priest following along as an observer, he took Binkton inside. Moments later, the captain and the priest returned and relocked the entry, and then stood waiting.

"Is he well locked in, Prelate?" called someone.

"Indeed," replied the priest. "Shackled tightly and locked in a cell from which there is no escape."

"How d'y' know he ain't got no lockpicks on'm?" asked another.

"I thoroughly searched him," said the captain. "There's nothing whatsoever that could've escaped me, not even a pin."

"Did y' look in his mouth?"

"I did."

"How about his nether parts?"

"That, too."

A quarter candlemark passed, and the crowd became restless, and Pipper sat glumly on the top step. The captain glanced up at the sun and then back to the audience and said, "Well, I do think a trice has passed." He turned toward the priest and said, "Come, Prelate, let us go and see how he's doing." Then he grinned and said, "I'm going to enjoy the meal he now owes me."

Moments later, with bewildered looks on their faces, the captain and priest came back out the door, and in the captain's hands were the small shackles, and he said, "He's gone."

"Where can he be?" shouted someone in the crowd.

"Yeah. Where is he?" cried someone else.

Babble broke out among the onlookers, and Pipper, grinning and completely at ease, jumped to his feet and held high his hands for quiet. When it fell, Pipper said, "Why, he's at the Black Dog and sitting at a table and waiting for his meal."

The crowd streamed back to the inn, and there sat Binkton at a table, and he stood in welcome and invited the captain to sit at his side while he partook of the Black Dog's finest food and its very best drink.

Graden Finster and his staff had never served such a noonday crowd as they did that very day.

"I say," said Pipper as he and Binkton made ready for bed that eve, "we ought to do this at every town."

"Do what?" asked Binkton, yawning.

"Challenge them to lock you in gaol, and then you escape. Did you see how many came to watch?"

"Of course I did, ninny. I was there, you know."

"No, Bink, what I mean is: it'll draw the crowds."

"Hmm . . ." Binkton frowned in thought.

"And if we send handbills ahead of us to the next city and put up broadsheets, well, then . . ." said Pipper, not completing his words, but Binkton knew what he meant.

Binkton frowned. "Wull, it might have been difficult to get out of the stockade had we not slipped down there last night so that I could try their locks."

"Yeah, but you didn't have any trouble then, and you were working in the dark. And it certainly wasn't any trouble in the light of day."

Again Binkton yawned and he slipped into his bed. "I suppose it is a good idea, Pip. But for now, blow out the candle and let's get some sleep."

The seven-day engagement at the Black Dog flew by, and Binkton and Pipper performed the variations of their Fire and Iron act every night—juggling, jesting, picking pockets, mind reading, swinging, flipping, escaping, appearing and disappearing. But soon nearly everyone in Junction Town had seen the performances, and the crowds began to wane.

"Where will you go?" asked Graden, when the buccen told him they were moving on.

"We'll work our way down to Argon Ferry Town," said Pipper. "We hear it's grown back since the war, and is quite prosperous with trade."

"I'd watch out for them Rivermen, if I were you," said Finster.

"Don't worry," said Pipper. "We know what they did back in the Great War of the Ban. And before that what they did at the Race and on Olorin Isle."

"Robbers and traitors," said Binkton, nodding.

The very next day, with the help of footmen, the Warrows laded their iron-gray, flame-painted, secret-paneled trunk, loaded as it was with chains and locks and ropes and other gear, onto the southbound Red Coach. The footmen also tossed up to the top the buccen's duffle bags, filled as they were with clothing and costumes for the Fire and Iron act, along with their personal kits. Finally, waving good-bye to Graden Finster and his boy Pud and a small gathering of townsfolk, as well as a few soldiers from the garrison, including the captain, the Warrows boarded the coach on their journey to acquire fame and glory, along with some of the good King's coin.

As the coach trundled out of town, Pipper turned to Binkton and asked, "Nervous?"

Binkton scowled. "Nervous, me? Pah. I mean, after all, what can possibly go wrong?"

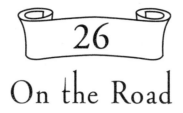

On the Road

FIRE AND IRON
MID AUTUMN, 6E6

Three rainy days and thirty-seven leagues after leaving Junction, Binkton and Pipper arrived in Luren, a town at the confluence of the Rivers Hâth and Caire, which then became the River Isleborne, those waters to flow on westerly and ultimately reach the Ryngar Arm of the Weston Ocean.

At the layover, they took rooms in the Luren Ford Inn, the establishment of two brothers who had fled from Gothon after a short-lived rebellion, the brothers having been on the losing side, or so it was they said. Others claimed the brothers were fleeing from harsh Gothon justice, having defrauded a handful of royalty. Regardless, when the brothers discovered that Binkton and Pipper were the Warrows they had heard about from Red Coach passengers who had previously fared through, they asked the buccen to stay on a few days and stage their performances at the inn. And although the ceilings were not nearly high enough for Pipper's aerial show, nor for Binkton's "Spikes of Doom," still Fire and Iron had many acts that required no lofty overhead. After a bit of negotiation, Binkton and Pipper agreed to a six-day stay, for that was when the next southbound Red Coach would come trundling through, given the weather got no worse. And so, they offladed their gear and took up residence at the inn.

That evening, in a short performance, with their sleight of hand and patter, they had the onlookers in stitches, finding eggs and newts and other such oddities nestling in and about various audience members' persons. Pipper juggled and Binkton escaped from tightly bound ropes, and they announced that on morrow eve and those after they would put on a full performance.

The next day they visited the local gaol, and while Pipper entertained the city watch, Binkton wandered about seemingly at random, but at last he invited the captain and his warders to come to the performance that night, and to bring their best irons, from which he would escape.

That evening, fair-haired Pipper, in scarlet and saffron and gold, put on a show of acrobatics, where he backflipped through flaming hoops, and landed on the chest, and vanished as black-haired Binkton appeared. As usual, some in the audience declared that Pipper was hiding in the chest, but when it was opened and tilted forward for the patrons to look within, no Pipper could be seen. As men carried the chest offstage, the Luren watch shackled Binkton hand and foot and tied him up in a sack. They cinched the last knot, and as instructed returned to their seats. The sack wriggled and thumped about, but finally came to rest, and a plaintive voice called out from within: "Would someone get me out of here?"

Even as the Luren watch grinned in triumph, "I will," called a voice from the back of the audience. When the spectators turned to see, the dark-haired Warrow in gray and white and black strode among the tables and to the stage, where he released the yellow-haired shackled Warrow in scarlet and gold and saffron.

"How did t'other Warrow get in there?" cried someone, "And the first one get out?" called another, even as the dark-haired buccan reached forward and took the suddenly unlocked irons from the fair-haired other and returned them to the captain of the city watch.

The Warrows bowed to the applause and then stepped into the wings, and after a moment returned to center stage and took another bow. And Binkton said, "As you can see, I simply escaped the bag when someone wasn't looking while Pipper took my place." As some in the audience laughed, while others scratched their heads, Binkton turned to the commander of the watch and asked, "Captain, is your gaol as unsecure as that bag?"

"No one has ever escaped our cells," testily replied the man.

Binkton smiled. "Well, how about we wager the best meal this inn has to offer that I will be out in a trice."

"I accept."

"We'll need a reliable witness," said Binkton, "just to prove that you and I are not in collusion."

"I'll be that witness," cried someone.

"As will I," said another, his voice rasping like gravel in a sieve.

One who had volunteered was the mayor of Luren, but the other, the raspy-voiced one, was a broad-shouldered Dwarf, who stood and said, "Brekka Ironshank, at your service."

He was the first Dwarf that Binkton and Pipper had ever seen. Dressed in leathers and standing some four-feet-six, he sported chestnut hair and a like-hued forked beard, and his shoulders were perhaps half again as wide as those of a man.

The spectators called out their approval of the Dwarf, for the honesty of Châkka was legendary. Oh, not that they didn't trust their mayor, but a Dwarf, well, his word would be unimpeachable.

Brekka stepped among the tables and came to stand with the Warrows, and he bowed to the gathering. Then as he turned and shook the buccen's hands, he quietly said, "Nice trick, changing clothes and donning wigs, for surely most Humans think all Waerans look alike and cannot see the differences between you twain."

Pipper looked at Binkton and shrugged, for clearly the Dwarf had discovered that he and Binkton had switched identities to perform the Buccan in the Bag trick, with Binkton in the sack becoming Pipper, while Pipper in the wings became Binkton.

At the mark of noon the following day, just as in Junction Town, spectators stood at the gaol, while Brekka and the watch captain and a thoroughly searched wrist-shackled and ankle-chained Binkton went inside, the Warrow shuffling. Pipper remained outside and paced back and forth and bit his lower lip and wrung his hands, his head down, as if worried.

From within the building there sounded a clang as the cell door was slammed to, and a rattle of keys and a clatter of a lock being thrown. A moment later the captain and the Dwarf reappeared, and the captain, twirling the ring of keys, said, "He's tightly fastened away and in irons."

"These irons?" a voice asked.

Brekka stepped aside, and just behind stood Binkton, the fetters in hand.

The crowd whooped in glee.

A few days afterward, Pipper and Binkton, along with Brekka, caught the next southbound Red Coach. The day was overcast with dark clouds, and light fell blear on the land. Under the glum skies, the coach trundled out from Luren and across the ford and into the forest of Riverwood, a broad treeland that would extend along both sides of the route for nearly seventy miles. The way between Luren and Gûnarring Gap was known as Ralo Road, stretching nearly three hundred fifty miles in all. But ere they reached the Gap, they would have to fare through the Grimwall Mountains, lying some eighty miles away, there where Ralo Pass cut through that mighty chain. After that they would cross Gûnar itself, a land sparsely populated.

As they rolled through the forest in dreary morn, Pipper looked out the window at the passing gloomy woodland and said, "Oh, Bink, it looks grim out there, as if the forest doesn't want us here. The trees seem on the verge of reaching out to grab us, and who knows what they might do?"

"What?" said Bink. "Trees reaching out to snag us?" Binkton shook his head. Where Pipper came up with such wild notions, Binkton didn't know. Oh, not that his cousin wasn't full of good ideas, for more than once he had come up with madcap schemes that really were quite clever. Yet time after time throughout their entire childhood and unto this very day Pipper had come up with harebrained imaginings to the point of fright, and Binkton always had to calm him down. But then again, time after time Pipper had also devised things that Binkton admired, things that perhaps in his entire lifetime he never would have thought of himself— things for the act, or pranks to pull, or quite practical things. And Pipper was always full of stories, and his curiosity seemed boundless. Binkton both looked forward to and somewhat deplored what might pop out of Pipper's imagination next.

Binkton sighed. "Pip, they are just ordinary trees."

"Are you certain?" asked Pipper, staring out the window, his eyes wide. "I mean, they look rather ominous to me."

"Brekka, would you talk some sense into this buccan?" asked Binkton. "Tell him that trees don't grasp anyone."

Brekka slowly shook his head. "In the Gwasp—a swamp in Gron—I am told there are trees that scream like women, and woe to the one who rushes to the rescue, for there are ropy tendrils that live among the roots and grasp the would-be hero and hold him fast. Then those clutchers and the so-called tree *feed* on the captured person."

"Oh, lor, oh, lor," moaned Pipper. "I'll dream about those awful things through the night."

"He's just joshing us," said Binkton. "You are, aren't you, Brekka?"

"Nay, wee one. What I say is true, or so I was told." As Binkton and Pipper both gasped in dismay, Brekka gestured toward the forest. "Yet these are ordinary trees, and not those foul things of the Gwasp. So fear not, Pipper, Binkton, the trees here are quite benign."

"Are you certain?" asked Pipper, yet doubtfully looking at the woodland.

In that moment the sun broke through, and the forest stood awash with light, banishing the gloom.

"Ah," sighed Pipper in relief.

Binkton, too, relaxed.

After riding a moment in silence, Pipper asked, "Where are you bound for, Brekka?"

"I am on a journey back to my home in the Red Hills," said the Dwarf. "I am returning from a three-year apprenticeship in Blackstone in the far-northward Rigga Mountains, where, among other things, I learned to set gemstones into sword and axe blades."

"Oh, Bane and Bale were set with blade-jewels," said Pipper, "Bane being returned to The Root after the Dragonstone War."

"I've heard of those weapons," said Brekka, "one a sword, the other a long-knife."

"Bane is the long-knife," said Pipper. "But it's like a sword to a Warrow, being as, um, being as tall as we are."

Brekka laughed, and Binkton asked, "Do you make weapons like Bane and Bale?"

"Would that I could," said Brekka. "But those two were made by Dwynfor the Elf, and are magical. Glow with an arcane light when Grg draw near, they do, and such magic is beyond me." Brekka sighed and patted a double-bitted axe that was never far from his reach. "But I do make fine steel weapons such as this in the Châkkaholt armories of the Red Hills."

"And now you'll be able to fit them with jewels," said Pipper.

"Aye."

"I say," said Pipper, his eyes lighting up, "perhaps you could fit Bink's bow with a gemstone. He's a fine archer, you know—or perhaps you didn't know, but that is neither here nor there. Me, I use a sling instead. But a jewel in his bow, well, that would look splendid."

Binkton frowned. "I don't need a gemstone in my bow, Pip; it'd probably just weaken it."

"Not if it were done properly," said Brekka. "I would put it just above your grip, and not in one of the arms. You see . . ."

Much of the rest of that day, Brekka explained the ins and outs of setting jewels into weapons—into hilts, pommels, blades, helves, butts, grips, and such, and both Pipper and Binkton fell quite asleep during the drawn-out oration. Other passengers nodded off as well, but Brekka continued to detail the fashioning of such as the road slowly rose toward the distant mountains, the Dwarf talking to himself as much as to anyone else.

Three days and several changes of horses later they reached the way station among the foothills at the base of the col. In the morning they would hitch up a fresh team and take a second unladed team in tow, for the pass itself was some twenty leagues from end to end, and, but for a few pauses partway through to feed and water and change teams, there would be no stopping, barring a broken wheel or such.

"And barring attacks by the Grg," growled Brekka as he oiled his crossbow that eve.

"You mean Spawn?" asked Pipper, his eyes wide in speculation.

"Of course he means Spawn," snapped Binkton.

"What I meant, Bink, is, are any likely to be there?"

Brekka set aside his crossbow and took up his double-bitted axe and said, "It's the Grimwalls, Pip, one of the haunts of the Grg."

Pipper's eyes widened. "Rúcks and Hlôks and Ogrus, you mean?"

"What else would he mean?" growled Binkton.

"Do not forget the Khôls," said Brekka.

"Ghûls," said Binkton before Pipper could ask.

"We've never seen any," said Pipper. "No Rûcks, Hlôks, Ogrus, or Ghûls. What do they look like?"

Binkton groaned. "You've read about them, Pipper."

"Yes, but I would have someone who has actually seen them tell me from firsthand experience."

Binkton started to protest, but Brekka pushed out a palm to stop him. "Ükhs are about a head or so taller than your folk. Dark they are, and skinny-armed and bandy-legged and have bat-wing ears and viper eyes; some Humans—notably the Harlingar—call them Goblins. They mostly use cudgels as their weapons, though some have skill with crooked bows loosing black-shafted arrows, poison-tipped, for the most part. Hrôks look about the same as their smaller kindred, though their limbs are straighter. They stand about Châk height or a bit taller, and they use scimitars and tulwars as weapons and loose black-shafted arrows as well. Trolls, now, they also resemble the Ükhs and Hrôks, though they stand about ten or twelve feet tall. They have stonelike hides that arrows do not penetrate, but they can be killed by a shaft through an eye or the roof of the mouth. The soles of their feet are tender, and caltrops do great damage to them. They fear fire. Like all Foul Folk, they also dreaded the withering death of Adon's Ban, but that is no longer in effect. Oh, and Troll bones are stonelike as well, and the Trolls fear water, for they sink like rocks and drown should it be over their heads. Their weapons of choice are great, long, thick, heavy iron bars—warbars, which they sweep through their enemies, mowing them down like a reaper cutting wheat. As to the Khôls, man-sized and dead-white and corpselike they are, and they use cruelly barbed spears and ride Hèlsteeds. Khôls are a most fearsome foe, for ordinary steel—whether they be piercing or cutting or crushing weapons—does little harm to them, though they can be killed by a silver blade or by a weapon of <power>, by wood through the heart, by fire, by beheading, or by dismemberment."

"See, Pipper," said Binkton, "you knew all of that."

"Yes, I know," said Pipper, a tremor in his voice. "But hearing Brekka actually describe the Spawn out loud is like to give me the blue willies." He paused and then added, "I'll probably be riding a haggard horse all darktide."

Binkton's eyes softened, and he said, "If you have a nightmare, Pip, I'll waken you and we'll wait till you settle down again."

Pipper reached out and touched his cousin's arm and said, "Thanks, Bink. I can always count on you."

They sat in silence for a while, and then Pipper turned to Brekka and asked, "Have you met them in combat, Brekka?"

"Aye," said the Dwarf. "Many times, for the war against the Grg never ends."

"How do you deal with Ogrus?"

"We use ballistas to launch steel-pointed spears."

"Ballistas?"

"Giant crossbows we mount on wheeled carriages. Though if we must, fifty or so Châkka gang up on each Troll and we try to bring them down by heel-chopping the tendons or hamstringing them using battle-axes."

Pipper turned to Binkton. "Lor, but I hope we don't meet any Ogrus in the pass ahead."

"If we do," said Brekka, "the drivers will whip up the team and we will flee. Otherwise we'll sacrifice one of the trailing horses to draw the Troll away. They cherish horsemeat, and that is what a Troll would be after."

"Oh, poor horse," said Pipper, and he reached out for Binkton again, who took him by the hand and said, "Pip, better a horse than us." Pipper glumly nodded his agreement.

"We are not apt to meet a Troll in the pass or a Khôl on a Hèlsteed, for that matter," said Brekka. "Ükhs and Hröks are more likely."

"Rûcks and Hlôks, eh?" asked Pipper, and he took a deep breath and turned to Binkton. "Well, then, you'd better fetch your bow and arrows, Bink, and I my sling and bullets."

Binkton nodded, and together the Warrows stepped out to the coach and climbed atop and unlashed their chest enough to open it. Binkton took up a bow case and quiver, while Pipper grabbed a pouch and looked inside. Satisfied, he tied the pouch to his belt, and then he and Binkton closed the chest and lashed it down once again.

Early the next day, a candlemark before dawn, the Red Coach pulled out from the station, trailing horses behind. Two additional footmen were atop, and all were armed.

And up through the remaining foothills they fared.

Sometime just after sunrise, the sky began spitting tiny flakes, for even though the days were not quite verging upon mid autumn, at these heights winter came early.

"In a fortnight or two," said Brekka, "this pass will be closed by snow."

"What'll happen to the Red Coaches then?" asked Pipper, and quickly, before Binkton could say ought, Pipper added, "What I mean is, how will they fare between Caer Pendwyr and Challerain Keep?"

"Up the Gap Road and through Gûnar Slot," said Brekka, "and then along the Old Rell Way to Luren, until that route becomes snowed in, in which case the coaches will not cross through the Grimwall at all."

Just then they reached the jagged maw of the pass, and one of the footmen atop swung down and rapped on a window, startling Pipper and Binkton along with other passengers. As Brekka lowered the sash, "Be alert," said the footman, and then scrambled back up as Brekka cocked his well-tempered, steel-armed crossbow and loaded a quarrel.

Brekka and Binkton were the only ones with bows, and so they took stations on opposite sides of the coach.

There was one female among the nine passengers, a nineteen-year-old named Rebecca, slender and black-haired and blue-eyed and quite pretty. They placed her in the midmost position, and two of the men mistakenly tried to place Pipper beside her, but Brekka said that a Warrow with a sling was almost as valuable as one with a bow. "Besides, I would remind you that the most deadly warriors in any combat are Waerans."

Pipper nodded sprightly and said, "Tuckerby Underbank slew more than eighty Foul Folk in just three days."

The men looked at wee Pipper and Binkton in wonder, and none made any further suggestions that the buccen remain anywhere but at the windows.

And as they entered the looming dark walls of the slot twisting upward through the mountain chain, Pipper looked out at the grim frowning stone and said, "Lor, but I wish we had Bane with us."

"Me, too," said Binkton, his bow in hand and an arrow held loosely.

"We left before dawn, and it will be after nightfall when we reach the far end," said Brekka, "but most of the journey will be made under the sun, and the Grg hate the light of day. Nevertheless, be on guard."

On they fared up into the pass for mile after mile after mile with sheer stone rising to either side, and the sun rode up into the sky. And still no threat appeared. Exhausted by remaining so alert, Pipper fell quite asleep, and he slept until the coach stopped to change teams partway along the rise. Here the passengers, cautioned to be vigilant, were allowed to debark and stretch their legs and take care of other needs, Rebecca given her privacy behind a large boulder while Brekka stood ward in front of it.

Soon the horses had been fed and watered and exchanged—the fresh ones now in harness, the others tethered behind—and the coach started out once more.

"You sleep, Bink," said Pipper. "I'll call you should the need arise."

Binkton looked at Brekka and received a nod, and so he curled up next to Pipper. But he tossed and turned—"Gah! I can't sleep!"—and after a while gave up and resumed his watch at the window.

It was a mark or two past noon when they crossed the crest of the pass, where again they took care of needs and changed the teams, and then started down the opposite side.

Pipper fell asleep again, and Binkton looked at Brekka and pointed at Pipper and said, "Some sentry, eh?"

Brekka smiled at Binkton and said, "In the never-ending war against the Grg, I have fought alongside comrades who could fall asleep at the drop of a helm, even though combat was but moments away. This I would say: a well-rested warrior is much better to have at hand than one worn down by fatigue. I believe your Pipper will make good account of himself should there be a need." Then Brekka looked at Binkton and said, "Not that all should sleep, for we do need those who remain on watch to signal should the foe draw nigh."

Down the long slope of the pass the coach went, the teams working nearly as hard on the descent as on the climb, and the driver stopped a third time to make one more exchange.

Soon they were on their way again, the sun sliding down the sky, and dusk fell as the pass widened and they came in sight of the foothills below and the plains of Gûnar beyond.

Even so it was full dark when they came to the way station. And as the passengers debarked, one of the men looked back toward the Grimwalls and said, "Well, that was nothing."

Brekka looked at him and gritted a warning: "Be glad that this time it was nought. Also be glad not only were there four stage guards atop, but also three warriors inside. And when next you fare through such, I advise you to come well armed—with bow and arrow and a sword or axe—else, somewhere within, you might not live long enough to regret it."

Two days later in midafternoon, in a small stretch of woods on the way through Gûnar, five brigands, armed with clubs and knives, stood afoot by a log they had felled across the road to stop the coach.

As the passengers debarked at the command of the leader of the bandits, Brekka loosed a quarrel to slay that sneering brigand; Binkton took down two more with his bow; Pipper killed one with a sling bullet; the fifth brigand fled, only to be brought down from behind by an arrow from one of the coachmen.

Brekka then looked at the man he had warned and said, "Waerans three, the rest of us two."

Raudhöll

FIRE AND IRON
MID AUTUMN, 6E6

Brekka stepped to one of the fallen outlaws and—*thuck!*—pulled out his quarrel. He also retrieved one of Binkton's two arrows; the shaft of the second had broken when that man had hit the ground. As for Pip's sling bullet, there was no chance of retrieving it, buried in the third deader's skull as it was.

Both Binkton and Pipper looked a bit nauseated, for ere now they had never slain ought but rabbits and other such small game. But even though these were brigands, still they were men, and their deaths sudden and violent, the battle over almost before it had begun.

"I-I never killed anyone before," said Pipper. "It's awful."

Pipper glanced at Binkton, only to see someone whose face was as stark as his own might be. Binkton nodded without looking at Pipper, his gaze fixed on one of the two men he had slain.

"I mean," said Pipper, "one moment they could be laughing and talking, and the next, they're just—just dead."

"Forget it," said Brekka, holding Binkton's arrow out to the buccan. "They are nought more than Ükhs."

"But, Brekka, even Rûcks, or Ükhs as you call them, are a walking, talking . . ." Pipper's words fell to silence.

"All Grg are vile," said Brekka. "They have no conscience, none of them, and act as Gyphon made them long past. And these foul men are even worse, for, unlike the Grg, they have a choice. Hear me, Châkka justice against the Squam is swift and sure, and these"—Brekka made a dismissive gesture toward the slain men—"these dregs deserve no better."

Binkton took the arrow from Brekka and stared long at it, and finally swallowed, and looked up at the Dwarf and nodded. Then he stepped to the side of the road and cleaned off the shaft and point in the grass.

The driver called for all to climb back into the stage.

"Shouldn't we give them a decent burial?" asked one of the men, gesturing toward the dead outlaws.

"Didn't you hear me?" growled Brekka. "They are no more than Ükhs. Leave them for the scavengers."

The man looked at the coachmen, and the driver said to the footmen, "You heard the Dwarf. Drag them to the side and leave them for the crows."

As the crew dealt with the bodies, nineteen-year-old Rebecca kissed both Warrows on the cheek, and this seemed to cheer them somewhat, but when she approached Brekka, he held up a hand to stop her and said, "It was nothing more than killing vermin."

The footmen then cleared the log from the road, and the coach got under way again.

That night, as they lay over at the way station, when the two buccen were alone and making ready for bed, Pipper said, "I did not like the feeling I had when I killed that man."

Binkton sighed and shucked out of his shirt. "Neither did I. But I've been thinking about what Brekka said."

"That Châkka justice is swift and sure?" asked Pipper, kicking off his boots.

"No. That these foul men were no different from Grg. And you know, I think he's right."

"How so?"

"Well, Pip, think of all that we have read and heard about Tipperton and Beau and Rynna, and of Tuck and Danner and Patrel and Merrilee, and Perry and Cotton, or Gwylly and Faeril, as well as Cousin Triss and Danby and Kipley."

"That's a lot to think about, Bink."

Binkton nodded, then said, "And then there is Aravan and Brega and Gildor and Vanidor and Vanidar and Riatha and Urus and a whole host of others, to say nought of the many High Kings."

"What's all this leading to, Bink?"

"Just this, Pip: none of them hesitated whatsoever in dealing swift justice to evildoers."

Pipper digested Binkton's words for long moments as he and his cousin disrobed. Then he sat on the edge of his man-sized cot, his feet dangling freely. "Yes, but those we killed were just highwaymen, robbers. Who knows, they might have been men who had fallen upon hard times and who had turned to banditry simply to feed their families."

"Perhaps, Pip, yet there are more honest ways of dealing with hard times. No, I think Brekka is right: they were no better than Rûcks."

"But couldn't we have simply captured them and turned them over to the King's justice at the next town? —Oh, wait, perhaps that's not practical. I mean, hauling prisoners all the way to the next gaol."

"You're right, Pip," said Binkton, yawning and pulling his cover up around his neck. "That would have been impractical. Evildoers they were, and swift and sure justice is what they deserved. And listen: dealing swift justice doesn't mean you have to like it; only that it must be done. Now blow out the candle and let's get some sleep."

Pipper snuffed out the flame and darkness descended, but sleep was a long time coming, as both buccen lay in the gloom and wondered if they were merely making excuses for their killing of those men, be they bandits or no.

Three days afterwards, the Red Coach rolled into Gapton, a town at the junction just beyond the Gûnarring Gap, a wide opening in the ringlike spur of the Grimwalls. In Gapton the road split and changed names: the Reach Road faring east to Vanar, the capital city of Valon; the Pendwyr Road running southeasterly, toward the Red Hills and past to the Argon Ferry and on to Caer Pendwyr beyond.

Brekka and the Warrows dropped off in Gapton, the Dwarf to rest and enjoy himself, the buccen to try for an engagement at one of the local inns. Binkton and Pipper found that once again their reputation had preceded them, and they made a commitment to the owner of the Red Foal to perform for the next five days, in exchange for room and board and a bit of the good King's coin.

Brekka stayed at the same inn, and it was he who arranged for the captain of the city watch to be at the very first performance.

Once again Fire and Iron thrilled the patrons, and here, too, Binkton proved no gaol could hold him.

The days flew by, and as time drew near for the buccen to catch the Red Coach and move onward, they debated whether to travel to Vanar, a city of considerable size, or to stick to their original plans and go on to Argon Ferry Town. They asked Brekka for his advice.

"Certainly in Vanar, the Riders of Valon, the Harlingar, would enjoy your show. And I believe you would make a small fortune there. But what I would ask you to consider instead is to come with me to the Red Hills, and perform for Dalek, DelfLord of my Châkkaholt."

"Put on a show for a king?" blurted Pipper.

"DelfLords are not kings," growled Binkton.

"I know that, Bink, but he *is* the leader of a mighty holt, and putting on our show would be just the same as a royal performance, and if that's not for a king, there's hardly a whit's difference between the two."

"Yes, but he's not a king."

Brekka listened to them quibble for long moments, and then called for quiet between the two and said, "I suppose you could say it's a choice between fame and fortune: fortune in Vanar, fame in the Red Hills, or at least in the Châkkaholt where I was born."

Binkton looked at Pipper and asked, "What do you think?"

"We can always go to a large city, Bink, but how often will we get a chance to perform before a king?"

"DelfLord, you mean."

"Oh, all right, DelfLord. But my question remains the same."

Binkton turned to Brekka. "The Red Hills it is."

Eight days later and travelling southeast, the Red Coach stopped at a stone-paved spur leading off to the right and into the ruddy hills looming up alongside Pendwyr Road. A flanking pair of Dwarven realmstones warded the pave, marking the boundary of a Châkkaholt. In the shade of a nearby tree a horse-drawn wain stood waiting, the driver, a Dwarf, sitting with his back to the trunk. Binkton and Pipper and Brekka descended from the coach, and with the aid of the footmen, they unladed the chest and their duffles and set them beside the road. The Red Coach then moved on, even as the wain driver stood and led the horses and waggon toward the trio.

"Brekka," he called.

"Anvar," replied Brekka.

As Anvar arrived, Brekka introduced the buccen. Binkton and Pipper eyed the second Dwarf they had ever seen. Nearly identical in stature to Brekka was Anvar, though his hair was ginger and his eyes a pale blue. Too, he seemed a bit younger than Brekka, or so Pipper whispered to Binkton.

The two Dwarves laded the Warrows' trunk onto the wain, Anvar saying, "This seems a bit heavy for the likes of you two."

"Oh, it is," replied Pipper. "When we have to handle it ourselves, we unload it and move things piecemeal."

"It is full of the equipment used in their act," said Brekka.

"Act?"

"We are Fire and Iron," said Binkton. He pointed to Pipper and said, "He's fire; I'm iron."

"I invited them to put on a show for Dalek," said Brekka. "They are quite good: Pip with his acrobatics, Binkton with his escapes."

"No gaol can hold me," said Binkton, beaming.

Anvar cocked an eyebrow, and Brekka said, "I would hesitate to claim that in Raudhöll if I were you, Bink, for you challenge Châkka locks."

"Raudhöll?" asked Pipper.

"The name of our Châkkaholt," said Anvar. "Or, if you prefer, Redhall."

They clambered into the wain, and Anvar clucked his tongue and the horses started forward, and up the paved spur and into the Red Hills they went, in among the tors and crags, ruddy-colored stone rising all 'round. Here it was the Dwarves mined iron-rich ore and smelted fine steel in their furnaces to fashion into arms and armor, thought by many to be the finest in all of Mithgar. They made, as well, superior implements: plow-shares and axes and levers and pry bars and saws and other such tools. Dwarf-crafted was a term of excellence in all of the High King's realms, and a work of armor or a weapon or a tool bearing the crimson mark of the Red Hills was held to be among the very best.

"How did you know we were coming?" asked Pipper.

Anvar laughed. "I did not. But when the Red Coach is due, north-bound or south-, someone is always assigned the duty to meet it in case there is a need. This sevenday it is mine to do."

"Oh," said Pipper. Then he frowned and asked, "Do you often get visitors?"

"On occasion."

"Well, I am glad that you were at the road to meet us, else Bink and I would have had a dreadful time with our gear."

Binkton nodded his agreement, and Anvar grinned and said, "Indeed."

The road wended among the rises, now and then passing a thicket or a stand of old growth clutched up against a slope or huddled in a deep recess. And at one-mile intervals stood rune-laden markers declaring to travellers that they were on Dwarven land.

It was late in the day, the sun in its descent having disappeared beyond the western tors, when around a sweeping turn they came in sight of the Redhall gate, the great iron leaves standing shut. Wide it was, some thirty feet in all, and tall, reaching up twenty feet or so, with an arrangement of arrow slits high up and across the broad expanse of metal. And its surface bore an arrangement of runes, declaring this to be the Châkkaholt of Raudhöll, or so Brekka explained. Out before the gate, two Dwarven warders stood, and one stepped in through a side postern when the wain came into sight.

Anvar drove the wain onto the stone forecourt and halted. After a mo-ment, the right-hand portal, a great, thick slab of iron, opened, revealing a large chamber, and in the shadows at the far end stood another gate, this one perhaps but ten feet across and ten feet high.

"Here gather warriors in times of strife," said Brekka, "should there be a need to charge an enemy at the gates."

Across this assembly area the waggon went and to the gate at the far end.

Once more the warders opened the portal, revealing a narrow passage that went forward a short way and then turned sharply leftward. Into this corridor they went, the way lighted by luminescent Dwarven lanterns. Pipper nudged Binkton and pointed overhead, where machicolations gaped in the ceiling, and high up to either side were arrow slits.

The passage jagged left and then right and then left again, and they came to another iron gate. When this one was opened, a vast, well-lit chamber stood revealed, and Dwarves crossed thither and yon, emerging from and disappearing into passages to left and right.

Anvar stopped the wain beside one of these openings, and Brekka leapt to the stone floor and said, "We are here." As the buccen scrambled down, Brekka and Anvar unladed the chest and duffle bags.

"Leave the case behind," said Brekka. "I'll make arrangements for someone to come and take it up. But first I'll show you to your quarters, and if you are in mind of a bath, I'll show you where that is, too. Then I will introduce you to DelfLord Dalek, to make arrangements for your show."

"Well, then," said Dalek, stroking his black beard shot through with silver, a glitter of anticipation in his dark eyes, "how can we aid you in putting on your performance?"

Pipper looked about the throne room and, glancing at Binkton, said, "Have you a chamber with high ceilings, one much larger than this?"

"The training chamber, DelfLord?" suggested Brekka.

Dalek pondered a moment and said, "The banquet hall, mayhap."

"Ah, yes," said Brekka. "The Châkia."

Frowning, Pipper looked at Brekka, but no further explanation was offered.

"Might we see both?" asked Binkton.

Dalek stood and motioned them to follow, and he and Brekka led the way through the twisting corridors.

Although the banquet hall was suitable, the training chamber was even better, for it had tiers of benches along the walls that could be moved to seat part of a large audience, and Dalek informed the buccen that additional benches would be brought in to add to the seating. Brekka and Dalek stepped to one side and held a brief whispered conversation, and finally Dalek turned to the Warrows. "The training chamber it is, yet what you will see here you must vow to never reveal."

Binkton looked at Pipper and that buccan shrugged; then together they agreed to the terms.

Much of the following day was spent with a multitude of Dwarves—all under the Warrows' guidance—driving pitons at different levels into the stone walls and the rock ceiling above and stringing lines between or hanging trapezes thereon or fitting fixed rods into the walls. They also constructed a stage with wings and a platform above concealed by a high curtain, with a ladder going up even higher. The tiered benches were moved out from the walls and arranged in a long, curving row facing the stage. Additional benches were set out before these in echoing arcs so that all in the hall could see. And, as they had in Junction Town and Luren and Gapton, the buccen arranged for the aid of two stagehands—Brekka one and Anvar the other—and instructed them as to their duties.

That evening, a great many Dwarves gathered in the hall for the first performance, but they took no seats whatsoever. Peering out from behind the curtain concealing the high platform, Pipper and Binkton looked at one another in puzzlement.

"What's that all about?" whispered Pipper.

"How should I know?" snapped Binkton.

"What I mean, Bink, is why aren't they finding places to sit?"

Binkton took a deep breath and slowly let it out. Finally he said, "I think they are waiting on something."

"Yes, but what?"

Binkton groaned. "Do you think I am an expert on Dwarven doings?"

"Maybe they are waiting for Dalek," said Pipper.

"Perhaps."

But Dalek came and still no one took seat.

But then chatter echoed down the halls, and moments later Dwarven children reached the entry, and fell silent as they walked past the assembled adults and to the front of the hall. But then they, too, stood waiting.

Finally, a large group of lithe beings entered, each one mantled from head to foot in swirling veils, their steps silent, their progress somehow elegant. And all the Dwarves, but for Dalek, knelt upon one knee as they passed by. These graceful creatures were a half a head taller than most of the Dwarves.

"Châkia," whispered Pipper. "These must be the Châkia."

"Females, you mean?" asked Binkton.

"Yes. Don't you remember the diary of Beau Darby?"

Binkton nodded. "Female Dwarves."

"Don't be too certain of that, Bink," said Pipper. "Beau himself wasn't sure, and Tipperton said they were beautiful. I can't imagine a Dwarf, male or female, as being described as beautiful. —And look. See how they are revered? What kind of creature would cause such regard?"

Binkton snorted and asked, "Why would someone not a Dwarf ever consider being the mate of a Dwarf?"

Pipper shrugged, but then said, "They tell that Elyn of Jord loved a Dwarf."

"That's just a legend, Pip."

"Maybe. Maybe not. Oh, Bink, perhaps this is what we are supposed to keep secret."

"That Elyn loved Thork?"

"No, no. The Châkia of this holt. The children, too. Mayhap we're supposed to keep quiet about how many there are. Perhaps the numbers of the Châkka, as well."

"I don't know what it is we are supposed to keep quiet about, except absolutely everything we see herein, just like we vowed. —Now, get ready, for it looks like they're all finding seats."

As the Châkia took places in the front rows midmost before the stage, and the Dwarven children—all males—sat alongside them, the remaining Dwarves spread out among the benches and tiers behind. They all sat when Dalek did so at the very front.

Anvar stepped to the fore of the stage and called out in the Dwarven tongue of Châkur, announcing Fire and Iron.

Pipper, now waiting at the top of the ladder, peered down through a space between the concealing foredrop curtain and the high platform, to watch as Anvar turned and pointed upward; that was Pipper's cue.

And Pipper in red and trailing orange and yellow ran to the end of the springboard and leapt outward and plummeted down, to the screams of the Châkia and the shouts of the Châkka and the cries of the children below.

As Pipper and Binkton ran back out from the wings to take another bow, 'mid the clapping and cheers Pip looked over at his cousin and said, "I thought those Dwarves were going to charge the stage and save you from the Spikes of Death."

They straightened and then bowed again to thunderous applause, and Binkton said, "I think they were simply trying to stop the Châkia from wailing for fear of my life."

On the next bow, Pipper said, "The Dwarves did seem to have trouble holding back when it seemed the Châkia were in distress."

And the very next bow, Pipper added, "I thought one of the Dwarves was going to throttle me when I almost touched a Châkia during our blindfold mental act."

"Keep that in mind the next time, bucco," said Binkton. "Now hush, while I make my challenge."

Binkton stood and raised his hands for quiet, and when it fell he called out to Dalek, "My Lord Dalek, no irons or gaol can hold me. Have you one in this holt?"

The next day they took Binkton to a seldom-occupied lockup, one now and then used to hold someone who had gotten too deep in his cups and had become belligerent. Not that being thrown in a cell was a common occurrence among the honorable Châkka. Typically, violence was settled with more violence, fists being the weapons of choice, but occasionally a winner of such a bout went on a rampage, in which case several Châkka would haul the perpetrator to the tiny prison and shut him in, much to his chagrin when he finally sobered.

Just like his jailers elsewhere, the warders thoroughly searched Binkton, and finding no lockpicks or other devices, they shut him inside. And then as agreed, they left him alone. When they were gone, he slipped the long length of wire out from his belt. The tip of one end of the wire had previously been bent at a sharp angle to act as a single lock-pick, and this was what Binkton first tried to use, to no avail. Carefully, he examined what he could see of the interior of his restraints, and then he bent the other end of the wire into a peculiar shape and tried again. It took Binkton four candlemarks to escape from the Dwarven fetters and cage, but escape he did. And when the Châkka smiths asked him how he had done it, Binkton showed them the weaknesses he had finally discovered in their shackles and in the lock on the door. "The irons were easier than the cell, but both were quite difficult," he said. "Even so, I stand by my claim that no gaol can hold me, not even a Dwarven one."

The locksmiths growled and one of them said, "Next time, Waeran. Next time."

Five days and four house-packed performances later found the Warrows waiting alongside Pendwyr Road for the southbound Red Coach to appear. With them were Brekka and Anvar.

"Where will you go?" asked Anvar.

"Argon Ford Town," said Pipper.

"And then maybe to Rivers End," said Binkton.

"But ultimately to Caer Pendwyr, where we hope to open our own theater and music hall," said Pipper.

"You'll need a King's license to do so," said Brekka, "and those are difficult to come by."

"To say nothing of the cost," said Anvar.

"Well, if all folks reward us like your DelfLord did, the coin shouldn't be too hard to acquire," said Binkton.

"Here comes your ride," said Brekka, pointing up the road.

The Red Coach rumbled to a stop alongside the junction, and no one got off. Anvar and Brekka hoisted the trunk up to the footmen atop, and then stepped back.

"Take care, my friends," said Anvar, "especially in Rivers End. They say it's a rough place, what with Rivermen and the like prowling the streets."

"I think they can handle themselves," said Brekka. "After all, I've seen them in action." Then he turned to the buccen and added, "Nevertheless, Anvar's advice is good, so watch out for those who would do you harm."

"Don't worry, we will," said Pipper, and he and Binkton clambered aboard the Red Coach, and the driver clucked his tongue and cracked his whip and off toward the mighty Argon River they went.

28

West Bank

FIRE AND IRON
MID AUTUMN, 6E6

When the Red Coach rumbled into Argon Ferry Town, Pipper and Binkton had the driver stop at the Sturdy Oar, an inn recommended by Brekka. They unladed their gear and took a room, and the next morning after breaking fast they asked the innkeeper, one Tarly Oates, a tall, skinny man, whether there were any theaters in town. He laughed and said, "Nowt in West Bank be there such a thing, and nowt across in East Bank nuther. Nar, you'd have to float downstream to Rivers End or fare across and all the way to Caer Pendwyr to find such."

"Wull, then," asked Pipper, "what about an inn with a stage and a high ceiling?"

The 'keep scratched his head, then said, "The Clearwater."

"The Clearwater?" asked Pipper.

"That's what he said," growled Binkton.

"What I meant, Bink, is just where is this Clearwater Inn?" Pipper looked up at Tarly.

"Bain't no inn, 'cause bain't no rooms, but a saloon instead, and adown by the water 'tis, at th' corner o' Mudlane and Tow. Used t'be a warehouse, it did, till they built them new ones up by the landings. But, fair warnin' 'bout the Clearwater; we call it th' Bilgewater instead, 'cause them drinks they serve—ale and such—bain't as fine as those here't th' Oar, and the regulars, well, much o' them be a lawless crowd, Rivermen that they are."

Binkton's face fell. "Oh. Rivermen, eh?"

"That's what he said, Bink," snapped Pipper.

"I heard what he said, Pip," Binkton snapped back. Then he turned once more to Tarly. "Only Rivermen frequent the place?"

"Nar. Now and again th' toffs 'n' their ladies and their bodyguards find it amusing to swagger along the 'front, 'n' they make a parade of it, and them gents and ladies sometimes even drop in t'sample the swill."

"Swagger along the 'front? You mean the waterfront?"

"Yar."

"How do we find this place?"

The man pointed leftward. "Go yon till y'come t'Mudlane. Then head f'r th' river. Right along the bank y'll find Tow. And right there'll be the Bilge."

"Why do you even want to know, Bink?" asked Pipper.

"I thought we'd go look at it anyway."

"But it's Rivermen, Bink. Lawless. Didn't you hear the man?"

"Yes, I heard him." Binkton started for the door, saying, "But he said the gents and ladies also come to the tavern. So, I'm going to take a look regardless."

"He said they only *sometimes* swagger along the 'front. It's not like they'll be there every night."

But Binkton simply shook his head and stepped out from the Oar.

"This is a big mistake," growled Pipper, yet he followed his cousin into the street.

Still quibbling, the buccen turned to the left and headed for Mudlane.

Unlike many of the thoroughfares in town, Mudlane had no pavestones, and the Warrows followed the narrow dirt lane down to a road running along the steep bank of the river.

"Oh, lor, Bink, look at the Argon," marveled Pipper. "Makes the Dinglerill look like a piddling leak, it does."

They stood and surveyed the width of the mighty flow: fully two miles across it was, and it meandered southward to empty into the Avagon Sea some three hundred miles hence. And more or less equally divided by the grand run was Argon Ferry Town itself. The half Binkton and Pipper found themselves in was known by the locals simply as West Bank, with East Bank being on the opposite shore.

The buccen turned and looked leftward, and on both sides of the river some two miles upstream, they could see the docks where the ferries were moored, while others plied across the waters both coming and going. As to the ships themselves, though neither Pipper nor Binkton knew the kinds of craft they eyed, some were swift pinnaces but most were barques, all ferries being fore and aft rigged and nimble in the wind, though each carried oars to be plied by strong men should the air lie calm.

And up at the piers where the ferries docked, the Warrows could see a bustle of activity, with carriages and wagons arriving and leaving, but the buccen could not tell what was afoot, though Pipper said, "It's probably the on-lading and off-lading of passengers, don't you think?"

"You're probably right, Pip," replied Binkton. "Cargo, too. It looks like goods are moving in and out of those warehouses at hand."

The Warrows then slowly turned about, taking in what they could see on both sides of the river: Extending southward from the ferry slips to run past the Warrows and reach far downstream, tow paths ran along the banks, nearly twelve miles in all—ways to be used by drovers and horses to pull wayward craft against the current and back to the piers should the need arise, especially on the days with no wind whatsoever during flood season, for then it was all the rowers could do simply to get from one bank to the other; hence, the street the Warrows stood on was simply called Tow.

And there at the southwest corner of Mudlane and Tow stood the Clearwater Saloon, clearly a former warehouse.

Pipper turned and looked at it and muttered, "Come on, Bink, let's go look at the Bilge."

The place was perfect for Pipper's aerial show, with numerous beams and joists high above, and down below and against one wall there sat a platform they could use as a stage. As for the Spikes of Doom escape, that act would work equally as well with a drape of canvas hanging down from a crossbeam to use as a high curtain, and behind that high curtain another crossbeam from which Binkton could dangle. And with more hanging canvas to serve as wings to the stage, they could as well use their secret-paneled, flame-painted chest in which to disappear.

They spent the rest of the day planning, and then most of the evening negotiating with Tager Lynch, owner of the Clearwater. Finally, they came to terms, the Warrows agreeing to pay for the canvas curtains should the act not bring a fair return to the tavern. Likewise, the buccen agreed to pay for the broadsheets and handbills, again under the same provisions. But should the performances bring in enough additional income, then the buccen would get a quarter of the new. Haggling over this last took the most time, for it seemed Tager set his nightly income higher than what it was in reality, but Binkton surveyed the meager crowd and bargained him down.

The next day the buccen went to a printer and arranged for handbills and broadsheets. The printer also offered to supply a group of urchins to put up the broadsheets and distribute the handbills all over town, but especially to the higher-class residents, for a fee, of course. As well, the Warrows paid the ferry fees for half the urchins to cross to the other side and post and distribute them there as well. That same day, Binkton and Pipper purchased the canvas and hired men to help set all up.

A day or so later the printing was done and the broadsheets went up in both town squares and all of the common marketplaces. And the handbills were distributed widely over both West and East Banks.

They announced that in three days, straight from the mysterious land of the Boskydells, the extraordinary and quite rare Warrows of Fire and Iron would put on their first remarkable show, with amazing aerial acts and incredible feats of escape, this last by a strange and wily Warrow that no gaol could hold.

Pipper and Binkton then went to the captain of the city watch and invited him to the first performance.

"I've heard of you, Binkton Windrow," said the captain, a tall, angular man with a scarred face that sported a narrow moustache. "Rumors travel fast by the Red Coach."

"I'm flattered," said Binkton. "But, you see, no rumors are these, but they are facts instead. The truth is, no gaol can hold me, not even yours."

"Ha! Challenge me and my prison, would you? Well, then, I accept. But hear me now: unlike those flimsy hardtack crates you've broken out of, you'll not master my locks or shackles, for I will strip you naked and examine every orifice and then throw you in a cell without a stitch. Then we'll see whether or no you escape."

Binkton paled, and the captain said, "What's this? Do I see you blanch?"

"Never," said Binkton defiantly, though his voice was a bit unsteady.

"Might we see this unbreachable stronghold of yours, Captain?" asked Pipper.

"Certainly," replied the man, grinning at the apparently cowed Binkton, and he took them on a tour. Pipper seemed fascinated and bubbled over with questions, occupying the captain's full attention, while Binkton lackadaisically lagged behind, wandering hither and yon, on the face of it completely discouraged and without purpose.

When they finally left the gaol, Pipper said, "Lor, Bink, what're you going to do? I mean, he said they'd lock you in wearing nothing whatsoever, but for the shackles and chains."

"Worry not, Pip, for you see, I have a plan."

As in every town they had played so far, the Clearwater Saloon was filled to its warehouse walls with the crowd that had come to see the extraordinary and quite rare Warrows from the mysterious land of the Boskydells. Many of the spectators were common folk; others were shady wharf denizens; yet, as the Warrows had been told, the toffs and gents and their ladies and bodyguards were present in goodly numbers as well.

And they screamed and shouted in fear for Pipper's life as he dived and swung and tumbled through the air high above, and swooped down to pass close over their heads only to fly back up and sail free through empty space to grab a bar and spin 'round, then leap and run along spidery ropes.

And then they cried out as Binkton slowly twisted and turned above tall, gleaming sharp spikes, and dropped once, then again toward the deadly points, only to drop once more, nearly to his doom.

They laughed at the antics of the mental act, and gasped as Pipper flipped through flaming hoops, and held their breath as Binkton escaped the tightly bound ropes.

At last, claiming that no gaol could hold him, Binkton challenged the captain of the city watch, and the challenge was accepted.

As promised, naked and with every orifice searched, and with his hands shackled behind him and fetters on his feet, Binkton was bundled into the cell and the door slammed shut and the lock thrown to.

The jailers then left Binkton to himself and went to the steps out front, where Pipper fretted and paced, while holding Binkton's clothes.

Back in the cell, Binkton slipped his manacled hands under his heels and brought them 'round front. Then he sat down and peeled off the well-blended, soft leather patch from the sole of his foot, and straightened the wire within, then began shaping one end.

Outside, the captain confidently surveyed the crowd and smiled and nodded and smoothed his moustache, clearly in his element. But that self-assurance was suddenly shattered when the locked front door of the gaol opened a crack and fetters and shackles clattered out on the stoop and a voice called, "Might I have my clothes now?"

With their fortnight engagement at the Clearwater successfully concluded and their gear packed and ready for pickup and shipment, the buccen sat at breakfast in the Sturdy Oar and talked of bypassing all other towns and taking their show straight to Caer Pendwyr. They speculated that High King Ryon and Queen Dresha and their children might actually come to see their performance. But as they pondered their future, Bandy, one of the printer's street urchins, came flying into the foyer, shouting, "Guv! Guv!" He dodged past innkeeper Oates, who had leapt forward in an unsuccessful attempt at capture, yelling, "Off wi' y'! Off wi' y'! I'll nowt ha'e no—"

But Pipper recognized the voice of the lad and called for him to come to the dining room, much to the shock of Tarly, who threw up his hands and wondered what was an innkeeper to do if just anyone could let riffraff in.

Bandy rushed into the room and to the table where the buccen sat. "I seen it, guv. I seen it floatin' by. Them what took it put it on a barge. It's off to Rivers End."

"What's off to Rivers End, Bandy?" asked Pipper.

"Why, that chest of yours, guv, th' one with th' flames and all."

29

Purloined

FIRE AND IRON
MID AUTUMN, 6E6

Both Warrows leapt to their feet, Binkton shouting, "*What?*" Even though Bandy was a good head taller than either buccan, the boy flinched back, as if expecting to be hit.

"He said, Bink, that our—"

"I heard what he said, Pip," Binkton snarled, "that some Rûck-loving, rat-eating thief has stolen our chest."

"It's got all of our rig in it, Bink," said Pipper.

"I know that! I know that!" snapped Binkton. "I was there when we packed it, remember?"

"What I mean, Bink, is: until we get it back Fire and Iron is more like Ashes and Mud."

Binkton smashed a fist to the table, setting the dishes arattle. "I know, I know, Pip."

"Well, then, Bink, we'd better get a move on."

"Where will you go?" asked Bandy.

"To the Clearwater," said Pip, "and then to the docks. We've got to find—"

"The rat eaters who took it," spat Binkton.

As Pipper and Binkton started for the door, Bandy muttered, "Rat-eatin', he says. Wull, I say roasted rat ain't too bad, guv." Then he trotted after the Warrows.

"As soon as we find out what we can at the Clearwater," said Pipper as they reached the street, "we've got to book passage to Rivers End and recover our gear."

"And deal swift and sure justice to the thieves," added Binkton.

Pipper skidded to a halt. "Hoy, now, wait."

Binkton pattered along a few steps and stopped. "What?"

"I'll be right back," shouted Pipper, and he bolted into the Sturdy Oar.

Binkton fidgeted for long moments, and then started toward the steps just as Pipper came bursting out, their duffles in tow.

"I settled up with Tarly."

"What for?"

"Just in case there's a boat or a barge leaving for Rivers End. I mean, it'd be a shame to miss the next one out."

"Right, Pip. Good idea," said Binkton, and he took his duffle bag from his cousin and hefted it over his shoulder. "Now, come on, let's go."

Down Mudlane to Tow they hurried, Bandy jogging along at their side. Into the Clearwater Binkton charged, Pipper following, Bandy stopping just inside the door. "Tager!" shouted Binkton. "Tager Lynch!"

A few of the habitués blearily looked up from their mugs. They were well into their cups this early in the morning; it was clear they had been here awhile. Serving the shoremen of the port, the Clearwater never closed, for comings and goings across the Argon were never-ending, day and night year-round, though it slowed in flood season. And so the customers eyed this small person—Ah, yes, one of the Warrows—and it seemed he was riled. With interest they watched as Binkton looked toward the barkeep, who jerked a thumb over one shoulder. Binkton's gaze swung in that direction, and he spotted the proprietor at a back table near the passage to the storerooms. Tager looked up from his ledger and cocked an eyebrow as Binkton stormed across the room, Pipper at his heels. "What Rûck-loving, rat-eating son of a Troll stole our chest?" demanded the buccan.

Carefully, Tager set down the pen and closed the book, as if he didn't want the Warrows to see any entry therein. Then he looked at Binkton. "Stole your chest?"

"That's what I said," growled Binkton.

Tager raised a hand of negation. "I know nothing about that chest of yours."

"Maybe Bandy was mistaken," blurted Pipper, and he darted into the hallway and to the small compartment he and Binkton had used as a dressing room. Moments later, Pipper was back. "It's gone, Bink."

Tager called to the bartender. "Jess, did you see what happened to their trunk?"

"The one with the flames?" called Jess.

"What other Rûck-loving one would there be?" snapped Binkton.

As Jess wiped a mug with a bar cloth, he strolled over. "No more'n two or three candlemarks ago, a couple of Rivermen came and took it. They said you sent them."

Binkton cast an accusatory eye at Pipper. Pipper shook his head. "Not me, cousin."

Binkton then glared at Jess. "And you just let them take it?"

"They said you'd sent them. And, after all, we knew you were leaving."

Binkton's lips thinned in anger and he spat, "Rivermen!"

"Do you know who they were?" asked Pipper.

Jess shook his head.

"What'd they look like?" asked Pipper.

"What good will that do?" growled Binkton.

"If we're going to find our chest, we first need to find them," said Pipper.

"Oh, right," said Binkton, then sighed and added, "At least one of us is thinking."

Again, Pipper turned to the barkeep. "What did they look like?"

Jess shrugged. "One was big and burly, the other small and skinny."

"Color of hair, eyes?" asked Pipper.

Jess shrugged. "I didn't notice."

"Aargh!" growled Binkton. "Big and burly. Small and skinny. That describes half the people in town."

"You're right," said Pipper, "but maybe the workers at the ferry docks will know who they are. Let's go, Bink."

Binkton shouldered his duffle and cast a glare at Tager Lynch, then spun on his heel and stalked off. Even as they reached the door, Jess called out, "Oy, now, something I just remembered."

Pipper stopped and looked across the wide room at the man.

"One of them, the big one, called the other Caker, or Waker, or something of the sort."

"Rats," muttered Binkton. "That's no help."

"Thanks, Jess!" called Pipper, and out onto Tow the buccen went, Bandy trailing after.

Tager watched the Warrows go, and then opened his ledger and looked at the figure he had early this morning jotted within and smiled to himself.

Pipper and Binkton spent most of the day asking questions and receiving shrugs in return, but then Bandy suggested that they talk to the pier master. Judd Leeks, though, was a very busy man, and his answers were terse. But he did tell them the barge that had gone downriver just after sunup was tended by the *Red Carp*, a barque assigned to the task of keeping the barge in the main river current and of pushing the flat-bottomed craft to Barge Bottom Shore just north of Rivers End. And, no, he didn't know of any flame-painted chest, nor of anyone named Waker or Caker. And, yes, there would be another craft going that way first thing in the morning, the *Otter*, another barge tender.

Binkton and Pipper booked passage on the *Otter*. They tried to give Bandy a silver for alerting them and the help he had been, but he took ten coppers instead. "That way, guv, I'm less likely to lose it all should anyone find out I've such wealth."

That night on the *Otter*, the ship yet docked at the barge piers, belowdecks Pipper started awake in his hammock. Lightly he swung down and padded to Binkton's canvas. "Bink, Bink," he hissed.

"Wh-what?" Binkton wildly grabbed at the sides of the heavy canvas sling. Not being the acrobat that Pipper was, Binkton had had a perilous time first just trying to get into and then to remain in the swinging bed. And as if unwilling to upset anything, while gripping the cloth tightly he carefully turned his head and, by the moonlight seeping in, he looked at his cousin. "What is it, Pip?"

"I believe I know who took our chest."

"Who?"

"I think the name of the small, skinny one wasn't Waker or Caker. Instead, I think it was Queeker. Recall those two at the Black Dog, 'cause if I'm right, the burly one is Tark, and they—"

"Rûck-loving, rat-eating—!" Binkton shouted and lurched up, and his hammock flipped over, the buccan to thud to the deck.

30

River Drift

FIRE AND IRON
LATE AUTUMN, 6E6

The *Otter* set sail just after dawn, tending a barge loaded with sawn timber, the lumber itself from the Greatwood, that vast forest a Baeron protectorate in South Riamon.

Pipper and Binkton stood in the bow of the barque and watched as the little tender sailed about and nudged the barge this way and that to keep it more or less midstream of the mighty Argon River.

Captain Vení, an Arbalinian by birth, who had left that isle years past to become a river pilot and then a captain, came to stand beside them.

"How long till we reach Rivers End?" asked Pipper.

"The city, she be some hundred leagues down the waterway; and the Argon, she flows nigh a league each candlemark, twenty-four candlemarks a day without rest. So, if all goes as planned, we be on the drift a hundred candlemarks altogether."

"Four days and a bit, then," said Binkton.

"You know your ciphering, I see," said Vení.

"We were well taught," said Pipper, "by Uncle Arley back in the Bosky."

"Ah, the Boskydells. I've ne'er dropped anchor there. Be it true a fanged barrier encircles the place?"

"Indeed," said Pipper. "The Thornring. It's kept the land free of trouble, all but during the Winter War."

"Speaking of trouble," said Binkton, "what did you mean when you said, 'if all goes as planned'?"

"Well, they be some islands we need slip past, but now and again a defiant barge takes it in mind to land."

"Did that ever happen to you?" asked Pipper.

"Nay. At least, not yet. But others do tell of the contrariness of the Argon."

"Contrariness of the river?"

"Aye, some say the river decides on its own to push the barge ashore, though others tell the river serpent takes it in mind to do so instead."

Binkton cast a skeptical eye toward the captain. "A river serpent, you say?"

"Not 'a' river serpent, lad, but 'the' river serpent."

Binkton snorted but said nothing, while Pipper, his eyes agoggle with wonder, asked, "What does it look like, this river serpent?"

"Yellow it be, they say," said Vení, and he waved toward the barge. "Three or four times as long as that scow, and as thick as a tree, with glowing green eyes as big as dinner plates, and a ridge of bloodred fur running the length of its black-spotted back. It has a mouth that'd swallow a cow whole, filled with long, backward-angled, pitchfork-like teeth so that once it grabs on it can't let go. At least, that's what they say."

Again Binkton snorted in disbelief, but Pipper, his eyes still wide, said, "Oh, oh, I don't ever want to see it. And I don't want it to come in the nightmare I'm now likely to have, either."

Captain Vení smiled and said, "Nor would I want such a thing; but be it the barge or the river or the serpent, I hope none take it in mind to do other than behave, and we'll reach Rivers End without incident to the contrary. —Now, if you'll excuse me, I do believe the scow needs another nudge."

Captain Vení stepped to the stern and gave his bosun orders, and soon the ship had circled to the opposite side of the barge and gave it a slight push.

Moments later, the captain and the bosun were laughing and looking in the direction of the Warrows.

"See, Pip, I *knew* the captain was just making fun. There's no such thing as the river serpent."

"I don't know, Bink. He seemed quite serious."

"Argh!" growled Binkton. "You'll believe anything."

"Maybe it just shows I have a more vivid imagination than you, Bink."

"Oh, yeah. Well, I have a vivid imagination, too," protested Binkton.

"Then why don't you think that it's possible there's a river serpent?"

"Because, Pip . . ."

The buccen continued squabbling as the mighty Argon slowly flowed southerly. Tall, stately trees lined the shores, and small boats at anchor bobbed here and there, the fishermen within watching their red-painted corks afloat. Now and again a dwelling could be seen beyond the tree line, usually upon high ground to avoid a calamity in flood season. Occasionally, the *Otter* drifted between high bluffs, but mostly the land beyond the shores was one of rolling hills or rising plains. Intermittently and far to the west, they could just see the crown of one of the Red Hills, just one of the many among which Raudhöll lay, and both Pipper and Binkton wondered what Brekka and Anvar and DelfLord Dalek might be doing, and they fell into speculation about the Châkia, this latter converse held in whispers, for the buccen were sworn to secrecy.

And the sun rose up and rode across the sky and fell toward evening. And ropes creaked and sails flapped, eased-off-all in the main, for only now and again did the ship have to get under way to give the barge a push. Both Binkton and Pipper lazed adeck throughout the idyllic drift, pausing from their leisurely chatter only to take a meal in the noontime, and another in the eve.

That night a thunderous rain hammered the *Otter*, but the storm blew up no violent wind, and so the barque maintained the barge well out in midstream.

Also that night, Binkton discovered that if instead of lying all tensed up he simply relaxed, the hammock wasn't difficult to sleep in after all. Even so, mounting and dismounting remained a challenge for him. Pipper, on the other hand, simply hopped in and out as if it were just another bed.

The next morning dawned to high-blue autumnal skies and fresh-washed air, and the day was much like the previous one except no longer could the buccen see the crown of one of the Red Hills. Instead, beyond the river border trees, to the west lay the plains of Jugo, and to the east those of Pellar.

Once again, all day they drifted, though Pipper asked Captain Vení if he could climb to the crow's nest and take a gander about. "Be of care, wee one," said Vení. "I wouldn't like you to fall splat on my deck." Vení burst into laughter and added, "We'd be candlemarks swabbing."

"Not to worry," said Pipper, and he scrambled up the ratline as if he had been a lookout all his life. Binkton followed Pipper at a careful and measured pace.

"Hoy, you can see for leagues up here," Pipper called down to Binkton, only to discover his cousin nearly at his feet.

Binkton clambered up and into the nest, and then took a long look about. "You're right, Pip. Leagues."

"Let me know if you spot the river serpent," Captain Vení called up. "We'd like to avoid him if we can."

"Oh, lor, I had forgotten all about the river serpent," said Pip, and he faced forward to peer downstream.

Binkton snorted. "River serpent. Pah!"

Much of the day the buccen spent in the crow's nest. Pipper's vigilance slowly waned, and soon he was slumped down and leaning forward against one of the rails, though he continued to chatter with Binkton about this and that.

That evening found the Warrows down on deck and playing tokko with members of the crew. One of the yeomen, Pick by name, was particularly good at the game, and he often captured the throne.

It was just after dawn of the third day on the river, when Pipper and Binkton, back in the crow's nest, espied in the distance to the east in Pellar a number of King's men in red and gold tabards galloping in pursuit of a band of riders, all the horses kicking up dust in their wake. Up and over rolling hills they rode and then down out of sight into the swales beyond, only to reappear topping the next crest to disappear in the following dip.

"Huh," grunted Binkton. "I wonder what that's all about."

"Maybe they're smugglers. Maybe bandits. Maybe they've captured the King's children. Maybe they're really Rûcks and Hlôks, now that the Ban is no more."

"Nah," said Binkton, "not Rûcks and Hlôks. They only do their misdeeds at night."

"Yeah, but what if they got rousted out and had to run?"

"Well, they wouldn't be on horses," said Bink, "'cause Rûcks and such eat horses."

"Oh, right," said Pipper. "Well, then, maybe they are jewel thieves, or Rovers of Kistan, or Chabbain or Hyrinian or even Fists of Rakka. Maybe they are . . ."

Pipper kept babbling, naming possibility after possibility, Binkton now and again snorting at some of the wild conjectures his cousin put forth. And he burst out laughing at Pipper's suggestion it could be that the King's men were after wild, blue-eyed, fair-haired women of the north to capture them as brides.

As Pipper continued rattling on, of a sudden Binkton sat up straight and stared at the water just ahead. "I-I don't believe it."

"Don't believe what?" asked Pipper.

Binkton pointed, and Pipper's gaze followed Binkton's outstretched arm.

Under the surface, it seemed, a long, dark, undulant shape slithered upstream, but perhaps it was no more than a rolling wave on the surface of the Argon reflecting light in an odd manner.

But Pipper had no doubt. "Captain Vení! Captain Vení!" he cried. "The river serpent! It's the river serpent!"

"What?" Vení looked up at the crow's nest.

Now Binkton, yet pointing, shouted, "The river serpent!"

"The river serpent?"

"Yes! Yes! That's what I said!"

"Where away?"

"Ahead and to the right."

"All hands starboard!" shouted the captain. "Gaffs and spears!"

The crew snatched up lances and long poles with iron hooks on the end. They rushed to the starboard rail, getting there just as a heave in the water coursed alongside, rolling the barque to port. And then it was gone, the shape diving deeper, or perhaps the strange rolling wave simply faded to nought. Neither buccan could be certain as to what it might have been, though Pipper maintained the rest of the day that it really was the river serpent, yet Binkton was not at all sure.

"I never heard of him being this far upstream," said Captain Vení at dinner that eve. "His usual haunts be around the Upper Isles, and we won't get there till nigh sunrise."

With a look of triumph on his face, Pipper smiled at Binkton as if to say, *See, I told you*, but Binkton merely shrugged noncommittally.

In the marks of the following dawn they passed the Upper Isles without incident, the dozen or so sheer-sided stone upjuts lying in midstream, two of them more than three miles in length and covered in tall grass and trees.

And just before dawn the next morn they passed the Lower Isles, also without incident, this group smaller than the other, though one was a mile or so long.

When the sun was well into the sky, "This is the day we reach Rivers End," said Binkton, "where we'll find the rat eaters who took our chest and, as Brekka said, deal out swift and sure justice to these worse-than-Rûcks foul folk."

"Um, Bink, I don't know how to tell you this, but your bow and arrows are in the chest, along with my sling and bullets."

"Well, then, Pip, we'll just have to get new ones in Rivers End, now, won't we?"

"Right. But shouldn't we find a town constable or the captain of the city watch or a King's man or someone to enforce the law?"

Captain Vení had just come within earshot, and he laughed. "Law? In Rivers End? I'm not certain there is any. Or rather, what law there is, well, it's in the pockets of those who run the city."

Even as he said those words, a barque hove into view downstream, and Captain Vení stepped to port and waited. As the ship passed, he called out something in a language neither Warrow knew and was answered in kind. The ship sailed on upriver, while the *Otter* continued down.

The captain turned to the buccen. "It was my brother, captain of the *Red Carp*."

"The *Red Carp!*" blurted Pipper. "That was the ship tending the barge bearing our stolen chest."

"You had a chest that was stolen?"

"By rat-eating Rivermen," growled Binkton.

"We were hoping to ask the captain of the *Red Carp* what happened to our case," said Pipper.

Captain Vení sighed. "I'm sorry, wee ones. Had I but known, I could have asked. Yet perhaps someone at Barge Bottom will know. —Oh, and if I be you I be not disparaging Rivermen, for there be a lot of them in Rivers End. They run the city."

Binkton looked at Pipper and said, "Then is it any wonder there's no law in that town?"

The Argon spread wide and slowed, and the barque and its barge came into estuarial waters filled with reed-infested low isles. Cyprus and cattails lined the water, and mangroves grew in dense thickets along the tidal shores, for they were in the grasp of the river delta, drawing ever nearer to where the Argon flowed into the Avagon Sea.

Here the captain and crew were most busy, herding the barge through shallow, fenny waters, the maneuvering room restricted. But at last ahead and to the right a long strip of cleared land came into view, and farther downstream the Warrows could see the near edges of Rivers End, its buildings marching away beyond sight.

"Lor, Bink," said Pipper, "I thought Argon Ferry Town was big, but this makes that look like a hamlet."

The barque maneuvered to the port side of the barge and began nudging it toward the shore. Pipper and Binkton could see workers dismantling other scows, now empty of their cargoes, salvaging the wood for other uses, and so the buccen reasoned the cleared strip of land must be Barge Bottom.

At last the *Otter* managed to shove the scow into the shallows, where it ground to a halt against the shoals. Men laid boarding planks from shore to barge, and secured the craft by hawsers to pile-driven posts on land.

The *Otter* then docked at one of the downstream piers.

Captain Vení met with the pier master and asked about a chest painted with flames and two men named Tark and Queeker; had he seen or heard of it or them?

The pier master shook his head and sent a lad running to ask the work crews if they had seen or heard ought of the trunk, or of a burly man named Tark and a skinny one named Queeker.

A half-candlemark later the lad returned and said as far as he could discover no one knew of the flame-painted chest or the men.

Sighing in disappointment, the Warrows then took up their duffle. They thanked Captain Vení and said their good-byes to the crew, and then they set foot ashore and began trekking the mile or so along the reed-bordered, log-paved riverbank road that led to the city of Rivers End.

Urchins

BURGLARS

LATE AUTUMN, 6E6,
TO EARLY SPRING, 6E7

As they trekked along Argon Way to the center of town, "Lor, lor," said Binkton, "there are people everywhere. How does someone stand to live in such crowds?"

"On their two feet," said Pipper, grinning.

"What?"

"You asked how someone could *stand* to live in such crowds, Bink, and I said—"

"Oh, Pip, you know what I mean. People all jam-packed together. No wonder this is a lawless city, what with folks all banging and bumping into one another."

"I don't see a lot of jostling," said Pipper.

"Well, if there isn't any, there should be," snapped Binkton.

With their duffle bags over their shoulders, the two buccen sidled their way through the throng, and Pipper said, "I don't see how we're ever going to find Tark and Queeker in this mess."

"I don't know either," gritted Binkton, "but find them we will."

They wove their way a bit farther, and then Binkton burst out, "Aargh! I've got to get away from this horde."

"Bink, it's no different from any jammed common room where we've performed. I mean, we draw packed houses and—"

"That's different," growled Binkton. "I mean, in a crowded tavern or inn we could always go to the outside. But this *is* the outside, and it's worse than any common room we've ever been in. Come on, let's go down one of these side streets and get free of this mob of towering Humans. I mean, we're like minnows swimming among trout, and I'm like to get swallowed up."

Pipper sighed. "All right, but we'll have to come back into the stream and swim with the fishes, if only to find a place to stay. I mean, I doubt if there are any inns whatsoever outside of this street."

They turned and made their way onto one of the twisting lanes leading off to the right. The narrow street was laden with shops of various sorts—curios, books, clothes, boots, and other such.

The route became less congested the farther they went, and finally Binkton heaved a great sigh of relief, glad to be able to walk without stepping this way and that to avoid being run over.

"I don't understand you, Bink," said Pipper. "I mean, they shackle you in chains and lock you in fetters and shut you up in little boxes and tie you up in ropes, and you don't seem to mind that a bit. But stick you in a crowd and it's as if you can't breathe. I would think it'd be the other way 'round."

"Maybe if it were Warrows instead of Humans," said Bink, "I wouldn't mind it so much. But the Big Folk, the Humans, well, they are just a menace, I think. I mean, how can they live that way, all bumping elbows, so to speak?"

Pipper said, "I am put in mind of what Uncle Arley said when I asked him to name the gifts of the various folk."

Binkton looked at Pipper, one eyebrow raised in an unspoken question.

Pipper smiled. "He said the gift of Elves is grace and ageless life, and that of Dwarves is never to lose their feet, for once they tread a path, it is with them forever. And he said the gift of Warrows is heart."

"Heart?"

"Yes. It seems we have the courage and will to follow through, once we take up a cause."

"What about Humans, then?"

"Uncle Arley said their gift is fecundity, and that's why there are so many of them." Pipper gestured back toward Argon Way. "So, you see, Bink, in this place we are witness to the Human flair."

Binkton turned and looked back toward the center of the city, and though the twisting street they followed blocked his view, he said, "Well, if they continue to try to fill up the world like they did this city, I think there will be no room for the rest of us."

"That's what the Elves say, Bink, or so Uncle Arley told me."

They strolled a bit farther, but finally Pipper said, "Bink, we've got to go back, 'cause we need a place to stay."

"Go back, Pip? Never."

"Well, are we just going to sleep on the streets like those urchins back in Argon Ferry Town?"

"No, Pip." Binkton pointed. "We're going to stay right there."

Pipper's gaze followed the direction of Binkton's outstretched arm, and above a small shop proclaiming itself to be Lady Jane's Millinery—Fine Hats for Fine Ladies—a sign in a second-storey window declared, "Room to Let."

"Well, I never had any of your folk ever stay in one of my rooms before," said the matronly woman, silver glints here and there in her hair.

"We won't be any bother, Lady Jane," said Binkton.

"Oh, it's not that I think you would be," she replied. "I mean, I am honored to have Waldana live here, heroes of the Dragonstone War and all. I mean, my Grady—that's my boy. Wounded in the war, he was. Took an arrow in the leg, he did. Walks with a limp, he does. Kept on fighting, though. Made it all the way to the Red Hills for the final battle. Anyway, my Grady, he says that when the Dragons came, all the Host were like to bolt, but then the little golden-armored Waldan blew on her silver horn, and the men looked to see the entire company of Waldfolc standing fast, and the Host took heart and stood fast as well."

"That was our cousin Triss who sounded the call," said Pipper.

"Was it now? Well, then, I'm doubly proud to have Waldana taking my room. Wait'll I tell—"

Pipper threw up a hand to stop her words. "Ma'am, I wish you wouldn't let anyone know that Warrows are in residence here. You see, we are on a mission of sorts. One that we'd rather keep quiet."

With a puzzled look, Binkton stared at Pipper, but Lady Jane peered about as if to spy eavesdroppers and, seeing none, she whispered, "Ooo, a mission. One for the High King, I suspect."

"We'd rather not say," Pipper replied.

"Well, then, mum's the word," said the woman. "Oh, and if I might, and to help keep your presence secret, I'll make you hats—caps, really—to cover those pointed ears of yours." Then she frowned. "But I don't see how to disguise those jewel-like eyes of yours—sapphire blue, emerald green. —Oh, wait, I know: hats with tall crowns and brims. They'll shadow your faces. I have some lovely fabric."

Pipper snapped his fingers as if at a sudden thought and said, "We'd rather look like urchins."

Binkton's jaw dropped a fraction.

Lady Jane frowned. "Urchins? Oh, I see. The better to blend in, you being so small and all. Well, then, I'll find something to make do."

Lady Jane bustled off, and Binkton looked at Pipper and asked, "What in the name of Adon was that all about?"

"Look, Bink, we can't let word leak to Tark and Queeker that we are in town. I mean, they might just hie out of here."

Binkton frowned a moment but then brightened. "Ah, I see. They probably heard about us dealing out swift and sure justice to those brigands, eh?"

"No, Bink, I was thinking more along the lines of—"

"Here we are," declared Lady Jane, rushing back into the room. She held a cloth tape measure in hand, and she wrapped it around Binkton's head. "Hmm . . . For one so small you have a considerable brow. All right. All right. Don't wiggle so. There now." She jotted a note on a pad from her pocket, and then turned to Pipper and made another set of measurements.

As she rushed out again, Pipper said, "Come on, let's unpack and then get something to eat."

"Without our urchin disguises?" Binkton snorted, and then added, "We have to blend in, you know."

"Oh, right," said Pipper. "We'll have to wait."

With dark, wide-brimmed hats pulled down over their ears to keep the tips from showing, Pipper and Binkton stepped out from the side entrance of the millinery and headed for the small inn Lady Jane had recommended as being one frequented by people of limited means. "The food is good, and you'll fit right in with other urchins who gather there. Just keep your hats on and don't let them see your eyes, and don't flash any silver or gold."

On the street, Binkton paused a moment to examine Pipper, who peered out from under his jammed-down hat like a mouse peeking out from a hole, and said, "Gah, Pip, but we look like a couple of simpletons."

"Simpletons or no, Bink, I think we need some seedier clothes. Right now we look too prosperous. —Oh, wait, all we have to do is smear a bit of dirt here and there and on our faces too; then we'll fit right in."

In distaste, Binkton stared at the gutter, running as it did with a thin layer of water over a grayish sludge. "Dirt?"

"No, Bink, not from the gutter. We'll find a better grade of mud."

A quarter candlemark later, a pair of street urchins entered the common room of the Yellow Lantern.

"Two bowls of your stew," said Pipper as they passed the barkeep on the way to a table.

"I need to see the color of your coin, lads," replied the man.

Pipper tossed two coppers onto the counter; then he and Binkton sat down and waited to be served.

"When are we going to get some weapons, Pip?" asked Binkton. "You a sling and some bullets, me a bow and some arrows."

"Bink, I don't think an urchin bearing a bow and a quiver full of arrows would blend in."

"Barn rats! You're right."

"But we can both carry slings and bullets," said Pipper.

Binkton sighed and said, "I'm not as good with a sling as you are, Pip, and not nearly as good as I am with a bow. But I suppose a sling'll have to do."

The buccen fell silent as their stew and bread were served. But as soon as the man walked away, Pip said, "Now, here's my plan. . . ."

Every day and part of each eve they spent on the streets of Rivers End, and over a fortnight they made friends with "other" urchins, at times springing for a meal for an underfed kid at the Yellow Lantern, and at other times sitting quietly in doorways and watching the traffic flow—pedestrians and carts and carriages and riders and the like. And idly they chatted with their newfound acquaintances—cadgers all—occasionally bringing up the subject of Queeker and Tark, but none of the urchins knew anyone by that name, though descriptions of the pair sounded familiar.

Most of the talk, though, was about the number of shops that had been damaged, burglarized, or set afire, and the fact that the city watch seemed helpless in the face of these deeds. Many businesses had begun paying someone for "protection" from such unfortunate events, which gave rise to the idea of a shadowy, so-called crime lord of Rivers End, yet none of the urchins knew who he might be. And just that morning another store had been broken into and the merchandise strewn about.

"It's the crime lord's doings, right enough," said Cricket, the smallest of the urchins, who stood about Pipper's height. "Wos a warning to pay up."

"Maybe it's Tark," said Binkton. "He'd do such a thing."

"The rumor is that the crime lord hisself, well, he's someone in high circles," said Weasel, the skinny lad pointing a finger straight up toward the sky for emphasis.

"Well, that lets Tark and Queeker out," said Pipper.

"Wot is it y've got agin this here Tark and Queeker?" asked Tope, wiping a sleeve across his ever-running nose.

"They stole our bindle," said Pipper. "Took nearly everything we have."

"The dirty rats," growled Cricket. "No wonder you're looking for them."

Weasel nodded and said, "Me and my friends, we'll all help you."

"Ri'," agreed Tope.

"We'll keep an eye out," said Cricket.

"Ri'," again agreed Tope.

But six full months passed altogether with nary a sight of either Tark or Queeker, and the buccen were quite discouraged. The reports of some shadowy crime lord continued to circle, but as to just who he might be, neither the urchins nor Warrows came across even a rumor as to his name.

Even though disheartened, Pipper and Binkton had never considered making their way back to the Bosky. Still enraged in spite of the lack of success, Binkton often declared, "We can't let those Rûck-loving, rat-eating, thieving bullies win, Pip." Pipper would sigh and nod his agreement, though his own anger had long since vanished. Even so, a pledge was a pledge, and Pipper was a Warrow through and through, and, as was the wont of his kind, it was ingrained in his very fiber that a mission undertaken was to be finished. After all, it took a millennium for Gwylly and Faeril, the Lastborn Firstborns, to finish the mission begun a thousand years before by Tomlin and Petal, distant ancestors of theirs.

And so they continued their surveillance of the streets, cadging a few coins from passersby, to pay for the rent and food. . . .

It was Binkton who finally spotted Queeker, the small, skinny man just entering a leather-goods store.

"Come on, Pip," snarled Binkton, fumbling in his pocket for his sling, "let's get that son of a Spawn."

"No, Bink, no!"

Binkton whirled on Pipper. "What?"

"We need to follow him so that he'll lead us to our chest."

Binkton stood glowering at Pipper, but then took a deep breath and slowly let it out and nodded. "You're right, Pip. We'll deal out swift and sure justice in good time, then."

"Right," said Pipper. "And surely he will lead us to Tark, too."

Again Binkton nodded, and then scowled. "Speaking of Tark, there he is."

Outside but looking in the window of the leather-goods store stood the burly man.

"Come on, Bink. Let's see what they're up to."

Like a couple of disinterested street children, the buccen meandered down the opposite side of the crooked lane. Inside the store they could see Queeker talking to a young woman, who had a look of distress upon her face. Queeker pointed over his shoulder at Tark. Moments later she handed the skinny man a small pouch, and Queeker stepped out into the street. Laughing, the two went on down the way and across the street to the very next establishment, where once again Tark hulked at the window, while Queeker went inside.

Opposite the leather-goods store, the buccen could see the woman inside weeping.

"You watch them, Bink," said Pipper. "I'm going to talk to her."

"Right, Pip, but you and I both know what they're doing."

Moments later, Pipper was back at Binkton's side. "As we suspected, they're collecting protection money."

They followed the pair the rest of the afternoon, always keeping to doorways and alley openings and other such concealment. Finally, Tark and Queeker seemed finished for the day, for they headed down a twisting street and entered no more establishments. At last they came to a small yellow house and unlocked the door and went inside.

"That's where our chest will be," gritted Binkton.

"Perhaps," replied Pipper. "But we need to wait and see."

They took station where they could watch the front of the dwelling.

A candlemark later, as evening fell, Tark and Queeker emerged. Queeker locked the door, and then he and his burly companion went back toward town, Tark whistling a tuneless air.

"Now what?" whispered Binkton. "Follow them some more? Me, I'd rather get our chest if it's in there."

"So would I, Bink. But if we can, I'd also like to find their stash of ill-gotten gains and give it all back to the merchants."

"Good idea," whispered Binkton, and he pulled the long piece of wire out from his belt.

As soon as they were certain Tark and Queeker were well out of ear-shot and sight, the two buccen slipped through the shadows and across the street. Binkton peered in the dim light at the lock. It was a new one, made of brass hanging through the hasp shackle. Moments later— snick!—the lock sprang open.

Quickly, they were inside, and they softly closed the door after. Pipper found a candle and a striker, and he lit the taper, its soft light barely illuminating the parlor. There were three other rooms within: one a little-used kitchen, as evidenced by the dust on everything but a table and chairs, on which sat a deck of cards; and two bedrooms, one larger than the other, but none held their flame-painted chest.

"Barn rats!" spat Binkton.

Pipper sighed. "I couldn't have said it better. Even so, if they hide the money they took from the merchants, well . . ."

"Say no more, Pip."

They went into the largest bedroom. Clothes fit for a burly man hung in the freestanding wardrobe against one wall.

"This has to be Tark's room," said Binkton.

"Then it's more likely to have the coin," said Pipper.

But a thorough search turned up nothing.

The same was true of Queeker's room.

And they found nought in the parlor.

Finally, in desperation, they went to the kitchen.

As they searched this chamber, Pipper frowned and glanced at the hooked rug under the table. "I say, Bink, what with the dust over everything but this—"

"Right!" said Binkton.

The two Warrows moved the table, and under the circular rug they found a loose floorboard, and under that—"Aha!" Binkton exclaimed—were sixteen pouches altogether, each holding five silvers.

"How many stores did they rob today?" asked Pipper.

"I would say sixteen," replied Binkton, grinning in the wavering light of the candle.

"Let's hie out of here," said Pipper, taking up half the pouches, while Binkton took up the other half.

They carefully replaced the floorboard, and then the rug, and finally the table. Pipper blew out the candle and put it back where he had found it. Moments later they were outside in the darkness, with the front door relocked, and off toward their own room they went.

On that night they had become burglars, though they made no profit from their deed, all monies being anonymously returned by urchins to the merchants who had been robbed.

32

Ashore

ELVENSHIP
MID SPRING, 6E7,
TO MID SPRING, 6E8

Over the next year, as was Aravan's wont, the *Eroean* made several stops along isolated shores, where, again, Aravan and Aylis and Lissa and the warband, as well as various members of the crew, went exploring, or made forays inland for water and fruit and other comestibles. Yet little else did they find.

But nigh the far edge of the Weston Ocean, as they passed a small atoll lying in tropical waters, they espied on one of the islands a tattered flag of Gelen tied to a tree and flying upside down.

"'Tis a distress flag," said Aravan, and then he called, "Heave to." As soon as the ship came to a gentle drifting, Aravan and Dokan and four of the crew rowed a skiff to the isle, where they found an old campsite and what appeared to be the remains of seven men. Weathered water casks sat at hand. Dokan tapped each of them and said, "All empty. Likely the crew died of thirst." On the lagoon-side shore, a heavily damaged pair of dinghies lay abandoned.

"Kapitan," asked Nikolai, "flag from Gelen; be *Gray Petrel* crew?"

"I know not, Nikolai," said Aravan. He turned to Noddy, now second bosun of the *Eroean*. "Fetch Aylis."

Noddy and two others rowed back to the ship, and within moments Aylis and Lissa and Vex boarded the skiff. The sailors turned the craft and began rowing back, with Vex in the prow and peering down into the crystalline waters as they approached the isle.

Aylis and the others disembarked, even as Aravan picked a lengthy bone out from the long-cold ashes of the fire.

Vex whined and postured, and Lissa said, "All right. All right." She looked up at Aravan, even as he squatted and examined the bone. "Captain, Vex says the atoll itself is lifeless: no birds whatsoever; and even the reef fish so plentiful in these waters were absent as we rowed over. And look at the plant life. It is nought but scrub and stunted trees. Vex thinks we'd better get back on the ship and leave."

At these words, Aravan realized his blue stone amulet dangled outside his jerkin. He pressed his palms against the token and said, " 'Tis slightly chill to my touch." He stood and looked about, adding, "Somewhere a distant peril lies."

Dokan unslung his war axe from his back and eyed the surround, even as others of the crew laid hands on the hilts of their falchions.

Aylis yet peered askance at the bone. "Let me do a <seeing>." She murmured an arcane word and looked upon the bone and then the remains of the castaways. Tears sprang into her eyes, even as a horrified gasp escaped her lips. "Oh, my."

"What is it? What is it?" asked Lissa.

"They turned to cannibalism, drawing lots to see who would be the next 'provider,' " said Aylis.

Now Lissa's face blanched, and she turned to Vex and buried her face in the vixen's fur.

"Be it *Petrel*?" asked Nikolai.

Aylis shook her head.

Aravan glanced at Aylis and Lissa and Vex. He touched the stone once more. "The amulet grows more chill. Noddy, return Aylis and Lissa to the *Eroean*."

Even as Noddy moved to comply, "No, Captain Aravan," protested Lissa, "you will need my arrows."

"And my <sight>," said Aylis.

Aravan sighed. "Then we shall all return to the ship."

They stepped to the skiff and rowed back to the *Eroean*. Even as they clambered aboard, the mainmast lookout called down, "Cap'n, you ought to come up and see this."

"What is it, Finn?"

"I don't rightly know, Cap'n. A darkness is all I can say."

Aravan scrambled up the ratlines to the crow's nest. "Where away, Finn?"

"Yon," said the lookout, pointing to waters central to the atoll.

In the center of the lagoon the sea changed from a pale crystalline green to a wide circle of deep blue.

"Make ready to get under way!" called Aravan down to Long Tom. "All sails! We might need to run as fast as the *Eroean* will fly!"

Even as James piped the orders, Long Tom cried up, "What be it, Cap'n?"

"A blue hole," Aravan replied.

"Oh, lor," breathed Long Tom, and he began barking commands as the ship heeled about and took up the wind and slowly gained speed.

"What is it? What is it?" asked Lissa. "What's a blue hole?"

"No one knows exactly," said Tarley, standing by the helm in case Fat Jim needed help with the wheel. "Though seldom sighted, 'tis said there be many. Each be a great hole, circular round as if driven by a giant auger. And deep, oh, deep . . . bottomless, some say, and almost always in a ring of islands. And there be things said to live down in—things dire deadly."

"Well, why didn't Finn know to call out a warning earlier?" asked the Pysk.

"This be Finn's first voyage, taking him on as we did earlier this year when Bri left. He bain't likely to know about the blue holes yet, I reckon."

Even as the *Eroean* gained headway, Aravan's gaze swept the circular extent of the blue hole in the lagoon bounded by the ring of isles. And with his keen Elven sight, he espied a broken ship's mast jutting just above the surface at the near edge of the rim of dark water, its splinters clutching at the sky as would a maimed hand.

Straight away from the atoll the *Eroean* sailed.

"What be there, Cap'n?" asked Finn.

"Mayhap a dreadful thing occupies the deep of that hole," said Aravan. "Dost thou see the ship's masts just this side of the dark blue?"

Finn stared long, but at last said, "Cap'n, my sight be sharp, but yours be e'en keener."

"Keep watch, Finn, for I fear our journey to the isle might have disturbed what lives therein, and I would not have it grasp the *Eroean*."

And after a while, as the atoll slipped over the horizon aft, Aravan clambered down from the crow's nest and to the main deck. And neither he nor the lookout above saw the welling of water as a monstrous green thing come heaving up from the depths of the blue hole, only to sink back down and out of sight once more.

Three months later, as the Elvenship sailed into Arbalin Isle at the end of her fruitless voyage, a message awaited Aylis . . . a message from Queen Dresha. Aylis had once paid her respects to the Queen during a time the *Eroean* had been in Caer Pendwyr.

Chicken Thieves

BURGLARS

EARLY SUMMER 6E9

Ah, then, so that's how we ended up in this unseemly business of burglary, thought Pipper as he and Binkton stealthily slipped down the alleyway.

"Where are these chickens you spoke of?" hissed Binkton, interrupting Pipper's thoughts.

"Just ahead," said Pipper. "I noticed them when I was watching Rackburn's manor. I saw that now and then they escape their yard, so chickens being on the loose shouldn't seem unusual."

Binkton snorted. "Don't you think that chickens on the loose in the *night* might be a bit strange?"

"You have a point, Bink, but even so, we aren't very far from the edge of the city, and who's to say a fox didn't somehow get in the henhouse and roust them out?"

"Ha! So we are foxes, now?"

"More like ferrets, I would think," said Pipper.

A few more paces down the lane and, "Ah, here we are," whispered Pipper, and he stopped at a wooden alley gate on the left. "We have to keep the chickens quiet, else the owner is like to fly a few arrows our way."

"Shall we wrap them in our cloaks?" asked Binkton, unclasping his. "—The chickens, I mean, not the arrows."

225

"Good idea," murmured Pipper, and he slipped out of his own cloak and lifted the latch on the back entry.

Moments later they were again in the alley, two hens each bundled in their wraps.

As they stealthily started down the way, Pipper fell into reflection again, recalling the past two years. . . .

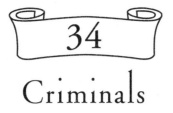

34

Criminals

BURGLARS
EARLY SPRING, 6E7,
TO EARLY SUMMER, 6E9

With the help of Weasel and Tope and Cricket and a few of their urchin friends, throughout the next two years they managed to follow a goodly number of "protection" collectors. And so, a wave of burglaries struck Rivers End, and even the corrupt city watch became involved in trying to discover just who the thieves were. And some of the places burglarized had the latest of locks and the best of strongboxes, but still they were opened and all monies taken. And other of the places had befanged walls and guards for protection, yet they were burglarized as well. The merchants simply shrugged and said they knew nought, for the only thing they understood was that they paid their protection monies, and what happened after that was a complete mystery to them. But on the sly, the storekeepers began donating five coppers to each of the urchins who brought back their silver coin.

And in one of the crowded marketplaces, as Tark and Queeker made their way among the stalls, a group of eight urchins or so, playing some game, went running and squealing past the pair, jostling and bumping as they ran. It wasn't until later that Tark noted all that was left of his money pouch were the ends of the thong that held it to his belt. He and Queeker rousted every known marketplace pickpocket and cutpurse in the city, but all claimed innocence, even after fingers were broken.

Meanwhile, Binkton, chortling and laughing, shared out the coin among the urchins and sent them to return the silvers to the merchants from whom they had been taken.

With their copper rewards, the urchins ate well that night.

Some of the merchants feared that the protection collectors would simply demand more, yet it seemed that whoever was behind the scheme realized that he could not get blood from stone, and so he left them alone. In desperation, though, the protection collectors began hitting up the very smallest of stores, ones they had never bothered before, and that was how Lady Jane had come to lose five silvers to the brutes.

The buccen were incensed, and over the next few days they set their small gang out to follow the trail of that particular collector, and it led to a manor occupied by one of the leading lights of Rivers End: Largo Rackburn, a man of means, though no one seemed to know how he had come about his wealth.

Pipper and Binkton and their urchins set watch on the Rackburn house, and they noted as collector after collector brought their loot to the place, Tark and Queeker among them.

It came to the attention of one of the lads that Lily Francine, an actress at the Rivers End Theater, was a favorite of Largo's, and he went without fail to every opening performance when Lily had the leading role.

"I thin' it be his child, Pip," said Tope, wiping his nose against his sleeve. "That'r she be his sweetie."

"And when will she be opening?" asked Binkton.

"In a sennight," said Tope.

"Then we've a sevenday to make our plans," said Pipper.

"Well, you're the acrobat," said Binkton, "so it's up to you to spot a way in."

"Right," said Pipper. Then he turned to Cricket, who had grown somewhat during the half year the buccen had known him. "Cricket, you and Weasel make certain of the date of the performance. Not that I don't trust you, Tope, but we've got to be sure, and since you've been there before, I wouldn't want anyone to think you've been snooping about."

Tope nodded and again wiped his nose against his sleeve and said, "'At's all ri', Cap'n. I ain't 'ffended."

And so it was that Pipper began in earnest watching and recording the comings and goings at the Rackburn house, and of the back wall and the balcony at the rear of the manor, and of the guards within. And by spying from a wall where he could see through the back windows, he noted what looked to be Rackburn's office. It was the most likely place for a strong-box, and it could be reached from the balcony. The spikes atop the back wall would pose little or no hindrance to the buccen. And the window to the room would prove to be no bar to Binkton's skills.

Pipper's plan was simplicity itself. Over the wall, across the yard, a padded grapnel to the balcony, up the rope, through the window, and to the strongbox. But if they couldn't get in through the window, there was always the balcony door.

On opening night at the Rivers End Theater, Pipper and Binkton watched as Largo Rackburn stepped into the carriage to go.

"Now's ours to do," said Binkton. "Let's get back Lady Jane's money."

"Right," said Pipper, and he and his cousin slipped to the back wall. As Pipper padded the grapnel, Binkton stealthily climbed to the top of the wall, only to discover several large dogs patrolling the yard.

35

Jade Carving

The message awaiting Aylis at Port Arbalin was written in Queen Dresha's own fine hand:

> *My dear Aylis:*
>
> *Some two years past, I received the gift of a small chest of black lacquerware decorated with exotic designs in gold leaf of Jingarian Dragons and landscapes and other such. It originally came from Janjong, to be exact. It is quite a lovely piece, and it would please us most dearly if you would fetch a variety of black lacquerware—bowls, chests, vases, and the like, whatever might strike your fancy—of similar design the next time you and your Captain Aravan are at that port city.*
>
> *With Our warmest regards,*
> *Dresha,*
> *Queen of Mithgar*

And so it was that in the spring of 6E8, Aravan set sail for Jinga to purchase lacquerware—bowls, chests, vases, and the like—as well as a cargo of fine porcelain.

They docked in Janjong, the principal port city of that realm. And even as the Elvenship tied up at the pier, peddlers and merchants selling

230

their wares crowded the wharf, calling out to the crew of the *Eroean* to come and look at their goods.

When Aylis decided to look for lacquerware as well as to explore the city, Lissa hid in the hood of her cloak, for she would see the city, too. Vex obediently trotted at Aylis's side, a very light leash 'round her neck—more of a string than a lead—the fox finally submitting to Lissa's commands to be ignominiously led by such.

And even as they embarked, the hawkers rushed forward, and then shied back, not only at the sight of the fox, but also at the pair of armed and armored Dwarves escorting this person and her familiar, for surely with such unusual guardians and a wild fox attendant she must be a *nyuwu*, a witch.

Yet one young man braved the escort of fox and fierce Dwarves, and he stepped discreetly to one side of the path and said, "I have been waiting for you, Lady Fox, for I had a dream you would come, and you must see what my father has carved."

Aylis laughed. "A dream, you say?"

"Oh, yes, oh, yes. In my dream I saw a great ship arrive, and you stepped from it, though in my dream you had no fox."

Again Aylis laughed, for she had never before had a hawker tell such a tale. "And this carving is . . . ?"

"Jade, my lady. Jade. The finest of gemstone, and carved by Master Luong, my father. You must come and see."

"Let's go look," whispered Lissa in Aylis's ear.

"I must admit, I am intrigued," said Aylis, replying more to Lissa than the youth.

And so "Lady Fox" followed the young man through the streets of Janjong, the merchant heading for his shop, the two Châkka trailing not far behind, their gazes ever on the alert for dangers that might threaten their charge.

And Aylis was led to a stall where the young man, Huang by name, showed her a carving of a jade tower. It was not the tower itself that arrested her curiosity, even though it somewhat resembled the Seers' Tower at the College of Mages; nay, rather it was the inscription in a strange tongue etched around the base of the figurine. With an arcane word muttered under her breath she read:

Thrice I dreamt the dream
The City of Jade I fled
Nought but shades now dwell

It was a particular form of Ryodoan poetry, yet not of Ryodo was this work. It was instead carved by a Jingarian jade master, or so said Huang, who again proclaimed it was his own sire, Luong. Aylis bought the statuette, but only under the condition that she meet the artist. The young man gave her directions to a dwelling where he and his wife and his father lived, but he warned her that Master Luong was a recluse. Undaunted, Aylis took the jade carving and hailed a jinricksha. The man who pulled the vehicle seemed both surprised and honored as well as awed to have Lady Fox as his passenger, for the word of the witch and her familiar had spread across the neighborhood. And he set off at a brisk pace toward the address given.

Behind her, two Dwarves scrambled into a jinricksha of their own and followed after.

It was the very fact that a lady and a fox came to call upon Luong that the jade master deigned to see this curiosity for himself.

Dressed in silks and soft sandals, he was a man of about sixty years, his hair and beard white and long, his eyes so dark as to nearly be black. When Aylis told him that she had come seeking knowledge about the statuette, he was amazed that she, a foreigner, spoke such flawless Jingarian.

[It did come to me in a dream,] said Luong, as soon as they had settled down upon tatamis, a small tea table between, a steaming pot of tea thereon. As he poured two cups of the pale drink, Luong said, [I don't know what it means. Not only that, but I suspect it is a form of poetry, one that I have never seen before.]

[It is Ryodoan,] said Aylis. [A strange form that never deviates from its syllabic count—five, seven, five, you see.]

[Ryodoan it may be, but it is not in that language, for I would know; written Ryodoan and Jingarian are much alike. Regardless, do you know what it says?]

[You don't know?]

[It is not in any language I have.]

[It is strange that you would carve it, then,] said Aylis.

[Yet carve it I did, even though I know not its meaning. As I said, it came in a dream, and I felt compelled to set it in jade.] Luong then turned up a hand toward the statuette, and he looked at Aylis in anticipation.

[These are its words,] said Aylis.

> [*Thrice I dreamt the dream*
> *From the City of Jade I fled*
> *Nought but shades now dwell.*]

[Oh, how mysterious,] said Luong. [Not words that I would choose to carve, nor a dream I would choose to dream, I think.]

[Only sometimes can we choose our dreams,] said Aylis, harkening back to the time she and Jinnarin had learned to dreamwalk. Aylis sipped her drink and added, [Perhaps it was a sending.]

[Sending? Sending? What are these sendings? Are they dangerous? My son Huang had a dream as well.]

[He did?]

Luong nodded. [He said a lady from a great ship would like to see my carving. He said nothing of a fox.]

Aylis nodded. [That's what he told me.] She laughed. [I thought it but a ruse to get me to see this beautiful jade figurine.]

[No, his was a dream, as was mine. Yet you call them 'sendings.' What are they?]

[A message from someone else—a spirit, a lost soul, a Mage—someone who fled the City of Jade. If so, then it is something I cannot trace back, for finding the source of dreams is beyond my ken.]

Luong's eyes widened. [You are one who can do <chiji>?]

Aylis laughed and shook her head. [I have only a bit of <yanli>.]

[Then how is it you can read those words?]

In that moment Aylis's hood sneezed, or so it seemed. Luong reared back, concern on his features.

"Oh, well," said Lissa, stepping from the hood and onto Aylis's shoulder. "I gave myself away. Besides, I'd like some tea, too."

Luong's mouth fell agape. [I-I . . . I cannot believe my eyes.] And he backed away and prostrated himself before the two. [Forgive me, mistress, I did not know you had such \<nengli\> . . . such power.]

It took some coaxing for Aylis to get the man back onto his tatami. And when she said that Lissa would like some tea as well, Luong did not call his servants, but rushed out to get a vessel himself. Moments later he was back with a porcelain thimble, and with trembling hands he poured a bit of tea into the improvised cup and proffered it to Lissa, who now sat atop the small table.

In that moment Aylis frowned, and she spoke a word and looked at the figurine. Then she sighed and said to Lissa, "There has been no casting, for it contains no \<power\>."

"What contains no \<power\>?" asked Lissa, looking up from her drink.

"The statuette."

Luong looked back and forth between the two females.

[I said it contains no \<nengli\>,] said Aylis, for Luong's benefit.

[Ah, then, so you can see power. Perhaps that is why you have such a companion and how you can read the words, eh, and mayhap as well speak such beautiful Jingarian?]

Aylis inclined her head in assent, and Luong smiled in his discernment, though his eyes yet held a glimmer of awe.

[Do you remember anything else about the dream?] asked Aylis.

[Only what I etched on the bottom, but I do not understand that either.]

Frowning, Aylis took up the statuette and looked at the bottom. Curving lines were scribed, but she had no idea what they might represent. She spoke another arcane word, yet her \<sight\> revealed nothing further.

Luong looked at Lissa and asked, [What are you called? What folk are you from?]

Lissa shrugged and looked at Aylis. "He wants to know what type creature you are."

"Tell him I am a sprite of great power, and should he ever speak to anyone of me, I will appear in a whirling cloud and carry him away to a fiery pit of darkness, where he will burn in shadow forever." To prove her point, blackness suddenly enveloped the Pysk.

[Wah!] exclaimed Luong, juggling his cup.

[You must never speak of her to anyone else,] said Aylis.

[No, no. I am sworn to silence.] Again he prostrated himself before the pair.

Aylis nodded toward the blot of darkness, and the shadow vanished, revealing the Pysk once more.

Once again Aylis had to persuade Luong to return to his tatami, after which they spoke for long moments, yet nothing else was forthcoming about the dream or the figurine.

Finally, Aylis and Lissa and Vex took their leave, much to Luong's relief, for to have such persons of power in his very own chambers, well, it was all quite beyond his ability to cope. Yet it was but moments after they had left that Luong began a new jade carving. One of a very small person, or perhaps it was nothing more than a tiny statuette.

"City of Jade, eh?" Aravan looked at the small sculpted tower. "Hmm . . . There is an ancient legend. One that was old when I first came to Mithgar. It tells of a city carved of jade that fell to some terrible fate. Perhaps this jade carving has something to do with that legend."

Aravan then turned the statuette upside down and looked at the lines on the bottom. "Hmm . . . This could be a map, for it resembles a coastline, yet there are thousands of places along many shores similar to this. Even so, there might be some hint of where to look in the archives of the libraries in Caer Pendwyr. If so, we will look for the City of Jade after we deliver the cargo to Queen Dresha."

"Good," said Lissa, taking a small sip of brandy from her thimble-sized cup. "Should we go off searching for a lost city, mayhap at last Vex and I will again have something to do to earn our keep."

Again Aravan looked at the figurine. He glanced at Aylis and said, "Following this to wherever it leads suits me well, for, as I said, this crew is meant for adventure, seeking out legend and fable. Mayhap this statuette will take us to something rare."

They sailed the Alacca Straits with their cargo of fine porcelain and black lacquerware decorated in gold leaf with exotic designs. And just ere reaching the jagged rocks known as the Dragon Fangs, they sank two junks and three sampans filled with Jungarian pirates who had foolishly decided to attack the *Eroean*; this time the Dwarven crew on the starboard side loosed the fireballs that set the pirate ships aflame. And with falchions and axes and hammers in hand, the sailors and Dwarves grappled and winched and boarded one of the burning ships, the men shouting, *Eroean! Eroean!* and the Dwarves roaring, *Châkka shok! Châkka cor!* The pirate crew leapt into the sea rather than face the wild savages of the Elvenship.

That night they celebrated as they sailed southwestward for the distant Cape of Storms.

Southwesterly and southwesterly she sailed, but at last the *Eroean* came to the shoulder of the cape. And the wind had risen in strength and had risen again, and now the Elvenship beat to the windward into a shrieking gale. For though it was the height of the warm season in the south, the air chilled to frigidity and the wind shrieked in fury, as if Father Winter and Rualla raged together to show just who was master and mistress in this polar realm. Great grey waves, their crests foaming, broke over the bow and smashed down upon the decks with unnumbered tons of water, clutching and grasping at timber and wood and rope, at fittings, at sails, the huge greybeards seeking to drag off and drown whatever they could, whatever might be loose or loosened.

In the teeth of the blow Aravan again ordered all sails pulled but the stays, jibs, tops, and mains. And Men had struggled 'cross decks awash— cold, drenching waves dragging them off their feet and trying to hurl them overboard and into the icy brine; yet the safety lines held fast, and the crew made their way up into the rigging, the frigid wind tearing at them, shrieking and threatening to hurl them away. But the Men fought the elements, haling in the silken sail and lashing it 'round the yardarms and spars, while all about them the halyards howled in the wind like giant harp strings yowling in torment, sawn by the screaming gale.

On the very next watch the wind force increased, and once again the crew was dispatched onto the dangerous decks and up to the hazardous spars, this time at Nikolai's command, and all jibs were pulled and the mains reefed to the last star. And now the ship ran mostly on the staysails and the upper and lower topsails, the *Eroean* flying less than a third of full silk.

The following watch Aravan took command, and after an hour or so, the wind picked up yet again, and the Elven captain ordered forth the crew to reef the mains and the crossjack to the full.

"*Diabolos,* Kapitan," shouted Nikolai above the wind, "I t'ink if this keep up, soon we be sailing on yards alone."

Aravan grinned at the second officer. "Mayhap, Nikolai. Mayhap. But if it's to bare sticks we go, then backwards we will fare."

Even though the galley was locked down for the heavy seas, its fire extinguished, still Nelon, ship's cook, managed to brew tea, and Noddy made his way up through the trapdoor and into the small wheelhouse, the lad bearing a tray of steaming mugs. That he managed to carry the cups in the pitching ship without spilling a drop spoke well of his agility and balance. With a grin he passed the tray about to Aravan and Fat Jim and Nikolai, then disappeared belowdecks once more.

As Aravan sipped his tea, he wiped the condensation from the window and peered at the raging sea. "Vash! Here comes a wall." Aravan quickly set his cup to the holder and called, "Pipe the crew on deck, Nikolai; we'll need to change course." And he took a grip on the wheel on one side while Fat Jim held the spokes across. "Prepare to come about. On the starboard bow quarter this tack."

At the moment Nikolai opened the trap to go below and summon the crew, a blinding hurl of white engulfed the *Eroean,* the Cape of Storms living up to its name as wind-driven snow slammed horizontally across the Elvenship.

A sevenday plus two it took to round the cape, sometimes the *Eroean* seemingly driven abaft while at other times she surged ahead. And at all times the savage wind tore at her, while the greybeards struggled to wrench her down. Snow and ice weighed heavily on her rigging, and Men and Dwarves were sent aloft to break loose the pulleys so the ropes would run free. Tacking northwest up across the wind and southwest back down, Aravan sailed by dead reckoning, for no stars nor moon in the short nights did he see, nor sun in the long days. Nor did he see the southern aurora writhing far beyond the darkness above, shifting curtains of spectral light draped high in the icy skies, as if a strange wind blew out from the sun to illumine the polar nights.

Still, battered by wind and wave, the *Eroean* took nine full days before she could run clear on a northwesterly course, free of the cape at last, Aravan's reckoning true, the crew superb in handling the craft and not a Man or Dwarf lost unto the grasping sea. Even so, all were weary, drained by this rugged pass, including her captain, a thing seldom seen by any of the crew. Yet finally the ship's routine returned to something resembling normality though the winds yet blew agale, but they were steady on the larboard. And running on a course with the wind to the port, mains and crossjack and jibs back full, up into the Weston Ocean the Elvenship ran, the log line humming out at nineteen knots, the *Eroean* flying o'er the waves.

And once the ship was out of danger, Aravan fell into a deep sleep, and Aylis did not see him awake for a full two days.

A week later across the Doldrums of the Goat the *Eroean* fared, this time heading north, the ship laden with all sail set, yet moving slowly in the light air—"Slipping past the Horns of Old Billy," as Noddy had said. Three days it took to cross the calms, three days ere the wind picked up again, now coming from abaft. North-northwest she drove, sweeping through the coastal waters of the wide Realm of Hyree.

Five days under full sail she ran on the northerly trek, the winds steady but moderate, until they came once more unto the Midline Irons, where they unshipped the gigs to tow the *Eroean* across the placid equatorial waters.

At last the winds returned, blowing lightly down from the northeast, and into these she fared, sailing through the gap between Hyree to the south and Vancha to the north, finally entering into the Avagon Sea along the Straits of Kistan. A day she coursed as the skies turned a sullen grey, and still to the north lay Vancha, but now to the south lay Kistan.

"Sail ho, crimson!" called the foremast lookout. "Sail ho on the larboard bow!"

Nikolai's gaze swept the horizon forward and left, then stopped. A heartbeat later—"Ring alarm, Noddy, and stand by to pipe crew."

Noddy hammered a tattoo upon the ship's bell, and moments later crew and warband spilled onto the deck as Aravan came to the wheel.

James stepped to Noddy's side, but left the bosun whistle in the lad's hands.

"Where away, Nikolai?"

"There, Kapitan," replied the man from the Islands of Stone, pointing.

Just on the horizon, scarlet lateen sails could be discerned, a two-masted dhow heading downwind in the general direction of the Elvenship.

"Nikolai, bring the *Eroean* to a northeast heading. Put this rover on our starboard beam."

"Aye-aye, Kapitan."

Aravan turned to the wheelman. "Wooly, ready to bring her to the course laid in."

"Aye, Captain."

"Noddy, pipe the sails and then fetch Brekk."

"Aye, Cap'n," responded the cabin boy, and he blew the command and then handed the whistle to James and sped away.

As the *Eroean* came to the new heading, Brekk stepped to the wheel, the Dwarf accoutered for combat. "Where away?"

Aravan pointed.

Brekk looked long, then glanced up at the pale blue Elven-silk against the somber skies.

Aravan said, "Armsmaster, we should know within half a glass whether this Rover will be foolish or wise."

Brekk grunted and said, "We will be ready."

Then the Dwarf made a circuit of the ship to all the ballistas, readying the crews of missile casters for battle.

Steadily the Kistanian ship ran downwind west-southwest, and just as steadily the *Eroean* haled crosswind, northeasterly, up and toward the track of the freebooter. Time eked by, and still the Rover ran on his straight course, as did the Elvenship.

"Keep her on our beam, Nikolai."

"Aye, Captain."

"Wooly?"

"Aye, Captain, I'm ready, too."

"James?"

"Ready as well, Captain."

"Then pipe away."

Gradually the *Eroean* headed up into the stiff wind, now running on an easterly reach. Still the crimson-sailed pirate fared southwesterly, running downwind, the vessel now nearing the Elvenship.

Of a sudden the raider changed course and fled toward the Isle of Kistan.

Down on the main deck, "Kruk!" barked Brekk. "Cowards all. She is afraid to take on *Eroean*."

Beside him, Dokan said, "I think the Rover captain didn't even see us until she was nigh upon us."

Once again, Brekk glanced up at the cerulean sails against the dark grey skies, and then down at the indigo hull. Finally he looked toward the fleeing ship. Then he sighed and said, "Sometimes I wish we were harder to see."

Ten days later in the heart of the night the *Eroean* haled into the wide waters of Hile Bay, and she docked at one of the stone piers below the city of Pendwyr.

All the next day and the one after the cargo was unladed, and new ballast was taken on to replace the weight of the porcelain ware, for it would not do to have the *Eroean* turn turtle at the first strong wind or great wave. When the ship was empty of cargo and laden with the proper ballast, Aravan had her tugged away from the docks to anchor in the bay.

He set the crew free to "do the town," and knowing the crew as well as he did, he knew that most of them would try.

The very next morning, Aravan and Alyssa and Lissa and Vex all paid their respects to High King Ryon and Queen Dresha, Aylis and Lissa and Vex standing by as Dresha *ooh*ed and *aah*ed and murmured over the golden designs on black, while Aravan and Ryon stepped into the courtyard and flew arrows at distant targets.

After a private midday meal with the High King and his Queen, Aravan and Aylis and Lissa—the Pysk once again hidden in the hood of Aylis's cloak—and Vex on his string tether, went to the libraries of Caer Pendwyr to see what they could discover about the City of Jade.

They carried with them a small jade statuette on which was carved a haiku in a strange tongue:

Thrice I dreamt the dream
From the City of Jade I fled
Nought but shades now dwell

Over the Wall

Burglars
Early Summer, 6E9

With their captives encloaked, as the buccen softly trod along the alleyway, Pipper shook himself from his reminisces. *Yes, burglars we became: with me the planner and smoother of the way in, and Bink the lock picker*—Pip glanced at his cousin and grinned, remembering that time in the marketplace—*cutpurse, too. Oh, how Tark must've raged over that.*

Pipper gave a soft giggle and said, "Burglars and chicken thieves we are, Bink, and you a cutpurse." Then Pipper sobered and asked, "What have we become?"

Binkton softly growled and said, "We are robbing the robbers, Pip, dealing out just retribution and returning to the victims what is rightfully theirs; never forget that."

"Yes, but we are taking the law into our own hands, Bink, and that isn't right."

"In a lawless city, Pip, what else can we do?"

"Notify the High King," said Pipper. "That's what. I mean, surely he'd send King's Men in to clean things up."

Binkton nodded and said, "Well, now that we've identified the crime lord, what you say seems like a good idea. Remember what the *Ravenbook* says."

"It says a lot of things, Bink."

"I mean the part where Brega told Tuck and the others that if you cut off the serpent's head, the rest of the snake dies. Well, if the King arrests Rackburn and all his henchmen, including the city watch, clearly Rivers End will be better off."

"It will indeed," said Pipper. "And after we get back Lady Jane's silvers, let's go to Caer Pendwyr and tell the High King. Surely he will break the hold of Rackburn and his Rivermen on this town." Pipper stopped, stopping Binkton as well, and Pipper said, "Speaking of regaining Lady Jane's silvers, here's what I think we ought to do. . . ."

After Pipper explained his plan, he and Binkton fell to complete silence as they neared Rackburn's house. Binkton took control of all the chickens as Pipper climbed the wall. When he reached the spikes, he cautiously peered over the top. In the moonlight shining down and into the yard, he could see two of the dogs lounging on the grass. Of the third dog, there was no sign. *Oh, well, if my plan works, he'll soon show up.* Pipper turned and signaled Binkton, pointing to the places where lounged the dogs. Binkton then reached within one of the bundled cloaks and pulled out a chicken by its legs and flung it over the wall. As it flew squawking through the air, quickly Binkton threw a second and then a third. The yard erupted in uproar, as the mastiffs chased after the three fowl. Lanterns were lit, and a door slammed open, and several of the house guards came rushing out. With barking and squawking and chickens running about, dogs in pursuit, someone yelled, "Wot th—"

And another shouted, "Ar, it's that stupid Wingard's chickens got loose ag'in."

"Rip! Slash! Render!" bellowed a third, trying to get control of the dogs.

In the roaring, squawking, yelling chaos and confusion, Pipper slid to the alleyway and clapped his hand over his mouth to keep from laughing aloud, giggles escaping from between his fingers.

"Har! I got me a hen!" whooped one of the men. "We'll have us a meal tonight."

Then came a growl and a snap and the sound of bones breaking like twigs as a chicken squawked its last, and in that same moment one of the hens flew over the wall, escaping with her life. Loud barking followed after, as if one of the huge mastiffs stood with its paws up against the barrier.

Then there came the sound of two of the dogs fighting, perhaps over the remains of the slain chicken, and the shouting of men trying to separate the brutes.

In nearby houses along the alleyway, lanterns were lit and sashes were lowered and protesting shouts rang through the night from outraged people who had been awakened.

Finally, the snarling, raging, and cursing quieted. Candles and lanterns were extinguished. Sashes were drawn up. And the neighborhood fell silent again.

That was when Binkton hurled in the last chicken over the wall.

Once more the night air was filled with uproar, and when it finally fell silent again, the dogs had been locked in their kennel, and the house guards had returned to preparing their dinner, now with two hens for their meal.

Pipper threw the padded grapnel across and onto the balcony, where it landed with a light thump. Carefully he drew in the rope, until the hooks caught on the rail. Then he pulled the line tight and tied it off against one of the wall spikes.

"But, Pip," whispered Binkton, "why don't we just do it as first planned: over the wall, through the yard, and climb up the rope?"

"Because, even though they are in their kennel, the dogs are still down at that level. We need a way to cross over without alerting them."

Binkton growled, but said nothing in return.

"Come on," said Pipper, "let's go." And he stood atop the wall and lightly ran along the line to the balcony.

Dangling underneath and with his legs thrown over the rope and pulling himself by hand, Binkton followed. He had almost reached the balcony when the door below opened.

Still hanging under the line, Binkton froze in place up against the edge of the balcony.

One of the house guards, a burly man whistling tunelessly, walked across the yard and threw chicken entrails in to the dogs. As the mastiffs snarled and squabbled for a share, the man strode back through the grass and into the house. Never once had he looked up.

Binkton scrambled up and over the rail. He stood a moment, trembling. Pipper put a hand on Binkton's shoulder, but said nought. Finally,

Binkton took a deep breath, and then softly stepped to the left edge of the balcony and examined the window just beyond.

In moments he had the sash lowered into its recess, and the buccen silently clambered in.

They waited for their eyes to adjust to the enshadowed interior.

"Now to the strongbox," murmured Pipper, and he faced the far wall and said. "My guess is it's over behind the desk."

They padded across and around, where they found: "Bink," hissed Pipper. "Look—" Faintly in the shadows they could see the orange and yellow flames painted on the side of the large case. "—it's our chest."

"Those rat-eating, Rûck-loving sons of a Troll—" Binkton began, but Pipper shushed him to quietness.

Even as Binkton knelt to spring the lock, the door burst open and four men charged into the room, one of them bearing a lantern.

Pipper nearly made it to the window, and Binkton to the door, but they were snatched up by strong grips they could not break.

And as they were dragged back into the light, "Well, if it ain't the pip-squeaks," sneered Tark.

37

Doom

"Har!" shouted Queeker, holding the lantern even higher. "Wot're they doing here, I wonder? Lookin' for their chest, d'y'think?" Queeker broke into nasal snorts, even as Binkton and Pipper struggled to get free.

"What do you think, Tark?" asked the huge man who clutched Pipper to his chest. "Kill them? Break their scrawny necks?"

Even as Tark nodded, an older, gray-haired, thin, and rather bookish-looking man entered the room. "Kill them? No. Instead we'll wait until Largo gets back. He'll tell us what to do."

Tark made a scoffing sound, but otherwise said nothing.

"Oi, now!" exclaimed Queeker. "Maybe these two are the ones what's been taking our silvers."

Tark looked in amazement at Queeker. "By the crabs, I think you're right." Even as Queeker thrust out his bony chest and strutted about, Tark turned to the gray-haired man. "Brander, I think Queek has hit upon it: These are the thieves who've been robbing us."

Binkton snarled and started to speak, but Pipper cut his cousin off, shouting, "Silvers? What silvers? We came to get back our trunk."

Tark snorted and said, "Trunk? Ha! As if that matters."

Queeker crowed and said, "Oh, Tark, Largo's going to love us. I mean, we've caught ourselves the thieves."

Binkton shouted, "You're the thieves, not us."

"Downstairs with them," said the man called Brander. "We'll throw them in the hole till Largo gets back."

With Binkton yelling curses and both he and Pipper kicking and twisting and wrenching and flailing, the two brutes holding the Warrows carried them downstairs and into a room, where Queeker threw back a rug and Tark lifted a trapdoor and the two men dropped the buccen into a small, unlit, rock-walled chamber and slammed the lid shut.

As Binkton shouted epithets upward in the dark, with but a step or two Pipper found his way to one side of the cell, and he began pacing out the dimensions: six Warrow strides by seven. He discovered a cot along one wall, with an empty lidded chamber pot beneath, along with a bucket, perhaps for water.

"This is a dungeon, Bink," said Pipper, when his cousin paused in his cursing to take a breath. "Does that trapdoor have a lock?"

Binkton seethed for a moment, and then got control of his breathing and said, "Yes, but it's a hasp on the outside in a recess, with a shackle and a keylock. I saw it just before they chucked us in. There's no way I can reach it. Not unless we cut a hole in that rat-eating door up there."

Even though Binkton couldn't see him, Pipper nodded, and then asked, "Did you get anything?"

"Get anything?"

"When they were carrying us downstairs, did you manage to get anything off the one holding you?"

"Oh, Pip, I'm sorry. I was so angry, I didn't even think of that."

"Well, don't fret, Bink. I didn't get anything either."

Binkton fumbled his way toward Pipper's voice, and found him sitting on the cot. As he took a place beside his cousin, Binkton said, "We'll have to make our break when they take us out."

"*If* they take us out," said Pipper.

"Oh, Pip, do you think they'll leave us down here?"

"Who knows what those"—Pipper grimly smiled to himself— "rat-eating, Rûck-loving sons of Trolls will do to us?"

The Warrows talked of what they might use as a weapon, but only the privy pot and water bucket came to hand, and neither one had a bail. The cot itself was built into the wall, and nothing could be broken away to use as a cudgel, and they couldn't find a single loose rock. Though Binkton still had the wire in his belt, he had lost his lockpick kit in the struggle upstairs, and neither he nor Pipper had even a cloak pin, for the pins, along with those garments, lay on the far side of the alley wall.

It seemed as if an endless time passed before the buccen heard a number of footsteps overhead, followed by a rattle and snick of a lock being opened and a hasp clacking back. The trapdoor lifted, and lantern light shone from above, and as the Warrows squinted in its brightness, a ladder came scraping down.

"All right, you two," snarled someone, Tark by the sound of his voice, "up here."

As they approached the bottom rung, Pipper whispered, "When you see a chance, Bink, take it."

As they clambered out from the tiny dungeon, they saw that one man stood before the closed door, and another at the window, each with a leashed mastiff in hand. Pipper's heart fell, for he knew they could not outrun the dogs, and even if they tried, with a snap and a crunch they would be brought down like the chickens running in the yard.

As soon as the buccen had emerged from the hole, Queeker and Tark stepped to one side and looked to their left, where gray-haired Brander stood to the right of a wing-back chair in which Rackburn sat. Largo was yet dressed in the finery he had worn when he had set out for the theater. He had black hair and dark eyes and a long, straight nose above the hint of a sardonic smile that touched his lips. With an elegance of motion, he tented his hands together, fingertip to fingertip, and canted his head to one side and peered at the Warrows. "So these are the burglars?"

"That's right, Mr. Rackburn, sir," said Queeker. "Snatched 'em right up, we did, 'cause they didn't know the windows and doors are connected by hidden bell cords to jinglies in the ward room. And we—"

Without taking his eyes off the buccen, Largo threw up a hand to stop Queeker's blathering. Then Rackburn once again tented his hands and said, "And you believe these are the ones who have been taking our . . . due?"

"Yes sir, we do," said Tark.

"Hmm. . . ." With a dark eye, Largo fixed Binkton and then Pipper. "What have you two to say for yourselves?"

"These rat-eating—" began Binkton, but Pipper cut in and said, "Tark and Queeker stole our chest. We were merely trying to recover our property."

Rackburn smiled and nodded. Then he reached into the inside breast pocket of his jacket and said, "If that's all you came for, then why carry this?" He held up Binkton's lockpick kit.

"Because you took Lady Jane's silvers!" blurted Binkton. "You're a bunch of Troll-begotten, Rûck-loving—"

Tark backhanded Binkton, knocking the Warrow sideways and down. One of the mastiffs snarled and lunged forward at the buccan, only to be brought up short by his handler's leash.

Largo lifted his right hand and snapped his fingers, and held open an upturned palm.

Brander gave him two small, capped bottles, each filled with a dark liquid.

"Force this down their throats," said Rackburn, holding the vials out to Queeker, who jumped forward to take the little containers.

Tark jerked Binkton to his feet, and Queeker uncorked one of the vials as Tark forced the buccan's head back. Queeker reached forward, bottle in hand, but Binkton slapped it aside, knocking it flying, and the thin glass shattered when it hit the wall, the dark liquid running down.

Tark smashed a fist into Binkton's temple, and the buccan fell unconscious to the floor.

"Bink!" yelled Pipper, and he sprang toward his cousin. But Tark caught Pipper up and grabbed him by the hair and jerked his head back. This time Queeker held tightly to the second vial, and he poured the contents in and clapped a hand across Pipper's mouth.

Pipper struggled and tried not to swallow the bitter fluid, all in vain, for the men were just too strong. In the end he could not help himself, and the liquid burned his throat on the way down.

Almost immediately the sides of the room seemed to draw inward. Darkness descended, and his knees gave way, and his mind began to fall toward blackness. Even though he could no longer see, he could yet hear, as one of the men asked, "What next?"

Rackburn answered: "Weight them down and take them out to sea and throw them in."

"Out to sea, boss?" asked one of the henchmen.

"That's what I said," replied Rackburn.

"Whatever for?" asked Tark. "Why not just cut their throats and throw them into delta mud for the crabs to strip?"

Suppressed rage sounded in Rackburn's voice. "Think, fool, think. The last thing we need is for a pair of Warrows to be found slain anywhere near Rivers End. It would call the attention of the High King, and that's the last thing we want to happen."

"He's right, Tark," said Queeker. "I hear tell ever since the big Dragonstone War, the Warrows, they be favorites of King Ryon."

Pipper could hear as Tark gritted his teeth, but then all consciousness fled.

Half-aware, the side of his head hurting there where Tark had hit him, Binkton heard the *chank* of heavy links clacking together, and felt something being fastened to his ankle. Then a manacle clicked shut on his left wrist. Someone lifted him up, and a voice said, "Throw 'em over, Tark. Throw 'em over." And then he was hurled outward.

Binkton came fully awake as he struck the water and, even as he realized his wrist was shackled to Pipper's, the remaining length of a long, heavy chain splashed into the water beside them, and it jerked Binkton under by his left ankle as it plunged toward the bottom, Binkton dragging Pipper along as down through the water they plummeted. Swiftly Binkton withdrew the wire from his belt and poked the sharply angled tip into the wide key slot on the ankle lock. *Come on, bucco, come on!*

He felt the tine catch on the single tumbler, and with a sharp twist the shackle sprang open. The chain fell away and continued to plunge onward, as Bink clamped the pickwire between his teeth and began kicking and stroking upward with one hand, dragging Pipper along by the manacle that held them together.

Binkton desperately needed to breathe, but there was no air.

Above he could see a glimmer of light, as if day had come.

Swim, bucco, swim, else you and Pip will drown.

Upward he stroked, and upward, Pipper a deadweight, but Binkton stroked and stroked one armed, his lungs heaving but not breathing in, for his mouth was tightly clamped shut.

And then he broke through the surface and took in a great gulp of air past the wire held between his clenched teeth, even as he pulled Pip up into the sweet morning breeze.

Pip, though unconscious, had not taken in any water, and he started breathing on his own.

Binkton took the pickwire from his mouth and stabbed the angled end into the fetter on his wrist. And even as the manacle opened, from a distance Binkton heard laughter—Queeker's nasally whine riding above Tark's deep roar. And Binkton could see a white sail on a small skiff, faring away, heading toward the land the buccan could just see.

I need to get Pip to shore, but I can't let Queeker and Tark see me. Oh, Adon, Adon, let them not look back.

In between buoying Pipper up, Binkton kicked off his boots and shed his shirt, but kept on his trousers. Struggling, he stripped Pipper likewise. Then, towing Pip, Binkton rolled onto his back and began swimming after the craft. He swam for long moments before he rolled back over to sight on the land. By this time the skiff itself had drawn far away, and he no longer feared that Tark or Queeker would catch sight of him and Pipper.

Again he rolled onto his back, and stroked for long moments more, but when he rolled over to take another sighting, he could no longer see the land or the skiff itself, though he did spot the top of its mast.

What's this, bucco, where did the land go?

Once more he rolled onto his back and swam for what he thought might have been a quarter candlemark altogether. But when he again took a sighting, not only was the land gone, but even the top of the mast had disappeared.

"What's happening here, Pip?" he asked aloud, but, of course, Pip didn't answer.

Think, bucco, think. Surely you know the reason.

A moment later it came to him: *The Argon. The mighty Argon. It flows into the Avagon Sea, and we are caught in that current. Adon, but I cannot swim against the force of that flood. What will I do? What will I do? Oh, come on, Pip, wake up. I need you to have one of your harebrained schemes to get us out of this mess.*

Slowly a full candlemark passed, and Binkton, weary beyond his means, struggled to stay afloat.

"Oh, Pip, oh, Pip," he called aloud, "please wake up. I don't think I can hold out much longer."

And as Binkton strove to keep his head above water and keep Pipper's up too, the relentless spillage of the Argon River pushed them farther out into the deep blue indigo sea.

38

Nearing Vengeance

DARK DESIGNS
EARLY SPRING, 6E9

Safely locked away in his sanctum, such that none could do him harm, Nunde's body lay slack, unresponsive, but for shallow breathing. For anyone who had the <sight> to see, out from his abdomen trailed a thin, dark, aethyrial cord, no thicker than a fine hair, for Nunde's spirit soared far away.

And the Necromancer watched as Malik and his cohort of Drik and Chûn, with one of the four Oghi in the lead, hacked their way through the last mile of the tangle lying between them and their goal. That Malik ineffectually swatted at the swarms of bloodsucking flies and mosquitoes and swiped at whining gnats and scraped leeches from his legs was of no concern to Nunde. After all, Malik was but an apprentice—valuable, perhaps, but expendable at need. One day Malik might achieve enough knowledge to strike out on his own, but that day lay far in the future; it certainly was not here yet. And by that time, Nunde himself would be so powerful that neither Malik nor anyone else would pose a significant threat. Why, Nunde would slap him down just as Malik had slapped that bloated thing feeding upon his cheek, leaving behind nought but a crimson smear and scarlet droplets oozing from the hole lingering in his skin.

After seeing that Malik neared the destination, Nunde sped on ahead. And before him, rearing up from the jungle, lay the pristine tower, made of stone so smooth and so seamlessly joined that no plant, no vine, not even lichen could gain a foothold upon its flawless surface.

To the top of the tower soared Nunde, and through one of the four cardinal arches carved in the dome and into the open chamber beyond. Ah, yes, his chosen one yet remained in place upon the pedestal.

I will call upon you if needed, crooned Nunde as his aethyrial self circled 'round, knowing that if he did so, it would take much <life force> to cast the spell that would loose and then cage the creature again, and would drain Nunde's astral being dreadfully. Yet he would not make the same mistake as that fool of a Sorcerer had made, for at that time the city had been laid to waste by an imperfectly cast conjuration. It was only by the efforts of many of Magekind in the years after that the warder had been confined again. As to the original imperfectly cast summoning that had set the warder free, the imbecile who had done so had paid with his life. Nunde knew that he would have to expend the <essence> to prevent the same fate from happening to him.

Then away he fled, back toward his sanctum. Nunde would have liked to find Aravan and see what that fool of a Dohl was up to. Surely by now he had taken the bait. Yet Nunde would not risk the gamble, for not only did Aravan have that cursed blue amulet that might warn him that Nunde was nearby, but he also was accompanied by the whore Aylis, a Seer with the <sight>. And Nunde would not reveal his aethyrial self to her. Oh, no. She was, after all, the one who had helped Aravan ruin all of Nunde's carefully laid plans in Neddra that hideous night when Aravan and his host attacked the Black Fortress.

Nunde smiled. In fact, he was depending upon that stupid trollop to help spring the trap he himself had devised. She *was* a Seer, after all.

What was it now? Seven, eight years since he had conceived his brilliant scheme?

To some that might seem a long time.

But Nunde was patient.

It didn't matter how long Malik and his cohort had to wait there in the steaming environs. After all, they were nought but lackeys, and obeying Nunde's slightest whim was the why of their very existence.

All this and more did Nunde contemplate as he sped back to his sanctum.

His trap was nearly laid.

Aravan would meet his doom.

39

Under Way

Aravan and Aylis and Lissa spent days upon days going through the ancient archives in the libraries of Caer Pendwyr, those that had survived the burning and destruction of the Winter War, when Caer Pendwyr had fallen to the Southerlings—Hyrinians, Kistanians, Chabbains, and the Fists of Rakka, all under the sway of Gyphon's surrogate Modru. But that was just over a millennium past, and the libraries had recovered some of the knowledge lost, though many ancient scrolls and tomes were gone forever.

The librarians had looked askance at Aylis leading a tethered fox into the buildings, yet the High King had sent word that whatever Aravan and Aylis did was under his personal aegis. And so the librarians had grumbled at this vermin being in their domain; still they had said nought. It wasn't until Vex had slaughtered a goodly number of rats and mice that the staff began considering getting a fox of their own, for after all there were vermin and there were vermin, and rats and mice shredded documents to build their nests, while foxes did not. Then again, there were those cats in the cities of Khem that were said to deal death to vermin as well, so perhaps . . .

Deep in one of the subbasements of the central library, where they had been directed by an ancient archivist, "Look here," said Aylis, whispering so as to not waken Lissa, the Pysk asleep in a pigeonhole of a nearby escritoire, Vex dozing 'neath. "It mentions the City of Jade."

She and Aravan stood at a waist-high scroll-scattered table, a lantern sitting thereon.

By the cast of yellow light, Aravan peered at the ancient broken clay tablet Aylis held. "What language is that?"

"I'm not certain," she replied. "But it is similar to the one scribed 'round the base of the statuette."

Aravan frowned. "Now that I think on it, the script looks somewhat like the runes of Jûng. That language I speak and read, for several times I rode through in my search for the yellow-eyed man. Yet, from those runes I know, these seem to be a much older form . . . ancient, I deem. What does it say?"

" 'In the near west lies the City of Jade, a place rich in spoils, but with a dreadful—' " Aylis looked up and said, "There is no more. Whatever else it might say is gone, broken away."

"Something dreadful there, neh?"

"That's what it says."

"Then it seems to correspond to the warning on the statuette. I deem this tablet might have told why the city was abandoned, what might have been so dreadful."

Aylis nodded and said:

> *"Thrice I dreamt the dream*
> *From the City of Jade I fled*
> *Nought but shades now dwell."*

Long had they speculated on the last line of the haiku, yet they had nought but conjecture as to why someone had fled from something in the lost city—be it disease, drought, invaders, madness, or other such.

Aravan glanced at the shard and asked, "Canst thou do a <seeing>?"

"I was just about to suggest that," said Aylis, smiling.

Aravan looked deep into her gold-flecked eyes. "I would not have it tax thee, Chier."

"I think it will not, though this tablet seems to be quite ancient and might take a while."

Aravan gently held her hand. "I would not have thee swoon, my love."

"Swoon I might," said Aylis, returning his concerned gaze, "yet how else can we discover what we might?"

Aravan looked about the shelves jammed with dusty clutter, and he turned up a hand of surrender.

Saying that the closer to the floor the less distance to fall, Aylis sat upon the tiles. Aravan knelt at her side. She pressed the shard between her palms and then spoke a word. After long moments she muttered an utterance in the tongue of Jûng, though an archaic form of that language.

[In the near west lies the City of Jade, a place rich in spoils, but with a dreadful past. Only shades and shadows now dwell therein. Citizens of Jûng, beware.]

Aylis took a deep breath and seemed to come to herself. "There is no more, my love. Yet I deem this a clear warning."

Aravan frowned. "We know little more than we did ere now."

Aylis nodded and then said, "Perhaps it is nothing more than a legend to keep looters away," said Aylis.

"Mayhap," said Aravan. Then he fell into thought and finally said, "So from somewhere in Jûng, the City of Jade lies nearby to the west."

Aravan suddenly stood and looked at marks on the bottom of the statuette. "I ween I know where this is." He turned and held an aiding hand out to Aylis and said, "Up, Chier. The maps on the *Eroean* will say yea or nay."

On her feet, Aylis wakened Lissa and Vex, and within moments they exited the library and headed for the switchback road down to the docks, where they would row out to where the Elvenship was moored.

It took several days to round up the crew, Long Tom and Brekk and several Dwarves scouring the taverns and bordellos and other such low places for those who had not answered the recall flag on the *Eroean*. But at last, all came aboard, some carried over the shoulders of others.

They sailed on the evening tide of an early summer day, and as the ship hauled out from Hile Bay, the second bosun, Noddy, asked, "Where be we bound, Cap'n? What be th' set o' th' silks?"

Aravan glanced at Noddy and then at Helmsman Tarley. "With this northerly wind, I would have ye keep the shore of Pellar a league or so off our starboard. When we pass the point of Thell Cove, we'll run straight for Port Arbalin. There we might make a short layover, no more than a candlemark or two; then we'll head for our next destination."

"And what might that be, Cap'n?" asked Tarly.

"We'll talk about that as we approach Arbalin," replied Aravan, "for I would propose the mission to the entire crew, one with an unknown danger, mayhap. And those who would forgo such a venture will be let ashore, while the remainder will go on."

Just after mid of night on the second day out, the wind slowly shifted 'round from the north to finally flow out of the west and toward the east, directly against the *Eroean*. Noddy and Tarley, again on duty, looked to Nikolai, who said, "Tack nor'west, by damn. We run that way to dawn, then back sou'west. In all, ship take four tack to Arbalin."

"What about th' Argon, Nick?" asked Tarley. "Th' flow be against us."

"Aye," replied Nikolai, "but flow with us when make next tack."

And so Noddy piped the sails to the night crew, and Tarley spun the wheel over.

Dawn arrived, and Fat Jim took the helm, and Long Tom the watch. First Bosun James appeared and assumed his duty, as did the day crew. Aravan came adeck as they piped the sails about to run southwesterly, and the *Eroean* tacked across the wind to take up the next leg.

In the second candlemark after making the turn, the foremast lookout cried, "Somethin' in the water, Cap'n, nigh dead ahead."

As Aravan and Long Tom strode to the base of the stem, the lookout added, "A bit starboard, sir. Oh, cor blimy, it looks to be a swimmer . . . no, wait a moment, it be two children!"

Aravan, with his keen Elven sight, peered ahead and slightly to the right to catch sight of the pair.

"Cap'n, they're sinking."

Of a sudden, from a bright flash of light, a falcon sprang, and hurtled ahead of the ship. O'er the water it sped to where the two had just gone down, and then in another flash of light, Aravan appeared and plummeted into the sea.

"Lower a boat," shouted Long Tom, racing to the starboard davits. "Now, by damn! Now!"

As sailors sprang to obey, Long Tom grabbed three crewmen and shoved them into the boat, leaping in after. "Faster, by damn, faster!"

Even as the dinghy dropped ten feet to the water, Long Tom yelled up, "Have Fat Jim and James heave to nearby." Then he grabbed an oar and turned to the crewmen in the boat with him. "Row, you sea dogs, row!"

Aravan arrowed down into the depths, stroking deeper into the water, all clarity clouded by the Argon outflow. *There!* Two forms, one clinging to the other, came into hazy view, and down Aravan plunged.

He caught both of them, and kicking and with one arm thrusting, the other holding the pair, he turned upward.

Moments later, he burst through the surface and took a great gulp of air, and then he looked at these children—Nay! Not children, but two buccen Waerlinga instead. And neither of them were breathing.

Long Tom and the crewmen pulled alongside, and Aravan let the big man take the two aboard, and then he clambered over the wale after.

With Tom working on one Warrow, and Aravan on the other, they turned them facedown to press water out from their lungs and then face-up and began breathing into them.

One of the buccen, the one with dark hair, the one with Long Tom, began hacking immediately, while the fair-haired one with Aravan exhaled a long sigh and gave a slight cough and began breathing on his own; but he did not come to. The Elf measured the Waerling's pulse beat, and gauged his breathing, and then, cradling the wee one's head in his lap, Aravan sat back and relaxed.

The other Warrow broke free of Long Tom and scrambled forward and cried, "Pip . . . Pip . . . Pipper . . . are you . . . all right?" the words ejected between wheezes and hacks.

But Pipper said nought, slack and unconscious as he was.

"He is safe, my small friend," said Aravan, "as art thou."

At these words, the dark-haired Warrow began coughing again and fell back against Long Tom. Moments passed ere the buccan got control of his breathing, and then he closed his emeraldine eyes and slumped wearily, as if on the verge of a swoon.

Even as Tom held the Warrow, the big man frowned and looked at Aravan and asked, "What'n th' w'rld was these two doin' way out here?"

With a free hand he gestured 'round and said, "Oi mean, there be no land nowhere near, and there be no flotsam from no sunk ship 'round about, neither. How did they get here? 'N' why ain't that one awake?"

Aravan looked down at the fair-haired Waerling. "I detected a faint trace of Nightlady on his breath."

"Noightliady? 'E wos drugged?"

Aravan nodded. "It would seem so."

"'N' j'st who moight've did that, eh?"

The dark-haired Warrow, without opening his viridian eyes, murmured, "Rûck-loving, rat-eating thieves did it, that's who. Rûck-loving . . . rat-eating . . ." His voice dwindled to a whisper, and he fell into exhausted sleep.

And there was nought to wake him or the other buccan but the quiet plash and pull and plash and pull of the oars as the crewmen rowed back to the ship.

40

Recruits

The men who had rowed the longboat fastened the davit hooks through the eyelets in the bow and stern, and other crewmen aboard the *Eroean* hoisted all up and to the rails. Quietly, Aravan and Long Tom handed the two buccen from the craft and into the waiting arms of Brekk and Dokan, who cradled the Waerans like wee bairns and took them below to the warband's quarters and laid them in hammocks. The ship's chirurgeon, a Gothan named Desault, stripped their wet breeks from them and wrapped the Warrows in blankets, then measured their pulses and thumbed back eyelids in the shining lantern light; he listened to their breathing and felt the cool of their pale flesh.

"We'll need to chafe them a bit to raise their warmth," said Desault.

As Aylis began rubbing the dark-haired one, and Aravan did the other, the chirurgeon pointed at the fair-haired buccan and added, "By the look of that one's pupils, Captain, I think he was drugged."

Aravan nodded and said, "His breath carries a faint trace of Night-lady, Desault. What of the other? He was conscious for a while after Long Tom got him breathing again."

"Him? I think he's just spent beyond his means to stay awake."

"Oi'd guess he moight o' been keepin' t'other one afloat," said Tom. "Oi mean, th' cap'n here says he wos still holdin' on when they went under. So as Oi suspect, he wos keepin' hisself 'n' t'other abobbin' f'r a good bit o' toime, he wos, Oi guess, Oi would, Oi do."

"Well, if the other is indeed drugged, he must have been keeping them both up," said Desault. "And I'd say he was long at it, for he is truly totally spent. I would think that all they each need is rest, one to get past the Nightlady, the other simply to recover from his ordeal. When they waken, they'll need warm drink, and mayhap a bit of broth, as well as a small bite to eat."

"I'll tell Cook," said Dinny, one of the two new cabin boys taken aboard when Noddy was promoted, Ebert being the other new boy. "Tea and honey and biscuits and soup 'tis." Dinny bolted up the ladder and out.

"I'll remain here awhile," said the chirurgeon.

"I'll sit with you, Desault," said Aylis.

"I'll stay as well," said Lissa, "though what I might be able to do, I can't say."

"Liss, you can let us know when they waken," said Aravan.

"Er, Cap'n," said Long Tom, "d'y' want them t'see that we've a Pyskie aboard? Oi mean, all th' crew be sworn t'secrecy, 'n' these two be not."

Aravan looked down at Lissa. "When they begin to come around, find me and then take to thy quarters. Though I deem we've nought to fear from Waerlinga, still I would they be sworn ere revealing your existence to them."

Lissa grinned and sketched a salute and said, "Aye-aye, Captain."

"I believe that's enough chafing," said Desault. "Their color is now good. We'll just wrap them in their blankets; that should be enough."

Moments later, Aravan and Long Tom headed for the ladder, Long Tom asking, "What be our course, now, Cap'n?"

"We still ply for Port Arbalin," replied Aravan.

It was late in the night when, "I have to pee," muttered Pipper. He groaned and opened his sapphirine eyes. "I have to—" He gasped and bolted upright. "Bink! Bi—! Ooh, I'm dizzy."

Pipper caught a glimpse in the lantern light of what seemed to be a fox darting away. He rubbed his face and looked again, but it was gone. Then he saw a beautiful female sitting nearby and just then rousing from a doze. Was she a Human? An Elf? Something in between? At that moment she opened her eyes and smiled at him.

"Wh-what happened?" asked Pipper, looking about at the swaying hammocks.

"You were drugged," said the female.

"Where am—? I'm on a ship!" blurted the buccan in realization.

Aylis stood and stepped to his side. " 'Tis the *Eroean*."

"The Elvenship?"

Aylis nodded.

"Oh, my, the Elvenship," breathed Pipper. "I've got to tell Bink. Where's Bink?" His voice took on an edge of panic as he wildly looked about. "Where's Bink?"

"Your friend?"

"Yes, my— Oh, there he is. He's on the *Eroean*, too?" Then Pipper said, "Oh, Bink would say you are a ninny, Pip, that's what. Of course he's on the *Eroean*, too."

"We plucked you both from the sea," said Aylis.

"From the sea? The last thing I remember is Tark and Queeker forcing me to take a drink of Rackburn's foul-tasting stuff."

"Forcing you to take a drink of Nightlady?"

"Look, I'll tell you all about it, but right now I have to take a— Um, er . . . I say, is there a privy nearby?"

Aylis laughed and said, "We thought you might need to go, and we've a chamber pot at hand."

"Wull, then I'll . . ." Pipper started to throw off his blankets but quickly covered up again. "Hoy, now, where's my clothes? I mean, I can't go traipsing about naked as a loon."

Aylis smiled and said, "I'll turn my back. The privy pot is right there."

She listened as he swung down from his hammock and, on unsteady feet, lurched the few steps to the privy pot. He made water for what seemed a very long time, and Aylis wondered how someone that small could hold that much. But at last she heard him stumble back and, with a grunt, swing up into the hammock. A moment later he said, "Now, if you don't mind, I'd like to dress and make certain that Bink is all right."

She turned about to find him once again under his blanket, his eyes closed. "I'm afraid," said Aylis, "the only thing we found you in were breeks."

"Breeks? No boots, no jerkin, no—"

"Just breeks."

"Well, if you could bring me—"

Roused by the noise, "What th—?" exclaimed Binkton, sitting up and then wildly grabbing at nought but thin air as the hammock flipped over and he fell out to hit the deck with a muffled thud. As he groaned to his feet and fought his way free of his blanket, he shouted to no one in particular, "Are we on a blasted rat-eating ship?"

By this time, Pipper had raised up enough to see Binkton, with the Human, the Elf, the whatever, now on one knee at his side. "Are you injured?" she asked.

"What?" Binkton whirled around and snarled, "Am I—?" But in that moment he discovered he was naked and facing a kneeling female. "Oh, goodness." He grabbed at his blanket to cover himself.

In that same moment, Aravan clambered down the ladder to the peals of Aylis and the fair-haired Waerling's laughter, while the dark-haired buccan seethed and glared at the two.

The Warrows slept the rest of that night and most of the following day, Pipper casting off the dregs of Nightlady, and Binkton recovering from his ordeal. That evening they told Captain Aravan of the events leading up to their near drowning in the Avagon Sea:

". . . and then they threw us overboard, the two of us shackled together, a great weighty chain dragging us down, Pip entirely unconscious. But I picked the lock on the chain and— Oi, now, wait a moment. Why, those dirty, rat-eating blighters, Pip, I'll wager it was our very own chain I sent to the bottom."

Pipper managed an "I wouldn't know, Bink," around a mouthful of soup-sopped bread.

"Our lock, too!" shouted Binkton in ire.

Aravan waited for the pique to subside, then asked, "And thou didst say this man, this Largo Rackburn, is the one responsible?"

"Yes," seethed Binkton. "He and Tark and Queeker and others. But it's Rackburn behind it all, him and his gang of ruffians, threatening shopkeepers and landlords and peddlers and whoever else they can take from."

Aravan and Aylis and the two buccen sat on the low foredeck of the *Eroean*, Pipper and Binkton now dressed in their breeks but nought else, their jerkins and boots and socks having gone into the sea. Yet the night was mild, and a light southern breeze spilled over the larboard bow and brought comforting warmth with it. A half-moon rode overhead, shedding silvery light down upon the decks.

The buccen's state of undress would not last long, for the sailmakers and leather workers had taken their measures and were even then sewing shirts and trews and cobbling footwear.

Aylis smiled at the fuming Warrow and said, "But you, Binkton, and you, Pipper, you took from them and gave back to those who had been wronged? Nicely done, I say. Nicely done."

Binkton, pulled from his vexation by her smile, nodded and said, "I'd rather you just call me Bink and him Pip."

Pipper managed a nod, even though he was at that moment taking a sip from his cup of tea. No sooner had he a mouthful than he choked and hacked and coughed and pointed, trying to say something, though it seemed more as if he were strangling. As Aravan patted the buccan on his back, Pipper finally managed, "B-Bink! Look. A tiny person."

Aravan laughed and said, "For a Waerling to dub someone else tiny, well . . ."

Lissa groaned and dropped her <wild-magic> cloaking shadow and said, "I forgot." She turned to Aravan and said, "I'm sorry."

But Aylis said, "Fear not, Liss; they have already taken the oath to reveal nought seen nor heard aboard the *Eroean*."

His mouth yet agape, Binkton stared at the Pysk, but Pipper, now past his choking fit and grinning with the wonder of looking upon someone so wee, said, "You forgot what?"

"That Warrows can see through Pysk darkness."

In that same moment, Vex scrambled up a ladder from belowdecks and came trotting toward Lissa.

"I *knew* I had seen a fox," said Pipper. "And now I know why." He turned to Aravan. "You've a Fox Rider aboard."

"Of course he's got a Fox Rider aboard," snapped Binkton, now past his own moment of awe.

"No, what I meant," said Pipper, "was why do you have a Fox Rider aboard, if I might ask—might I?"

"I am a scout," said the Pysk. "And by the bye, my name is Aylissa, but everyone calls me Liss or Lissa."

"Pipper Willowbank at your service," said Pipper, leaping to his feet and bowing, "but everyone calls me Pip. And that one over there is Binkton Windrow; but you can call him Bink."

Binkton, too, got to his feet and bowed, and Lissa curtseyed in return.

As Pipper and Binkton resumed their seats, Lissa clambered up the ladder to the foredeck and sat down as well, Vex curling up beside her. "A scout, you say," said Pipper. "Oh, I've always wanted to be a scout aboard the Elvenship. I mean, legend has it that way back when, Warrows were known to do such."

Aravan nodded. "Aye, 'tis true. Betimes in the High King's First Era, I did sail with Waerlinga as scouts, for none can move quieter than they."

"Hmph," snorted Lissa. "Not even Pysks?"

Aravan held a hand out level and waggled it. "Wert thou afoot, mayhap so, but afox, I think not."

Lissa cast a skeptical eye, but said nought.

Aravan turned a speculative look upon the buccen. "Ye didst say ye performed as Fire and Iron. And thou, Binkton, canst pick locks?"

"Haven't come across one yet that I couldn't open," said Binkton proudly.

Pipper nodded in agreement and said, "It was all part of our act. Why, as a challenge, Bink even broke out of the gaol cell they have in Raudhöll. Opened the Dwarven shackles, too."

"Thou didst pick the locks in Redhall?"

Binkton grinned and nodded.

"Hai!" said Aravan, casting the buccan a salute.

"Is that a difficult thing to do?" asked Aylis.

"Well," said Binkton, "I don't like to brag, but—"

"It took him four candlemarks," blurted Pipper, all agog at the skill of his cousin. "Whereas, in the Human gaols"—Pipper snapped his fingers—"it took but mere moments."

As Aylis covered her smile with her fingers, her eyes dancing in merriment, Binkton sighed and said, "Pip's right. It took a while, but I finally did get loose."

"To open Dwarven fetters and one of their gaol doors in but four candlemarks is quite remarkable," said Aravan.

"Well, I would have done it sooner," said Binkton, "but all I had left after the Dwarves searched me was but a piece of bent wire."

Aravan rocked back in amazement, while Aylis and Lissa and Pipper clapped in applause.

Even as Binkton blushed in response, Aravan now turned his gaze upon Pipper. "And thou art an acrobat?"

Now Binkton bubbled over and said, "Pip can tumble and juggle and he walks tightropes and swings from trapezes and makes incredible flying leaps from one to another at heights that take your breath away and all without a net, too. And he's the one who figured out how to get into places where we retrieved the stolen coin, and some of those were quite tricky. —Oh, and he thinks up these clever illusions, to make it seem we've done something impossible."

"Ar, but you are the master of the sleight of hand, and can pick pockets and juggle, too, though not at the same time," said Pipper, "to say nothing of managing to get out of the tightest bindings, as well as chains and locks." He turned to Aravan and said, "We were taught by our Uncle Arley."

Aravan cocked an eyebrow. "Was his name Arley Willowbank? And didst thine uncle spend some time in Caer Pendwyr?"

Pipper nodded and said, "Lots of other places, too."

Aravan smiled. "If I be not mistaken, thine Uncle Arley was an agent of the High King."

Both Binkton's and Pipper's mouths dropped agape. "He was?" asked Pipper, while Binkton said, "Of the High King?"

Aravan nodded. "He was oft sent on missions where places needed to be gotten into and locks picked and items found or retrieved."

Aylis turned to Aravan. "He was a King's thief?"

"Indeed," said Aravan. "His public performances were merely his way of allaying suspicion as to his real endeavors."

"But we just thought he was . . ." said Pipper, his words falling to a whisper. But then a puzzled look filled his face and he looked at Aravan and asked, "Well, why wouldn't he tell us so?"

"Because, my friends," said Aravan, "the High King isn't supposed to condone thievery, much less have one or more of his own thieves at his beck and call. Your uncle was one of these."

"See, Pip?" said Binkton. "What we did in Rivers End wasn't so bad after all. I mean, like uncle, like nephews."

"Yes," said Pipper, "but he was working for the King."

"And who's to say we weren't?"

Aylis grinned and said, "For all practical purposes you were . . . at least, in your own way."

"What were they doing in Rivers End?" asked Liss.

"Taking ill-gotten gains from thieves and returning them to those who had been wronged."

"Good!" declared Lissa.

"Speaking of those Rûck-loving, rat-eating thieves," said Binkton, "I can't wait to get back to Rivers End and deal with Rackburn and Tark and Queeker and the others."

"And get our stuff back, too," said Pipper.

"Stuff?" asked Lissa.

"The gear for our act," said Pipper.

"All but the chain and lock and shackles now lying at the bottom of the Avagon," gritted Binkton. "Just get me a bow and Pip a sling and we'll make 'em pay for that."

"Ho, now, wait but a moment," said Aravan. "Stealing from thieves is one thing, but mayhap ye should think ere killing without a warrant. —Not that I haven't done the same, yet—"

"Yet, nothing!" spat Binkton. "Those that deserve death will—"

Aravan threw out a hand to stay Binkton's words and asked, "Have ye twain e'er slain brigands?"

Binkton looked at Pipper, each one paling. Finally, Binkton said, "Three on the road in Gûnar. I slew two, Pipper one. Five of them tried to rob the Red Coach we were on. None of them survived."

"It was awful," said Pipper, his face yet ashen, his gaze lost in remembrance.

"Aye, 'tis. Taking a life in self-defense be one thing, but to murder be another thing entirely."

"What about killing someone or something that needs killing?" asked Binkton. "I mean, surely someone like Rackburn should be laid by the heels, even without a warrant."

"Mayhap. I admit that I have done so on occasion. Of recent when two of thy Kind had been poisoned by a wicked emir across the Karoo. Yet it is not a decision to be made lightly."

"Well, I want Tark and Queeker to meet their just ends," said Binkton. "I mean, they would have murdered Pipper and me had I not been quick with a piece of wire. We almost drowned as it was, but for you."

Aravan fell into thought and after a moment said, "Let me propose this, my friends: we are on a mission that might be perilous; make no mistake about that. Yet we are not certain that the danger ever was or, if it was, yet exists; on that, we cannot say. Regardless, our mission might call for someone who can open the unopenable, and might require someone who can breach the unbreachable. Ye twain were trained by the best for doing so, and we can use such skills."

Bink started to protest, but Aravan said, "I would have ye consider doing this: write down all ye know as to Rackburn's illicit activities. We will then give the record to King Ryon's agent in Port Arbalin as to the doings in Rivers End, and let him call for the High King to intervene."

"Won't King Ryon need witnesses?" asked Aylis. "In addition to any documents Bink and Pip might provide, I think he would ask for some people in Rivers End to speak to these vile deeds. And if the merchants and landlords and such are sufficiently cowed, then—"

"The urchins!" blurted Pipper. "Tope and Weasel and Cricket and Squirrel and the others. They'll tell what's going on. —Oh, and Lady Jane, too."

"Urchins?" asked Lissa.

"Children living by their wits on the streets of Rivers End," said Pipper. "They were our allies against the ruffians: they followed the 'collectors' on their rounds and found out where they lived, so that Bink and I could regain the stolen coin. The merchants were kind enough to reward us for doing so, and we in turn passed most of that compensation to the urchins for food and drink and clothes and other needs. I'm certain that they will be glad to bear witness against Rackburn and his ilk."

Binkton let out a burst of air and said, "But, Pip, I'd rather personally see Rackburn and the others get what's coming to them, instead of putting the burden on our friends."

"What about the city watch?" asked Aylis. "Where were they when these ruffians were afoot?"

"Ar, the watch was deep into the pockets of Rackburn and company," growled Binkton.

"Oh, it'll take the Kingsmen to set things right," said Pipper. "I mean, we had decided to go to High King Ryon straightaway after we finished with Rackburn, but his henchmen caught us in the act." Pipper turned to Binkton and said, "Oh, don't you see, Bink, we were going to get the High King to clean up the city anyway, and Captain Aravan's plan will do the very same thing."

"Yeah, but we won't be there to see it, to see Rackburn and the others get what they deserve, especially Tark and Queeker."

Pipper frowned and then brightened. "Tell you what, Bink: let's sail with the *Eroean* on this mission. I mean, Captain Aravan says he can use someone of our skills, and who better than the nephews of a King's thief? And when we get back, well, we'll just go and visit Tark and Queeker in the High King's gaol and show them that they failed to kill us, and tell them what we did to bring about their downfall."

Binkton smiled. "Oh, that would be sweet. I can just imagine the surprise on their faces."

"If they haven't been hanged," said Aravan.

"Oh," said Binkton. "I hadn't thought of them being hanged."

Aylis's heart reached out to these Warrows as she looked at the buccen's faces, gone ashen at the thought of anyone being hanged, even the two who deserved it.

Finally, Binkton looked at Pipper and nodded, and Pipper turned to Aravan and said, "Well, Captain, it seems you have two more crew to feed."

"Welcome aboard," said Aravan, smiling.

And even as the buccen grinned and Lissa clapped her hands, the foremast lookout called, "Land ho, Cap'n. Port Arbalin be dead ahead."

41

Fair Warning

When the Isle of Arbalin hove into view, Aravan called for the *Eroean* to heave to and, as the ship glided to a halt, he ordered a general muster. After the crew entire had assembled, warband and sailors alike, Aravan stepped to the forerail of the aftdeck and said, "I remind ye of the oaths ye have taken. Do ye affirm?"

All called out their yeas, including a Pysk and two Warrows, as well as a female Mage.

"This then I would tell ye: in the City of Janjong, Lady Aylis came upon a jade statuette"—Aravan held the figurine up high—"and wound 'round the base is a strange poem, Ryodoan in nature, yet the words are not written in that tongue. The carver who fashioned the statue claims that he knew not what they meant, yet carve them he did, for they came to him in a compelling dream. Lady Aylis translated the verse, and these are the words:

> *"Thrice I dreamt the dream*
> *From the City of Jade I fled*
> *Nought but shades now dwell."*

A mutter murmured about the deck, Humans and Dwarves looking at one another, and glancing at Warrow and Pysk as well.

"This we do know," continued Aravan, recapturing the quiet. "The

City of Jade lives in legend—a place rich in that precious stone. Yet where the city lies, none seems to know. But on the base of this carving are lines which might or might not represent its locale.

"Lady Aylis, Lady Aylissa, and I went to the libraries in Caer Pendwyr, and we did find something else of the City of Jade: 'twas an ancient clay tablet that warns the citizens of Jûng to beware."

Aravan turned to Aylis and nodded, and she stepped forward to stand beside the captain and intoned, " 'In the near west lies the City of Jade, a place rich in spoils, but with a dreadful past. Only shades and shadows now dwell therein. Citizens of Jûng, beware.' "

Again a ripple of muttering washed throughout the crew. As it died down and before anyone could ask, Aylis added, "We know not why the city was abandoned, be it disease, madness, drought, war, or other such. The clay tablet might have been written simply to keep looters away."

From amid the crew, Dinny called out, "Wot be these here shades, Cap'n? Be they ghosts? I mean, a shade is a ghost or suchlike."

Several of the sailors made warding signs at this suggestion.

Aravan glanced at Aylis, and she shrugged. "We know not what is meant by shades and shadows dwelling therein," replied Aravan. "Referring to ghosts might merely be to keep seekers away. 'Tis a mystery, I say, for we found nought else in the libraries concerning the City of Jade but the fables told to children at their mothers' knees."

Pipper leaned over to Binkton and murmured, "I think fables often have their roots in things real."

"Pshh," scoffed Binkton. "Like the River Serpent, I shouldn't wonder."

"Oh, that was real," said Pipper, his eyes wide in memory.

"Bah. It was nothing but a wave."

"Oh, yeah? Well, then, Bink, why did you cry out like a youngling?"

"Did not."

"Did too."

"Did—" But Binkton fell silent as Aravan went on.

"This then I say: the *Eroean* will sail from Port Arbalin in but three days. Any and all who would not dare this found warning may stay behind, with no disgrace attached. As to whatever peril might be, it can be but something there or not. If not, then no doom will befall; if there, it might strike. If it strikes, mayhap we will defeat it, mayhap not. Even if we defeat it, there might be nothing of consequence to find. If we do not defeat it, we might all be slain, though some might live to flee. As ye can see, there are many unknowns, and so, upon this great lack of information, each of us must within three days decide to go on or not. It is a decision only each of us individually can make.

"Remember thine oaths and say nought in Port Arbalin as ye take shore leave, nor ought in all the days thereafter, lest I give ye leave. Yet know this: the *Eroean* sails on the evening tide three days hence."

With that he dismissed the crew and called for the ship to make sail again. And within a candlemark or so, the *Eroean* hove into the harbor at Arbalin Bay to drop anchor under the light of the moon.

42

Spy

DARK DESIGNS
EARLY SUMMER, 6E9

*H*as the vile Dolh yet taken the bait? Surely, he must have. The jade carving is in his murderous, god-slaying hands, and he would not resist the challenge.

From leagues away, an incorporeal Nunde watched as the *Eroean* sailed into the bay at Port Arbalin.

Nunde did not dare fly any closer, for Aravan's trollop could invoke <sight>, and Nunde would not risk being revealed. No, he would stay a safe distance away. In fact, from now on, he would track the ship in the candlemarks following mid of night, when the slattern was most likely to be asleep, or at least in her quarters wildly rutting with that execrable Dolh.

Nunde glanced up at the half-moon slipping toward the west, the lit face ebon to his astral gaze, and then he turned eastward to speed toward the place where he had commanded Malik to lie in wait.

Leagues passed and leagues more, but at last he came to the site, and indeed Malik and the Chûn were there, just as Nunde had ordered.

The Necromancer chortled unto himself, for surely none would escape this trap. Yet, if by some miracle the foul Dolh and his crew managed to prevail, there was always the dread creature in the tower, and *that* would of certain prove fatal to Aravan.

43

Augury

On the evening tide of the third day after mooring in Arbalin Bay, the *Eroean* weighed anchor and raised sails and haled away from the port city. During their stay, Binkton and Pipper had written all they knew of the corruption in Rivers End, listing dates and places and names, including those they thought would bear witness—urchins and landlords and merchants alike—against Rackburn and his minions. Aravan had then escorted the two Waerlinga to the High King's representative in town, a realmsman named Tanner.

After he heard the buccen's tale and accepted their documentation, he said, "We knew that something was amiss in that city, but not that it had gotten this far. After the war, with the loss of realmsmen, we found ourselves quite shorthanded—still are, in fact—and I believe that Rivers End is one place where the station is yet vacant. But, as with other places, it was and is left up to the mayor and the city watch to see things remain orderly."

Binkton snorted and said, "The watch? The mayor? Pah! Rat-eating Rûck-lovers all."

Tanner smiled and said, "Obviously, from what you have seen, indeed they have succumbed to bribery."

"What now?" asked Pipper.

"We'll dispatch these papers to King Ryon on the next packet to leave."

"What about the birds?" asked Pipper.

Binkton looked at his cousin as if he had gone quite batty. "Pip, what in the—?"

"Don't you remember, Bink?" said Pipper. "Uncle Arley told us that the realmsmen have messenger birds."

"Oh, right," said Binkton, catching up to Pipper's thought.

Tanner shook his head and held up the papers and said, "There is much too much here for a bird to carry."

"Couldn't an eagle do it?" asked Pipper.

Tanner laughed and said, "We only have pigeons at our beck, Pip."

"Oh," said Pipper, somewhat glumly.

Tanner glanced at Aravan and shook his head in amusement, then said, "Regardless, a packet will get the papers to the High King rather quickly; I thank you for what you have done. And as far as stealing from thieves and returning the ill-gotten gains to those so wronged, well, let me just say, nicely played, lads. Nicely played. I believe the High King himself might even pin medals on your chests."

Pipper looked at Binkton, grinned, and received a smile in return, and Aravan said, "They come by it honestly, Realmsman Tanner. Mention to King Ryon that their granduncle is one Arley Willowbank. The King might have to look into the records of his sire and grandsire to find that name, yet it has a bearing on this duo."

Tanner cocked an eyebrow, and Pipper blurted, "Uncle Arley was a King's thief."

Binkton nodded his agreement.

"Ah, I see," said Tanner. "Then he was a realmsman—or, rather, a realmsWarrow."

Binkton sighed and murmured to Pipper, "Uncle Arley and his secrets. Why, he was a hero, don't you think?"

Pipper's eyes flew wide and he turned to Binkton and said, "The rider!"

Binkton threw up his hands in exasperation and demanded, "What in all of Mithgar do you mean by that?"

"Uncle Arley's pension. The Human who brings it to the Boskydell Bank. It's a High King's stipend."

Enlightenment filled Binkton's gaze. "Ohhhh. Why, Pip, I do believe you've hit upon it."

Even as the buccen nodded to one another and whispered about Uncle Arley and his secrets, Realmsman Tanner dashed off a quick note and placed it and the Warrows' document into a small leather bag and locked and sealed it with wire and wax. Then he and the Warrows and Aravan went to the docks where a mail runner was moored, and they gave over the pouch to the captain, with instructions to deliver it straightaway into the hands of the High King.

After that, they all four went to the Red Slipper for a celebratory mug of Vornholt ale. The Warrows and the full of the Elvenship complement, along with the captain and his lady, spent the rest of that day and the following two, as well as the nights between, in that wild bordello and inn, where, in the depths of the second dark night, Brekk and Dokan and the Dwarves, as well as Lissa the Pysk, officially inducted Binkton and Pipper into the *Eroean's* warband.

The next day the buccen's heads did ache, but they grinned in spite of the pain.

But on the evening tide of the third day they did sail, and the entirety of the crew—sailors and warband alike—came aboard. In spite of the warning of an unknown danger that might or might not be waiting, they all were eager to be off.

As crewmen sailed the ship westerly 'pon the indigo waters of the deep blue Avagon Sea, "Where be we bound, Cap'n?" asked Long Tom.

He stood at the map table in the captain's salon, along with others of the crew—Nikolai, Fat Jim, Tarley, James, Noddy, Dokan, and Brekk. There also were the scouts, Lissa and Binkton and Pipper—Lissa on the tabletop, the buccen standing in chairs, all the better to see.

"Here," said Aravan, stabbing a finger down onto the spread-out map, indicating a coastline of a realm, the interior of which was largely blank. "'Tis a land that has had several names throughout the eras: Amanar, Dinou, and Ladore among them. But whatever its name, it lies between the realm of Jûng to the east and that of Bharaq to the west."

Aravan then pointed to where the chart showed the mouth of a river out-flowing into the Sindhu Sea. Here, too, the map beyond the river outlet showed nought of the river course itself. "I deem from the marks on the bottom of the statuette"—he gestured at the figurine sitting in the mid of the table—"represent this very river, for the coastline corresponds."

Long Tom reached out and took up the jade carving and turned it upside-down and aligned the etching thereon to that of the map. After a moment of comparing the two, he grunted his approval and passed it to his left, where Noddy stood.

"Aye," said Noddy, after his own examination, "but how do y'know that this be the particular river, Cap'n?"

"From the clay tablet," said Aylis. "Recall, it was written in ancient Jûngarian and said, 'In the near west lies the City of Jade,' and this is the only nearby coastline west of Jûng that seems to match."

"What we know of river, Kapitan?" asked Nikolai.

Aravan shook his head. "Only that it is named the Dukong, and that here it flows into the sea."

"By the marks on that jade, if Oi've read them aright, Cap'n, Oi note th' lost city be upstream somewhat. Be th' channel woide enough t'sail upriver?" asked Long Tom.

"Aye, 'tis wide, yet whether it is deep enough is another question."

"We can always send boats to row and plumb, Captain," said Tarley.

"Aye, we can. And if it is deep enough and remains wide, 'twould be best to take the *Eroean* upchannel; 'twill shorten the trek to and from the city. And, given a friendly lay of the land, it will ease the haul back to the ship of any cargo we might find."

A general murmur of agreement met these words.

"But what about the peril?" asked Pipper.

"Oh, Pip, no one knows anything about that," said Binkton.

"What I mean, Bink, is I believe there is one among us who can discover something about any perils we might face in the lost City of Jade."

Binkton sighed in exasperation. "And just who might that be?"

"I will do a first reading," said Aylis.

At these words, Noddy backed away a step from the table, though Pipper looked at Binkton and grinned as if to say "See!" while Binkton mouthed a silent *oh, right.* Then Pipper looked across at Aylis and, fairly jittering in eager curiosity, asked, "May I watch?"

Binkton, on the other hand, frowned, as if considering whether or not he would like to witness a Seer casting a spell.

"Not me," said Long Tom. "Such and such gives me th' goosey flesh."

"Me, too," said Noddy, his head bobbing up and down in agreement with Long Tom's words, his accent slipping back to his East Lindor origins. "Oi'll pass up sich a diminstriation, if y'don't moind."

"I would like to know of anything that might put the crew in peril," said Brekk, glancing at Dokan, who grunted his agreement. "So, if we might, we also would witness this casting."

"Of course," said Aylis. "Yet, for detecting peril, 'tis better done in the depths of night." She pondered a moment and then said, "At the end of the first watch, I will do the reading here in the salon."

"Then it be eight bell," breathed Nikolai.

"Aye," said Aravan.

"Eight bells?" asked Pipper.

"Just count the ringing," said Lissa, who was now an old hand at timekeeping at sea. "When the ship's bell tolls eight, then it'll be time."

"But I just heard the bell ring eight times," objected Binkton.

"It marked the end of the dog watch," said Lissa. "Now we begin first watch."

"Argh!" spat Binkton. "Bells. Watches. Just tell me how many candlemarks till Lady Aylis does her reading."

"Old candlemarks or new?" asked Pipper.

"I don't care!" shouted Binkton, totally frustrated. "Just tell me."

Aylis held out a soothing hand. "I will do the reading at mid of night, Binkton."

"That's the end of first watch, when the bell tolls eight," said Lissa.

Even as Binkton growled, Pipper said, "Liss, perhaps you ought to teach us all about these watches and bells." He turned to his cousin. "We do need to know, Bink. I mean, after all, we now are part of the crew."

As Binkton grudgingly nodded his acceptance, Aylis said, "I welcome any who would like to participate in the reading."

"Lady Aylis, I would ask a question if I may," said Pipper.

Aylis inclined her head.

"Why now?" asked Pipper.

"It's not now, Pip," snapped Binkton, still riled. "Didn't you hear: it's at eight bloody bells."

"No, Bink, what I mean is, why did Lady Aylis wait until now to decide to do a reading? I mean, she and the captain have known for a long while about a peril that might or might not be in the city. So why did Lady Aylis wait until this night to do a reading?"

"Oh," said Binkton, now catching up to another of Pipper's mental leaps.

"Because," said Aylis, "'tis best when all who will be on a given venture are assembled. You see, the acts of one might affect the deeds of many; hence, the presence of the crew entire influences the cards. Even so, I will do another reading when we are at the mouth of the river, to see if ought has changed."

At mid of night, when the ship's bell tolled eight, Pipper, Binkton, Lissa, Nikolai, and Aravan joined Aylis in the salon. Noddy, Tarley, Fat Jim, and James had all bowed out, leaving the others to witness such doings.

They were seated 'round a side table in the captain's lounge. Lissa sat cross-legged on the board, and Vex lay curled up below.

Upon the table as well sat the jade figurine and a small wooden box made of sandalwood. A tiny golden hasp latched the box. Aylis opened the clasp and raised the lid. Inside was a black silk cloth wrapped about something. Aylis unfolded the cloth to reveal a deck of cards.

"This is the gift of Lady Katlaw," said Aylis.

"Are the cards special?" asked Pipper.

"Pish," murmured Binkton, cocking a skeptical eyebrow.

"Perhaps, Pipper," Aylis answered as she spread out the cloth. "'Tis said some decks are more powerful than others, yet to a Seer it is the casting that reveals whatever might be." Taking the pack in hand, she began shuffling, blending and cutting the cards time and again, and on the final shuffle she murmured, *"Simplicia, propinqua futura: Aylis."* Setting the pack before her, she fanned the deck wide across the silk and selected a card at random and turned it faceup. It showed a lightning-struck tower bursting apart, stone blocks flying wide, a person falling from the castellated top. Aylis glanced up at those watching.

"What does it mean?" asked Lissa.

Pipper blurted, "Disaster? Trouble?"

Aylis nodded. "In this orientation, you are correct."

Nikolai glanced from the card to the jade figurine. "This tower, that tower, all same?"

Aylis shrugged. "Mayhap, Nikolai. Mayhap." She reached out and slowly canted up and over one of the end cards of the lapping, spread such that the remainder of the deck turned faceup. Revealed were a variety of illustrations—people and places and animals, the sun, moon, and stars . . . cups, swords, wands, coins, more—each card different: some apparently representing the ordinary, others depicting the arcane.

Nikolai drew slightly back at the sights revealed, but Pipper leaned forward, the better to see.

Aylis looked at Lissa. "Would you care to try?"

Lissa drew in her breath sharply but said, "All right."

Again Aylis shuffled and muttered, "Simplicia, propinqua futura: Aylissa." Then she fanned the cards, and Lissa walked to the spread and dragged one free and flipped it face up.

"'Tis the Knight of Swords, upright," said Aylis.

"What does it mean?" asked Lissa.

"Victory over a dire foe, in this orientation, though perhaps at great peril."

Pipper's eyes widened in speculation. "Is it somehow related to the tower?"

"Mayhap," said Aylis.

Nikolai refused to draw a card, but Aravan, Binkton, and Pipper each in turn selected, respectively turning up the Tower, Strength, and the Fool, all upright.

Aylis said, "My love, you and I share trouble. And you, Binkton, the way your card, Strength, is oriented, you must not surrender, else all will fail. As to your card, Pipper, the Naïf, indicates that you will be at a crossroads and face a decision, and you must choose wisely."

"Oh, my," said Pipper. He turned to Binkton and asked, "When ever have I chosen wisely?"

"Oh, Pip," said Binkton, reaching out to place a hand on his cousin's arm, "you always seem to come up with something."

"Like the chickens?" asked Pipper, grinning.

Binkton laughed. "Yes, Pip. Like the chickens."

"You must tell me of these chickens," said Lissa. "And then I'll explain the watches and bells."

"Agreed," said Pipper, "though in the end my idea of using chickens didn't lead to one of our finer moments."

Aylis looked at the others and said, "I now seek the fate of all of us on the *Eroean*." She then again shuffled and cut, and this time she uttered, "Propinqua futura *nautae Eroean*," then swiftly dealt out ten cards face down, placing each one precisely upon the silk in a particular spread, muttering strange words as she did so. When she set the remainder of the pack to the lower left corner of the black cloth, she said, "This is the simplest and perhaps the most reliable spread. It is called the Rwn Cross, and it speaks of the past, the present, and the future, of negatives and positives, of companions and foes, of causes and outcomes."

Then she turned up the cards, carefully leaving each one in its precise place in the pattern.

Long did Aylis study the arrangement, and finally she took a deep, shuddering breath and said, "Swords. There are many swords in the layout and all reverse, all opposed, which means conflict and battle. As to the individual cards, this is what I see. . . ."

Aylis pointed to the first of the cards she had laid down. "Death covers us. Someone or something threatens our very existence."

"As have many in the past," said Aravan. "Yet we prevail."

Aylis smiled at Aravan and nodded. She then lightly touched the card lying athwart the first one. "The King of Swords crosses us, and in this orientation he is someone who is intolerant and cruel."

"Modru," breathed Pipper.

"Pip, you idiot," said Binkton, "Modru is dead."

"No, Bink, what I meant is that Modru was intolerant and cruel. So, this could be someone like him, Lady Aylis?"

Aylis shook her head. "The King of Swords is not powerful enough to be Modru. Instead, he likely would be the card named the Emperor, for when reversed, it can be even crueler than this king."

She pointed at the next card, this one lying directly downcloth from the first two. "The Ten of Swords is the basis of the situation. It means broken goals and deep distress lie at the heart of the matter."

"Perhaps it's why the city was abandoned," suggested Lissa.

Aylis shook her head. "No; 'tis more likely goals the King of Swords had."

"Well, could not that king once have ruled the city?" asked Dokan.

"Perhaps," said Aylis. "Yet the King is what crosses us now, and though that might be something rooted in the distant past, I think instead the broken goals refers to events more recent."

Moving deasil and to the left of the first two, at the following card she said, "Behind us is what has gone before: still more conflict, as is shown by the Chariot, which placed as it is represents a triumph in the past. Mayhap in battle or war."

"The Black Fortress?" murmured Aravan.

"Perhaps," said Aylis, "though it could be the War of the Dragonstone or even triumph over Gyphon, or even any one of the many conflicts and struggles upon the Planes. It is unclear as to which triumph it represents, though given the number of swords, I deem it lies in war."

"Say on, my love," said Aravan.

Yet moving deasil, Aylis pointed to the card lying directly upcloth from the first two. "Justice is next, and, as it lies, it means possible loss, which could come into being."

Brekk growled and said, "My Châkka warband will see that it doesn't."

"Wait a moment, now," protested Binkton. "Your warband includes two Warrows and a Pysk."

Brekk's hawklike gaze swept to Binkton, then to Pipper, and finally to Lissa. Then he smiled at Binkton and said, "Forgive the omission?"

"Well, er, aye-aye, Armsmaster," said Binkton, now mollified.

When none said ought else, Aylis moved to the next card. "The Knight of Swords follows, and in its reversed orientation it represents someone who is underhanded, perhaps an associate of the King of Swords. It lies before us."

Lissa stood and stamped her foot. "But that's the card I drew, and I'm not underhanded."

284 / Dennis L. McKiernan

Aylis smiled. "Nay, Liss, you are not. Yet this Knight of Swords represents someone else, someone who is not you. And in this spread and in the reverse orientation, it is perhaps the pawn of the King of Swords, who, as I said, is someone quite cruel."

Somewhat placated, yet with a remnant of disgruntlement lying upon her face, the Pysk sat down once more.

Aylis looked about the table, and then pointed at the next card in the spread, the lowest of four lying in a vertical line to the right of the first six. "The Ace of Swords represents the negative, and in this reversed orientation it means the seeds of defeat are taking root and could come to fruition."

Again Brekk growled, but otherwise said nought.

Aylis moved to the next card up the line. "The Wheel of Fortune reversed represents the feelings of all of us, and even in the face of apparent defeat we must remain strong and have courage."

"Châkka shok. Châkka cor," muttered Dokan, then adding, "Hai, Pyska; hai Waerans."

"Is that our battle cry?" asked Pipper. "Me, I'd settle for Châkka shok, Châkka cor."

"Dwarven axes, Dwarven might?" asked Binkton. "But we're not Dwarves. Why that, Pip?"

"It's shorter," replied the buccan. "Easier to call out in the midst of battle." He looked at Lissa.

She shrugged and said, "All right."

Smiling to herself, Aylis touched the third card in the line. "Now we come to the Hermit upright. It represents positive actions, as of a door being opened, as of a seeking and finding. In the context of all the other cards, I think that even when things seem lost, still there is a way."

"I can open doors," said Binkton. "Do you think that means something I have to do?"

"Mayhap. Yet I deem it more likely it is something all of us must be aware of."

"Oh," said Binkton, disappointed.

"Finally, the tenth and last card," said Aylis. "Here again we see the Tower, but this time it is upright. In this complete layout, it means things can change rapidly, whether for good or ill, I cannot say, yet change they will."

Aylis then held out the remainder of the pack to Aravan and said, "And now one final trial: you, as our captain, must draw a single card from these, for it might tell us what the spread does not show, what we do not know; mayhap it will be the key to all."

Aravan took the cards as Aylis muttered another arcane phrase. He cut the deck and looked about at the others, and Pipper and Binkton sat up straighter, while both Nikolai and Lissa got to their feet.

Aravan then drew out a single card and turned it face up.

"Thaimon!" hissed Nikolai, and he made a circle of protection upon his chest, even as Lissa blenched and turned her face away. Both Dokan and Brekk copied Nikolai's gesture, and Dokan uttered several words in Châkur, "Elwydd" among them.

"What? What is it?" cried Pipper, leaning forward to see.

Aylis sighed and shook her head and said, "The Demon."

44

Crossing

"Demon?" blurted Pipper.

"Aren't you listening, Pip?" snapped Binkton. "That's what she just said."

"No, no, Bink," said Pipper. "What I mean is, does it have anything to do with Grygar?"

"The Demon Plane?" asked Binkton. "Why didn't you say so? And what would that have to do with anything?"

"Well, if it does," said Pipper, his voice quavering, "it means the reason the city was abandoned was because of a Gargon or such."

Brekk and Dokan glanced at one another, being from Kraggen-cor as they were.

"I mean," continued Pipper, "those Fearcasters are demons, or so it is I hear."

"Oh, my," said Lissa.

Both Warrows and the Pysk looked to Aylis for confirmation.

"Gargons are indeed Demons of a kind," said Aylis. "But this card, the Demon, has little to do with such. Upright, and in relation to this layout, the card means an evil external force, a dreadful influence that one must take steps to break."

"Oh, well, that's better," said Pipper, heaving a sigh of relief.

Aylis shook her head. "Take no solace in what I just said, for, given the import of the casting, still it could mean something just as vile as a Gargon, though more likely it is incorporeal."

"Incorporeal?" asked Pipper.

Binkton groaned in frustration at Pipper, for he knew that his cousin meant to ask something else altogether instead of merely repeating a word.

"What I mean, Bink," said Pipper, now glancing at his cousin, "is how can something incorporeal hurt us?"

"A Gargon's fear is incorporeal," suggested Lissa.

Pipper looked at the Pysk and nodded, saying, "Oh, right you are."

"And fear that strong can burst a person's heart," said Binkton.

"There are other nonmaterial things that can do harm," said Aravan.

"Oh, don't tell me," said Pipper. "It'll give me bad dreams if you do. Won't it, Bink?"

Binkton nodded. "Ever since I've known Pip, he's been given to nightmares, especially when told some ghost story or tale about dreadful Dragons and such, or grisly doings."

"Now I'll dream about those things, Bink, just because you said them."

"If you do, I'll waken you, like I've always done."

Nikolai said, "Ghost?"

"You mean as an incorporeal being?" asked Aylis.

Nikolai nodded. "Ghost, shade, like in poem."

"I suppose," said Aylis. "Yet I've not heard of a shade being able to do harm, other than to cause alarm."

"Oh, now you've done it," groaned Pipper. "I'll dream of ghosts all night."

Binkton reached out and laid a hand on Pipper's forearm and again said, "I'll waken you."

Brekk cleared his throat. "Is there anything else you need tell us, Lady Aylis? Anything else the cards reveal?"

Aylis looked at the spread and the lone Demon card and sighed. "Only that there appear to be dark forces arrayed against us, and it seems we'll have a fight on our hands when we reach the City of Jade. We must go well armed"—she glanced at Pipper and Binkton and then Lissa—"and well equipped to deal with whatever we face." She turned to Aravan and added, "Your stone of warding, my love, perhaps will prove to be key, in that it will warn us of peril at hand."

Aravan's hand strayed to the blue amulet on its thong at his throat, next to the falcon crystal. "The stone does not give notice against all things of evil intent, and so we depend on scouts—and perhaps Valké—to detect things lying in wait."

"You can depend on Vex and me," said Lissa. "If it's there, we will find it."

The vixen, hearing her name, raised her head from her doze. But when no command followed, she went back to sleep.

Binkton started to protest—"I say, Pip and I, we're scouts, too, and—" but Dokan, speaking at the same time, said, "If it is the Grg, we will deal with them."

Brekk nodded and said, "We will be ready, Captain."

Lissa stood and asked, "Is there more?"

Aravan looked at Aylis, and she turned up her hands. "I can see no more."

"We are finished," said Aravan.

"Good," said Lissa. "Dinny and I are in the middle of a tokko game, and I am about to stun him with a move of an eagle."

Brekk and Dokan got up from their chairs, and Pipper and Binkton hopped down from theirs. As Nikolai lowered Lissa from the table, he said, "When play Dinny tokko, he be sly one. Probably already know move you make."

Lissa called Vex and mounted up, saying, "We'll see, Nikolai. We'll see."

As all trooped out but Aylis and Aravan, Pipper overheard Aravan say, "Would that I yet had Krystallopŷr or a sword like the one Riatha bears, then I would feel more—"

Following Binkton, Pipper passed beyond hearing whatever else the captain then had on his mind.

Faring southwesterly, past Hoven and Tugal the *Eroean* ran, the early summer wind braw and steady and off the stern port quarter. Down through the Northern Strait of Kistan she fared, the rover isle to larboard, the realm of Vancha starboard. Past the inlet to the city of Castilla the ship sped, that port of call notable for cargos of a wine called Dark Vancha, perhaps the finest in all of Mithgar, though the winemakers of the Gothon vineyards would say otherwise.

Rovers fled before the many-sailed Elvenship for, in the long-ago past and then again in the present, they had come to fear the fireballs and arrows cast by this swiftest of all ships in the seas.

Finally, broaching out into the waters of the Weston Ocean she went, to turn southerly and make a run toward the Calms of the Crab and the Midline Doldrums beyond, and the Calms of the Goat past that, for once again the *Eroean* was aiming for the frigid waters of the Cape of Storms. At this time of year the wrath of winter, raging in the dread waters of the South Polar Sea, made the opposite passage through the Silver Straits all but certain death. Not that verging 'round the tip of the dark lands would be an easy course, yet it was measurably better than the other choice.

And so, past the Calms of the Crab they sailed, the winds light and shifty, the passage slow, but when they came to the Midline Doldrums, a gale-force blow, rare for this latitude, sped them across. Yet they had to row four days in all to pass the Horns of the Goat, as those calms are sometimes called.

And then they reached the South Polar Sea. . . .

The shrieking wind howled easterly around the bottom of the world, hurling the *Eroean* before its brutal blast. Great greybeards loomed over the ocean, the tall Elvenship riding toward each towering crest, her sharp prow to cut through, her hull to slam down—*whoom!*—upon the far side to plummet into the chasm below; then up she would ride again, sailing on slopes and crests and slants, for not even the knife-sharp prow of the *Eroean* could cut straight through the bulk of these mighty waves. Her masts creaked and groaned, and her halyards wailed in the wind as of a malevolent spirit calling out for a toll of souls, as 'round the nadir of existence hurtled the Elvenship, driven by a tearing wind dire. With her decks awash in deep brine, the ship flew only her royals and gallants and her goose-winged tops, her pulleys and rigging clogged with ice. It was too dangerous for crew to go above, and Fat Jim and Aravan manned the helm from the enclosed wheelhouse adeck, with waves slamming over that haven.

In the crew's quarters below, the pitching and heaving and rolling ship had no noticeable effect upon Pipper, but Binkton, on the other hand, was tossed about like a balled-up wad of parchment.

Lissa and Vex remained in their tiny underbunk chamber, the vixen sliding to and fro, but curled about her mistress.

Aylis lay in her bed in the captain's cabin, the deck of cards in hand. As she had occasionally done throughout the long voyage, she muttered an arcane word and drew a pasteboard out. *The Empress upright. The whole cannot be seen at this point.* Aylis shook her head in mild frustration. *We are left with no more knowledge than that which the spread revealed.* She sighed and put the deck away, and returned to the book she read by swaying lantern light, just as a wall of snow hammered across the decks and masts and sails and rigging of the magnificent ship.

Three days later, in eerie calm the crew rowed dinghies across placid but frigid waters, towing the *Eroean* after, the sea nought but a slowly rolling mirror as long, gentle swells passed across the surface, reflecting stars shining above in the clear skies, for at this time of year the day was but moments long.

To the starboard and on the horizon, icy walls loomed, the endless glacier concealing a continent, or so lore would have it be.

In the rigging above, both Humans and Dwarves hacked away at caked ice, while Pipper and Binkton and Lissa helped others chip away at the coating adeck, all tethered by safety lines, for to slip into the frigid brine meant nigh instant death.

Soon the rigging and sails were free of the encrustation, and the crew unreefed the silks and shook them out. And before the next day dawned, the wind returned, gentle in its aspect.

The arrival of autumn found the *Eroean* faring east of Bharaq, the Elvenship now heading for a meridian at the point where the Dukong River spilled into the Sindhu Sea, Aravan navigating, for as it is with all of Elvenkind, he knew at all times exactly where lay the sun and moon and lights of the celestial sphere, including the wandering stars.

Running in a northerly direction, once again they had passed the Calms of the Goat as well as the Midline Doldrums, where they circled this part of the world. They would not reach the Calms of the Crab, for in this hemisphere that latitude was far inland from where the *Eroean* was bound.

And as midautumn arrived, so, too, did the ship come to the league-wide mouth of the river, where she dropped anchor.

Warband and crew alike stood at the railings and surveyed the coast rising up into nearby hills, with lush greenery steaming and seeming impenetrable.

"Jungle," said Dokan. "Miles of jungle."

Nikolai groaned. "It mean bug bite."

"Aye, it does," said Fat Jim. "Swarms of stinging flies and mosquitoes and gnats and midges. And if we have to pass through streams, blood-sucking leeches, too."

"You'd better watch out, Liss," said Pipper. "I mean, if a leech latches onto you, you'll be gone in a trice."

Lissa shook her head. "Not if I can reach one of my arrows and stab the thing. It's the leech that'll be gone, and in a lot sooner than a trice."

Both Pipper and Binkton eyed the small quiver of arrows at Lissa's hip. The lethality of those tiny barbs was legendary. And Liss had told them the tale of her sire saving Alamar by bringing down a full-charging boar in midstride; between one step and the next the massive swine had dropped, just an instant after being pricked.

Aravan said to Long Tom, "Lower all dinghies and stand by, for we'll need to plumb the river to see if we can sail the *Eroean* up it to a suitable place to dock. In the meanwhile, I'll fly as Valké upstream to see if what we think might be the old road from the river to the city yet exists, though given the denseness of the foliage I see, I ween it's overgrown and lost."

"Take care, my love," said Aylis, embracing Aravan. He kissed her, and then disengaged, and in a flash of silvery light, a falcon took to wing.

"Oh, my!" breathed Pipper.

Binkton's jaw dropped agape.

Neither buccan had seen Aravan transform into Valké ere now.

"How does he do that?" said Pipper, looking to Aylis for an answer.

She shook her head. "I know not, for it is <wild-magic>."

Binkton cocked an eyebrow.

"Like my darkness," said Lissa, "or your ability to see through it."

Aylis nodded. "My gift, as with all of Magekind, is to use the aethyr to cast spells, but Aravan's transformation does not use aethyr at all, or if it does, I cannot detect it. Instead, he uses the crystal he bears to shift from Elf to falcon and back again."

"Wull, I wish I could do that," said Pipper, now watching the bird in flight.

Aylis shook her head. "Mayhap you would not, Pip."

"Why not?"

"Aravan tells me that when he is a falcon, he truly is nought but a wild thing. He is not a bird that thinks like an Elf, but is a raptor true. 'Tis only by concentrating beforehand upon what he would have the bird do that he gets ought done. The danger is, he might never shift back to an Elf, but be a falcon forever. Just as is the danger to the falcon that Aravan will never become the bird again."

"You mean he might be trapped in the form of a falcon forever?" asked Binkton.

Glumly, Aylis nodded. "Indeed."

"Oh, Adon," said Pipper, not taking his gaze from the dark bird. "That would be terrible. I think you're right, Lady Aylis: mayhap I would not like to be able to be a bird."

With keen raptor eyes searching, Valké flew up the flow, and soon was lost to the vision of those remaining behind. O'er the river he soared, and along the verge of the jungle, looking this way and that. No immediate prey did he sight, yet he was not out for game. Instead, his unfalconlike thought was to survey and remember and then to return to the floating thing with the tall trees jutting up from it.

And as the bird flew, Long Tom had the dinghies lowered, and he chose those who would row and plumb.

No sooner was that done than the werebird returned and transformed into Aravan. "Valké espied the tower—in fact several towers—yon"—he gestured a point or two forward and to the right—"and two leagues upstream is a stone quay, where we can dock the *Eroean*, should the river be navigable. A path runs through the hills toward what must be the city, though it is well overgrown. Tom, with the pier upstream, I suspect the river will be navigable. Send out the crew to confirm or refute our assumptions."

"Better safe nor sorry, Oi allus say, Oi do, Oi say," replied Tom, and he gave the signal for the men in the dinghies to begin the mission.

Many yards apart, four abreast they rowed, Dinny and Ebert in the bows of two of them, Noddy and Wooly in the bows of the remaining pair, the quartet swinging bobs to plunk into the water just ahead and calling out depths for crewmen in the sterns to record. The *Eroean* would need but thirty-five feet fully laden, and should they sail upstream, they would do so on the inflowing tide.

In the Captain's Lounge below, Aylis, Aravan, Pipper, and Binkton gathered 'round the side table, Lissa sitting atop. Once again Aylis dealt out the Rwn Cross upon the black silk cloth. After studying the spread for long moments, she said, "The layout is but slightly different, with many swords indicating conflict. Again it seems there is someone or something opposing, yet I know no more than before. We must go in caution, and choose wisely, should violence come our way. I can say nought else."

Once again she held the deck out to Aravan, and once again he drew the Demon.

45

Lurking

DARK DESIGNS
EARLY SUMMER TO MID AUTUMN, 6E9

High in the night sky in his incorporeal form, Nunde gloated as the Elvenship set sail from Port Arbalin.

Perhaps Aravan has *taken the bait. We shall see. We shall see. Yet whether or not he has done so, surely he will someday. And no matter how long it takes, Malik will be waiting. After all, he has my orders.*

Nunde continued to haunt the *Eroean* from afar, knowing what course the ship must take if it were indeed bound for the City of Jade, as he, Nunde, had planned.

As they sailed southerly, Nunde began to worry, for if catastrophe struck and the ship were to sink to the bottom in the raging South Polar Ocean, Aravan would be dead and beyond Nunde's revenge.

And when the ship entered those perilous waters, Nunde made it a point to watch as the *Eroean* pitched and yawed and plunged through crest after crest, the Necromancer's aethyrial heart hammering in dread of the upset of all his schemes, for tons upon tons of icy brine engulfed the ship, and it disappeared as waves roiled over it, only to reappear time after time.

But then the Polar Seas calmed, and Nunde shouted in glee as the *Eroean* turned northerly, and sailed on what appeared to be a course for Bharaq. *Surely vile Aravan is heading just where I planned; I knew he could not deny the siren call of what he thinks will be a grand adventure. But little does he suspect what lies in wait. My plan is coming full circle.*

Nunde raced ahead to see if Malik and the Chûn were in position. They were.

Not that they had any choice. After all, Nunde had decreed.

The voyage went onward, and at last Nunde, daring to spy during the day, though remaining well away, watched as the ship dropped anchor at the mouth of the Dukong.

But then, out from a brief flash of light—*What's this? They have a trained bird? A pigeon, a dove—no, a raptor of a sort, mayhap a small hawk. Never mind, for it cannot— Oh, wait, perhaps that slut of a Seeress is looking through the bird's eyes. Regardless, the jungle is thick, and Malik and the others well hidden. Whatever the hawk and trollop are up to, it will do them no good.*

Two nights later, Nunde watched as the *Eroean*, under sail, rode the night tide upriver. A candlemark later, the Elvenship tied up to the stone pier.

I have triumphed! Yes! And Aravan is mine!

46

Strife

It took the rest of that day and all of the next to plumb the key part of the river, for not only did the main channel need to be found and its depth charted, but the measure across its width as well. Too, when the rowers came to the stone quay, they had to sound up to and all along the length of its brim and somewhat beyond to see if the *Eroean* could safely tie up without becoming grounded.

A map was made of the findings, and, running on staysails alone, on the inflowing night tide the Elvenship fared upriver to the pier, where the crew moored her. They left the staysails up but luffing, in the event they needed to move away from the dock quickly. Yet the *Eroean* was much like a floating fortress, with its ballistas and the warband's crossbows and lethal quarrels and their mêlée battle gear, as well as the sailors' own bows and arrows and falchions and boarding axes.

Mindful of Lady Aylis's reading, they set a sharp watch and made ready for combat, should ought come to wage war 'gainst them.

The next morning, Brekk and a squad of Dwarves marched down the gangplank, Lissa on Vex running ahead. Valké soared high above in his natural element, for the falcon was wild, and for the raptor to fly below the jungle canopy and among branches and leaves went against Valké's nature.

Aylis and the sailors and Dokan and the remainder of the warband watched them go, including Pipper and Binkton, Binkton complaining mightily: "What kind of a rat-eating decision was that? Brekk leaving us behind when we are scouts, too?"

"Right you are, Bink," said Pipper. "We should be out front with Liss. I mean, what good is a scout that doesn't find out what's ahead?"

Dokan rumbled deep in his throat and said, "Given Lady Aylis's readings, this is just a quick probe to see if enemies lie to the fore. And a Pysk on a fox is swifter than Waerans afoot."

"Yes, but—" Binkton started to respond, yet Pipper said, "He's right, Bink. Much as I don't like staying behind, Dokan is right."

High above the thick jungle Valké soared. Only now and then did the raptor catch a glimpse of the warband below, for the interlace of leaves and limbs of the tall, vine-laden trees with little or no gaps was simply too dense to see through no matter the keenness of sight. And of the fox and its rider, he saw nothing at all.

Valké soared toward the towers he could see in the near distance, and as he approached the falcon sensed danger, but what it might be, the raptor could not say, only that peril lurked . . . somewhere.

Down within the green and humid and close jungle, Lissa and Vex coursed, the fox swift and ranging in a sweeping zigzag run. Past huge banyan trees they ran, where widespread aerial branches descended to plunge into the soil and become additional rooted support. Forest giants, too, soared upward, their flanged trunks like buttresses. Liana vines twisted out from the damp loam and about the trunks, and drooped like dangling ropes high above. Massive roots snaked across the soil among the undergrowth down within the canopy-shadowed dimness, the shade pierced now and again by errant shafts of sunlight. Tiny rills trickled toward the river, only to vanish among the ever-thirsty foliage. Gnats and midges swirled in swarms, seeking warm-blooded creatures, and an occasional bird winged among the branches high above. Amid ferns and broad-leafed plants did fox and rider weave, and past slender trees, saplings struggling to find light and growth of their own. The land rose as Lissa and Vex approached the hills, and back and forth and up the slant they fared. Of a sudden the vixen froze, her nose in the air, quietly taking in a scent.

"What is it, Vex?"

[Bad,] the fox indicated with her ears.

"What is it?"

[Many bad.]

"Foul Folk?"

A quick bob of Vex's head confirmed that Spawn were somewhere nigh.

"Where Foul Folk?"

Vex raised her nose into the faint breeze flowing toward the river. Then she stealthily ranged left then right. Finally she indicated, [Ahead.]

Somewhere to the fore lay Foul Folk in wait, or so the vixen did say.

Lissa turned the fox, and back down the hint of a trail she sped. Swiftly she came to the Dwarves, slowly making their own way up the trace through the undergrowth. When the Fox Rider appeared, Brekk signaled a halt.

"Spawn," said Lissa.

"Where?" asked Brekk, taking a firmer grip on his war hammer.

"Ahead."

"How many?"

"That I cannot say, though Vex indicates many."

Brekk growled. "This, then, is the peril Lady Aylis foresaw in her sword-laden spread?"

"Perhaps."

Brekk nodded. "Then, Scout, as planned, we will return to the *Eroean*, while you get closer and gauge their numbers, but stray not too near, for Ükken archers can be deadly."

Without another word, Lissa turned Vex and slipped off to the side of the trail, while Brekk and the squad started back for the ship.

"I counted nearly two hundred Spaunen, four Trolls among them. The rest are Rucha and Loka, nearly fifty of the latter. And there is a Human with them as well, or so I surmised he was, yet I couldn't see him closely."

Aravan nodded, and Lissa sat down atop the table.

"What we do about Troll, Kapitan?" asked Nikolai.

Brekk nodded and added, "They are the most formidable of a Grg band. Alone, they could devastate us."

"We can deal with the Ükhs and Hrôks, and the Human, but the Trolls be another matter," said Dokan.

"I have a plan for the Trolls," said Aravan, "but the one who might be a Human, what if he is a Mage instead?"

All eyes turned to Aylis.

"Magekind is just as vulnerable to slings and arrows and blades as are others," said the Seeress. "It is simply a matter of getting close enough to take him unaware."

"The King," blurted Pipper.

Binkton groaned.

"What I mean, Bink," said Pipper, "is the King of Swords. Could this Human or Wizard be the King of Swords?"

Again all eyes turned to Aylis. "Perhaps."

"He might also be the Knight of Swords," said Lissa.

"Wull, then," said Long Tom, who hadn't been to Aylis's reading but who had heard all about it, "j'st who be th' King if this'n be th' Knoight?"

Aylis turned up her hands. "There's no way of knowing which is which, or if even the cards spoke of this person who mingles with the Spawn, whether or no he is Human or Mage."

"I think it matters not at all," said Aravan, "if he is the Knight or the King. What matters most is that we come up with a means to deal with this threat, and for this I have a plan."

"Wull, Captain," said Long Tom, "that'd be more'n Oi got, for Oi can't think o' nothing but sailin' off 'n' wiaitin' f'r another day, 'r sneakin' 'round 'em."

"Uncle Arley!" blurted Pipper.

"Oh, Pip, you nobberjowl," said Binkton. "What in the world popped into that head of yours?"

"Stealth and guile," said Pipper. "That's what Uncle Arley'd recommend. Show them one thing, but give them something else altogether."

Aravan laughed and said, "Exactly so, Pipper. Exactly so."

Aravan then turned to Long Tom. "Other than me, who among the crew are fleetest of foot? Four of us will do."

"James be swift," said Long Tom, scratching his jaw, looking across at the bosun. "'N' then there be Dinny and Noddy, 'n' me with m' long-leggedy stroide."

Aravan shook his head. "Dinny is too young, Tom, and I would have thee aboard the ship, and I can't risk both bosuns."

"Wull, then, Oi'd say James be swifter'n Noddy."

Aravan looked at First Bosun James. "Are you up to a risky, mayhap fatal venture?"

James nodded. "I am, Captain."

"All right. Then James and I are two. Who else?"

The planning went on throughout the rest of the day, but at last all was decided.

In the darkness, Aravan, Long Tom, and four crewmen rowed a dinghy away from the ship. They payed out a hawser attached to the port-bow anchor winch of the *Eroean*, the other end tied to the shaft eyelet of that anchor in the rowboat with the crew. They fared some two hundred feet upstream and perhaps fifty toward midriver, where Aravan called a halt. All six aboard lifted the heavy weight and dropped it overside, its blunt but heavy tines turning as the mass fell to the bottom. When they returned to the Elvenship, Long Tom and the crewmen cranked the winch to make certain the anchor had dug deep into the river bottom.

When the hawser grew taut and the mooring lines tying the ship to the pier groaned under the strain and the men could wind no more, "She be well anchored, Cap'n, she be, she is," said Long Tom.

"Then, we are ready."

In the light of dawn, Lissa on Vex led the way down the footway ramp, followed by Aravan, with James and Finn after, and Dinny coming last. In spite of his youth and in face of arguments to the contrary, Dinny convinced Aravan he should be allowed to act as bait with the others, for he was truly swift. Each bore a bow and two oil-soaked fire-arrows.

Aboard the *Eroean*, the warband made the ballistas ready, and Long Tom and other sailors with boarding axes stood by the mooring lines as well as the staysails, should they be needed.

Pipper counted his sling bullets, and Binkton his arrows, while Aylis, her heart pounding in fear for Aravan, stood by, a bow in hand as well.

Sailors with nought to do fingered the hilts of their falchions as if making certain the weapons were there, or checked their bows and arrows again and again. . . .

. . . And all waited, as into the jungle along the path went Aravan and three others, with a Fox Rider ranging far ahead of the quartet.

In the concealing foliage crept Vex and Lissa, until she had the Spaunen in sight. The Ruch acting as lookout was completely unaware of the tiny scout.

Lissa fingered a lethal shaft. *It would be so easy, but no, he must see Aravan and the others, for we must draw all to the ship, especially the Trolls.*

Lissa turned Vex, and back toward Aravan and the others she stealthily went.

"Now 'tis no more than thirty of your paces, Captain," whispered Lissa, and she pointed in the direction of the Ruchen sentry.

"And the Trolls?" murmured Aravan.

"Another twenty paces beyond."

"What of the Human?"

"Him I did not see. Would you like me to—?"

"No, Lissa. 'Tis enough. Now, hie thee back to the ship."

Off into the foliage slipped Lissa and Vex, while Aravan silently used his bow and a single shaft to indicate to the three others the direction and angle to loose the arrows. They each set two shafts to the string, all but Aravan, who held the striker. When they were ready, Aravan lit the oiled batting wrapped about the arrowheads that James had, and then Aravan and the others lit their own fire-arrows from those two.

Then all drew the shafts to the full and aimed and yelled and loosed, the flaming arrows to arc through the air past vines and greenery and into the waiting trap.

Trolls roared in startlement at the fire flashing down among them. Hlôks yelled, and Rûcks squealed, sounding much like swine.

Still shouting battle cries, Aravan and James and Finn and Dinny turned tail and fled. The Rûcken sentry cried out, and moments later, and upon the orders of their leader, the dreadful mob howled in pursuit of the fleeing four, for their ambuscade no longer held any surprise.

Shouting, *Eroean! Eroean!* down the trace the four sprinted, the ship some half mile away.

"Save thy breath for flight!" called Aravan, as soon as he heard the shouts of the rout in pursuit. "They will soon be on our heels."

"Not mine," called Dinny, and he slowly pulled away from the others, all of them running flat-out but Aravan, who deliberately brought up the rear.

Yowling, shrieking, Rûcks and Hlôks and Ogrus thundered after, their quarry just then coming into view.

Several Rûcks paused and nocked black-shafted arrows to their twisted bows and let fly, the missiles to fall short and left and right and long.

As the arrows sissed down among the runners, Aravan called, "If ye have anything left, now is the time to use it."

James managed to add to his speed, but Dinny ahead began to flag, while Finn maintained his own swift pace.

The *Eroean* came into sight, and those aboard burst into cheers, and then into shouts of encouragement . . . and then into cries of anxiety, as the Spawn in pursuit also came into view.

The great Trolls with their mighty strides began overhauling the four. More black shafts whistled down among the runners.

And then James fell, pierced through and through.

Aravan paused at his side and knelt down.

The Trolls thundered toward him.

Aylis screamed and loosed a shaft, and it flew a long flight, only to shatter against the stonelike hide of an Ogru, even as the creature hurtled toward Aravan.

Dinny ran up the gangplank, Finn right after.

Captain! Captain! shrieked sailors and warband alike, even as the massive Troll reached for Aravan.

But then, in a silver flash of light, Valké exploded forward in a hammer of wings, and Long Tom shouted to the crewmen with the boarding axes, "Now!"

Chnk! Whnk! The axes sheared through mooring lines, and in the river current and tethered by the anchor upstream, the *Eroean* slowly began to swing away from the pier, the gangplank to slam down onto the stone.

Howling in frustration at being denied the prey that had suddenly turned into a bird, the Trolls thundered forward, racing for the ship.

"Hold, hold," called Brekk to the Châkka at the ballistas.

Even as Brekk gave that command, Valké swooped to the deck, but from a bright flare 'twas Aravan who landed afoot.

In that same moment, the *Eroean* stopped swinging outward, and she lay off some fifty feet from the dock, where she fared at the end of the anchored hawser in the flow of the Dukong.

Aravan called for Desault and, as the chirurgeon came running, Aravan turned to see where the Rûpt had gotten to, just as the two charging Ogrus in the lead reached the pier and could not stop, and, shrieking in fear, they slid across the stone and into the water.

Down like rocks they plummeted, their massive bones too heavy for them to be able to swim. And in water forty-seven feet deep, they clawed at the vertical rock face of the pier, but found no purchase. They fought one another, trying to climb each other's back and, still struggling, they drowned.

Even as those first two fell into the river, the remaining pair of Trolls managed to stop ere doing so.

"Loose!" cried Brekk.

T-thunn! sang two ballistas, and fireballs smashed into the Ogrus and set them ablaze. Shrieking and burning, unable to cast off the tarlike clinging fire, back toward the oncoming rout they fled.

"Loose!" cried Dokan.

T-thun! two more ballistas sang, hurling lances to slam through each of the fleeing Ogrus, and yet aflame, they fell slain.

"So much for the Trolls," grunted Brekk.

But still, there were two hundred Spawn to deal with.

Desault, his satchel in hand, reached Aravan. "Are you hurt, Captain? Wounded?"

"Nay, Desault. But James is wounded, and as soon as we can, we must return to his side."

"He yet lives?"

"Aye, he does. And if the Spaunen think he does not, then there is a chance he will survive this battle."

Even as Aravan spoke, black-shafted arrows and heavy slingstones flew at the *Eroean*, to be answered by arrows and crossbow quarrels in return.

Sling bullets, too, hammered into the Foul Folk, as again and again Pipper rose up from behind the railing and let fly. "Got one!" he shouted. "That makes six in all."

"Pish!" sneered Binkton in return, loosing another arrow. "Seven for me."

As Pipper squatted behind cover to load another sling bullet, he scanned the deck. "Scout!" he blurted.

Binkton, also squatting to nock another arrow, growled.

"What I mean, Bink, is, Where's Lissa?"

Now Binkton looked about. "Didn't she and Vex come running up the gangplank?"

"I don't think so."

"Well, she's got to be here somewhere," said Binkton, though the bleak look in his eyes claimed otherwise. He rose up and loosed another arrow. It flew wide of its intended target.

But grume-coated Ruchen arrows hissed among the crew, and some fell pierced, crying out in shock and pain. Others fell with bones broken by heavy slingstones. Desault and his aide rushed thither and yon, and Aravan and Aylis joined the chirurgeon, and they stanched the flow and cleansed away grume and administered sops of ease for those in dire need.

Arrows and sling bullets flew from ship to shore, to be answered in kind in reverse. The ballistas sang, and fire fell among the Grg, though for the most part the flaming missiles were dodged.

But then a great howl of elation rose up from the Spawn.

"Kapitan! Kapitan!" shouted Nikolai. "Look!"

Aravan gazed toward where Nikolai pointed.

Out among the tall foliage, a burning Troll wrenched upright. Aflame and fully skewered by a ballista-flung lance, the Troll jerked to its feet.

"Wot th' . . . ?" Long Tom gaped at the fiery apparition.

Aylis muttered an arcane word, and with her <sight> she peered at the jerking, wrenching Ogru just as it took up a large slab of stone and juddered about to come toward the ship.

"Aravan, it is not alive," she called. "There must be a Necromancer near."

"Where away?" called Aravan.

"I cannot <see> him. I ween he is shielding himself from my <sight>."

Bearing the heavy stone, the Troll afire—its flesh sizzling and popping, greasy gray smoke swirling upward from the blaze—lumbered toward the pier.

"Oh, Gralon, but Oi do think he's thinkin' o' throwin' that monstrous rock at us, Oi do," cried Long Tom. "He be aimin' t' hole th' hull."

Swiftly cranking, the Châkka recocked the ballistas. "Lade stone!" cried Dokan.

"Stone?" asked a nearby Châk, even as he reached for one of the granite balls.

"Neither fire nor spear has slowed him," growled Dokan. "Mayhap we can break him apart."

Again, the Foul Folk erupted in jubilation, and aboard the ship Pipper said, "Adon, Adon, look," as the second burning Ogru wrenched itself up out from the tall foliage growing along the shore.

Arrows and sling bullets flew, all to no effect against the first of these hideous creatures.

Thunn! sang the ballista, and the rocky missile hurtled through the air to strike the burning, spear-pierced, slab-bearing Troll along the left side of its abdomen, punching through, leaving a gaping wound behind. As the monster staggered sidewise a step, viscera slid out from the hole to hiss and sputter in the fire. Yet in spite of his entrails spilling forth to burn, the creature recovered and lumbered on.

"If ye can, take off its head," commanded Aravan.

Châkka adjusted the aim.

Thunn!

"Kruk! Missed!"

As the Spawn jeered and flew arrows at the crew, onto the pier thudded the Troll, the second Troll afire following yards behind, a small boulder in its grasp.

"Kapitan, cut hawser?"

"Nay, Nikolai. They will throw ere we move away."

T-thunn! Two more ballistas loosed, one to miss, the other to slam into the first dead thing's right shoulder. It dropped the slab to the pier, and jerkily stooped to pick it up. And still the second Troll came on.

The monster on the pier lifted the slab and jerked upright and raised the hunk overhead to throw.

"Oh, lor! Oh, lor!" cried Binkton, even as he loosed another ineffective arrow at the Ogru. "It's going to sink us."

Among the dense riverside foliage, Lissa looked at her last arrow, the small missile with its dark barb deadly and nigh instantly lethal. She had slain eighteen Foul Folk with her shafts—all of them bow-bearing Rucha and sling-bearing Loka, for with the ship out in the stream, these were the long-range foe.

She had disobeyed Aravan's last command, though were she to be questioned about it, she *could* claim that he had told her only to hie back to the ship. And certainly she had nearly done so. Still, she knew that she would be more valuable ashore than to be stranded afloat, where her bow-cast missiles would be somewhat outside decent range. And so, riding Vex she had slipped among the growth and had slain eighteen Rûpt in all. And as she had done so, several times Loka or Rucha had spotted her, and she and Vex had fled through the growth, veering this way or swerving that, dodging black-shafted missiles, or escaping wide cuts of hard-swung tulwars or the smashes of hammering cudgels, and each time she and the fox had avoided the death-dealing strikes and had managed to lose the pursuit, for none of the Rûpt was as swift as the vixen.

And now Pysk and fox lurked in the weeds, and Lissa was down to a single arrow; surely she needed it for protection.

But then she heard the Spaunen cheering and jeering, and she risked standing on Vex's back, the better to see.

A burning Troll? But it's dead. How can such a thing—? Of a sudden she knew why, and who her last target had to be. She slipped back astride Vex and gave the fox her orders.

Through the tall growth slipped the vixen, her nose questing, and another cheer rose up from the Rûpt. Still the fox searched. Finally, she leaned forward as if on a point. "Go," whispered Lissa, and ahead the vixen skulked.

They slipped up behind one who must be a Mage and, Mage or no, Lissa with her single remaining arrow had to try. For had not Aylis said, "Magekind is just as vulnerable to slings and arrows and blades as are others; it is simply a matter of getting close enough to take him unaware"?

Even as the being gestured toward the two Trolls afire, and as the one lifted the slab overhead to hurl, Lissa nocked the tiny arrow and drew aim and loosed.

Malik was dead between one breath and the next, and certainly before he hit the ground.

On the pier the Troll collapsed, the slab crashing down upon it. The other Troll crumpled as well.

The dead were dead again.

The jeering Rûpt fell silent, and a Hlôk near their newly slain leader howled in dismay.

Without any Spawn shouting a command, of a sudden the entire force of Foul Folk fled away, most running upriver, a few running downstream, none running toward the City of Jade, for they dreaded what lay within.

47

Respite

ELVENSHIP
MID AUTUMN, 6E9

With the Rûpt fled away, Long Tom sent sailors in two dinghies to the stone quay, the boats pulling mooring lines from the ship to the shore. They landed and once again tied the *Eroean* to the pier. Then, using long iron pry bars, they rolled the dead Troll into the water, and down it sank like the heavy-boned thing it was, to become fish food along with the two drowned Trolls some forty-seven feet below. After the ship was tethered to the dock, Long Tom had the crew loosen the port-bow anchor winch and pay out the hawser, and with the mooring lines along the starboard side they drew the *Eroean* back to the pier. Yet, when safely tied up, they once again cranked the anchor hawser tight—"Should we need t' pull th' same trick agin', lettin' th' river 'n' anchor rope swing us away from th' quay."

As soon as the crew ashore lifted the gangplank back into place, Aravan and a litter crew hurried to where James had fallen. The bosun was yet breathing, though unconscious. A grume-slathered Ruchen arrow jutted out from his back. The crew carefully placed him onto the litter and bore him back to the ship. As they went up the footway, Lissa and Vex followed.

"Where were you?" asked Pipper.

"Killing Spaunen, mostly Rucha," she replied.

"I got seven with my sling," said Pipper. He smiled, but it did not reach his eyes, for killing of anyone, even maggot-folk, did not set well on his mind. "And Bink, here, got eight."

"I had twenty arrows," said Lissa, "but I wasted one against a Troll. It did not penetrate that thick hide of his."

"What of your other arrows?" asked Bink.

"Eighteen Rûpt and one Mage."

Even as Binkton gaped at the Pysk and breathed, "Eighteen?" Pipper blurted, "The Trolls!"

"Pip, she just said her arrows didn't penetrate their hide."

"No, Bink. What I meant is that by Liss killing the Mage, that's what brought down the dead Trolls."

"Oh," said Binkton, the light dawning. "You're right, Pip." Binkton turned to Lissa. "You saved us all."

"The Knight!" Pipper exclaimed. And even as Binkton groaned, Pipper said, "Lady Aylis's reading. Liss drew the Knight of Swords upright, and Aylis said, 'Victory over a dire foe, in this orientation, though perhaps at great peril.' Don't you see, Bink, Lady Aylis had it right all along, for a Necromancer is a dire foe." Pipper turned to Lissa, adding, "And out there among the Rûcks and such, well, you were indeed at great peril."

"Vex kept me safe," said Lissa. Then she looked about the ship. "What of the others? How did the warband and sailors fare?"

"Some took wounds," said Binkton. "Arrows and slingstones. Most of the Dwarves avoided the missiles, or their armor kept them safe. The sailors took the largest part of the hurt. Desault has commandeered space belowdecks to be an infirmary, where he's taken the wounded for treatment."

Lissa said, "Well, I hope he knows about Ruchen arrows. They can be quite nasty, you see, as vile as they are."

Even as Lissa spoke, as he carefully worked the shaft back out from the chief bosun belowdecks Desault said, "It is essential for us to get all wounds as clean as we can, for these Rûcken arrows, they bear a festering disease. A person can die days, even weeks after taking such a wound. They turn the flesh black, and a dreadful rot sets in. Were it an arm or a leg, and that were to happen, we would amputate. But where James is injured, all we can do is wait and see. So, let the wounds bleed freely for a short while, and probe gently with these cleansing swabs to clear out as much of the dark filth as you can, even though it will pain the patient." Desault then held up vials of yellowish liquid. "Then hold them down and pour this fluid in the gash."

And so, amid groans of the injured, Aylis and others helped Desault treat the wounded—cleansing, pouring, bandaging, and giving the worst of them sops of poppy juice to ease the agony. As well, they set and splinted the bones of five sailors, bones broken by the large slingstones of the Spawn.

And up on deck lookouts watched as along the shore Dwarves dragged slain Grg into a pile, heeding the Pysk's warning to touch not any of her shafts that might be protruding from Ükhs or the back of the neck of the Mage. And as to the dead Troll yet ashore, it took nearly all of the Dwarven force to drag that still-burning corpse to the pile. When that was done, they splashed oil thereon and the licking flames on the corpse of the Troll set the whole afire.

As black and grey smoke spiralled into the sky, Nikolai turned to Aravan and asked, "When we go City of Jade?"

"On the morrow, Nick. Tonight we rest and recover."

And so that night, weary from the stress of battle, and glad to have survived, the crew entire took turns at watch and at sleeping, all but the wounded, that is, some of whom fell into drugged stupors, others to lie awake in pain. The captain and Aylis and Lissa and Binkton and Pipper and other comrades moved among them and spoke quiet words of support.

And even as they did so, the sky began to darken, and a wind began to stir, as of an oncoming storm.

48

Calamity

DARK DESIGNS
MID AUTUMN, 6E9

At the onset of night and smiling to himself in his aethyrial form, Nunde flew out from his tower in the Grimwalls and headed for the City of Jade. Surely by now, Malik had triumphed and had Aravan's corpse in his possession. *I will have to reward my loyal and clever apprentice for succeeding in his task. Yet, wait: should I reward him for something I planned? After all, he is merely an extension of my own hand. Oh, why not? Surely a reward will confuse him, and I would add to his distress, and that will please me much.* And so, in astral contentment, Nunde sped toward that far-distant land.

Yet when he neared and with his reversed aethyrial vision he saw along the shore a thin spiral of white smoke rising up as from a dying fire. Nearby and peacefully docked lay the Elvenship. Human and Dwarven lookouts aboard kept watch, yet these Nunde did not fear, for they could not see him. Only that trollop who consorted with Aravan had the <sight> to do so. Yet careful observation showed him the whore was not adeck, and so Nunde swooped low over the dwindling blaze, where he saw the massive bones of an Ogh amid the ashes.

Shaken, he sped toward the col between the hills where the ambush had been set. No one was there. Where had they gone? Surely they couldn't have been—

Nunde sped back to the smoldering remains of the fire. Not only were there Ogh bones among the ashes, but a medallion that Malik had worn. Malik had failed! Malik had failed! Aravan, no doubt, yet lived.

How did they discover his trap? The hawk! That must be how. That slut of a Seeress must have flown the bird under the canopy and had peered through its eyes and had found the ambush waiting. And that fool of an apprentice had somehow lost all in an attack on the ship. Four Oghi and a hundred Drik and another hundred Ghoki: more than two hundred Chûn in all. How could he have done so, with the ship bound to the pier and as vulnerable as a puling child? *Idiot! Imbecile! May he rot forever! May he have died in unbearable agony!*

Now I must do that which will put me in peril.

Nunde sped back to his distant tower, where he ordered the roundup of hundreds of Drik. And in an orgiastic frenzy of killing, not only to vent his rage, but also to bloat his being with <fire>, he began an all-day slaughter. For what he now needed to do, in fact had been *forced* to do by that foul Dolh, was to cast a spell while in his aethyrial form, and to do that took energy beyond compare. And so he slew and slew, and tortured and flayed and sucked up the life force needed to perform the deed. But even then, even though swollen with power, he knew he might not survive the loosing of the *thing* he was about to set free to do his bidding, for if he could not reconfine it, the creature would come after him next.

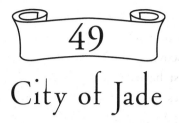

49

City of Jade

B lustery dawn came dismal.
Long Tom looked up at the flying wind pennants atop the masts
and the glowering sky above, and then he turned his attention toward the
swaying forest canopy in the near distance. "We be in f'r a blow, Oi
think, Oi do," he said to no one in particular.

"Aye," replied Nikolai, raising his voice to be heard above the flapping
of the luffing staysails. "You t'ink we be go lost city today?"

"Aye. The cap'n, he says y' be, j'st as soon as th' warband finish briakin'
their fast."

Noddy came topside, a glum look on his face.

"Oy, naow, Noddy, y' be all chapfallen, y' be," said Long Tom, when
the bosun came up the stern ladder.

"Oi wanted t' go to th' city with th' others," replied Noddy.

"Wull, y' can't, what wi' James all wounded and such. Oi mean, we
can't leave th' ship wi' no bosun."

Nikolai nodded in agreement with Long Tom's words, but Noddy
said, "Ar, they ain't no enemies left, what with the Mage and Trolls bein'
deaders, and the livin' Foul Folk all run away."

Nikolai shook his head. "Lady Aylis, last night she say she t'ink bad
Mage might be Knight of Sword. If right, King of Sword still enemy. Ship
might need sail."

"Wull, that's easy f'r you to say, Nick," Noddy dolefully said, "'cause you get t' go, while me 'n' Long Tom have t' stay j'st in case some runaway Rûcks 'r th' like show up 'n' th' ship has t' be moved. 'N' wot 'r th' chances o' that, eh? Nought, I say. Nought."

Nikolai smiled and said, "I tell ever'ting we see."

"Won't be th' same," grumped Noddy.

Long Tom sighed his concurrence.

As Aravan and Aylis came out onto the main deck, Aylis said, "You will need my <sight>. Besides, with scouts running ahead and your blue stone amulet and the warband about, I will have forewarning as well as protection should peril be nigh."

Nikolai leaned over to Long Tom and whispered, "Cap'n, he no win this battle."

"Aye, he won't," murmured Long Tom in reply.

Aravan looked long at the jungle ahead, and then at Aylis, and then the jungle again. Finally, he said, "Fetch thy weaponry."

Aylis smiled and said, "They're already adeck." She gestured to one of the crewmen, and he stepped forward to hand Aylis her bow and a full quiver of green-fletched arrows.

"I don't think we'll need climbing gear," said Binkton, looking back downward as he reached the top of the ladder up from the main hold.

"We might," came Pipper's voice from below. "I mean, Bink, who knows what lies past that col the Foul Folk were camped in? There might be cliffs and—"

"All right. All right," said Binkton, clambering on out. "Bring it if you wish. But, me, I just think it's extra weight."

Moments later Pipper emerged, a backpack strapped on. Just as his cousin did, Pipper also bore a small horn to signal the band, should there be a need.

"You've got your sling and plenty of bullets, right?" asked Binkton, he himself well armed with bow and arrows.

"Right," said Pipper, patting a pocket and touching a bullet case affixed to his belt.

"Can't be too careful, you know," said Binkton. "As Uncle Arley says, 'Be prepared.'"

"That's why I'm bringing climbing gear," said Pipper, a superior smile upon his face.

"Argh!" growled Binkton, shaking his head.

Brekk and Dokan and the warband emerged, twenty of whom were going on the march, while the remainder of the Dwarves would stand watch on the *Eroean*, all but the two wounded below.

A squad of nine armed sailors made ready to march with the warband as well—cargo handlers and other such, for they would make estimates as to hauling and lading in the event they all came upon something the captain would have them eventually stow in the holds.

"Where's Liss?" asked Pipper, looking about.

"She and her fox have gone ahead," said Fat Jim. "They left just a wee while ago."

"That little sneak!" burst out Binkton. "Come on, Pip, let's go. I don't care if her fox is faster than us; we'll show her what Warrow scouts can do."

"Hold," commanded Aravan.

As the buccen swung about, Aravan said, "I would have ye two no more than three hundred of your paces ahead of the main body. Stay alert, for we know not what lies to the fore."

"Three hun—?" Binkton started to protest, but Pipper said, "You heard the captain. Three hundred it is." Then he saluted and said, "Aye-aye, sir."

And so, as the warband and sailors assembled, along with Aravan and Aylis, Binkton and Pipper started down the gangplank, Binkton grumbling, Pipper whistling a merry tune.

"One-two-three," growled Binkton.

"What are you doing?" asked Pipper.

"Counting off three hundred bloody paces," snapped Binkton. "Don't want to get too far ahead, you know. Where was—? Oh, how about six-seven-eight—"

And on they went: Binkton stubbornly counting, Pipper sighing at his cousin's unseemly behavior.

When Binkton reached the three-hundred mark, he stopped, Pipper stuttering a few steps before stopping as well. Binkton looked back toward the ship through the swaying foliage, the plants rocking in the wind. "Huah! I can see the top of the masts, but nothing else," said Binkton. "You know, it's quite far away."

"Well," said Pipper, "give me a boost and I'll see if the warband is following."

Binkton cupped his hands, and Pipper stepped into the finger stirrup and looked back. "Ah, they're just now starting. And you're right: it is quite far we've come."

He turned and looked the other way. "The trees are just ahead."

"Time to go in caution," said Binkton, as Pipper stepped back down. Binkton lowered his voice and added, "Spread wide, but keep the path in sight."

Binkton slipped left of the overgrown path as Pipper moved off rightward. And into the canopied forest they went. All about them, giants of the rain forest reared upward, their trunks buttressed with flanges. Banyan trees, too, huge and many-trunked, added to the interlace overhead. But the forest was not silent, for the wind caused wood to creak and vines to swing and the leaves above to whisper *shssh*.

Neither Pipper nor Binkton could see or hear the other, with Binkton somewhere off to the left and Pipper off to the right, and they moved stealthily onward, now and again making certain they had not strayed too far from the overgrown path.

Far behind came the warband and sailors. And Aylis said, "Even with my <sight> invoked I cannot see the Warrows."

"They are stealthy, my love," said Aravan. "I think neither of us will espy them unless they deliberately make themselves visible."

"Do you think they will remain within three hundred paces?"

Aravan laughed. "Mayhap not. Yet I gave them that command so that they would not run off completely willy-nilly."

"Think you they would do so?"

"Pipper sometimes strikes me as impulsive, but I also would not put it past Binkton to do so just to show Lissa that he and his cousin are scouts as well."

"Are they scouts or not?"

"I deem someday they will be very good at the task, yet I think them more valuable as two who can get into places others cannot."

"Lock picking and acts of stealth and guile, you mean?"

"Aye. After all, they were taught by one of the best."

Binkton froze in place, for, in spite of the wind in the forest, he heard quiet movement ahead. He nocked an arrow to his bow and silently stepped behind the bole of a tree.

The stealthy movement continued to advance toward him, and Binkton envisioned a monstrous snake or dreadful jungle cat sneaking upon him. He listened, and as it drew closer he knew this was no snake, for it did not slither but stepped softly instead.

And he waited. . . .

And on it came. . . .

Until . . .

It paused on the opposite side of the trunk.

And then a voice said, "Don't shoot. It's just me."

Binkton exhaled the breath he had been holding. "Lissa?"

"Of course."

Binkton stepped 'round the tree to see the Pysk and fox. "How did you know it was—?"

"Vex told me."

"Ah . . . yes."

"Where's Pipper?"

Binkton waved off to the right. "The other side of the path. Somewhere yon."

"I'll find him. —Or, rather, Vex will," said Lissa.

"To tell him what?" asked Binkton. "For that matter, why are you here instead of out there?" He gestured upslope toward the hills.

"I came back to say the way ahead is clear. No one lurks in the col, though there be Troll scat and other Rûptish dung and filth. The stench is quite strong, especially to Vex. And the city lies a bit beyond."

"You've been there?"

"Not in the city. Just to within sight of it. Vex seems uneasy, but just why she cannot tell me. Whatever it is, it's not Spaunen."

"Well, then, if there's nothing ahead in the way of Rûcks and such, is there any need for stealth?"

"Not until you reach the city, and mayhap not even then."

"What do you intend to do, Liss?"

"Find Pipper and tell him what I told you, then report back to the warband. Where are they, by the bye?"

Binkton gestured behind and growled, "About three hundred bloody paces back along the trace."

"All right, then. I'll see Pipper and then report to Aravan."

"Tell Pip to meet me in the path. We'll go on ahead to the city."

Lissa frowned and started to say something, but Binkton said, "We'll be all right." And so she and Vex darted off toward the opposite side of the overgrown trail, while Binkton followed more slowly. When he reached the weedy way, he waited.

Some long moments later, Pipper appeared, uphill of where Binkton stood. Binkton trudged up to Pipper, and then together they went east through the dimness under the swaying forest canopy, a swirling wind below, a glum sky high above.

"And Binkton and Pipper?"

"They went on ahead, Captain," said Lissa. "The trail is clear of Rûpt: no ambushes, no squads, or lone assassins. I think it safe, though Vex senses something ominous about the city, yet what it might be she cannot say."

"Sniff strange smell?" asked Nikolai.

"The fact the city be dead?" asked Wilfard, one of the cargo chiefs.

Lissa frowned and shook her head. "No. It's more like the time we went ashore at that set of islands ringing 'round the blue hole. Vex just seems uneasy."

Aravan turned to Brekk. "Remain alert, Armsmaster."

Brekk grunted an assent.

Aravan then glanced at Aylis.

"My <sight> is invoked," she said, without being asked.

"Then let us catch up to our wandering Waerlinga," said Aravan.

"Would you have me try to overtake them ere they reach the city, Captain? Vex is quite swift."

Aravan shook his head. "I deem they have enough caution to be the scouts they fancy themselves to be."

With Pipper whistling snatches of a merry melody and singing a few words between, he and Binkton strolled out from under the jungle canopy to come to the edge of a forsaken place. Pipper's tune came to an abrupt stop, and only the groan of the wind broke the stillness.

"Whoa," said Binkton. "Would you look at that."

Spread out before them lay the ruins of an abandoned city, with some buildings yet standing while others lay in shambles. Cracked pave made up the streets winding among dwellings and establishments and a temple or two, and all of the structures were made of stones of various hues. Vines twined among the rock and cascaded down the sides of walls, the leaves fluttering in the moaning wind as of green waterfalls tumbling. Here and there trees had taken hold and throughout the long eras had become huge, their massive roots snaking across the streets and diving into the earth, to fracture and tilt the pavement upward, splitting the stone with an inexorable, steadily increasing pressure as the trees had grown.

"Hoy, there," said Pipper, pointing.

Dwarfing the other structures, in the near distance ahead in what appeared to be the city center stood five towers: a central one hemmed in by four.

"The middle one looks like Lady Aylis's statuette," said Binkton.

"Other way about," said Pipper.

"What now?" asked Binkton.

"It's the other way about," said Pipper. "Lady Aylis's statuette looks like the tower."

"Isn't that what I just said?"

"No, Bink, you said it just backwards."

"Did not."

"Did too."

Bickering, in among the ruins they went, heading for the towers, while dark sky roiled above and the wind keened across stone and over walls and 'round corners, wailing as would a thousand ghosts lost in the cracks of time.

"Jade," said Brekk. "This stone, all of it is jade."

Aravan and Aylis, along with Lissa and the warband and sailors, had reached the edge of the ruins.

"The entire city is jade?" asked Lissa, even as she leaned forward and ran a hand along Vex's neck, trying to soothe the vixen, who yet indicated that they should leave, even though she didn't know why.

"At least this part of it is," replied Brekk.

"But not all green," objected Nikolai.

"Jade comes in many colors," said Aylis. "Green, yellow, white, grey, black, orange, and even in pale violet."

Brekk nodded his agreement.

"Speak of green," said Nikolai, pointing.

"The tower," breathed Lissa.

"I suspect that's where we will find Binkton and Pipper," said Aravan. He looked at Lissa and said, "Take point."

As the Pysk and reluctant fox trotted ahead, Brekk gestured left and right, and Dwarves moved to flanking positions, and all set out, war hammers, crossbows, bows, or falchions in hand, though Aravan bore a spear.

With the moaning wind whipping his shoulder-length hair about his face, "It has no door," said Pipper, as he and Binkton finished circling the midmost tower, central to four others close-set in a square, there in the heart of the city plaza.

"No doors, Pip? You noticed, eh?" said Binkton. Then he grinned and added, "Well spotted, bucco."

Pipper looked up at the smooth, virtually seamless stone. "Wull, then, how does anyone ever get inside?"

"Mayhap they weren't meant to," said Binkton.

Pipper stroked his fingers across the pale green, almost translucent surface. "I don't even think our climbing gear will be of any use."

"I *told* you it would just be extra weight," said Binkton smugly.

Pipper looked at an adjacent tower. "That one has a door. —Say, maybe there's a secret passage from that to this."

Binkton sighed and said, "Let's just wait for— Oh, here comes Liss now."

"There you are," said Lissa. "I don't think the captain is very pleased that you didn't wait."

"Oops," said Pipper, glancing at Binkton.

"Well, that's all water under the bridge now," said Binkton. He looked back in the direction Lissa had come. "Where is the captain?"

"He and the others are on their way," said Lissa, gesturing hindward. Vex whined.

Lissa petted the fox along the neck. "It'll be all right, Vex."

"What's the matter with her?" asked Pipper.

"As I told you back along the trail," replied Lissa, "there's something about the city that seems to bother her."

"Perhaps she scents something we cannot smell," said Pipper.

"No, it's not an odor," said Lissa. "But something else that she cannot make me understand."

Pipper looked about as if seeking hidden foes, and Binkton said, "Perhaps it's this blasted wind, shrieking among the stone as it is. That or the darkness in the middle of the day. I mean, we're in for a storm, and Vex knows it."

"Arm hair," blurted Pipper.

"What in the world—" began Binkton, but Pipper said, "What I mean is, sometimes when a storm is coming, the hairs on my arms stand straight up. Then there is a flash and a boom, and lightning streaks the sky."

Binkton turned toward Pipper. "And what does that have to do with anything?"

"Well, Vex is hair all over, and—"

"I don't think that's it, Pip," said Lissa.

"Oh," said Pipper, then added, "Why don't we wait here till the others arrive?"

Lissa turned the vixen. "I'll tell the captain where you are."

As Pysk and fox trotted away, Pipper and Binkton sat down on blocks of dark green jade, Pipper again looking about for . . . what? He did not know.

Amid the warband and sailors, Lissa and Aylis and Aravan entered the city square. At Aravan's side, Brekk growled, "There they are," gesturing toward the buccen, even as Pipper stood and began trotting toward the group, while Binkton followed at a more leisurely pace.

In that very same moment, as Aravan's stone of warding grew icily chill, Aylis looked up at the pale green central tower and gasped in alarm. "Aravan, something, a thing dark to my <sight>, just flashed into—"

Before she finished saying what she <saw>, a great blast of aethyric energy exploded out through the openings high above, and, shielding her eyes, Aylis jerked her face to the side, just as a vast cloud of darkness boiled out from the top of the tower and swooped down toward them. "Châkka shok, Châkka c—" called Brekk, even as Aylis cried, "Oh, Adon, it's not ali—" and Aravan hefted his spear, shouting, "'Ware—"

And then the darkness clenched them all—all Dwarves, all sailors, Aravan, Aylis, Lissa, Vex, and, at the far edge, Pipper.

And they fell to their knees and toppled sideways and began to scream in unendurable agony.

Yet within that seethe of anguish, though engulfed in unbearable pain as he lay upon the tiles, Aravan managed to reach out and take Aylis's hand ere the torment o'erwhelmed him.

And even as Binkton ran toward fallen Pipper, to his Warrow sight he saw dreadful roiling within the darkness, and it seemed as if a monstrous twist of blackness descended upon one of the sailors, and the man screamed and screamed and writhed as if the life were being sucked out of him, and the darkness itself grew.

Binkton reached for Pipper—"Ahh!" he yelled in pain—as his hand entered the shadow. He jerked back. Yet Pipper shrieked in anguish. And, gritting his teeth, Binkton reached into the shade again. Screaming in dire hurt, still Binkton grabbed Pipper's ankle, and gripping tightly and bawling, he fell backward while yet hanging on. Jerking, hauling, he dragged Pipper free of the *thing*. And then he sat sobbing, as Humans and Dwarves and a Pysk and her fox and a Seeress and an Elf thrashed in torment beyond bearing.

And the twist of blackness within rose up from the sailor and moved to another, the one left behind unmoving. And once again it coiled about its victim and began sucking away his life essence.

Binkton grabbed Pipper and began shaking him. "Come on, Pip. Come on. It's killing them all."

Pipper groggily opened his eyes—"Wha-wha-?"—and then snapped awake. "What is it?"

Binkton jerked Pipper about. "Look! Oh, Adon, look!"

"Oh, oh, oh no, oh no," cried Pipper. He got to his feet and started toward the fallen. But Binkton grabbed him and hauled him back, shouting, "We can't go into the darkness! It's deadly!"

"Deadly?"

"It had you, Pip. It had you. Watch, watch the thing inside."

Pipper turned and looked and cried out, "Oh, Elwydd, what is it? Adon! Adon! It's killing them, killing them!"

"What'll we do, Pip? What'll we do?"

The knot of darkness released a now-dead sailor, and it descended upon a Dwarf.

"We can't let this go on," shouted Pipper. "What is it? Where did it come from?"

Binkton slued about, and his Warrow vision followed a dark, twisted, ropy strand of the *thing* back up to the top of the central tower. "There!" he cried. "Pip, it's from there."

"We've got to get to the top," cried Pipper. "Perhaps we can somehow stop it."

"But how? There is no door," shouted Binkton above the wail of a strengthening wind and the screams of agony.

Pipper whipped the pack off his back and dragged out the rope and grapnel. "It's too high," wailed Binkton.

"We're going to the other tower," shouted Pipper, "the one with the door."

The twist inside the darkness moved from the Dwarf to another sailor and embraced the man, and again began sucking away the life. Yet at the same time, lo! Kalor, a descendent of Brega, Bekki's son, stirred upon the tiles, and, screaming in pain, levered himself up to one knee. And he took his war hammer in hand and, yelling in agony, he swung at the knot of blackness, but the hammer passed through without effect. And the thing turned upon its assailant and took all his essence from him.

Pipper and Binkton ran to the tower with the door. Binkton tried the handle. "Locked!" he spat, and reached for the wire in his belt.

And wind howled among the streets of the City of Jade, wailing about corners and screaming over walls and sobbing through broken windows.

The *thing* within the void now sucked upon another Dwarf, while all about the creature its victims-to-be shrieked, all unknowing, all unthinking, all unseeing . . . unable to do ought but shrill.

"Hurry, Bink. Hurry!"

"Shut up, shut up!" snarled Binkton, and he bent the tip of the wire at a different angle and probed again.

Another Dwarf died ere Binkton succeeded. But at last the lock fell to his skills, and he and Pipper, grunting and shoving, managed to wedge the stone panel open.

They found the insides completely hollow, but for a spiral stair winding upward.

"Come on," shouted Pipper, and up they ran, turning, winding, ascending. At the very top they came to a jade trapdoor. And together and straining, with stone grating, they managed to lift it and throw it back.

They climbed onto a flat roof, a low parapet running about. They ran to the lip closest to the taller central tower; four openings could they see—the nearest fifty feet away.

"I can't throw that far," said Pipper.

"Give it to me," said Binkton.

And as the wind howled, and darkness roiled in the sky, and a *thing* below sucked the life out from another Dwarf, Binkton whirled the grapnel at a short length of line, while Pipper held the far end, the rope coiled so as not to impede the flight.

Binkton threw.

The grapnel fell short.

Swiftly he recovered the line and hook, and whirled and threw again.

It clanked into the side of the tower and dropped.

Once again Binkton whirled and threw, and this time the hook flew through the opening.

Pipper pulled the line taut and looked about, and only a runoff slot at the far side did he see. "Oh, Adon, there's nought to tie this end to."

"Yes, there is," shouted Binkton above the shriek of the wind. And he took the line and wrapped it about his waist thrice and lay down with his back to the roof and his feet against the parapet, the rope taut. He looked at Pipper and said, "I hope I can hold this."

"Remember, Bink, your card, the one you drew for Lady Aylis, it was Strength."

"Oh, Pip, the wind, it's—"

"And mine was the Naïf," shouted Pipper, stepping to the parapet. "A decision to be made, and I've made it."

And gauging the force of the swirling wind, Pipper stepped onto the line.

And as the rope took Pipper's weight, Binkton grunted and gritted his teeth and held on with all his might, his legs trembling with the strain.

Across the line, sloping slightly upward, Pipper ran, praying to El-wydd and Adon that Uncle Arley's training in the pines would see him through. *Don't place a foot wrong, don't place a foot wrong, Pip!* And the howling wind tore at him, as of a creature seeking to hurl him to his death on the jade stone far beneath.

And the swirl of darkness within the *thing* below moved on to another sailor. Just beyond writhed screaming Lissa, yowling Vex twisting at her side.

Pipper lost his balance just as he reached the arched opening, yet with a final lunge he managed to grasp the sill and pull himself in.

He jumped to the floor and looked about, and did not see the shadowy grey form slumped against the far wall, an astral being who had spent too much power loosing the deadly creature, a *thing* that had just finished sucking the life from a Human and now descended upon a Pysk.

But up above in the tall tower, Pipper could see an urn at rest on a high pedestal. Yet, what did that have to do with—? But then with his Warrow sight he saw the twisted rope of darkness extending from the footed vase and leading out and down to the plaza below.

As Pipper loaded a bullet into his sling, he did not see the astral form that struggled to its feet and limped to that same opening, nor did he hear the frantic aethyrial shout.

And the blackness below sucked up into a ball and flew toward the arched opening high above.

With a whirl and a snap, Pipper loosed the bullet, just as he was engulfed by darkness and hideous pain once again.

Yet the missile flew true, and it shattered the delicate, rune-marked vase, scattering the ashes of a deadly wraith.

And the howling wind whirled up those ashes and hurtled them out from the tower, scattering them wide, spinning the motes spiralling away like the long-dead dust they were, the wraith mewling even as its unnatural life bled away on the storm.

And Pipper fell unconscious, released from unbearable agony.

And even as an astral being fled toward a far-distant mountain fastness, the skies opened and a torrential rain thundered down and down on the long-lost City of Jade.

50

Escape

DARK DESIGNS
MID AUTUMN, 6E9

Nunde expended nearly every bit of the remainder of his essence just to reach his stronghold in the Grimwalls. It had been a close call, for he had spent too much of the stolen <life force> as well as his very own merely to release the wraith. He certainly had not retained enough <essence> to imprison the Shade again, and he knew that when the fiend had finished with Aravan and his band, he, himself, would be the next victim. Yet even as Nunde had been gathering his strength to flee back to his fortress, where he planned to slay many more Chûn for their <fire>, enough to defeat the wraith, that fool of a Warrow had entered the sanctum of the jade tower.

And when the Necromancer had seen the Warrow ready his sling to break the funerary urn, he knew that only the Shade could stop the intruder. And Nunde, at peril of his own life, had cried out a warning. Yet the Warrow had succeeded, and though Aravan was most likely slain, mayhap his trollop had survived. Nunde could not risk that whore of a Seeress discovering who he was, for she would send legions of Magekind to track him down, and he would spend the rest of his existence in flight.

And so Nunde had fled, and now he was back in his own body and wheezing for each feeble breath, while locked away safely in his chamber, locked away from Ghoki and Driki and Oghi and all other Chûn, any of whom at an opportune moment might try to slay him, and he was oh, so very weak.

And it was a frail, greatly aged Necromancer who struggled up from his dark throne to totter to his bed and collapse. On the morrow he would slaughter many Drik and wrench their fire from them to restore his own youth and essence. But for now, totally spent, he needed rest, and he fell into a black and dreamless sleep.

51

Recovery

A ravan awakened in a drenching rain to the sounds of someone
shouting in the distance and the whines of a fox nearby. Slowly he
rolled to his side to see Aylis, lying as if dead. Up he wrenched and scrambled to her and took her form in his arms. *She breathes.* He looked about.
Dwarves lay strewn like tenpins—sailors, too. But Brekk was stirring, as
were some of the other members of the warband. Water runnelled everywhere, it seemed, and Vex whined and licked the face of Lissa, the Pysk
not moving. And Aravan swung his gaze about, trying to locate and identify who was shouting.

Atop one of the towers, with water cascading from runoff slots, he saw
Binkton standing at the lip of what looked to be a parapet, with a rope
strung loosely from where the buccan stood to one of the high openings
in the central tower. Aravan could just discern that Binkton called for
Pipper, but the swirling wind and hammering rain drowned out what else
he cried.

Aravan looked down at Aylis. Her eyelids twitched, yet she did not
come awake.

Brekk heaved himself to his knees and took his war hammer in hand,
the armsmaster glaring about, seeking foe. Yet there were only felled
Dwarves and fallen sailors at hand. He glanced across at Aravan.
"Captain?"

"See to the others," said Aravan, yet cradling Aylis. The cold rain beat on her upturned face, and he leaned over a bit to shield her from the worst of it, though it was rather like trying to stem a flood.

As Brekk slowly moved among the crew, others came to.

And still the rain hammered down.

"Find us some shelter," said Aravan. "One of these structures will do."

Brekk looked about. "There is a door open to that tower." He looked up. "And what is Binkton doing atop?"

"I know not," said Aravan, rising to his feet, Aylis yet in his arms.

Nikolai regained consciousness and got to his knees.

Aravan paused at the side of his second in command and said, "See to Lissa, Nick." Aravan inclined his head toward the Pysk. "Bring her to the tower where I go." And, carrying Aylis, Aravan crossed to the door and in.

Nikolai got to his feet and stepped to where Vex whined over Lissa. "*Aylos* Garlon!"

"What is it?" asked Brekk.

"See?" said Nikolai.

Brekk looked. The Pysk lay on a yellow jade pavestone laced with metallic streaks.

With a puzzled gaze, Brekk looked up at Nikolai. "I don't—"

"Pysk brown hair now gold," said Nikolai, even as he squatted and took tiny Lissa up. Cupping her away from the rain next to his chest and, with Vex trotting at his side, off toward the open door he strode, leaving an astonished armsmaster behind.

Still the rain poured down, and Brekk sent Bruki to discover just why Binkton was shouting. Occasionally Brekk would look up, and long moments later he saw Binkton shinnying along underneath the rope to get to the central tower. The armsmaster could see Bruki standing at the edge of the parapet, one end of the line cinched about the Dwarf's waist.

"Pip, Pip, wake up, Pip," urged Binkton, soaked to the skin, holding his cousin close.

Pipper moaned, but did not awaken.

"Come on, Pip. Come on." Binkton patted Pipper's face, and his cold hands seemed to rouse Pipper. So Binkton drew Pipper to one of the openings, where rain swirled in on the wind.

Pipper sputtered and wakened. "Oh, Bink, I was having the most terrible dream; there was this darkness and—" He looked about. "It wasn't a dream, was it? Oh, my"—his face filled with alarm, and he struggled to get up—"we've got to get out of—"

"No, Pip, no," said Binkton, pressing his cousin back down. "You killed the thing. It's gone, wailing away on the wind."

"Gone?"

Binkton smiled, nodding.

"Dead?"

"Blew away on the wind."

"Good," said Pipper. "Say, how did you get here?"

"The rope."

"But there was nothing to tie it to," said Pipper.

"Bruki is anchoring it," said Binkton, releasing Pipper.

They both got to their feet, and Pipper asked, "Shall we get out of here now?"

"Aye," said Binkton. "Beware, though, the rope is wet: slick as an eel."

"Eight Châkka and five Humans, Captain," said Brekk. "That's how many the *thing* slew."

"Where are they?"

"We bore them out of the rain and into another building, a low one with a roof."

As Aravan nodded and glanced about at the survivors, Brekk looked at Aylis, kneeling at Lissa's side. "Know you what the dark thing was?"

"A wraith, I think," said Aylis. "Some call it a Shade."

" 'Only shades and shadows now dwell therein,' " said Aravan, quoting the clay tablet they had found in the Caer Pendwyr archives.

Pipper and Binkton, now down from the roof, having shinnied across the line, sat shivering, yet cold from the chill rain. And Pipper quoted the writing from the statuette:

"Thrice I dreamt the dream
From the City of Jade I fled
Nought but shades now dwell."

He looked at Aravan and said, "Perhaps we should have fled as well."

Even as Aravan glumly nodded, Aylis shook her head. "'Twas an aethyrial presence who loosed the Shade."

All of those within hearing looked in astonishment at her, and Aravan asked, "Aethyrial presence?"

"Aye. Just as did I assume an aethyrial form to explore the Black Fortress, so, too, did someone enter the tower and set the Shade upon us."

"Who?" asked Binkton, an angry glint in his eye.

"The King," said Pipper, and as Binkton turned to look at him, Pipper added, "the King of Swords."

Aylis glanced over at the Warrow. "Most likely, Pipper. Most likely."

"Kapitan," said Nikolai, kneeling beside Aylis, both of their faces showing concern, "little one, she no wake."

"We've got to get back to the ship," said Aravan, "for warmth and food and respite. Once there, Desault can treat her."

"In this rain, Captain?" asked Willam, one of the cargo men.

Aravan looked at the trembling Warrows. "We must. The forest is drenched, and even should we find wood, starting a fire is uncertain at best."

"And impossible at worst," said Binkton.

"And there be no wood in this city of stone," said Tarley.

"It's not that far," said Pipper, "and perhaps the canopy will shield us from the worst of the downpour."

Aravan looked at the others and said, "We will return when the storm has passed and take up our dead for decent burial."

"Stone or fire," said Brekk. "Nought else will do." And he cast his hood over his head, as did all the surviving Dwarves.

And so, with Nikolai carrying Lissa, and Vex following at his side, the entire band headed for the *Eroean*.

Pipper was right in that the canopy sheltered them from the worst of the torrent, though the path itself ran ankle-deep with water, and the noise of rain in the leaves above drowned all speech. It was a grim-faced, sodden group that came up the gangplank.

Counting Vex, thirty-five had set out for the city, but only twenty-two returned.

When all had been warmed and fed and dressed in dry clothes, Aravan had called the crew together and had told them of the dreadful events in the city, Binkton and Pipper relating what they had done to destroy the dreadful Shade. All grieved at the fate of their shipmates—sailors and warband alike—yet they knew that death was a risk they each faced, and though it didn't lessen the sorrow, it somehow helped them to deal with it. Aravan then had held a meeting with his officers, and they decided what they would do in the days to come. Night had fallen, and still it rained, but the wind had slackened. And after making the rounds of the first watch, and having spoken to the wounded, Aravan entered his sleeping quarters. "Is she awake yet?"

"No, my love," said Aylis, "and I am worried."

Aravan sighed and looked at the wee Pysk, lying as she was in a soft bed of eider that had been stripped from one of the all-weather cloaks. "What says Desault?"

"That he cannot help her. And he says that he has seen others who have suffered harm, never to waken again. He deems that their spirits fled away. Oh, Aravan, mayhap the Shade has done permanent harm. Perhaps she will never waken." Aylis began to weep.

As if she understood Aylis's words, Vex whined, the vixen lying on the cabin floor at the foot of the tiny bed.

Aravan lifted Aylis up from the chair where she sat and embraced her and stroked her hair. Aylis returned his embrace and laid her head against his chest. After a while he asked, "Canst thou do ought with thy magery to find her lost spirit and waken her from this sleep?"

"No, I—" Aylis gasped and turned from Aravan and peered at Lissa. "Oh, love, you might have hit upon it."

In question, Aravan turned up a hand.

"She sleeps," said Aylis.

"Aye," said Aravan, not yet following her.

"And I but pray she dreams. If so, I can—"

"Dreamwalk," said Aravan, "and—"

"Mayhap find her soul," said Aylis.

Concern filled Aravan's features. "Wilt thou be in danger?"

"I don't think so," replied Aylis.

"Thy mentor, Ontah, was slain while dreamwalking, and thou and Jinnarin didst meet that same Gargon in Farrix's dream. What if thou dost meet the Shade in Lissa's sleep?"

Aylis pondered a moment and finally shook her head. "'Tis a risk I must take, Aravan, else she might be lost forever."

The cabin was lit by a single candle. Lissa lay in her eider bed, Vex at the foot. Aravan sat in the shadows, silent but for his soft breath. With her back to a wall, Aylis sat cross-legged with her hands resting on her knees, her mind calm, her body relaxed. And she closely watched the Pysk. The moment Lissa's eyes began whipping back and forth beneath her closed lids, "<*Añu*>," said Aylis softly, using one of Ontah's dreamwalking <words> of <suggestion>.

Aylis slipped into a state of deep meditation and used another of the ingrained <words> of <suggestion> taught to her by Ontah, and she began to dream:

She sat on a rock high in the mountains. Far below, a waterfall tumbled and became a river winding through a vale. Yet this was a dream Aylis could control, and she muttered a <bridge word>, one that allowed her to slip into another's dream. And she stepped through a crevice to cross over onto a flat yellow plain, for that was the 'scape of Lissa's dream. The sky above was aureate, as if begilded, and glittering metallic strands floated all about, as of spider silk on the wind, but spun of gold instead. A topaz sun shone brightly down on the plain, which itself was made of precious stone—yellow jade, it seemed, and it ran to the horizon and beyond.

Nikolai said he found Aylissa on a yellow jade pavestone, one shot through with metallic strands. Mayhap the Shade drove her spirit down and within. Yet, where is she?

Aylis rose up into the auric sky and slowly turned 'round, her gaze seeking—

There! Movement!

Swiftly, Aylis flew to overtake the figure.

It was Aylissa, trudging across the jade-stone land and sobbing.

Aylis landed in front of the Pysk, and she and Aylissa were of the same size.

Yet weeping, Lissa looked up through her tears. "I am lost," she said. "Can you help me?"

"Do you know who I am?" asked Aylis.

Lissa shook her head.

"Some name me Brightwing," said Aylis.

In spite of her tears, Lissa managed a frown and then said, "My mother told me of someone named Brightwing."

"I know your mother," said Aylis. "I called her Sparrow."

"Can you help me, Brightwing? I am lost."

"Yes, I can and will. Take my hand."

The Pysk took Brightwing's hand, and together they rose up into the sky.

"Oh, my," said Lissa. "I am flying."

"Then I will call you Wren," said Brightwing.

"Where are we going?" asked Wren.

"To see a fox," said Brightwing.

"Where?" asked Wren.

"Just across a bridge," said Brightwing. "But first you must learn a special <word>."

"What kind of <word>?"

"A <word> of <suggestion>."

"All right."

And Brightwing spoke to Wren the <word> and had her repeat it several times. When Brightwing was satisfied that Wren had the nuances well learned, she said a different <word>, and a hole formed in the yellow sky. In they flew—

—to emerge in a candlelit cabin.

"There is the fox," said Brightwing. "Her name is Vex." And she pointed at the vixen, who looked up at them both and made a yip.

"And there you are, Wren," said Brightwing, and she pointed at the Pysk.

"Is that me? Am I found?"

"You only need to say the <word> I taught you."

And so Wren spoke the <word> of <suggestion> and vanished. . . .

. . . And Aylissa opened her eyes.

Moments later Aylis opened her own eyes, and she wept to see Lissa sitting up and Vex bounding about in joy.

"What happened?" asked Lissa, peering into the small silver mirror held by Aylis. The Pysk pulled a tress of her hair in front of her eyes. "Why is it gold?"

"I don't know," said Aylis, shrugging. "Mayhap it had something to do with the pavestone you were on when the Shade, bloated with the <fire> of those it had slain, descended upon you."

"Pavestone?"

Aylis nodded. "Yellow jade streaked with gold."

"What would that have to do with ought?"

Again Aylis shrugged. "They say that jade is a special gemstone, yet what its properties might be, I cannot say. Those in Jinga call it 'yu,' and they attribute various powers to the different colors. I believe yellow jade is aligned with joy and fortune."

"And my hair turned golden just because I was lying on a piece of yellow jade?"

"No. If I had to guess, I would say instead it was because your spirit was driven into it by all the <fire> the Shade had stolen."

In that moment, Pipper and Binkton and Nikolai came bursting into the captain's lounge. "Liss! They said you were awake!" cried Pipper.

"I give you hug, but it crush you," said Nikolai.

"Something to celebrate," said Binkton, smiling, and Binkton seldom smiled.

"I'm so glad you survived," said Pipper.

"Me, too," said Lissa. "—I mean, I'm glad each of you survived as well. And Aylis says you two saved us all."

Pipper grinned and said, "Not bad for a pair of chicken thieves, eh?"

The lounge filled with laughter.

The next day the rain stopped, and the jungle turned into a steaming tangle of growth. The slain sailors and Dwarves were recovered from the jade structure where they had been placed, and were brought to an area near the ship. Even as fellow crewmen laid the five slain sailors to rest in stone cairns, the Dwarves hewed dead wood into billets, though it was wet from the storm, and constructed pyres, adding dry wood from the ship's stores. They poured lamp oil over all, and placed their slain atop.

All the wounded who could be were brought to the deck to witness the rites. The captain made a solemn speech at the cairns, and many wept, and then he spoke of the fallen resting atop the pyres. And he called out each of the names of the slain—comrades, shipmates, sailors, and warriors—each one to be entered in honor in the *Eroean*'s log. Finally, at a signal from Brekk, members of the warband thrust torches into the wood. As the flames caught and smoke rose, Aravan and Aylis sang their souls into the sky, and not an eye was dry when they fell silent.

The river rose over the next four days as the upstream runoff found its way to the course, and throughout those same four days, sailors and warband laded precious jade into the ship's holds.

The *Eroean* set sail on the outflowing tide of the swollen river the next morning.

She was on her way to Arbalin.

52

Homeward

ELVENSHIP
LATE AUTUMN, 6E9, TO EARLY SPRING, 6E10

James died of his wound six days after leaving the City of Jade behind. The Rûcken arrow had borne a festering disease, and a terrible dark rot had set in. There was nought Desault could do to stay the dark putrefaction, though poppy juice held back the pain somewhat. Ere James became too weak to talk, he had said to Aravan, "Cap'n, I've spent nearly all of my life asea, and so let it have me when I am gone." And so, when he died, they sewed James in canvas weighted with a ship's ballast stone, for that was what he wanted, and they gave him over to Gralon, god of the oceans.

Noddy was devastated, and during the ceremony he reverted to his East Lindor accent, saying, "He taught me everything Oi know, fro' the settin' o' th' sails t' get th' most outta th' wind t' th' blowin' o' th' poipe. 'N' e'en though Oi allus wanted t' be head bosun on th' *Eroean*, Oi allus thought it'd be when James took t' th' land, 'n' not loik this, oh, no, not loik this."

In these same six days, one sailor lost a foot to the Rûck-arrow blight, and another his left arm, Desault wielding his bone saw to save the lives of these men.

The wind was too strong for even the *Eroean* to make passage around the Cape of Storms, and so they came about and headed for the Silver Straits, which at this time of year was passable, for it was the warm season in the south.

They stopped off at the Great Isle in the Silver Sea to take on fresh water and provisions, after which they sailed onward, entering the South Polar Sea on Winterday.

Sailors warned the Warrows about the Grey Lady, and Binkton scoffed, while Pipper's eyes grew wide in wonderment. But then he said, "Oh, Bink, I'll have nightmares about a ghost ship, her sails all tattered, and a crew of lost spirits aboard."

"Pip, you've already faced the worst wraith you'll ever see, and look what you did to it. So, if any ghost ever tries to get you, just remind it of the fate of the Shade, and the ghost'll run away screaming in fear."

They sailed the Silver Straits without incident.

At the Calms of the Goat they spent nearly three weeks rowing through still air, and two weeks crossing the Midline Doldrums, and then another three weeks at the Calms of the Crab.

But finally, the wind returned and the *Eroean* sped across the water, to finally come to the Straits of Kistan and the Avagon Sea beyond.

Six days later and running before a westerly wind, the Elvenship *Eroean* came on and on, churning a white wake astern, with every bit of silken sail she could fly—mains and studs, jibs and spanker, staysails, topsails, gallants and royals, skysails and moonrakers and starscrapers—filled to the full. Eastward through the indigo waters of the deep blue Avagon Sea she ran, bearing some points to the north, the strong driving winds on her larboard beam aft. No other ship in the waters of Mithgar was faster; no other ship even came close.

Above the waterline her blue hull bore blackened smudges, as if she had taken damage from raiders, as of fireballs cast upon her. And indeed she had been set upon by a fleet of the Rovers of Kistan in the perilous long strait north of that isle. But she had given better than she had gotten, for three of the crimson-sailed dhows now lay at the bottom of the sea, while two others drifted aimlessly in the waters, their masts and sails and much of their decks in ruin, their foolish captains dead.

Yet that had occurred some two thousand sea miles astern, though it was but six days ago.

At her helm stood Aylis, brown-haired and tall and slender, a sprinkle of freckles high on her cheeks. Now and again she made slight adjustments in the set of the wheel, as if an occasional minor movement in response to a twitch in the wind kept the ship running swift and true.

Standing back on the aft deck and watching the lady helmsman maintain the course of the ship stood Fat Jim, his left arm in a sling, for it had been shattered by a hurled slingstone. Even so, still his hands twitched in synchronicity with each slight shift the lady made, and he nodded vigorously in agreement at every small turn of the wheel.

Aft of them both and with one elbow against the taffrail lounged Aravan, his tilted, sapphire blue eyes atwinkle, a slight smile on his face as he watched.

In the late-afternoon sunlight lying aglance 'cross the waves, up the ladder to the aft deck came Long Tom, tall and sandy haired and as broad as a great slab of beef. "M'lady Aylis," he said as he passed the helm, but she was concentrating on the wind-ribbon above, high atop the raked-back mizzenmast, and she did not reply, but made another slight adjustment instead.

"Fat Jim," said Long Tom, nodding to the rotund Pellarian, the *Eroean*'s first steersman.

"Tom," replied Fat Jim, without looking at the big man, but instead shifting his gaze from the streaming ribbon above to watch the lady's corresponding nudge of the helm.

"Cap'n Aravan," said the huge man.

"Long Tom," replied Aravan, shifting his attention to the first officer.

"Cap'n," said Long Tom, "th' crew has cleaned up the last o' th' damage done to th' decks, and they've replaced the two silks what was ruint by the bluidy Kistanee-flung fire. An' Brekk says that th' ballistas are as good as new, him 'n' his Dwarven warband settin' them t'rights. Th' only thing left is t'take th' soot 'n' smudge off th' sides o' th' hull and t'lay on a bit o' fresh paint, there where th' other fireballs struck. Soon as we drop anchor in Port Arbalin, I'll see the men get right to it."

Aravan shook his head. "Nay, Tom. After those yet injured are taken ashore and put in the care of the healers, as soon as the cargo is unladed and we moor in the harbor beyond, we'll take some time aland—a moon and fortnight at least, mayhap more—for this voyage has been hard on us all, and we deserve a goodly rest and time for wounds to heal, both those we can see and those we cannot. Hence, apart from a watch, we'll set the crew to shore leave, rotating the ward until all have had a fine fling, and until those with the most severe injuries and who would sail on with us have had a fair chance to recover.

"And we'll have to wait for Brekk to ride to the Red Hills and recruit eight Drimma to replace those we lost, and that will take three fortnights in all for the trip there and back."

"Cap'n, Oi'd loike t'help sign on th' Men we'll need t' bring th' sailor crew up t' full complement."

"Fear not, Tom, for when it comes to recruiting more Men for the crew I would have thee at my side along with Aylis, for I would have nought but the best; hence, I'll send word to thee.

"But as for staying aboard the ship, I know thou wouldst rather hie to that redheaded wife of thine, as well as thy boy Little Tom, and I would not deny thee that."

"Cap'n, Larissa understands Oi've a duty t'th' *Eroean*."

"Mayhap . . . yet I think Little Tom doesn't."

A great smile of relief lit up Long Tom's face, and he said, "Oy, naow, Oi do b'lieve y'r roight about that, Cap'n. Oi do b'lieve y'r roight."

Aravan stepped forward and surveyed the main deck teeming with sailors and warriors at the last of their chores, some of them, as did Fat Jim, yet bearing the remnants of hurt. In addition, Binkton and Pipper and Lissa were adeck, doing what they could to help with the cleanup and repairs. And belowdecks and under the care of Desault, there remained several of the more severely wounded, some who couldn't seem to recover from the Rûcken arrows, yet they had none of the rotting blackness; still, three couldn't quite get a full breath, while two others had numbness in arms and legs. And then there were those who were yet knitting severely broken bones. However, the majority of the cuts and bruises and punctures the crew had suffered had healed on the voyage home.

"We'll put up at the Red Slipper," said Aravan, turning once again to Long Tom.

"Oy, th' crew'll go f'r that," came the reply. "Oi mean, we've been asea a goodly long spell, 'n' they'll welcome some toime wi' th' laidies o' th' Slipper."

"I ween the ladies themselves would welcome that as well," said Aravan, and he glanced at Aylis.

A low, throaty laugh was her response, but she took not her eye from the wind pennant above as she made a minor adjustment in the wheel, Fat Jim behind her twitching his hands in concert, the hefty helmsman's mouth pursed in concentration.

"Besides," added Long Tom, stepping forward and looking down on the main deck, "they c'd use some gaiety to help 'em get over their grievin' for good comrades lost, 'n' t' help 'em forget our bad toime ashore."

"Land ho!" came the cry from above. "Port Arbalin dead ahead!"

As Second Officer Nikolai came up the ladder to the aft deck, Aravan said, "Stand by to hale in the studs and full reef all others; we'll take her in on nought but the stays."

"Aye, Kapitan," replied Nick, and he called orders to Noddy, bosun of the fastest ship in the world, and Noddy piped the commands to all.

And as the crew made ready, swiftly did the *Eroean* cleave the indigo waters of the deep blue Avagon Sea.

In gathering twilight, the elegant *Eroean* slid into the harbor, now running on staysails alone, and then even these were loosed to luff in the wind, and dinghies were lowered and towropes affixed to hale the Elven-ship to dockside.

There she would deliver her wounded unto the care of healers, as well as off-lade the hard-won treasured cargo she held in her hold: prized, precious, translucent stone the crew had wrested from a ghostly foe in the long-dead City of Jade.

The Red Slipper

ELVENSHIP
SPRING, 6E10

The crew put up at the Red Slipper, the large, rowdy inn and bordello a favorite gathering place for warriors and sailors and travellers of all sorts. At times Elven warbands would come through, or battle-hardened Dwarves. Fjordsmen, Vanadurin, Gelenders, occasionally the dark men from the far south, as well as others of various nations seemed to cluster here on their way to or when returning from distant realms. Traders, trappers, hostlers, shippers, merchants, minstrels, Mages, tradesmen, even passing royalty: all seemed to make it a point to stay awhile or even to just stop by. And whenever the *Eroean* was in port, townsfolk themselves came to spend an eve, all to see and hear of the adventures of the Elvenship's crew.

And the ladies of the Slipper—Yellow Nell, Dark-Eyed Lara, Laughing Jane, and the others—enjoyed the company of these men, especially the crew of the *Eroean*, for they seemed the best of the lot.

Burly Jack, owner and bartender, always had a tun of the Vancha Dark held in reserve especially for this crew, and he had a standing order for kegs of ale from the Holt of Vorn to be delivered on short notice whenever the Elvenship came to port.

And the local cadgers were happy to see the *Eroean* moored in the bay, for Captain Aravan's crew loosened their generous purse strings. And this time, on the day the Elvenship was sighted, Dabby the Cadger, making his way around a barroom brawl in the Red Slipper's common room, was the first to report it to Burly Jack, and received the reward of a mug of the Vornholt for the welcome news.

And so, that eve, after off-lading their wounded and the cargo of jade, and after mooring the Elvenship in the bay, the crew descended upon the Red Slipper and procured rooms and hot baths and laughed and drank and partook of the other amenities of that splendid inn.

But though they seemed joyous at being in port again, there lurked in the backs of the eyes of some of the sailors and the Dwarves and the two Warrows, as well as the captain and his lady, a painful memory or two, something it seemed they'd rather not discuss. And the only glimmering of what it might be was when the captain called for quiet, and when it fell he raised his glass and said, "To absent friends."

And so said they all.

Some of the patrons not of the crew found it odd that Captain Aravan seemed to have a pet fox—"A marvelous ratter," declared Burly Jack, hastily adding, "Not that the Slipper has rats, mind you." But now and then those who worked at the inn would glance from the fox to a small cluster of darkness lurking here and there, and they would nod to themselves and say nought of the shadow to others.

The crew spent nearly the full of the spring resting, relaxing, and celebrating. And every night, it seemed, a small group of them gathered about the fireplace and told tales to one another until the wee hours of morn. And the next day patrons would overhear references to Gelvin's Doom, and a wyrm in a well, and other such mysterious things, yet what they might be about, none but a few of the crew seemed to know.

Four signal events occurred during the stay of the captain and his mates, each of which caused ripples of excitement to flow through the town: the first was when Bair and his sire and dam and his truelove came sailing in one day, for Bair was known as the Dawn Rider, the one who brought the Silver Sword to Mithgar, and that was the sword Aravan used to slay Gyphon. His sire and dam—Urus the Baeran, and Riatha, the legendary Dara with the darksilver sword—were also famous in Mithgarian lore, and Jaith, Bair's truelove, was a bard beyond compare. The Red Slipper was packed night after night to hear their tales and to listen to Jaith sing. And many citizens dropped by during the days on the chance they might catch a glimpse of these famous folk.

The second event of note was when Dalavar the Wolfmage and his pack of Draega came to call, the 'Wolves as big as ponies. He stayed but two days, and he and the captain were as thick as thieves, and with a few others they sat in a far corner and spoke quietly to one another. What they said, none of the townsfolk knew, but when Dalavar and his Silver Wolves left, they took Bair and Jaith with them. And just after they were gone, Urus and Riatha sailed away, heading for Caer Pendwyr, or so someone said.

Over the next days the captain and a small circle continued to talk together quietly, while the crew of the *Eroean* relaxed and fought and gambled and sang and drank and dallied with the ladies of the Red Slipper.

As for the arc of friends at the hearth, they continued to gather each eve, and they spent a moon and a sevenday telling tales in the wavering candlecast shadows. Toward the mid of this time, Urus and Raitha returned from Caer Pendwyr and rejoined the hearth-tale group.

The next event of note was when Aravan and Aylis and Long Tom spent the afternoons meeting with the glut of men who wanted to sign aboard the *Eroean* and fill any of the positions now open on the sailing crew. One by one they came into a small room, where Long Tom and Aravan asked each of them questions as to his experience and skills. Aylis sat apart and jotted notes in a journal as she peered intently at every one of the applicants, and each of them felt as if she were seeing to the depths of his very soul.

In the latter days of the interviews, the fourth event occurred: a ferry from Merchants Crossing arrived, and with it came Brekk and eight Dwarves, enough to bring the *Eroean*'s Châkka warband up to the full strength of forty. And one of these Red Hill Dwarves the Warrows seemed to know—'twas the Châk named Brekka, apparently an acquaintance of old.

Finally, in concert with Long Tom, and relying heavily on Aylis, Aravan chose the men to fill out the remainder of the crew.

The dreadful events in the City of Jade had taken their toll, yet once again the Elvenship was up to her full complement of sailors, forty men in all.

Aravan settled the bill with Burly Jack, and a hefty sum it was, and he left a generous bonus for each member of the staff of the infamous inn—cooks, maids, and bottle washers all, including the Red Slipper ladies.

Then the crew entire—warriors and sailors and scouts—spent the next few days aboard ship.

Upon arrival at the *Eroean*, Long Tom assembled all hands on deck, and with Aylis looking on and Aravan leading, the sailors and warband took an oath to reveal no secrets of the Elvenship: the old hands renewing their pledge; the new hands vowing for the first time. Then all pledged a second time to never divulge to anyone the fact that they would sail with a Pysk, for she was one of the Hidden Ones, and preferred to keep it that way. Finally, the Dwarves and Men took an oath to reveal nought of this voyage whatsoever to anyone not of the crew. And when the pledging was done, Aravan looked to Aylis, and she nodded in satisfaction.

Under the tutelage of Nikolai and Brekk, the new crew members spent days familiarizing themselves with the ship and their duties, while the old hands spent time setting things to shipshape, some removing the scars the hull had taken in combat with the Rovers of Kistan, and laying on new paint where needed.

And as they readied the craft, Aylis spent time recording in her journal the tales they had told one another in the nights before the hearth. And the Châkka warband stripped and cleaned and regreased and reassembled the ballistas, or laded fireballs and round stones and huge arrows aboard, or sharpened axes or polished war hammers or oiled crossbows and such. And sailors swabbed or painted or coiled lines, or practiced reefing and goosewinging as well as running out the studding sails, and other such duties of seamanship.

As they worked at familiarizing themselves with the Elvenship, one of the new crewmen asked Aravan, "Beggin' pardon, Captain, but what be the name *Eroean* mean?"

" 'Tis an Elven word, Jules, and difficult to translate into Common, yet as close as I can come, it means *Dancer on the Wind*."

"Ar, then *Wind Dancer* be her name, eh?"

Aravan smiled and said, "Not quite, but close."

Within a sevenday all was ready, and Aravan had rowers in dinghies hale the *Eroean* to a pier, and there he tied up; and with the docks and ship abustle and cargo nets on booms swinging up and across decks and below, they laded on kegs and crates and barrels and bales of food and water and other such goods for the long voyage ahead. When the last of the provisions was lashed down in the holds, Aravan granted the crew a final day of shore leave, for they would sail morrow's eve, and it would be many a moon ere they saw these shores again.

To the Red Slipper the sailors and warriors went, while Aravan and Aylis and Urus and Riatha stayed aboard, along with Pipper and Binkton and Aylissa and Vex.

Even as the crew took their leave, a man rowed a dinghy to the ship. "Ahoy, the deck!" he called.

Aravan stepped to the rail.

It was Realmsman Tanner.

"I have a gift for two of your shipmates," called the realmsman.

"And they would be . . . ?"

"Binkton and Pipper."

Hearing their names, the Warrows stepped to the rail as well.

"Hand it up," said Aravan, lowering a rope and board ladder, "and then welcome aboard."

Tanner hefted up a large chest, one painted with flames. "It's empty, I'm afraid."

As Aravan leaned down and took hold of an end handle and hauled the chest adeck, "King Ryon," blurted Pipper.

Binkton sighed in exasperation, and Pipper said, "What I mean, Bink, is that the High King must have cleaned out Rivers End, else we wouldn't have our chest."

"Ah," said Binkton.

"The High King did at that," said Tanner, climbing aboard. "Cleared out Rackburn and the mayor and most of the city watch. Kingsmen now run the government there."

"What about that rat-eating Tark and his toady Queeker?"

"Sorry, but it seems they escaped," said Tanner.

"What?" demanded Binkton. "What Rûck-loving idiot let them get away?"

"I think they were elsewhere when the High King led the raid," said Tanner.

"I wouldn't call the High King a Rûck-loving idiot if I were you, Bink," whispered Pipper.

"Ah. Well." Binkton took a deep breath and slowly let it out.

Tanner and Aravan laughed.

"Wull, they're on wanted posters, right?" blustered Binkton.

"Indeed," said Tanner, controlling his mirth.

Binkton turned to Pipper and said, "When we get back from this voyage, Pip, we'll run them down ourselves, if they are still on the loose. After all, they tried to kill us."

Pipper sighed and said, "Oh, Bink."

"Wouldst thou have a brandy?" asked Aravan.

"Indeed," said Tanner.

As they started for the Captain's Lounge, Pipper turned to Binkton and said, "Come on, Bink, empty though it is, let's get our chest below."

Late the next afternoon the crew returned, a few carrying others over their shoulders. The ladies of the Red Slipper, some weeping, came down to the docks as well, for they would see the crew off. Long Tom and his family were there, Little Tom with his eyes agog at the magnificence of the ship. Long Tom gave Little Tom a hug and a kiss; then he scooped up his tiny wife, Larissa, in his arms and kissed her long and deeply. He set her afoot and turned and boarded the *Eroean*, last of all of the crew.

As the sun set and dusk drew down and the tide began to flow outward, "Get us under way, Tom," said Aravan, when the big man reported in.

"Aye-aye, Cap'n," replied Tom.

He turned to Noddy and Nikolai. "Cast off fore, cast off aft, hale in the gangplank, and rowers row."

These two called out orders, and dock men waiting on the pier cast the hawsers from the pilings, while crewmen drew the large mooring lines up and in and coiled them on the deck, as others pulled up the footway and stowed it in its place below. Rowers in the dinghies haled the ship away from the quay and turned her bow toward the mouth of Arbalin Bay.

Even as the dinghies were lifted up to the davits, Noddy piped the crew to raise the staysails, and on these alone did the craft get under way;

and in the deepening twilight, folk on the piers called out farewells and blew heartfelt kisses, some on the *Eroean* returning the sentiments in kind.

As the Elvenship cleared the mouth of the harbor and rode out on the ocean prime, "Where to, Captain?" asked Fat Jim, steersman again, his arm no longer in a sling. "What be our heading? Where be we bound?"

Aravan looked out across the broad Avagon Sea, the cool night air filling the silks above. Then he stepped up behind Aylis at the aft starboard rail and pulled her close and she leaned back into him. With men standing adeck and looking up at the captain embracing his lady, he reached 'round and cupped her right hand in his and pointed her finger and raised her arm and aimed at a bright gleam in the western sky. "Set our course on the evening star yon, all sails full, for we go to the rim of the world and beyond."

The bosun then looked at Long Tom, and at the big man's nod he piped the orders, and sailors scrambled to the ratlines and up to the yardarms, where they unfurled silks, the great sails spilling down in wide cascades of cerulean, while others of the crew stood ready at the halyards and sheets; and as this was done, Noddy strode along the deck and called out, "Look smart, men. You heard th' cap'n. Set those sails brisk, f'r surely we're bound on a venture grand th' loiks o' which th' w'rld has ne'er seen."

And with all silks flying in a following wind and filled to the full—mains and studs, jibs and spanker, staysails, topsails, gallants and royals, skysails and moonrakers and starscrapers—and with a luminous white wake churning aft in the night-dark Avagon Sea, her waters all aglimmer with the spangle of light from the stars above, westerly she ran, the Elvenship *Eroean*, the fastest ship in all the seas.

She was bound for the rim of the world and beyond....

. . . the rim of the world . . .

. . . and beyond. . . .

Dark Designs

DARK DESIGNS
SPRING, 6E10

In a tall tower hidden deep in the Grimwall, that long and ill-omened mountain chain slashing across much of Mithgar, a being of dark Magekind sat in his dire sanctum and brooded about retribution.

A single thought occupied all of his waking hours. . . .

. . . Aravan must die.

"Not bad for a pair of chicken thieves, eh?"

—Pipper Willowbank
Mid Autumn, 6E9

Afterword

For those who might wonder, most of this story, *City of Jade*, occurs in the time between the ending of the novel *Silver Wolf, Black Falcon* and the beginning of the collection *Red Slippers: More Tales of Mithgar*. For clarification purposes, I do "steal" a bit of *Silver Wolf, Black Falcon* to start this tale, and I steal a bit of *Red Slippers* toward the end of this story as well. And I go just a bit past *Red Slippers* at the last of this tale.

I also refer to several events occurring elsewhere in the series, although *City of Jade* stands on its own, as do all the other books in the chain (with the exception of anything called a trilogy or a duology; naturally, they must be read as a whole).

For those of you who are new to Mithgar, if you are interested in the sweep of the entire saga, a chronological list of the books in the series is printed at the front of this tome.

—Dennis L. McKiernan
Tucson, 2008

About the Author

I have spent a great deal of my life looking through twilights and dawns seeking . . . what? Ah, yes, I remember—seeking signs of wonder, searching for pixies and fairies and other such, looking in tree hollows and under snow-laden bushes and behind waterfalls and across wooded, moonlit dells. I did not outgrow that curiosity, that search for the edge of Faery when I outgrew childhood—not when I was in the U.S. Air Force during the Korean War, nor in college, nor in graduate school, nor in the thirty-one years I spent in research and development at Bell Telephone Laboratories as an engineer and manager on ballistic missile defense systems and then telephone systems and in think-tank activities. In fact I am still at it, still searching for glimmers and glimpses of wonder in the twilights and the dawns. I am abetted in this curious behavior by Martha Lee, my helpmate, lover, and, as of this writing, my wife of over fifty years.